MW00846801

THE DOLL'S HOUSE

NATASHA BOYDELL

Boldwood

First published in Great Britain in 2025 by Boldwood Books Ltd.

Copyright © Natasha Boydell, 2025

Cover Design by Head Design Ltd

Cover Images: Shutterstock and iStock

The moral right of Natasha Boydell to be identified as the author of this work has been asserted in accordance with the Copyright, Designs and Patents Act 1988.

Every effort has been made to obtain the necessary permissions with reference to copyright material, both illustrative and quoted. We apologise for any omissions in this respect and will be pleased to make the appropriate acknowledgements in any future edition.

A CIP catalogue record for this book is available from the British Library.

Paperback ISBN 978-1-83533-320-4

Large Print ISBN 978-1-83533-321-1

Hardback ISBN 978-1-83533-319-8

Ebook ISBN 978-1-83533-322-8

Kindle ISBN 978-1-83533-323-5

Audio CD ISBN 978-1-83533-314-3

MP3 CD ISBN 978-1-83533-315-0

Digital audio download ISBN 978-1-83533-317-4

This book is printed on certified sustainable paper. Boldwood Books is dedicated to putting sustainability at the heart of our business. For more information please visit https://www.boldwoodbooks.com/about-us/sustainability/

Boldwood Books Ltd, 23 Bowerdean Street, London, SW6 3TN

www.boldwoodbooks.com

PROLOGUE

Have you ever wondered what your life would be like if just one thing had been different? A single event which sent you down another path and, in turn, changed the course of your future? What if I hadn't lived in that particular place at that time? What if I hadn't accepted that job? What if I hadn't met that person?

What if I hadn't met her?

This thought consumes me as I lie in my prison cell, staring at a solitary photograph on the wall. A joyful and painful reminder of better days. Now I am completely alone, and the silence is deafening. There is no child running around making a racket. No cat fussing, begging for food. No friends texting to see if I fancy meeting for a coffee. There is nothing, and no one.

I suppose there are plenty of people right outside my door in this overcrowded prison, but I don't want to talk to them. I am afraid of them, of what they will say to me, what they will do. I am an outsider here. I am different to those women who act like they own the place, forming hierarchies and making deals. They've accepted their fate, and they've made this godforsaken place their home. But I can't do it because I don't belong here. I am the innocent party, a doll that has been played with and then discarded, forgotten by the people who are supposed to love me.

Other than the photograph, my cell wall is bare, a vast stretch of nothingness. We, the inhabitants of this prison, are also nothing. We are blots on society, the unsavoury, hidden out of sight so that our only interaction with the outside world is a phone call, a letter or a brief visit from family or friends for those fortunate enough to have anyone who still cares. But I don't want to be nothing, I want to be something again. Someone. I want it so much it hurts.

I stare so hard at the photograph that it begins to blur. It has been ripped in half, an action I now regret, but these are not normal times. I have been pushed to my limits and sometimes I've struggled to control my emotions.

Until recently, I led a regular life: work, the school run, playdates, socialising with friends. I didn't have a criminal record. Yet here I am and all I can think is, *How did this happen to me?*

And it all comes down to one thing. Her.

She has turned everyone against me. The people who I thought were my friends chose their side. The police, they decided too. They asked themselves, who is the victim? And they picked her.

She has stolen everything from me, and I hate her. She is the reason why I am here, the reason why everyone who adored me now despises me. So where do I go from here?

And then I have a thought.

My heart begins to race with anticipation. I've been feeling so lost but I know what the solution is now. I've realised how I can fix this. How I can get my life back on track and punish her for what she's done to me. There is one person left who still loves me, who would do anything for me, when everyone else has turned their backs. It's so obvious that I can't believe I didn't think of it before. I've been feeling too sorry for myself but now I can see clearly again and it's like I'm being reborn. This is going to work, I'm certain of it.

She will not win, I will.

I locate a pen and some paper. And then I start writing.

1

A YEAR EARLIER

'You've got to be kidding me. No way. No way.' I scowled furiously to emphasise my outrage, even though the caller couldn't see me. 'I can't believe this is happening.'

Freya and Bella looked up from their cereal bowls and stared at me. A splash of milk dripped off Freya's spoon and splattered on her freshy laundered school jumper. For God's sake.

'I understand it's disappointing, but I do also have some potentially good news,' the caller said in a soothing tone. This man was clearly experienced in dealing with stressed and irrational people.

I clung to his words like a leech. 'Tell me.'

'I may have found you a new buyer. She was one of the people who put an offer in the first time around, but she couldn't match the highest bid. So I called her last night and she's still interested. She's a lovely lady and the best thing is that she can move quickly.'

I narrowed my eyes. 'How quickly?'

'I've explained your situation to her and she's willing to do what it takes to secure the property. I think we can get things tied up within a few weeks.'

My heart rate began to slow down, and I closed my eyes and exhaled with relief. 'You know,' I said in a more conciliatory tone, 'you really could have opened with that bit.'

'I got there as quickly as I could,' he replied, and I could hear his smile. 'I'll email you her formal offer now but it's only three thousand pounds less than you agreed with your previous buyers, which I think is reasonable under the circumstances. She's a single mother and she's moving into the area from—'

'We accept,' I said quickly. 'Get the ball rolling.'

'If you could just read and reply to the email...'

'Yes, yes, yes, but we accept. Thank you so much for your help, you're a lifesaver.'

I hung up the phone and looked at my daughters, my gaze drifting down to the milk stain on Freya's jumper. I considered how long it would take for her to go up to her bedroom and change it. Adding in at least six minutes of unnecessary faffing time, I estimated ten minutes minimum. Sod it, the jumper could stay put. You couldn't win them all and I hoped we could claim victory to the most critical one. I hastily typed out a text message to Oliver, my husband.

'What is it, Mum?' Bella asked, standing up and putting her cereal bowl by the sink.

'The buyers of our flat pulled out at the last minute,' I told her.

I saw the girls' eyes widen and knew what they were thinking. Freya: *OMG, this means we're not moving! I get to keep sharing a room with Bella!* Bella: *OMG this means we're not moving. I have to keep sharing a room with Freya.*

'But I think it's all sorted,' I added quickly. 'Another buyer has stepped in.'

Freya's face fell, as Bella cheered.

'You almost had me there, Mum,' Bella, my twelve-year-old, said with relief. 'I thought we were going to have to stay here after all.'

I pictured the beautiful home that we had only been a couple of weeks away from securing the purchase on and thought, *No way, Jose. That house is ours.*

'Nope, the move is still on,' I said brightly.

Seven-year-old Freya sniffed huffily. 'I still don't get why we have to move.'

Freya had been against the idea from the start, but then that was Freya. She was a creature of habit, she liked things just so, and the idea of leaving the home where she had spent her entire life to date horrified her. Bella, on the other hand, was thrilled because after years of sharing a bedroom with her annoying younger sister, she would finally have her own space. I had lost count of the number of bedroom decor mood-boards she had already presented me with.

I looked at the time and habitual panic surged. 'We're late, girls, let's go.'

Bella grabbed her bag, blew me a kiss and let herself out of the house to make her own way to the local secondary school. Freya, however, stayed stubbornly put.

'Come on, Freya,' I said irritably. 'We'll be late if we don't leave now.'

I saw her little lip wobble and my heart sank. Freya always timed her meltdowns to perfection. My expression softened and I took her hand. 'Freya,' I said pleadingly. 'I know you're upset about us moving, but come on, sweetheart, we can talk about it on the way.'

'Does the new buyer have children?' she asked.

'Yes, I think so,' I replied, thinking of my hasty conversation with the estate agent, wondering where Freya was going with this, and fretting about the time all in one go.

'Do you know how old they are?'

'No.' I glanced at the clock and cursed inwardly.

'Will they sleep in my bed?'

'No, Freya,' I said with forced patience. We'd been over this many times before. 'Your bed will come with us to the new house. And all your toys.'

'But they'll sleep in Bella's and my room.'

'Well, yes.'

'I don't like it. This is our home.'

Yes, it was our home, and it had been mine and Oliver's for more than fifteen years, long before Freya came along. We loved it and we'd made some wonderful memories here. But it was time to move on. We desperately needed more space and we were finally in a financial position to buy a house without having to move to a new area. The town where we lived, which had been up and coming when we first moved, was now just up and we were lucky to have found a house we could afford on our dream road. Everyone understood this apart from Freya.

'You'll love the new house,' I told her, aware that I sounded like a broken record. 'But, Freya, we really need to get to school now.'

I looked at my daughter, silently pleading with her to capitulate. She stared back, the storm of indecision clear in her eyes. *Do I put my shoes on, or do I kick off?* In desperation, I pulled out my trump card. 'If we leave now, we can buy a chocolate croissant on the way.'

It had the desired effect. Freya was standing by the front

door with her shoes on before I'd even found my handbag. But as we began our walk to school, she was still brooding.

'Are you all right, sweetheart?' I asked her. Now that we were en route, I was feeling less tetchy and more amenable again. 'Shall we talk about it?'

'I don't want strange people living in our home.'

'They might not be strange. They might be lovely.'

She looked up at me with her big brown eyes. 'They might be strange.'

I don't care if they're freaking weirdos as long as they buy our flat, I thought. But Freya's words got me thinking. I'd done some sleuthing on the couple who had originally been going to buy the flat. They were in their late twenties, buying their first home together. According to his LinkedIn, he worked in property management. According to her Instagram, she enjoyed taking selfies in trendy bars. They had seemed like a nice couple, who would have fun times in the flat, just like Oliver and I had done when we first moved in, before the babies and the toddlers and the school runs. I had imagined them having dinner parties and cosying up on the sofa together after a long day at work and I had felt good about it, imagining leaving our home in good hands.

But I knew nothing about this woman, not even her name. As we walked, I pulled out my phone and saw that the estate agent had already emailed me her formal offer. I scanned the email and read that the woman, who was called Summer, wanted to come back and have another look at the flat. I quickly sent a response, accepting the offer and saying that she was welcome any time. Then I turned my attention back to Freya, who was dragging her feet along the pavement.

'Are you excited about the last day of school?' I asked her.

'S'pose.'

'I imagine it will be all fun and games.'

'Yeah.'

'And hopefully by September, we'll be in our new house and you can tell all your friends about your amazing bedroom. We could arrange a sleepover with Aanya. Would you like that?'

We were interrupted by the phone ringing. It was the estate agent and I panicked as I answered. 'Don't tell me she's changed her mind.'

'No, not at all. She's just in the area and she asked if she could come this morning.'

I pictured the dirty dishes by the sink. The unmade beds. 'What time?'

'Is in an hour okay? She says you don't need to be out. In fact, she'd love to meet you.'

I thought of the school gate chit-chat with my school mum friends that I had been looking forward to and the groceries I had been planning to pick up on the way home. And then I remembered how critical this sale was. 'That's fine, I'll see you then.'

With my plans out of the window, the last school drop of the academic year was a hurried affair. I wiped croissant crumbs off Freya's face, kissed her goodbye, waved at my friends and hurried straight home to begin Operation Tidy Up. By the time the doorbell rang, I was sweating, the open windows offering little relief from the brief British summer. I mopped my brow with the back of my hand and threw open the door with a welcoming smile.

'Hi there!' I said, shaking hands with Greg, our estate agent, and immediately assessing the woman standing next to him. She looked a few years younger than me, and her long blonde hair was tied up into a messy bun. Her face had a slight colour to it, a back garden tan rather than a fortnight in the Caribbean glow. She was wearing a pink sundress with spaghetti straps which hung off her slender frame. She was beautiful, not in a traditionally pretty way but strikingly so, and I self-consciously ran a hand through my own hair.

'I'm Summer,' she said, and her voice was soft and lilting. 'Thank you so much for letting me come at short notice.'

'Not at all,' I replied, wishing that I wasn't wearing one of Oliver's old T-shirts and denim shorts with the button undone because they were too tight. 'You're very welcome, come in.'

She didn't so much as walk but glide into the house and I inhaled a sweet, floral scent. She smelled fresh and clean, like summer, which, given her name, suited her perfectly.

'Oh yes, it's just like I remember it,' she said, looking around in wonder.

'Greg said you're new to the area?'

'That's right, we're moving from Devon.'

'Lovely.' I wondered why, if this woman lived in Devon, she was able to get to the flat in an hour. But then I reasoned that she may have been here already, looking at other flats. I had a momentary panic, in case she was seeing more properties that day which might turn her head.

'We've been so happy here,' I gushed. 'It really is a lovely flat and in such a nice area. There's a huge common only a few minutes' walk away and it's close to the Tube station if you commute. Plus there are lots of great coffee shops and bakeries on the high street.'

I caught Greg's eye and he gave me a look which said, *Steady on, woman. Selling the flat is my job.* Then he took up the conversation, extolling the many virtues of the north London market town of Barnet, with its rural feel combined with easy access to central London. I fell into step behind them as they walked from room to room. With Greg running the show, there wasn't much for me to say or do, but I didn't want to miss anything important. We needed this sale.

Touring a two-bedroom flat was not a time-consuming process and we soon found ourselves back in the kitchen again.

'Would you like a cup of tea?' I asked Summer.

'Oh, thank you so much, Naomi, but I wouldn't want to intrude.' Gosh, she was sweet.

'It's no intrusion, I was just going to make one myself.'

'Well in that case, I'd love one.'

We both looked at Greg, who was hovering.

'You're welcome to head off, Greg, if you have other viewings,' I told him.

Greg looked conflicted, as though he didn't trust me to be alone with Summer. Maybe he thought I'd unwittingly scupper the sale if he wasn't there to supervise. But I gave him my most reassuring smile and, with a quick glance at his watch, he nodded.

'I'll call you this afternoon,' he told Summer. 'To get your thoughts.'

'Oh, no need,' she said in a captivating sing-song voice. 'I stand by my offer.'

This woman is my hero, I thought as I did an internal victory dance. If I could have hugged her, I would have done. Given how glorious she smelled, it would have been no hardship. But I didn't want to seem full on and scare the poor woman away. She seemed so lovely. A good soul, I thought. I was already imagining picking Freya up from school later and confirming that the new owner was not strange. If anything, I thought Freya would be rather taken with Summer.

We saw Greg off and then I busied myself with the teas, taking them over to the table and joining Summer, who was gazing around the room with a beatific smile. Then she turned her beam directly on to me, and she was simply glorious. As she reached for her tea, I admired the bracelets on her wrist and the plethora of gold rings she was wearing on her fingers.

'I'm so glad that you're still interested in the flat,' I told her. 'I almost had kittens this morning when Greg told me that our buyers had pulled out. I'm sorry we didn't accept your offer in the first place.'

'Oh, no need to apologise, you had to go with the highest bidder. But I must say, I was thrilled when he called to tell me the flat was available again.'

'You didn't find anywhere else in the meantime?'

'Nothing as perfect as here. This flat was meant to be our new home. I can just feel it.'

Our. 'Ah yes, Greg mentioned that you have a child?'

'That's right.' Summer smiled, almost wistfully. 'Luna. She's seven.'

'Oh, that's the same age as my youngest, Freya! Do you know what school she'll go to?'

'Not yet, I can't apply until we've moved. Where does Freya go?'

'North Hill Primary. It's fantastic, I can't recommend it enough. Actually, I heard that a child in Freya's class is leaving so there might be a place available.'

Summer smiled gratefully. 'Thank you, I'll apply there then.'

'I'd apply to some other schools too,' I warned her. 'Just in case.'

'Well, if you say it's the best, then that's where I want Luna to go.'

I felt obliged to stress the importance of Summer considering other schools, rather than basing her decision solely on my recommendation. To remind her that choosing a school for your child was an incredibly personal choice and her opinion might differ to mine. But as I opened my mouth to say all of this, I stopped. Summer was new to the area and she was probably clinging on to my local knowledge because the myriad of choices was overwhelming. Anyway, the place might have already been snapped up.

'I hope we can move over the holidays, ready for September,' Summer said.

'We're ready to go as soon as you are,' I told her. 'What made you decide to move to Barnet?'

'It was time for a change,' Summer said. 'A new adventure.'

I remembered Greg telling me that Summer was a single mum and wondered about Luna's father, and what he thought about his daughter moving so far away. If he was still in the picture, that was. But it was far too personal a question to ask someone I barely knew.

Instead, I played it safe. 'Will you miss Devon?'

'I'll miss the sea,' Summer admitted. 'But I'm excited about being on London's doorstep. I can take Freya to museums and galleries, and I think it will be marvellous for her.'

I felt a pang of guilt that, despite living on London's doorstep, as Summer called it, I could rarely be bothered to take the girls into town. I should arrange some trips over the summer holidays, I decided. Drag the girls to the Natural History Museum. A bit of culture would do them both good, especially Bella, whose idea of culture was TikTok.

'You're so beautiful,' Summer said suddenly. 'Just like your home.'

'Thank you.' I smiled with surprise. It had been a while since anyone had called me beautiful, and at forty-three, with rapidly greying hair and an even more rapidly expanding midriff, I had been feeling far from it. Oliver and I had a strong, happy marriage but most of the time we barely had time to notice what the other one looked like. The other week he'd had his hair cut shorter than usual, and I hadn't clocked it for two days. He still hadn't let that go.

Summer was watching me and the intensity of her gaze began to make me feel uncomfortable. I took a sip of my scalding tea and tried to think of something to say.

'Do you work, Summer?'

She nodded. 'Yes. I used to be a performer but now I work as a virtual assistant. It means I can bring all my clients with me when we move.'

'A performer. How fabulous! Were you on stage?'

'Yes. I did West End shows and toured globally. It was a long time ago now though.'

'Wow!' I thought of Bella, who went to stage school every Saturday and dreamed of becoming a famous actress. 'My daughter would love you. She's mad about the stage.'

'I'd love to meet her too. What do you do, Naomi?'

'I'm a freelance accountant. Not as exciting as you.'

'Oh, I don't know. You get to have a nose through other people's financial information. That sounds interesting to me.'

I laughed. 'Well, when you put it that way.'

As we drank our teas, I gave Summer the lowdown on Barnet and the best cafes and restaurants to eat at. She asked me about the girls, and what clubs and activities they did in the local area. By the time we'd finished our drinks, I felt like I'd been sitting with a friend for the past half an hour, rather than a stranger whose relationship with me was purely transactional. Summer was delightful company and so easy to talk to. But my to-do list was playing on the back of my mind. I'd lost a couple of hours already and it was the last day before the summer holidays, when I would be juggling work with looking after the girls for six weeks. As well as hopefully moving house. And visiting the Natural History Museum. I looked at the clock and thankfully Summer got the hint. She stood up to leave, taking her empty mug over to the sink.

'Thank you so much again for letting me visit,' she said. 'I do appreciate it.'

'Of course, and with any luck I'll be seeing you around very soon.'

Summer smiled. 'I do hope so.'

I waved her off and closed the door, exhaling with relief. The visit had gone even better than expected and I was confident that Summer would go ahead with the purchase. Which meant that Operation Move was still on. We'd hit a bump in the road, but we'd quickly got past it and I was giddy with excitement. I couldn't wait to move into our new home and put our own stamp on it. By September, that dream could well be a reality.

By the time I'd called Oliver to fill him in, put a load of washing on and finally sat down to do some work, I'd almost forgotten about Summer. But as I walked down the hallway to use the bathroom, I caught a trace of her beautiful floral scent, her presence still lingering in the air.

2

'Day drinking now, are we?' My friend Asha looked at me with raised eyebrows as I opened the door with a glass of wine in hand. She was holding a bouquet of flowers and a present.

'Cut me some slack, I've had the most stressful few days of my life.'

'They do say moving is up there with death and divorce.'

'Well, I feel half-dead and I'm quite up for divorcing Oliver, so I'll go for the hat-trick.'

Asha laughed and gave me a hug as she stepped over the threshold. Against all odds, we'd completed the sale in six weeks and had moved into our new house the previous afternoon. This morning, I had packed the girls off to friends' houses so that I could roll my sleeves up and get unpacking, but every room was full of towering piles of boxes and I had never felt more overwhelmed. Yesterday had been a whirlwind of excitement: seeing the removal van pulling up outside the flat, getting the email to say that we could pick up the keys, driving over to the new house and standing outside it, knowing that it was finally ours. But there had been lows too: desperately trying to find our cat Sparkle, who had gone into hiding, managing the logistics of a house move around a seven-year-old who was playing up because she was unsettled, rebuilding furniture, and attempting to locate bedding so that we could actually go to bed.

Today, the effects of it all had taken its toll and I was both exhausted and on edge. So, I had decided that a lunchtime tipple might cheer me up, and Asha had caught me in the act.

But this was Asha, so instead of judging me, she said, 'Pour me a glass then.'

I grinned and led her to the kitchen, where I took the bottle of Sauvignon Blanc out of the fridge and located a spare glass. Asha put the flowers and present on the table then stood looking around with her hands on her hips.

'This is lush, Nims.'

I flushed with pride and, suddenly, all the stress that we'd been through seemed worth it. Just that one comment from my friend validated the entire upheaval of our lives.

'Thanks. I love it too. I just can't believe how much there is still to do.'

'There's no rush. Take your time.' Asha took the glass from me. 'So do I get a tour then?'

'Of course.' I showed her around the house, feeding off Asha's murmurs of appreciation. Asha and her family lived in a gorgeous house a few roads away and I'd always been envious of it. I still couldn't quite believe that we now lived in one too.

Once we'd finished the tour, we headed back to the kitchen, sitting down at our old dining table, which looked out of place but would have to do for now.

'So, what's this about you divorcing your husband then?'

I laughed. 'It was just a tough day yesterday, that's all. And

Oliver couldn't take today off as he has a big meeting, so I'm on my own. Don't worry, I love him really.'

'Well, the house is beautiful. Congratulations.' Asha raised her glass and clinked it with mine. 'Were you sad to say goodbye to the flat?'

'I did actually get emotional yesterday,' I admitted. 'It really felt like the end of an era. That flat was a big part of our lives, it's where Oliver and I first lived together, where we raised our babies. I think I've been so focused on the sale that I didn't stop to think about the impact it would have on me when we left for good.'

'You're moving on to bigger and better though, Nims.'

'I know. But now we've handed the keys over, I can't help but feel a bit funny about it. Like the new owner has stolen my boyfriend or something.'

Asha chuckled. 'You said she was nice, though?'

'Yes, she was lovely.' I thought back to that scorching summer's morning when I had met Summer and wondered how she was getting on. Whether she'd found a school place for Luna. What her furniture looked like in our flat. If I would see her again.

'There we go then. Your flat is in safe hands and you're now the proud owner of this incredible house. Oh, I almost forgot, I've brought you something.' Asha picked up the flowers and present and proffered them at me.

'Thanks, you shouldn't have.' I took the parcel and ripped it open, laughing when I saw the novelty tea towel, which said 'Do one thing every day that scares your family.' It was typical Asha.

'Who have you seen over the summer holidays?' I asked her. North Hill Primary was a close-knit community where everyone knew everyone. Sometimes it got a little too close for comfort and there were definitely a few interesting characters who liked to spice up the class WhatsApp groups. But most of the time it was wonderful to feel part of it and to know that there was always someone on hand to help if you needed it, and I was grateful to all my friends who had looked after the girls while Oliver and I were packing up the house.

'Just the usual,' Asha said, which meant Rachel and Victoria. Their children were in the same class as ours and we had become a little foursome, meeting up for dinner every month.

'Freya is at Rachel's today, but I haven't spoken to Victoria for a while. Is she okay?'

'She's fine. We should do drinks to mark the start of the new school year.'

School reopened for the autumn term in a few days, and I was looking forward to it. With all the upheaval, I was ready for some routine again and I had got horribly behind on my accountancy work, so it felt like I'd be playing catch up until Christmas.

'How did Freya cope with the move?' Asha asked me.

'She was difficult yesterday and she refused to go to sleep for hours. But she seemed better this morning. I think she'll settle in, she just needs some time.'

'And Bella?'

'Oh, Bella's thrilled. She's already on about going to the shops for supplies so we can paint her room this weekend. I'm hoping her enthusiasm will rub off on Freya.'

Asha looked at her phone. 'Crikey, I'd better go. I've got to pick Aanya up from my mum's house in fifteen minutes.'

I stood up to see her out. 'Thanks for stopping by. And let's organise those drinks.'

After Asha left, I poured the rest of my wine down the sink. Drinking during the day always made me woozy and I had too much to do. Instead, I filled up the kettle and rummaged around for the teabags while simultaneously fretting about which room to get stuck into next. I was just about to tackle the crockery when the doorbell rang again.

I went to open it, wondering if it was a delivery or if Bella had forgotten her keys. But the woman standing on the doorstep was the last person I had expected to see.

'Summer!' I exclaimed, unable to keep the surprise from my voice.

'I'm so sorry to intrude.' Summer looked mortified. 'I know you must be super busy.'

'No, it's fine.' I mentally ran through a list of why she might be here. Was there a problem with the flat? Had we not cleaned it enough? Had she changed her mind about buying it? No, I was being ridiculous. The sale had gone through, there was no going back now.

'It's nothing urgent,' Summer said. 'It's just that I was passing by and I wondered if you still had the instructions for the oven. I just can't seem to work it at all.'

I frowned. The oven had been in that flat longer than Oliver and I had. 'No, I'm sorry. It's really old but it's always worked just fine.'

'I think some of the symbols have rubbed off the knob,' Summer continued.

'Oh yes, I'm sorry.' I slapped my forehead. 'I should have left you a note, but it completely slipped my mind. Come in and I'll draw you a diagram of which function is which.'

I opened the door to let Summer in and she followed me into the kitchen, where I looked around for any sign of a notepad and pen.

'Oh, this is beautiful,' Summer said, taking in the kitchen. 'Lucky you.'

'Thank you. Did your move go smoothly yesterday?'

'Yes.' Summer was still looking around, her eyes wide like saucers. 'Gosh, your kitchen is stunning. And look at that garden!'

I grinned. 'It's lovely, isn't it. Although I'm not very green-fingered, I must admit.'

Summer walked over to the patio doors. 'It's quite low maintenance, you'll be fine.'

Triumphantly locating a pen, I made a diagram of the oven knobs and handed it to Summer. 'Here we go, that should do it.'

'Thank you.' She took the paper from me and put it in her bag. Then the kettle clicked off and she looked at me expectantly. My heart sank. Summer seemed lovely but I had so much to do and Asha's visit had already thrown me off schedule. However, years of being taught the importance of good manners were too strong to ignore.

'I was just about to have a cuppa. Would you like one?'

'Oh, yes please, that would be lovely.'

I pushed my stress to one side and located another mug, rinsing it out and putting in a teabag. Summer sat down at the kitchen table and watched me.

'Where are your children?' she asked me.

'They're with their friends. What about your daughter. Is it Luna?'

'Yes, that's right, Luna. She's with her dad but I'm picking her up tomorrow.'

'Is she excited to be moving?'

'Oh yes. She's really looking forward to starting at her new school. And I managed to get her a place at North Hill!'

'Oh, that's fabulous news. It's such a great school and

everyone is so friendly. I'll introduce you to the gang on the first day.'

'That would be great,' Summer said gratefully. 'I don't know anyone in Barnet.'

'You'll know everyone soon, trust me. It's a very close community.' I handed Summer her mug of tea and sat down opposite her. 'Are you settled into the flat?'

'I still have piles of unpacking to do but I'm getting there. That's why I left Luna with her dad. I wanted things to be a bit more settled for her when she arrived.'

'Where does her father live?' I asked curiously.

Summer sighed and looked out of the window, and I imme-diately sensed that it had not been a harmonious split. 'He lives in Devon,' she said flatly.

'Is he okay about you moving?'

Her head swivelled towards me and I saw a flash of anger. It almost seemed as though it didn't belong there, on such a sweet, peaceful face. But then I barely knew her, or what she had been through in her life. 'He doesn't get to have a say, I'm afraid. He's been next to useless since we split up. I had to beg him to have Luna for a couple of days while we moved as he said he was too busy to have her.'

'Oh gosh, I'm sorry.'

'He has a new family now,' she said. 'A son and a daughter. It's like he's forgotten Luna.'

'It must be so hard,' I said, acutely aware that I had no idea how hard it was because while I had joked about divorcing Oliver, I had never seriously considered it. And if we ever did break up, I knew for certain that Oliver would always be in the girls' lives.

Summer smiled. 'It was at first. But Luna and I are doing just fine.'

'I'll make sure Freya keeps an eye on her at school. Do you have all the uniform you need? I can lend you some if you don't get a chance to buy it in time?'

'I've ordered some online already, so we're good to go, thank you.'

Summer seemed distracted, and I wondered if the conversation about her ex had upset her. And I then thought about my own frazzled nerves after days of packing and moving and I understood how she might feel. I hoped that Freya and Luna would get along. Perhaps they might even become good friends. Then I wondered if Freya might find it strange that Luna was living in the flat, presumably sleeping in her old room. It could make playdates tricky.

'Penny for them.'

I started and realised that Summer was watching me with that intense gaze again.

'Sorry, I was miles away.'

Summer drained her tea. 'I've kept you too long. I'll let you get back to your unpacking.'

'And good luck with yours,' I said as I followed her out. She smiled and waved before drifting off down the road, her sandals flip-flopping on the pavement and her wavy blonde hair hanging loose down her slender back. I watched her for a moment before heading inside. I could smell her perfume in the hallway. We had been lucky to find such a great buyer for our flat. The sale had been a breeze, with none of the endless questions and attempted renegotiations that had happened with our previous purchasers. Summer had been the perfect buyer and Greg, our estate agent, had even commented on how amenable she had been throughout the process.

It was only as I was clearing up our empty mugs that something occurred to me. I had only met Summer once before, when she visited the flat, and I was sure that I hadn't told her which house we were moving to. So how had she known our new address?

* * *

'Maybe the estate agent told her.'

Oliver, home from work and changed into shorts and a T-shirt, was making a pasta sauce.

'Surely not. Wouldn't that be a breach of privacy?'

Oliver shrugged as he chopped an onion. 'How else would she know our address?'

'Well exactly.'

'I wouldn't overthink it.'

I snorted. Overthinking was my speciality and we both knew it. All afternoon, while I had been unpacking and cleaning and sorting, I had been trying to work out how Summer had found us. Had she seen us moving the previous day? Had the address accidentally been included on an email thread between our solicitors or the estate agent? Now I wondered if Oliver was right, and if Greg had told her where we lived. But it seemed unlikely.

'I'll call Greg and ask him if he told her.'

Oliver gave me one of his looks. 'Let it go, babe. Do you not like her or something?'

It wasn't that I didn't like Summer. In fact it was the opposite. She was friendly, easy to talk to, and she had a glow about her that seemed to warm the entire room when she entered. She seemed worldly too. I imagined that she had lived an exciting life, far more adventurous than mine, and I was curious. And yet, the idea of her actually being in our lives, of seeing her at school every day, felt odd, almost like an unwelcome intrusion. I tried to explain this to Oliver.

'Buying and selling tends to be anonymous,' I began. 'So it just feels odd that she's going to be around even after we've moved. It's almost like a constant reminder of the flat. And when we said goodbye to it, I felt like we were closing that chapter of our lives.'

Oliver nodded thoughtfully but I could tell he didn't get it. It was just bricks and mortar to him. I knew he had an emotional attachment to the flat, but I also knew that it wouldn't fester inside him like it would do with me. I was already afraid of walking past our old home and feeling the loss of it, even though I knew the sensation would pass over time. So it wasn't that I didn't like Summer, I just didn't like the idea of our past mingling with our future. And I certainly didn't like the idea of our past turning up on our new doorstep unannounced.

'Actually,' Oliver said slowly as he scraped the onion into the frying pan, 'I think it's cool that we know the new owner. And if she's as nice as you say, maybe you'll become friends. We might even end up going over to the flat as guests. Wouldn't that be fun?'

Fun wasn't the word that sprang to mind. 'And what about Freya? Won't it be strange for her that her new classmate lives in her old home? She already feels unsettled about it.'

'You know what children are like. In a few weeks she'll barely remember the flat.'

I admired Oliver's optimism, even if I didn't share it. As if on cue, Freya wandered into the kitchen and sat down with the heavy sigh of a ninety-year-old woman riddled with arthritis.

'Are you okay, darling?' I asked. On closer inspection, she

was looking peaky. I placed my hand over her forehead with concern. 'Are you feeling poorly?'

'No.'

'Are you hungry?'

'No.'

Poor Freya. It was like she had the weight of the world on her shoulders and it was too heavy a burden for a seven-year-old. I just had to hope that Oliver was right after all, and that in a few weeks Freya would be happy and settled in the new house. I resolved to be as upbeat and positive about it as I could, even though I was dog-tired and irritable myself. I had to show Freya that this move was the best thing that had ever happened to us. I was relieved when Bella skipped in, talking about how awesome it was that she now lived on the same road as a schoolfriend, and about how they were going to walk to school together every day next term. Bella's enthusiasm reminded me of Summer, a positive ray of sunshine, and I decided to make an effort with Summer and not let my own silly quibbles stand in the way of us becoming friends.

But late that night, as I lay awake in our new, unfamiliar room, listening to the noises of hungry city foxes rummaging through the bins on the street outside and the constant drip from the bathroom tap, which we had just discovered was leaking, I wondered if we had made the right decision in buying this house. There was so much to do to get it how we wanted it and the task seemed impossible. Oliver's DIY prowess was not legendary and the thought of interior design terrified me. Had we bitten off more than we could chew in our greed to have more space? Should we have stayed in our lovely, easy flat? And all I could think about was Summer, tucked up in the cosy bedroom that used to be ours, sleeping soundly.

And for a brief moment, I envied her.

3

The playground was buzzing, and that was just the grown-ups. The kids were on another level, running around as though they'd just been freed from solitary confinement, rather than having spent their summers swimming in the Spanish sea or bodyboarding off the Cornish coast.

I was delighted to see the school gang again. We shared hugs and brief snippets of how we'd spent our holidays, while simultaneously telling our children to calm down. Even Freya seemed to be caught up in the excitement as she proudly put on a friendship bracelet that Aanya had bought her from her holiday to Greece. I stood in a huddle with a few of the parents, catching up on their news and telling them all about our wonderful new house. I omitted the bits about the leaky tap and the damp we had just discovered behind the bath.

'I wonder who's taken Charlie's place in the class,' Richard, one of the dads, said. 'His family moved to the States over the summer. I imagine there'll be a new pupil starting.'

'Oh yes, her name is Luna,' I replied, pleased to be the

bearer of this juicy gossip. Everyone leaned in to hear more. 'Her mum, Summer, has moved into our old flat.'

'What's the child like?' Angela's eyes were beady. Her son, Sebastian, was top of the class and that was how she liked it. She was probably eager to make sure that Luna wasn't a usurper.

'I haven't met the little girl yet. But her mum is really nice.'

'Is she new to the area?' This was Richard.

'Yes, she's moved from Devon.'

'Well then, we must make her feel welcome.'

I looked up then and saw her. She floated through the school gates, her hair swinging loose around her shoulders. Her pale pink maxi dress swayed gently in the breeze. It was as though she moved at a different pace to everyone else, her gait in slow motion against the chaotic backdrop. My eyes moved down to the child clutching on to Summer's hand. In contrast, Luna looked nothing like her mother. Her hair was dark and straight, her movements awkward. Her eyes kept darting here and there nervously, yet she was avoiding eye contact with anyone. It was clear that the little girl was anxious, and my heart went out to her.

'Summer, over here,' I called, and Summer looked at me with relief.

'Naomi, hi!' She made a beeline for our little group, and I beckoned Freya over.

'That's Luna, the girl I was telling you about,' I whispered. 'Remember to be kind to her.'

Freya glanced over at Luna and nodded. By the time they reached us, a gaggle of children had formed, and they were all staring at Luna curiously. Freya, bless her heart, stepped forward.

'I'm Freya,' she said, and Luna looked at her with the

saddest eyes I'd ever seen. So much for being excited to start her new school, I thought. But first day nerves could be brutal.

The other kids continued staring in the unabashed way that only children can get away with. But after a minute or two they began to lose interest and drifted away. Only Freya remained, firmly stuck to my side, keeping a watchful eye on Luna.

Summer, meanwhile, was having questions fired at her from all directions. Where had she moved from? What did she do? How was she finding Barnet? She answered them all with good grace, as though her interrogation was a pleasure. She had everyone's attention and by the time the school bell rang, we had almost forgotten about the children.

After some hasty hugs and kisses, the kids ran to their lines and snaked their way into school, the commuting parents hotfooted it to the nearby train station and a few of us lingered, torn between getting on with our days and suggesting a quick coffee first. I had a mountain of work to do but it was so lovely to see everyone again and I thought a quick caffeine fix wouldn't derail me too much. So, when Richard suggested it, I was the first to put my hand up.

'Summer, would you like to join us?' he asked.

'Oh, yes please.'

In the end there were five of us: me, Richard, Summer, Asha and Victoria. We all trooped to the nearby cafe and found a table at the back.

Asha leaned in towards me. 'You're right, Summer is great.'

I smiled and nodded, glad to see that Summer was fitting in already. She seemed relaxed, but it must have been full on to meet so many new people. Richard was right, it was up to us to make her feel welcome. Victoria was asking Summer how she was settling into the flat, and as Summer described how she'd spent the weekend painting Luna's bedroom yellow, I ignored my uncharitable flare of indignation that someone was messing with our home. Because it wasn't our home any more and I needed to get over myself.

'Naomi has been wonderful,' Summer said, smiling in my direction.

'Oh, I haven't done anything,' I said modestly.

'And she made the flat so perfect, really there's not much I need to do,' Summer added quickly. It was as though she could read my thoughts.

The coffees arrived and, cross-questioning of Summer complete, we moved on to other topics. Angela's obsession with secondary schools even though our children had only just started in Year 3, the upcoming vote for the Parent Teacher Association members, the new pizza takeaway on the high street, Richard's family trip to Malaysia. When I had finished my coffee I could easily have stayed for another but those accounts weren't going to do themselves. So, reluctantly, I stood up to leave.

'I'd better dash,' I said, taking my bag from the back of the chair.

Summer sprang up too. 'I'll come with you.'

We said goodbye to the others and made our way outside. It was still warm, with only a hint of autumn around the corner, and I enjoyed the feeling of sunshine on my face as I began to walk back home, with Summer by my side.

'Everyone is so friendly,' she said. 'I knew moving here was the right decision.'

'Is Luna okay?'

'Oh yes, she's wonderful. She was so happy to go to school and make new friends.'

I thought of the little girl on the brink of tears that I'd seen this morning and frowned. Luna had seemed petrified, not excited. I hoped that Freya was being nice to her.

We reached the end of my road and I turned to say goodbye.

'I'll see you at pick up,' Summer said.

'Oh, I do a late pick up on Mondays,' I explained. 'Freya goes to gymnastics club.'

'Really? I must enrol Luna too.'

'Does she like gymnastics?'

'I'm sure she would.'

'There are plenty of other clubs to choose from. Have a look on the school's website.'

'I think she'd like gymnastics,' Summer said with an air of finality to her voice.

'Well, erm, great. Maybe I'll see you tomorrow.'

I waved and began to make my way up the road. But as I walked, I could feel her eyes burning into my back and I began to feel self-conscious. I couldn't shake off the beginning of a feeling that, as delightful as Summer was, there was something odd about her. Something I couldn't quite put my finger on. Was it her intensity? The fact that she turned up at our new house unannounced? Or just an unanchorable instinct? Unable to resist, I spun round to face her. But there was no one there. Summer was gone.

* * *

As I walked home with Freya after gymnastics, I asked her about Luna.

'How did the new girl get on? Was she okay?'

'She was very quiet,' Freya said.

'Did you play with her?'

'I tried, but she didn't want to.'

'Well, I'm sure she'll settle in soon. Just remember to keep asking her to join in your games, okay? If she doesn't want to, then that's fine.'

'Okay.'

'Any other news?'

Freya looked at me slyly. 'Aanya has a crush.'

'Oooh!' I loved playground gossip. 'Who is it?'

'I promised I wouldn't tell.'

'Oh, go on! I won't say anything.'

I grinned, enjoying the familiar banter between Freya and me. She had been so quiet and sullen for the past few weeks, and it was a tonic to see a hint of her old self again.

Freya looked around, as if checking to make sure no one was listening in. 'Sebastian.'

I stifled a laugh as I imagined the look on Asha's face if she knew that. Sebastian was a show-off who took pleasure in telling other children that they were stupid. It wasn't his fault, it was his mother's. That's what two hours of tutoring a week from the age of five did to a child.

'Well, they'd make a beautiful couple,' I said diplomatically. It didn't matter anyway. At Freya and Aanya's ages, crushes were as fickle as the British weather.

When we got home, Bella was already there, her homework sprawled across the kitchen table. It had been a wrench when Bella first started making her own way to and from school because I'd finally had to admit that she wasn't my little girl any more. But now, in all honesty, it was a relief not to have to worry about getting two children to two different schools at the same time. And Bella was more than capable, she was a lioness compared to Freya, my delicate butterfly. Bella took after her father, she was confident and self-assured. Freya had inherited my tendency to over-analyse everything and become anxious about things we couldn't control. It meant that I could easily empathise with her, but I wanted to make her as resilient as possible because all I dreamed of for my girls was that they would have happy, carefree lives.

I'd found coping mechanisms for my anxiety though, and the older I got, the less I cared what other people thought. Plus, the relentlessness of juggling family life and work filled my brain to capacity, which often left little room for worrying about the small things. But occasionally, when I was feeling low, tired or overwhelmed, the old feelings came creeping back. Social anxiety. Pangs of paranoia. And after the stress of the move, I was still in a state of high alert, which was making my brain fizz with too many unanswered questions. Should we have sold the flat? Could we really afford our mortgage? Did we need a new tap? Could we afford a new tap? What about the damp? What other problems were we going to discover in this house? Would Freya be okay? And then another one crept into my head. Where is Sparkle?

'Have you seen the cat?' I asked Bella.

'No.'

I looked around the room. I hadn't seen Sparkle all day, which was unusual. We'd had her for six years, ever since she was a kitten, and she had been named by Bella, who had been going through a glitter-obsessed phase at the time. Sparkle was a home-girl and she didn't venture far. Usually, she could be found curled up on a chair or sofa, snoozing near me while I worked. But the house move had thrown her, and she hadn't been herself since.

I went to the back door and started calling her name, waiting for a flash of tabby and white to appear from the end of the garden. But there was no sign of her.

'Mummy, what's for dinner?' Freya was always hungry after a long day at school.

'I'll put something on for you in a minute,' I said distractedly, pacing around the room and looking under chairs to see if Sparkle had found a new hiding place. Then I had a thought. What if she'd gone back to the flat? It was only a couple of streets away and she had lived there since she was a baby, so it was possible her homing instinct had led her back there.

After a thorough search of the entire house, I made up my mind.

'Girls, I'm going to pop back to the flat to see if Sparkle has gone there,' I told them. 'Do you want to come?'

'But Mummy, I'm soooo hungry,' Freya protested.

I plucked a banana and handed it to her apologetically. 'It'll only take fifteen minutes.'

'I'll stay here with Bella.'

'Fine. I'll be as quick as I can. Don't answer the door.'

I located my keys and let myself out, walking the short distance to our old flat. As I got closer, I resisted the urge to turn back. I didn't want to go to the flat, it was almost painful, like visiting an ex who had broken my heart. It was unjustified because I was the one who had abandoned the flat, who had moved on to another property, but I couldn't help how I felt. Then I thought about poor, disorientated Sparkle and I forced myself to keep going.

Summer answered the door and looked at me in surprise. 'Naomi!'

'I'm so sorry to bother you,' I said apologetically. 'I just wondered if you'd maybe seen our cat?'

Summer ushered me in and closed the door behind us. I took in the hallway, with the new, unfamiliar wooden sideboard and the plant sitting on top of it. There were some scented candles on there too and the flat smelled clean and fresh. Summer had furnished the place exquisitely, but I still couldn't help feeling like she, and all her things, were imposters in our home. I quickly pushed the thought out of my mind and turned to the matter at hand.

'She's not been right ever since we moved,' I explained. 'And I wondered if she had got confused and come back here. I can't find her anywhere.'

'Don't worry, we'll find her,' Summer assured me. I followed her into the open plan kitchen and living room, my eyes scanning over Summer's belongings, which seemed alien in a space that Oliver and I had inhabited for so many years. I sensed Summer beside me, waiting expectantly for me to make a comment, and I knew that I owed it to her to be generous.

'It looks fantastic in here,' I enthused.

'Thank you,' Summer said and I saw relief on her face. 'But let's try and find this cat.'

She opened the patio doors which led out onto a small, empty courtyard garden. Nowhere for a cat to hide. I called Sparkle's name a few times, in the hope that she might suddenly appear over the wall from a neighbouring garden, but there was no movement.

'I haven't had the door open anyway, so there's no way she would have got into the flat,' Summer told me.

My heart sank. 'Never mind, I'm sorry to have bothered you.'

'Give me your phone number and I'll call you if she turns up.'

We swapped numbers and I tried to hide my distress from Summer. I loved that cat and if anything had happened to her, I would be devastated, not to mention the poor girls.

'She'll be okay,' Summer said reassuringly, placing a hand on my arm.

'Thanks.'

As we walked into the hall, we passed Bella and Freya's old room. The door was closed and I assumed that Luna was inside. But then I heard a noise, and I stopped in my tracks.

'What was that?' I asked.

Summer stopped too. 'What do you mean?'

'I thought I heard a miaow?'

'I don't think so.'

I stood stock-still, unsure. I didn't want to cause a scene but I didn't want to leave either, not if Sparkle was trapped inside the flat somewhere.

'Shall we have a quick look in the bedrooms, in case she snuck in?' I suggested.

'But I told you, I've not had the door open all day. She couldn't have got in.'

I listened eagerly, hoping for another miaow which would be irrefutable evidence that Sparkle was *in situ*. But there was only silence and Summer was looking at me curiously, waiting for me to say my goodbyes and leave.

But it didn't feel right. The niggle was back, an instinct telling me that all was not as it seemed. 'I'd just feel so much better if we checked the rooms.'

Summer's brow creased with annoyance. 'Luna is resting and I really don't want to disturb her. She had a long day at school, and her senses are overloaded. And I think she might be coming down with something too, as she looked very pale this afternoon.'

'Of course, I understand.' With one last, reluctant look at the closed bedroom door, I made my way outside.

'I'll call you,' Summer said, giving me a wave before closing the front door.

Aware that Bella and Freya were home alone, something I rarely allowed, I power-walked back to the house. But I couldn't stop thinking about the miaow I was certain that I'd heard. The closed door. Summer's insistence that Luna not be disturbed, even though it was only just gone five o'clock and far too early for bed. By the time I got home, I was confused and upset.

When I stepped into the kitchen, the first thing I saw was Sparkle, sitting by her empty food bowl and staring up at me with huge, accusing eyes, as if she'd been there all along and I was the one who had been missing. And as relief flooded my body at the sight of our beloved cat, now home safe and sound, I immediately felt embarrassed about my earlier behaviour.

'Where did she come from?' I asked the girls who, by now, were watching TV.

'Dunno, she just showed up,' Bella said, not tearing her eyes away from the screen.

'Did she come in through the cat flap?'

'Dunno.'

I stared at the cat, and she stared back. One of us was losing the plot and I was pretty sure now that it wasn't Sparkle. I quickly put the oven on so that I could get cracking on the girls' much-needed dinner and then got a tin of cat food out for Sparkle. Once everyone was fed, I would text Summer and apologise. Then I would make sure I had a few early nights.

I'd be fine in a few days once the stress of the move had worn off and we were back into our usual routine. Things always took a while to settle down after a major life event. And I hadn't been sleeping well since we moved, which always made me tetchy.

But I was fine. Sparkle was home, Freya seemed happier, and soon Oliver would be back from work. Perhaps we'd open a bottle of wine, something we usually tried to resist during the week. And we could toast to our new house again, and our exciting future.

Yes, everything was okay. Better than okay. We were living the dream and I wasn't going to forget it, no matter how hard my own insecurities tried to sabotage our new start.

4

I looked out of the window and sighed with pleasure. I'd set up an office in the smallest upstairs room, which meant that I could look out over the street as I worked. I'd never had my own office before and it felt like such a luxury. It was also excellent for people-watching and for reminding me that we now lived on the road that I'd walked up and down for years, drooling over the stunning properties. And it took the sting out of the problems we'd found in the house.

A terraced house with wonky windows might not have been everyone's idea of the perfect home, but it was for us. We'd saved for years and then an unexpected bonus from Oliver's work had got us over the finish line. We finally had enough to sell the flat and buy a house. And as I gazed at the tree-lined streets, staring at the leaves that were slowly beginning to change colour, I ignored the leaks and the damp and succumbed to happiness.

I fingered my brown hair as I moved my gaze back to my emails. I'd had it cut into a bob the previous week and I was still getting used to it. I'd had long hair for as long as I could remember but I had decided that it was time for a change. Oliver had given me a wolf whistle when he got home that evening, which had made me giggle, and he had teased me that at least he noticed when I got my hair cut, unlike someone else he knew. I had started going to the gym again too, something I'd got out of the habit of doing months ago. I knew that a quick workout after the morning school run was an excellent mental health boost and I was already feeling so much better. My mind was clearer and the flat was starting to become a distant memory as I remembered how cramped we had felt, how we had always been clambering over each other. How the girls had asked every year for a trampoline but there was no room for one.

It was one of the first things we had bought for the new house. Oliver had ordered one online and had spent hours putting it together, cursing under his breath as I plied him with beer, snacks and compliments about his handyman skills. When it was finally finished, the girls had wasted no time in giving it a test run. Even Bella, who was allegedly too cool for a trampoline now, had laughed with delight as she tried to bounce as high as she could. And as Oliver and I had watched them, with our arms around each other, I had felt such a rush of happiness that I couldn't work out why I'd ever had any doubts, however brief, about our decision.

I wondered it again now, as I sat at my new desk, scanning my emails. Oh, the joy of having my own office. Oliver rarely worked from home, but I was here every day and it had made such a difference to be able to close the door at the end of the afternoon, rather than hastily tidy up the kitchen table, where I'd worked in the flat, ready for dinner duty.

My phone rang and I looked down to see my dad's name on the screen. Although I should be working, I always answered the phone to Dad. He had lived on his own – not far from here – for twelve years, ever since my mum died, and his health wasn't great so I tried to visit him as often as I could. He'd had a stroke five years ago which had left him with limited mobility, meaning he didn't get out much but he loved spending time with the girls and I knew he was happiest when he was with them.

'Hi, Dad.'

'Hi, Naomi, is this a good time?'

'Of course. Is everything okay?'

'Fine, sweetheart. I just fancied a chat.'

I leaned back in my seat and relaxed, happy to shoot the breeze with my lovely dad. After a while, my computer went into sleep mode, and I turned my gaze to the window again. A movement outside caught my eye, and I saw a black and white cat dashing across the road.

I was still embarrassed about what Oliver had dubbed 'cat-gate'. When I had told him what happened, he had failed to hide his amusement.

'So, you accused the poor woman of stealing our cat?' he'd said, snorting with laughter.

'No,' I had insisted defensively. 'I thought I heard a miaow, that's all.'

'Sure, the miaow of the mind.'

I had wanted to be cross with Oliver but I hadn't been able to resist smiling. That was the thing about Oliver, he could make me laugh even when I didn't always feel like it.

'God knows what I heard, if it wasn't a miaow,' I'd continued.

'Maybe it was a miaow after all. Perhaps Sparkle is playing a cruel game. She's playing you off against each other, pretending she lives here and there, that she loves you both, as she runs between the two of you like a tiny little feline polygamist?'

I'd thrown a cushion at him. 'Shut up. I've texted her to apologise, anyway.'

'For wrongly accusing her of stealing our cat.'

'Oliver, I didn't accuse her of stealing our cat.'

Summer had replied to my text message within minutes, telling me not to give it a moment's thought. *I know how traumatic it is to lose a pet*, she'd written. *I totally understand xx*

Since then, I'd resolved to make more effort with Summer. I'd considered inviting Luna round for a playdate but Freya hadn't been keen and I didn't want to push it. She was still adjusting to her new home and class teacher, and it took her a while to get used to change. Just like me, I thought now. But even though I'd made no social plans with Summer, I saw her often, not just at the school gates but also walking up and down our road. It was on the way to the high street, so I knew she used it as a cut-through. And slowly I was beginning to get used to her, her presence in our lives and the fact that she now owned our flat.

'Naomi, are you still there?'

'Sorry, Dad, I was away with the fairies.'

'Ah, I'll let you get off, I know you're busy. Will I see you on Sunday?'

'Of course, I'll bring the girls over in the morning.'

'I'll look forward to it.'

I hung up and went back to my work. I was so busy that I didn't even stop for lunch and by the time it reached three o'clock I was hungry and in danger of being late to pick up Freya. I rushed down the stairs, slipped on my jumper and hurtled out of the door.

Friday was always the busiest day in the playground. As I

walked in, I saw the usual crowd huddled near the benches and I went over to say hello.

'The weather's turned,' Asha said as she rubbed her bare arms vigorously.

'Yep, autumn's well on the way. We'll need to sort out the Halloween costumes soon.'

It was an annual tradition to go trick or treating together, followed by a party at Victoria's house, and we all made an effort to dress up. Freya was already planning her bat outfit.

'We never did sort those drinks,' Asha said. 'We need to get something in the diary.'

'How about tonight?'

'Ooh, I'm free. I'll put a message on the WhatsApp group.'

Asha meant the one between us, Victoria and Rachel, but I could see Angela's neck craning and my heart sank.

'Did someone say drinks?' she cooed.

Asha gave me a look before turning to Angela. 'Yes, we were thinking tonight. But if it's too short notice...'

'Not at all. Count me in! The usual place at 8 p.m.?'

Asha was trying not to grimace. 'Sounds good.'

'What's this?' Rachel sidled up to us, with Victoria behind her.

'Drinks tonight,' I said. 'The usual place.'

'I'm in,' Rachel said. 'I've had a honker of a week.'

'Paul's out tonight so I can't make it,' Victoria said apologetically.

'We should invite Summer,' Asha suggested.

'We should,' I agreed. 'Although I'm not sure she'll get a babysitter at such short notice.'

'Look, she's just arrived so we can ask her.'

As I followed Asha's gaze, I frowned. Something about

Summer was different and it took me a moment to work out what it was. Then it hit me. She'd had her hair cut into a bob, just like mine. And it wasn't just that. She'd coloured it a light brown too so that it was almost identical to my shade. My initial reaction was, *what the hell?* And I was too shocked to hide it.

'Summer, I love your hair!' Asha called. 'When did you have that done?'

'Oh!' Summer put a hand to her hair. 'This morning. It's not too much?'

'No, it looks fabulous.' Asha turned to me, waiting for me to agree. But the words were stuck in my throat and Asha eventually filled the silence. 'We're going out for drinks tonight, can you make it?'

'I'd love to, thank you!' Summer was addressing Asha, but her eyes were on me.

I had to say something. Anything. 'We were worried you wouldn't get a babysitter.'

'I've met a lovely girl who lives in one of the flats upstairs and she's happy to babysit.'

I'd lived in that small block for years and yet I couldn't for the life of me think of who Summer was talking about. I was pretty sure I knew everyone in the building.

'Are you okay, Naomi?' Summer was looking at me with concern.

'Yes, I'm fine,' I croaked. 'I'm just getting used to your new hairstyle.'

'I went to the hairdresser you recommended. Thank you so much, he was brilliant.'

So, she'd gone to my hairdresser, and she'd got an identical cut and colour to me. Summer was right, Lorenzo was brilliant, the best hairdresser I'd ever had. He was more than capable of perfecting a multitude of different styles, so who had suggested this one – him or her?

Thankfully, Summer had turned her attention to Asha now. 'The hairdresser warned me that all the blonde bleach I'd been using for years was wrecking my hair, so he suggested I go back to my natural darker shade. I wasn't sure at first but now I'm really pleased with it.'

'It looks fab,' Asha enthused. 'You definitely need to come out tonight to show it off.'

As Asha gave Summer the name of the local pub that we always went to, I couldn't get rid of the feeling that Summer had deliberately copied my hairstyle. But why would she do that? Summer was the epitome of style, and I was just a regular, run-of-the-mill mum. There was no reason in the world I could think of why Summer would be inspired by me. Was I being unnecessarily paranoid? I wasn't sure but suddenly I wanted to talk to someone about it.

'Asha,' I said quietly, so that Summer couldn't hear. 'Do you fancy coming back to ours for a cuppa after school? Freya would love to play with Aanya.'

'Go on then, thanks.'

'Great.'

The children began to pile out into the playground, and I gave Freya a hug. Her face lit up when I told her that Aanya was coming over to play.

'Can she stay for dinner?' she asked hopefully.

'Maybe,' I said. 'We'll check with her mum.'

The four of us began to walk home and when Freya and Aanya skipped on ahead, I took the opportunity to broach the subject that was playing on my mind.

'Asha,' I said hesitatingly. 'Do you think Summer's hair looks like mine?'

Asha scrunched up her nose. 'Now that you mention it, it does a bit. But didn't she say she went to the same hairdresser?'

'Yes. But why go for the same style? And the same colour?'

'Well, she said it matched her natural colour.'

'I know.'

'And it's not that similar. It's not like it's identical or anything.'

But it looked identical to me. 'I suppose so.'

Asha turned to me. 'Do you not like her?'

I was painfully aware that Asha wasn't the first person to ask me that. Oliver had done the same. 'It's not that I don't like her. She's great. It's just…'

How could I say what I meant? I didn't even know myself. It was a jumble of thoughts, a conflict of emotions. And at the heart of it all was the fear that I was projecting my own irrational feelings about leaving the flat unfairly onto Summer. It was as though I was jealous of her for stealing my prized possession. But she didn't steal it, we sold it to her, so that we could buy the home we had dreamed of living in for years.

'Forget it,' I said. 'Tell me about your new boss at work.'

As Asha launched into a description of her new manager, I tried to concentrate on what she was saying. I did my best to force all thoughts of Summer out of my head. But all I could think about was her walking towards us in the playground, with her perfect new haircut and her stunning dress, looking just like a better version of me.

5

Angela could be a pain in the backside, but her organisational skills were second to none. When I walked into the pub and saw how busy it was, I was thankful that she'd had the foresight to reserve a table for us. None of the rest of us had even thought about it.

I was running late because Freya hadn't wanted me to go out and had used every delay tactic she had up her sleeve to detain me. So I was the last person to show up at the pub and the table was full of mums, as well as Richard who worked freelance and did all of the school runs because his partner worked long hours at a law firm. There were nine, not a bad turnout given the short notice. And at the centre of the table, holding court, was Summer.

The sudden flare of jealousy I felt shocked me with its intensity. I was acting Freya's age, not my own. I was a grown woman turning into a green-eyed monster because my friends had found someone new to play with. What was wrong with me? I plastered a smile on my face and went to get a drink before sitting down on a stool, sandwiched between Angela and Richard. Summer, sitting opposite, leaned over to kiss me and I breathed in her perfume.

'I'm so happy to see you,' she said, and I smiled at her, remembering how nice she was. I gave myself a stern talking-to, just as I would do with the girls. *Don't be a silly sausage.* Meanwhile, everyone was gushing over Summer's new hairstyle and asking where she had got it done.

'Naomi recommended this wonderful hairdresser,' she said. 'His name is Lorenzo and he's just fabulous. So really it's all down to her.'

Angela scrunched up her nose. 'I get my hair done in central London. I just find that the quality is so much more superior than in these suburban salons.'

'Oh, me too,' Richard said, stroking his bald head. 'Only the best for me.'

We all tittered, while Angela tried to work out if he was making fun of her.

'How is Luna settling into school?' Asha asked.

'Very well, thank you.' Summer smiled widely. 'Your lovely children have made her feel so welcome. She particularly speaks highly of Aanya. I think they're becoming good friends.'

My heart sank a little at this. Freya and Aanya had been besties since nursery and three could be a tricky friendship dynamic. What if Freya got pushed out? I'd asked her about Luna a few times since term started, but she hadn't been forthcoming with information.

'You and Luna must come over for a playdate,' Asha said.

'We'd love that.'

'Oh, and you must join us for our annual Halloween event.'

'What's that?'

'We all dress up, even the mums and dads, and go trick or

treating and then everyone goes back to Victoria's for an after-party. It's always a lot of fun.'

'I don't really approve of trick or treating. It's very tacky,' Angela piped up.

'Luna will be so excited to join in. She's never been trick or treating before.'

'I've got loads of different costumes,' Rachel said. She had four children and her oldest was seventeen. 'Feel free to drop by and see if there's anything suitable. Save you wasting your money on an outfit Luna will only wear once.'

'Thank you. Oh, you've all been so welcoming. I can't thank you enough.'

After a few minutes the effort of keeping a group conversation going became too much and we broke off into smaller clusters. On the other side of the table, Summer was chatting easily with Asha and Rachel, while Angela cornered me to discuss whether I had found a suitable tutor for Freya yet. I kept stealing glances at my friends, wishing that I was laughing along with them, rather than being lectured on the importance of preparing my child for the eleven plus exams.

I finished my first glass of wine a little too quickly and when I went to the bar, I decided to order a bottle as I figured that a few people would be up for sharing. I was waiting to order when I saw Sharon Harding, the headteacher at North Hill, walk in with her husband. Sharon was a lovely woman and I had got to know her after helping out with the PTA over the years. I knew she lived locally, but I suspected that she'd rather not spend her Friday evening being interrogated by school mums as to the progress of their little darlings.

'Over there,' I hissed, gesturing to the corner of the pub with my thumb. 'School mum alert. You might want to sit on the other side of the bar.'

Sharon laughed and came over. 'Thanks for the tip. How are you?'

'Great, thanks,' I said. 'We've recently moved house.'

'Oh yes, I saw that you had emailed the office with a change of address. Congratulations.'

'Thank you. Can I get you a drink?'

'Don't worry, my husband's already on the case. So how are you settling in?'

'Up and down,' I admitted, the wine making me loose-lipped. 'We love the new house but all the skeletons are coming out of the closet. You know, the ones they hide when you go and view it. I guess that's the downside of buying a period property.'

'What kind of skeletons?'

'Oh, just the usual. Leaky tap, a bit of damp. Nothing fundamental.'

'You'll get it all sorted, Naomi. How is your friend Summer getting on?'

I'd hardly call her a friend yet, and I wondered why Sharon thought we were. 'I don't really know her that well, but she seems to be settling into the area.'

'Oh, I thought you were close buddies.'

I frowned. 'What do you mean?'

'Well, when she applied for a place at North Hill, she was very insistent that she wanted Luna to be with Freya. She kept calling and leaving messages on the office answerphone, even though it was the school holidays, and I got the impression that she was good friends with you.'

I glanced over at Summer, who was still deep in conversation with Asha and Rachel. Why would she have implied that we were already good friends?

'I suppose she wanted to ensure that Luna got a place,'

Sharon reasoned. 'Not that the calling made any difference. It was just down to the other pupil leaving, in the end. Anyway, I'll leave you to it. Have a lovely evening, Naomi.'

'You too, Sharon.'

As Sharon returned to her husband and I caught the eye of the barman and placed my order, I tried to make sense of what the headteacher had told me. Why had Summer been so insistent that Luna be with Freya? And why had she tried to use a fictitious friendship with me to boost her chances of getting a place? I looked at her again and this time she caught my eye and waved. Her expression was so open and kind, and I felt another pang of guilt. Yet, as the wine I'd guzzled too quickly took effect, I started compiling a mental dossier of evidence against Summer to help me justify why I was starting to feel the way I was about her.

One: She had turned up on the doorstep of our new home. When I had finally summoned up the courage to ask her about it, she'd said that she had been walking down our new road and had recognised our car from when it was parked outside the flat. It was a bit strange but hardly incriminating. Then there had been cat-gate, which I was still embarrassed about. The hair thing was definitely odd in my opinion, but Asha didn't seem to think so. And then there was Sharon's insistence that Summer had suggested we were friends.

It was flimsy, even I knew that. And yet that tiny feeling inside me was growing stronger. Suddenly, I didn't trust Summer. I didn't know why but I didn't. And now I just had to work out why.

* * *

When I got home, Oliver was lounging on the sofa with a beer in one hand and the remote control in the other. Sparkle was lying on his lap, curled up in a ball.

'Hey, did you have a good time?'

'Yes thanks.' I slumped down next to him and took off my shoes, causing Sparkle to jump off and scurry out of the room.

'Any juicy gossip?'

'No, just the usual chit-chat.'

'Was Summer there?'

My head swivelled towards him. 'Why do you want to know that?'

'I was just wondering. Don't bite my head off.'

'Sorry. I've had a strange evening. Yes, she was there.'

Oliver turned the TV down. 'Everything okay, babe?'

I told him about Summer's new haircut and colour, and my conversation with Sharon, hoping that he would understand.

'You know, imitation is the sincerest form of flattery,' he said, stroking my back.

'So, you think she did want to imitate me?'

He shrugged. 'I have no idea. But I wouldn't blame her if she did. Look at you, Nims. You're gorgeous.'

I snuggled up into him. 'Thanks, Ol. But she's more gorgeous.'

'Not to me.'

'You haven't even met her!'

'No one is more gorgeous than you.'

I smiled, enjoying the reassurance from my husband even though I knew I shouldn't need it. 'You know, she used to be a performer. She was in the West End and everything.'

Oliver was nuzzling my neck now. It had been a couple of months since he'd kissed me like this and I was amazed at how quickly my body responded to it.

'I don't care if she was the star of *Les Mis*. She's not a patch on my wife.'

I laughed and closed my eyes, enjoying the sensation of his mouth on my neck.

'And actually I have met her, so there.'

My eyes sprang open and I moved away from him. 'What did you say?'

Oliver looked at me, surprised by my reaction. 'I have met her.'

'When?'

'She popped round at the weekend, when you were out shopping with the girls.'

'What did she want?'

'She couldn't find the keys to the mailbox and wondered if we had a spare.'

'Did we?'

'Yes, I still had one on my key ring so I gave it to her. I should have left it at the flat to be honest, but I totally forgot about it.'

I was staring at Oliver, confused and slightly resentful that Summer had somehow managed to ruin the intimate moment between us. Oliver seemed equally as perplexed.

'Did I say something I shouldn't have?' he asked.

'I'm just wondering why you didn't mention it before.'

'I forgot about it. It wasn't a big deal.'

Oliver was right. It wasn't a big deal. And yet here I was, brooding on it. 'Why didn't she call me or ask me about it at the school gates?'

'She said she was passing and thought she'd knock on the off-chance.'

'What did you think of her?'

Oliver was now looking at me in the way he used to look at

Freya when she had a tantrum because he had cut her toast the wrong way. Wary but also slightly amused.

'She seemed okay. I only spoke to her for a few minutes, if that.'

I looked into the eyes of my lovely husband and realised I was being ridiculous. 'Sorry, Ol. I'm just tired and a little squiffy.'

Oliver stifled a yawn. 'Yeah, I'm tired too. Shall we go to bed?'

I smiled with relief. The mood for any romance had well and truly passed. 'Good plan.'

As we clambered off the sofa, checked on the girls and went to bed, I thought about how lucky I was to have such an amazing husband. Oliver and I had our ups and downs, but we'd always been strong. We had met in our early twenties, when Friday night drinks after work were a given. I was out with my colleagues from the accountancy firm where I was training, and Oliver was with his mates from the marketing agency he worked at. We'd got chatting at the bar and I'd immediately fallen for his Geordie accent and his confident charm. We had ended up going home together, something I'd been embarrassed about in the cold light of the next day, assuming that I was now a one-night stand and I'd never hear from him again. But he'd ended up hanging around for breakfast and then we'd gone out for lunch together too. By the evening, we'd decided that he might as well stay for dinner. And then, of course, it was too late for him to go home so he stayed over again. He had finally left on Sunday and when he said he'd call me the next day, I had known that he would.

We'd gone out together for a few years before buying our first flat together, the one that we had just sold to Summer. We'd always known that we wanted a family but we'd decided to enjoy our twenties first and we'd certainly made the most of it. We'd entertained friends, gone on amazing holidays and generally lived life to the full. After we got married, I fell pregnant with Bella and we had to readjust to our new roles as parents. It had been a shock, but we'd muddled through and Oliver had always been a supportive, hands-on dad. We had assumed that after Bella was conceived so easily, we'd have no trouble getting pregnant again and it had been a blow to learn that wasn't the case. It had been a low point in our lives, as I had become increasingly obsessed with having another child, and then increasingly disappointed when it didn't happen.

Oliver had held my hand throughout. Even when I was constantly going on about ovulation cycles and not much else, he had never once complained. He wanted another child too, but not in the way that I did. It took over my life and each monthly disappointment was like a stab to the heart. I wasn't the easiest person to be around, but he had been my rock. When Freya was finally conceived, he'd shared my joy unequivocally because we had been on the difficult journey together.

It all seemed so long ago now. The girls would always be our babies but they were growing up fast, and soon Bella would be a teenager. Over time, my relationship with Oliver had changed and we were no longer the head-over-heels couple we'd once been. But with Oliver by my side, I'd never felt alone. I'd always had someone in my life who had my back.

It made me think about Summer, who was a single mum. Being a parent was an incredible and rewarding privilege, but it was also relentless and she had no one to share the responsibility with. And she had moved hundreds of miles away where she didn't know anyone. She had no support network, no friends in the area. She hadn't mentioned any family. So, if she had clung on to me a little tightly, if she was a tiny bit too intense, then could I really blame her?

Already my paranoia was beginning to deflate as I began to think reasonably again. I climbed into bed next to Oliver and cuddled up close to him.

'I love you,' I said.

'Love you too, Nims,' he replied in a sleepy voice.

Oliver was asleep within minutes, and I wasn't far behind. But I tossed and turned that night, having strange, abstract dreams where I was back in our old flat, except that it was vast, with dozens of doors lining a long corridor. I could hear the children calling, and Sparkle's miaow, but I didn't know where they were and I became frantic, desperately trying to open the locked doors. And then I saw Summer, walking down the corridor towards me, carrying Freya in her arms. She was wearing my favourite dress and she was laughing. Beside her, Sparkle walked at her heel like an obedient dog. And behind her was Oliver, holding Bella's hand. I called out to them over and over again, screaming their names, but no sound came out. And then I realised that they couldn't see me because I didn't exist in their world. Summer had replaced me.

6

'Crikey, Naomi, you look awful.'

Rachel didn't pull any punches when she saw me at the school gates the following week. Freya had caught a sickness bug at the weekend and had been up vomiting in the night. I'd spent most of the early hours changing bed sheets and comforting her. And then the next day, Bella had picked it up. I thought I'd managed to escape but on Monday, I'd woken up feeling peaky and it hadn't taken long to work out why. Only Oliver had somehow got away with it.

'I'm just glad to be out in the sunlight again,' I said, after I explained that we'd all been sick. 'I've been at home for days and Oliver's been doing the school runs.'

'Noah mentioned that Freya was off school at the beginning of the week. I'm so sorry, I should have checked in. I've just had a crazy week.'

'Don't worry, it's fine. What have you been up to?'

'Oh, the usual ferrying the children to their many activities and we're also having our bathroom done. Plus, we had our first meeting of the PTA.'

'Oh yes, of course, I'm sorry I missed it.'

I wasn't officially on the PTA but I always went along to the meetings and volunteered to help out whenever I could. The school had given my girls so much over the years and I wanted to give something back. Plus, I enjoyed the camaraderie of it, if not the politics.

'Don't worry, you didn't miss much. We've started planning the Christmas fair. Are you okay to organise the raffle again?'

'Yes of course, count me in.'

'Thanks.' Rachel looked sheepish. 'I kind of already did.'

I laughed. 'That's fine.'

'You should speak to Summer too, she's offered to help you.'

I forced a smile. 'That would be lovely. I'll give her a call.'

'And she's donating a free private singing lesson as one of the raffle prizes. Isn't that fabulous? A lesson from a West End star! I think it might end up being the top prize.'

A West End star. Sitting at home feeling sorry for myself had given me too much time to dwell. And I had found myself thinking about Summer more and more. What was her story? Rachel's words got me thinking. If Summer really was that successful, then she'd be all over the internet and it wouldn't hurt to do a bit of googling and see what came up about her. It was essential research, I decided. I needed to write a short bio about Summer if we were offering a lesson from her in the raffle, so it would be good to know more about her background and the shows she'd been in. I knew Bella would want to win that prize when she found out about it.

I lingered by the gates until I saw Summer arriving with Luna. Although she had been at school for a few weeks now, Luna still looked terrified. She clutched her mother's hand like she never wanted to let go, and I noticed how reluctant she was to move away when the bell rang.

I subtly averted my eyes, so as not to embarrass them, and when I looked back, Luna had walked away from her mother and was making her way to her classmates, her expression downcast. Summer, on the other hand, was waving as though nothing at all was amiss.

'Hi, Summer,' I called to her and she smiled at me and walked over.

'Hi, Naomi, how are you feeling? I hear you've been unwell.'

'Much better now, thanks. Have you got time for a quick coffee?'

'Oh, I'd love that!'

'I thought we could talk about the raffle. Rachel mentioned you're keen to be involved.'

Summer's face was a picture of concern. 'Only if I'm not stepping on your toes? I don't want to intrude.'

'Not at all.' I smiled. 'Any help is more than welcome.'

'Great!'

We watched the children troop into the school building and then began to make our way to the local coffee shop.

'Is Luna okay?' I asked.

'Yes, she's fine.'

'It's just that she looked a little nervous.'

Summer was quiet for a few moments. Then she said, in a soft voice, 'I think she's having some trouble fitting in.'

'I'm so sorry to hear that. I'll speak to Freya and make sure that Luna isn't left out.'

Summer opened her mouth as if to speak and then closed it again. 'Thank you.'

We reached the coffee shop and found a table by the window. As Summer took off her coat and hung it over the back of her chair, I stared at her dress. Sensing my gaze, she looked down and then back up at me.

'Oh, I hope you don't mind. I saw you wearing it at the pub the other week and I loved it so much, I bought one for myself. It's just so flattering, isn't it?'

Imitation is the sincerest form of flattery. I tried to focus on Oliver's words. But this was too much, first the hair and now the dress. I gritted my teeth, determined not to seem childish.

'It looks lovely on you,' I said, and I meant it. The dress hung perfectly on Summer, exposing the tiniest bit of cleavage but not too much. My boobs practically spilled out of it when I wore it, so it was reserved for evenings only. And with Summer's extra few inches of height on me, I noticed as I looked down at her legs that the dress ended at the perfect point on her calves, which meant that she could get away with wearing it with trainers.

If it had been Asha, or Rachel, or Victoria, I don't think it would have bothered me. But because it was Summer, I was burning with indignation. Was I the only one who saw what was going on here? Was everyone else blind to the fact that Summer was clearly copying me? But I still had no idea why and I couldn't think of a way to ask her. So instead, I started explaining how the raffle worked and the best way to secure prizes. But I kept glancing down at the dress from time to time, trying to suppress my frown.

'I have a few clients who might be able to help,' Summer said.

'That would be great. What kind of prizes do you think they could offer?'

'One of them writes cookbooks and she'd be happy to donate some signed copies. And I work with a successful masseuse who is based in London, so I'm sure she'd offer a session.'

'Wow, thank you, Summer!'

Despite my rapidly growing reservations about Summer, I was impressed. The most I could usually muster for the raffle was a free brunch at the local coffee shop and a few bottles of wine. The PTA are going to love her, I thought.

'Leave it with me.' Summer was typing a reminder on her phone and as I watched her, I was impressed with her efficiency.

'Do you miss your old work?' I asked her suddenly.

She stopped typing and looked up at me. 'The stage work?'

'Yes.'

Summer put her phone down and seemed to be carefully considering the question. 'Sometimes, yes. I took Luna to a pantomime last Christmas and I felt very envious of all the actors treading the boards.'

'What made you stop?'

'It wasn't a steady job. There'd be times when I was so busy, I had no time for anything else. I'd be working every day, every night. Other times there'd be nothing, no income, and I'd have to find casual work to get by. It was manageable when it was just me to think of, but when I got together with my ex and we wanted to start a family, I knew the lifestyle would have to go.'

'Would you ever go back to it? When Luna is a bit older?'

Summer shook her head. 'I don't think so. I feel like that part of my life is over now. Sometimes it almost seems surreal, like it never really happened in the first place.'

'Are you still in touch with anyone from those days?'

'Not really, no. After I moved to Devon, I lost touch with pretty much everyone.'

'Is that why you came back to London, though? Did you miss it?'

Summer looked at me with her head cocked and I couldn't

read her expression. Was she annoyed with me for asking so many questions, or flattered that I was interested in her?

'Yes and no,' she said. 'I've always loved London and, because I lived here before, I guess it felt familiar to me. But the main reason was to get Luna away from her father.'

'We don't have to talk about this,' I said quickly.

'No, it's fine, I don't mind. You see, in Devon, he was there, which was a constant reminder of what a useless dad he is. When he cancelled planned outings with Luna, we both knew that he was only a couple of miles away, with his new family. And we used to bump into them sometimes, in town or at the supermarket. It was confusing and upsetting for Luna.'

'I can imagine.'

'So, I thought, if he's not going to be in her life properly, why not put some distance between us? I thought it would be easier for Luna, and for me.'

'Did he mind that you moved so far away?'

'He got huffy about it at first, started talking about lawyers and court orders. But when I reminded him that he'd had Luna to stay twice in a year, it soon shut him up.'

Twice in a year. I couldn't believe it. Oliver would rather die than see his children so little. What a horrible, selfish man her ex must be. My heart went out to Summer, and to Luna, and I made myself look at her directly in the eye, forcing my gaze away from her dress.

'If there's anything I can do to help, please let me know,' I said, and I meant it.

'You've done so much already, Naomi. You've welcomed me into your community and I really am grateful. To be honest, I was very nervous about moving.'

'I'm not surprised, it's quite a wrench.'

'Yes, it is and yet I feel like I've already made more close friends here in Barnet than I did living in Devon for a decade. And people say London is unfriendly!'

She'd only been living here for a few weeks, so 'close friends' was a bit of a push, but I let it go. My head was all over the place, oscillating between liking and disliking Summer. Twenty minutes ago, I was suspicious of her. Now I was in awe again.

By the time we finished our coffee, I was immensely relieved that I'd suggested it because, despite a rocky start, I felt it had cleared the air. Summer and I had got along well and there had been no strange vibes, other than the fact that she was wearing my dress, of course. But she had been honest about why she got it and I had recently bought a jacket after admiring it on Victoria. Oliver was right, I thought; if Summer was inspired by my hair and clothing choices, then I should be flattered, not dubious.

When I got home and opened my laptop, I couldn't resist googling her. I was expecting hundreds of hits, so I was surprised when nothing related to the stage came up. And when I clicked on social media profiles belonging to a Summer Caldwell none of the photos matched the Summer I knew. Did she use her maiden name instead? I wondered. But I was certain she'd referred to her ex as a partner and not a husband, so I didn't think she'd been married before.

Maybe she used a stage name. I started googling terms like 'Caldwell' and 'stage' and before I knew it, half an hour had passed, and I was well behind schedule with work. Reluctantly, I closed the browser and opened my email instead, trying to immerse myself in my tasks for the day. But I was preoccupied. Why was there no trace of Summer online? Why were there no photographs or interviews with her if she'd really been a big West End star back in the day? And why, for that matter, was there no trace of her virtual assistant business either?

I'd gone round in a circle again, my unease about Summer returning. It was almost impossible not to have a digital footprint these days and yet Summer had succeeded. But why would she be so keen to remain anonymous? I started to wonder if I had been right after all, if there was something off about Summer. Had she really been telling us the truth about her past or was she keeping a secret from us? If she was, I wanted to find out what it was.

Deep down I knew that I was fixating. I'd done it before, not on a person but on a particular issue or worry. It was what I did when I was anxious, my thoughts became more obsessive and intrusive. However, although I knew that the stress of the house move had triggered my anxiety, I still felt sure that Summer's behaviour was partly to blame. This wasn't all in my head, I assured myself. It had been caused by Summer's over-interest in me. And yet hadn't I just spent the morning googling her?

I'd talk to Oliver tonight, I decided. Tell him how I was feeling. Oliver was great at reassuring me and helping me to see the world for what it was again. And once we'd fixed the problems with the house, I'd feel much better. I'd see the property for what it was, a promising family home which just needed some TLC. I'd stop putting the old flat on a pedestal and remember it wasn't so perfect after all. But the pang of regret was still there, lingering at the back of my mind and it was beginning to haunt me. If we'd stayed in the flat, everything would be just as it should be. It was only when we moved that I started to feel this anxious.

And a single thought went round and round in my head. *We've made a mistake.*

7

'Why are you so obsessed with her?'

Oliver was washing the dishes as I stood beside him with a tea towel in hand, ready to dry. The dishwasher had just packed up too. It seemed like everything was going wrong with the house and we'd put all our savings into buying it, leaving us with little contingency for emergencies. To say I was stressed was an understatement and the conversation with Oliver, which I had been looking forward to, was not going to plan either.

'Oliver, I'm not obsessed with her.'

'Sounds like it. You won't stop banging on about her. I think you have a crush on her.'

Oliver's wry humour usually amused me but today it rankled. 'That's not funny.'

'Should I be worried? Are you about to embark on a passionate affair with the mysterious Summer? Will you move back to the flat and take Sparkle with you?'

I scowled at him. 'Stop it.'

He grinned. This was a joke to him, but I was struggling to

find it funny. 'Look,' he said. 'I've only met her once but she seemed harmless. So she bought your dress. It's a nice dress.'

'It wasn't just the dress though, was it? She also got the same hairstyle as me. And I can't find anything about her online. You must admit that's a bit strange.'

'So what? You think she's moved all the way from Devon just to mess with you?'

'No, of course I don't think that. I just think she might not be who she says she is.'

'You mean she might be your long-lost lover?'

'Oliver, stop it.' This time I couldn't suppress my smile.

'From what you've told me, it sounds like she's had a rough time. So maybe cut her some slack, okay? If she does want to keep herself offline, so what? Maybe she wants a fresh start.'

'I guess so.'

'Anyway, I'd better go freshen up. I don't want to be late for the dads.'

Oliver was going out for drinks with some of the school dads. They didn't meet up anywhere near as often as the mums did, but they tried to organise something a couple of times a year. Oliver got on particularly well with Asha's husband and, as they both lived in houses full of women, I imagined they'd spend a glorious evening talking about man-stuff.

'You go, I'll finish up here.'

'We need to get someone round to fix the dishwasher. And the tap.'

'On the to-do list after payday.'

Oliver disappeared up the stairs and I finished the dishes and went into the front room to see what the girls were up to. Freya was playing with Lego and Bella was on her phone.

'Bella, it's nearly phone curfew time.'

Bella rolled her eyes. 'Yeah, I know.'

Oliver emerged, wearing a fresh shirt and he smelled of aftershave. I leaned in to give him a hug. 'You smell lovely,' I told him.

'Thanks. Maybe I'll pull tonight.'

'Good luck, mate.'

He gave me a kiss and I sat down on the sofa next to Bella and put the TV on.

'Want to watch a film, girls?'

'Sure,' Freya said.

'Bella?' I asked.

Bella's eyes were still glued to her phone. 'Yeah, whatever.'

I started browsing until I saw the eighties film *Girls Just Want to Have Fun*. 'Ooh, I used to love this film,' I said. 'Let's watch it!'

Bella looked up briefly. 'What's it about?'

'It's about a teenager who wants to be on a famous dance television show.'

Now I had Bella's full attention. 'That sounds cool.'

'Hold fire, I'll get some snacks.'

I dashed into the kitchen, excited about introducing my girls to an eighties classic, and located some popcorn and chocolate. Filling my arms, I headed back into the living room and deposited the goodies on the coffee table. The girls immediately dived in.

'This is the best film ever,' I said. 'You'll love it.'

I started the film and as Bella and Freya cuddled up to me on the sofa, munching on popcorn, my heart filled with happiness. This was the perfect cure for my stress – a night in with my two favourite girls. Ever since we'd moved house, I hadn't been sleeping well. My mind was too overloaded with worries and things that needed to be done. So it was no wonder that I was frazzled. But I could almost feel the tension seeping out of me now and I put my arm around both girls and settled in for a relaxing evening.

Halfway through, Bella got up and started dancing around the room. 'Mum, this film is so cool! I wanna be a dancer like Janey!'

Then Freya, who had no interest in performing arts, got up and started dancing too, giggling as she twirled around the room. Soon I was up with them, laughing as I struck some poses. I turned the volume up and we went for it, prancing around the room, as high as kites, and I thought that this was the happiest I'd been since we moved into this house. This was the reason why we'd put ourselves through all that stress. We'd finally found our forever home, with the space that we had craved, and now we could enjoy it and live our best lives. Already I was seeing the house in a different light, like a high-maintenance but beautiful and special friend. The peeling paint in the front room was blurring at the edges and I could see the future version of me, laughing about how stressed I'd been when we moved, how the broken dishwasher had almost tipped me over the edge but now it seemed so trivial.

A movement caught my eye and I looked out of the window, peering into the darkness. Had it been Sparkle, jumping up onto the sill and trying to get our attention? She had a cat flap but she was lazy and preferred us to open the front door for her. Then I saw the movement again and I froze with instant terror. That wasn't a cat, it was a person.

'Stay here, girls,' I said, and my tone made them both stop and stare at me.

'What is it, Mum?' Bella asked. Freya went and stood closely by her sister's side.

'Nothing,' I said, trying to keep my voice calm. 'I just thought I heard the doorbell.'

I went out into the hall, my heart pounding, as I tried to decide if I was doing the right thing. If there was an intruder out there, surely opening the door was a terrible idea? But I had to put my mind at ease, I had to know if someone was out there.

I opened the door slowly and peered out into the darkness, listening keenly for any noise but all I could hear was the soundtrack to the film we were watching. I stepped out tentatively, all my senses on high alert, and called, 'Is anyone there?'

Once I stepped off the porch, I had full view of our front garden and a quick check confirmed that no one was there. But I was certain that I'd seen someone at the window. I gave our car the once-over to see if anyone had tried to break in, but it was untouched. Then I walked to the window myself, looking into the house. There were Bella and Freya, helping themselves to more popcorn, the light from the floor lamp giving the room a soft glow. If someone had been watching us, they would have had full view of the three of us dancing our socks off.

I looked around again and then peered into the flower beds underneath the window and that was when I saw it. I reached out and picked it up, staring at it in confusion. It was a camera, not an expensive one but a cheap pink one. Did it belong to the girls? Bella had asked for a camera a couple of years ago, before she was allowed a phone, but after a few weeks she'd lost interest and I hadn't seen it since. I couldn't even remember what colour it was now.

I glanced back up at the girls and then turned the camera around and switched it on to have a look at the saved images. But the memory card was blank. Was this just Bella's old camera? Perhaps it had fallen out of a box when we moved in and I'd only just noticed it?

But it didn't feel right. Someone had been watching us, I

thought, as fear gripped me. They had been planning to take photos of me and the girls before they were frightened off. But who would do that? Was it a burglar, scoping out a potential site or was it personal? A shiver ran up my spine and I quickly dashed inside and closed the door, craving the comfort of being back in the warmth again. I wanted to call Oliver, or the police, but I wasn't sure if I was overreacting, so I leaned up against the door to catch my breath and consider the options.

Summer. Her name popped into my head and once I'd thought it, I couldn't stop. Had it been her at the window? She'd already shown what I suspected to be an unhealthy interest in me, even if Oliver didn't agree. Was she becoming obsessed with me? It seemed so far-fetched that I almost laughed. And then I remembered Oliver accusing me of being obsessed with her.

What the hell was going on? I was confused and afraid. The girls, bored of waiting for me, piled out into the hall and looked at me.

'What are you doing, Mum?' Bella asked.

'Nothing,' I said as brightly as I could. 'False alarm, there was no one there.'

'But you were ages.' Bella's eyes moved down to the camera in my hand. 'What's that?'

'I found it outside in the flower bed. Is it yours, Bella?'

Bella stepped forward and took it from me, turning it over in her hand. 'Nope.'

My heart began to beat even faster. 'Someone must have dropped it,' I said.

'It's quite cool. Can I keep it?'

'No,' I snapped, and Bella looked at me in alarm. 'It doesn't belong to us,' I said in a more conciliatory tone. 'We should leave it out on the wall, in case someone's looking for it.'

Bella was pressing some buttons. 'There's no photos, it must be new.'

I caught Freya's eye and tried to give her a reassuring smile. 'Never mind. Shall we go back and watch the film?'

We went into the front room and I closed the curtains tightly before sitting down on the sofa again. Bella came to sit next to me, oblivious to my discomfort but Freya hovered and I could feel her eyes boring into me. She could sense that I was unsettled and if I called the police now, she'd be terrified. Anyway, what would I tell them? That I had found a camera in my front garden? It was hardly the crime of the century. No, I decided. I would let it go and speak to Oliver about it when he got home. He'd know what to do.

I leaned back and beckoned for Freya to join me, which she did eventually, and then put the film back on. But it was like my earlier joy had been sucked out of me, and I think the girls felt it too because neither of them got up to dance again. After a few minutes Freya went to sit on the floor and started playing with Lego. And then Bella covertly started peeking at her phone, even though it was past curfew. By the time the film ended, none of us were paying attention.

When Oliver came home, after the girls had gone to bed, I'd worked myself up into a bit of a state. The moment he walked through the door I rushed towards him and threw myself into his arms, craving the familiar warmth of his body.

'Whoa there,' he said, staggering backwards and I knew immediately that he was tipsy.

'Sorry,' I said. 'It's been an odd evening.'

'Why? What happened?'

I led him into the kitchen and told him what had happened. His eyes widened when I mentioned the camera.

'But who would be taking photos of you?'

'Well,' I began hesitatingly, knowing how absurd this was going to sound. 'I wondered if it was Summer.'

'Why on earth would Summer take photos of you?'

'I don't know, Oliver.'

Oliver looked at me for a few moments, almost as though he was trying to work me out. And because he was drunk, it took him longer than usual.

'It wasn't Summer,' he said, and there was a note of certainty in his voice.

'How can you be so sure?'

'Because she was at the pub.'

I stared at him in shock. 'She was what?'

'She was at the pub.'

'With you?'

'Well, not just with me, with all of us.'

'The dads?'

'Yeah.'

I couldn't believe what I was hearing. Why would Summer go out with all the dads?

'She's a right laugh,' Oliver continued, clearly oblivious to my discomfort.

'But how did she even know about it?'

'Dunno. Maybe Richard invited her. He was there too and I think they're good pals.'

This revelation blew my theory out of the water. If it wasn't Summer at the window, then who was it? And clearly Oliver was wondering the same thing, as he said, 'Are you sure you saw someone?'

Was I sure? Now that a few hours had passed, I couldn't be certain. Perhaps I'd seen a light from a passing car, or someone walking along the pavement.

'But what about the camera?' I asked him.

Oliver shrugged and I could see that he was sleepy. He always passed out after a few drinks. 'Maybe it belongs to the old owners.'

Was Oliver right? Had I got myself all worked up for no reason? I was starting to feel ridiculous, especially after hearing that Summer had been out that evening. My mind was playing tricks with me and I didn't like it. But I also didn't like the idea of Summer being out with all the dads either.

'Did you talk to her?' I asked Oliver.

'Talk to who?' Oliver was almost drifting off at the kitchen table now.

'Summer.'

'You really are obsessed with her.'

'I'm not, okay? I'm just interested.'

'A bit.'

'What did you talk about?'

'Can't really remember.'

It was clear that I wasn't going to get any sense out of my husband tonight. I stood up to get us some water and then followed Oliver up the stairs. He fell asleep without even brushing his teeth but as I lay in bed beside him, I couldn't nod off.

I thought about Oliver's words. *You're obsessed with her.* Even my own husband thought I had an unhealthy interest in Summer, and yet I was convinced it was the other way around. So who was right, Oliver or me? And why was I letting this woman get into my head so much? I tried to force her out of my mind and go to sleep but I couldn't. I kept thinking about Summer getting home from the pub where she'd been drinking with my husband, walking into my flat, pouring a glass of water from my sink and going into my bedroom. And then I thought about the pink camera I'd found. Could she have nipped over halfway through the evening, saying she was going to the loo or had to check on Luna? The pub was only a couple of minutes' walk away, so she could easily get away with it. I'm going mad. The thought swirled around in my head until the early hours, tormenting me, and still, all I could think of was her.

8

———————

'Are you okay, love?'

Victoria was working from home and we'd met for a quick weekday lunch at the local cafe. I was distracted and she'd clearly noticed.

'I'm fine,' I said quickly.

But Victoria didn't buy it. 'What's on your mind?'

I'd been wondering this myself. Why I was so on edge. Why I'd been convinced that someone was watching us through the window the other week. Why I'd immediately suspected it was Summer. And I had a possible explanation, which I needed to get off my chest.

'It's the new house.' My heart sank as I said it. 'I built it all up in my head, turned it into this perfect, dream home and it's not living up to it.'

'Why not?'

'It's old and leaky and it seems like such a huge mountain to climb to get it to how we want it to be. We can't afford to fix anything right now, we've spent all of our savings and our mortgage payments are ridiculously high. It just doesn't feel like home, and I miss the flat.'

Victoria nodded sympathetically. 'Of course you do. But you'd outgrown that flat, you said so yourself.'

'I know that but now I'm seeing it with rose-tinted spectacles. I've selectively forgotten all the bad stuff and I only remember the good. Nothing ever seemed to go wrong there, everything worked just fine. And it was cosy and easy. It was home.'

'The house will feel like home soon too, Naomi, I promise. It's just teething problems. I remember when we moved house, I cried for a week.'

I looked at her incredulously. 'Really?'

'Yes. I was so tired and stressed. And everything we'd loved about the house when we first bought it, I suddenly hated. I thought it was the biggest mistake we'd ever made.'

'And now?'

She laughed. 'Now I adore it and I'm never leaving. You'll have to wheel me out of there.'

I grinned. 'Thank you, Vic. I really needed to hear that.'

'You'll make it yours, Naomi, over time. You'll fix all the problems and put your own stamp on it. Just like Summer has done with the flat.'

I looked at her sharply. 'You've been there?'

'Yes, she invited us round for a drink. I thought it might be odd, because I've only ever known it as yours and Oliver's place, but it had a different feel to it now, you know?'

But I was barely listening. All I could think was, Who is 'us'? And why didn't she also invite me?

'Maybe she thought it might be odd inviting you back to your old flat,' Victoria said hurriedly, realising that I might have felt excluded. 'It wasn't everyone, just a few people.'

I tried to keep my voice neutral. 'Who else was there?'

'Just Asha, Rachel and Richard.'

So all my good friends, then. This conversation, which had started to make me feel so much better, was now troubling me and Victoria had clearly clocked it.

'I shouldn't have said anything,' she said with a worried expression.

'No, it's fine,' I said dismissively. 'I'm not at all offended.'

But I was. That was the truth of it. One minute Summer was telling me I was beautiful, styling her hair like mine and buying my dress. The next she was inviting all my friends over but not me. Could I blame her, though? I was polite but I hadn't been overly friendly recently. In truth, I had started to keep my distance from her. Maybe she thought of me as more of an acquaintance, as she slowly started to build solid friendships with the others. Or maybe Victoria was right and she just thought it would be awkward to invite me to my old flat.

I was tempted to confess to Victoria that I wasn't sure about Summer. But I was worried that she would think I was stirring, or being bitchy because Summer hadn't invited me round for drinks. I didn't want to be a victim of the school mum rumour mill, preferring to keep myself out of any politics. And although I adored Victoria, I could hardly expect her to believe me about Summer, especially if I wasn't even certain how I felt about her myself.

But yet again, I was thinking about Summer, and it infuriated me. It was like she had infected my life and I couldn't get away from her. She seemed to come up in every conversation, she was everywhere I went, she was even helping me out with the damn raffle. I'd been grateful for the October half-term break, so that I could switch off from it all for a bit, but now the children were back at school, I'd been thrown head first back into it again.

I shook my head, trying to forcibly remove all thoughts of Summer and abruptly changed the subject, asking Victoria how her job was going, how the kids were getting on at school. By the time we parted ways, I only had a couple of hours left before I had to pick Freya up and I threw myself into work, refusing to think about anything else but numbers. By the time I left the house again, it had started raining, and I pulled an umbrella out, fretting about the window in our bedroom which had started leaking. It was yet another thing to add to the endless to-do list. I thought about my conversation with Victoria earlier, about how all these problems would get fixed in time, and I would learn to love the house. I hoped she was right. And I felt ungrateful for even feeling the way I did because we were so lucky to own a house and to live where we did.

Then I thought about the Halloween party the following evening and hoped that the rain would clear before then. The kids were so looking forward to it and I'd spent hours making a bat costume for Freya. For the first time, Bella had decided not to come this year and was going to a party at a friend's house instead. It felt like the end of an era and I wanted to cling on to the childhood tradition for a tiny bit longer. I imagined the warm cosiness of Victoria's house, the pumpkin spiced cupcakes she was famous for, and the delicious red wine and my mouth watered. Then I thought about Summer being there and it was like she had tainted it.

When I arrived at school, the other parents were huddled under the bike shelter, looking miserable, and I headed over to Asha.

'This is grim,' she said.

'Tell me about it.'

'I hope it clears before tomorrow.'

'I was thinking the same thing, otherwise trick or treating will be a washout.'

'I'm picking up Luna today. She's coming over for a playdate.'

This mundane piece of news shouldn't have upset me, but it did. 'That's nice.'

'She's become very friendly with Aanya.'

I thought again of Freya and hoped she wasn't feeling left out. Like mother, like daughter. But Asha was oblivious to my discomfort. 'She's a sweet girl, once you get to know her. Aanya's very taken with her.'

The doors opened and the children began to spill out. I spotted Aanya and Luna, holding hands, as the teacher dismissed them and they ran over to Asha. But where was Freya? Then she appeared at the door, with her head down, and my heart sank. She was upset, I realised, and it was most likely because she had heard about the playdate she wasn't invited to.

I plastered an enormous smile on my face and spread my arms out wide to welcome her. But she trudged over, refusing to meet my eye and hovered in front of me.

'Hi, darling,' I said, putting my arms around her. 'Did you have a good day?'

Freya glanced at Luna and Aanya, who were ripping open a snack that Asha had brought for them. Then she looked up at me and her expression broke my heart into a million pieces.

'Shall we go to McDonald's for dinner?' I asked hopefully, desperate to cheer her up.

'I'm not hungry.'

I wanted to cry. I knew that this was all part and parcel of growing up, that friendship dynamics could be tricky, and that you couldn't be invited to every playdate, but all I wanted to do was protect my daughter. I spotted Noah, Rachel's son, and had an idea.

'Shall we see if Noah wants to come with us?'

Freya's face brightened a fraction and hope surged through me. But then I saw Noah running off with Sebastian and realised that Rachel wasn't here to pick him up. Dammit. But I was in too deep now and I was determined to salvage something from this mess.

I walked over to Angela. 'Are you picking up Noah today?'

'Yes, he's having supper with us.'

'Do you all fancy coming to McDonald's?'

Angela pulled a face. 'I don't like Sebastian eating fast food.'

'Come on, just this once. For a treat.'

'I'm not sure Rachel will approve.'

I thought of the numerous times I'd been to McDonald's with Rachel. 'She won't mind.'

Angela looked uncertain, evidently torn between accepting the surprise invitation to socialise and sticking to her healthy eating guns. I held my breath.

'Okay, just this once,' she said, and I exhaled with relief.

'Great!' I beckoned Freya over. 'Noah and Sebastian are going to come with us.'

Freya looked uncertainly at Sebastian, but she smiled slightly. 'Okay.'

We walked towards the high street and I noticed that the boys ran on ahead, leaving Freya walking alongside Angela and I. Already I was beginning to regret my hasty decision. In my attempt to buoy Freya, I might have made her feel even more excluded.

When we reached the restaurant, I made sure that the kids all sat together while I went to place the order. By the time I returned, they were chatting together and I immediately felt better. I dished out the meals and took a sip of the cola I had ordered for myself.

'This is nice,' I said.

Angela looked around, her nose wrinkling. 'It's very busy.'

'It always is at this time. But the kids are enjoying themselves. So, how are you, Angela?'

She looked at me warily. I rarely asked her how she was. In fact, I usually went out of my way to avoid her because, although her heart might be in the right place, she was hard work.

'It's not working out with the tutor,' she said with a heavy sigh. 'She's not challenging Sebastian enough.'

'I'm sorry to hear that,' I said, even though I couldn't care less. 'Have you found another?'

'I'm trying but the waiting lists are huge.'

'That's tough.'

'And Sebastian is having a hard time at school. That's actually why I invited Noah to play today.'

I looked at her sympathetically. 'I'm sorry.'

'I don't understand why he's not making friends.'

I did, but I didn't want to say that to Angela. 'It's common to have friendship issues at this age. It'll sort itself out. And the three of them seem to be getting along well.'

We both turned to look at the kids, who were tucking into their fries.

Angela was the last person in the world I'd usually confide in, but something about the candidness of our conversation made me unexpectedly want to open up.

'I'm worried about Freya too,' I whispered.

She looked at me keenly. 'Why's that?'

'Well, she's been best friends with Aanya for years and now Aanya has palled up with Luna. I think she's feeling left out.'

Angela leaned in towards me. 'I heard something about her,' she hissed.

'Who?'

'Luna.'

She had my full attention now. 'What did you hear?'

Angela looked at the children to make sure they weren't earwigging. 'Well, Sebastian told me that she can barely read or write. It's like she's never been to school before.'

I frowned. If this had come from another child, I'd be inclined to believe it, but Sebastian was convinced that everyone else was academically inferior to him.

'And she seems to be creating a divide in the class,' Angela continued. 'She acts all meek but she's trouble. Sebastian doesn't like her at all.'

Again, I wasn't sure that Sebastian was the best child to rely on for a character assessment. But I was intrigued, nevertheless. Freya had offered little information about Luna and I decided to broach the subject when we got home and see what I could find out.

Freya was in brighter spirits on the way home, despite the rain. We made a dash for it and as soon as we reached the house, we took off our shoes, peeled off our wet coats and headed into the kitchen. Bella was at choir, so we had the place to ourselves. I put the kettle on to make a cup of tea and then sat down next to Freya at the table.

'Are you excited about the Halloween party?' I asked her.

'I guess.'

'What is Aanya dressing up as?'

'A witch.'

'Lovely. How about Luna?' Freya's face fell and I wondered if I'd gone about this the wrong way. But I was determined to get my daughter to talk to me. 'Is everything okay at school?'

She looked away.

'Freya, darling,' I said in a soft voice. 'Is this about Aanya and Luna?'

Her nod was almost imperceptible.

'I've heard that they've become friendly but that doesn't mean that you can't be friends with Aanya too, darling. She's still your best friend.'

'No, she's not.'

Freya's eyes welled up and I gave her a cuddle. 'Oh darling, I'm sorry. I know it's hard.'

It was like I'd opened the floodgates. Once Freya had started, she couldn't stop and it was clear that she'd been carrying the weight around with her for some time.

'Aanya is best friends with Luna now,' she said, the words spilling out of her. 'And they don't want to play with me any more.'

It was typical schoolgirl politics, but this was my daughter, and it hurt to hear it.

'Do you want me to speak to their mums?' I suggested.

'No!' Freya said vehemently. 'No, Mummy, don't do that.'

'Okay,' I said quickly. 'But listen, Aanya is a lovely girl. Maybe she doesn't know that you're feeling left out. Have you tried speaking to her?'

'Luna won't let me.'

I pulled away and looked at my daughter in surprise. 'She won't let you?'

'She won't let me talk to Aanya any more.'

I thought of what Angela had said about Luna and

wondered now if she'd been right. How had I not realised this was going on? Why had Freya not told me sooner?

'That isn't kind of Luna, and I think you should tell a teacher.'

Freya's lip wobbled. 'I don't want to.'

I put my arm around her again. 'I know, sweetheart, but it might help.' Already I was thinking about calling the school myself to have a word. 'Why don't I arrange a playdate with Aanya? Just the two of you. And you can have a chat without Luna being there.'

'She won't want to come.'

'I'm sure she would.'

'No, thank you.'

I thought about what else I could offer up. 'What about Noah? Could you play with him?'

'Noah only wants to play with the boys at school.'

An image popped into my head of Freya in the playground, alone and sad, and tears pricked at my eyes. I wanted to march round to Asha's house and have it out with the girls.

'What about some of the other girls?' I suggested.

Freya shrugged.

'There are lots of other lovely children in your class, darling. Maybe you should try and play with them a bit more. And I'm sure Aanya will realise how much she misses you. This friendship with Luna might only last five minutes. You two have been friends for a long time.'

'Everyone hates me.'

Her words were like a punch to the gut. 'No they don't, darling.'

'Yes, they do.'

'Why would you say that?'

But Freya just looked down at her socks.

'Freya?'

She had shut down and I knew she wouldn't open up again, not right now. I just hoped that she would talk to me more when she was ready. But what did I do until then? I'd never faced this problem before. Bella had the usual spats with her friends from time to time but never anything serious. And Freya and Aanya had always been buddies, a mutual security blanket which had helped to ease the transition from nursery to primary school. Now, it seemed that the dynamic had shifted and I was trying to work out how best to support my daughter.

I'd observe them at the party the next day, I decided. See if I could work out what was going on for myself. It might all be a fuss about nothing and the three of them would be the best of friends by the end of the week. If not, I'd speak to the teacher and ask him to keep an eye on Freya. And if I felt it was necessary, I'd speak to Asha and even Summer, even though Freya had asked me not to. I'd do whatever it took to fix this for my daughter.

Later, when Freya had gone to bed and Bella was upstairs reading, I relayed the conversation to Oliver.

As always, he was philosophical. 'Sounds like the usual playground stuff to me.'

'I know, Oliver, but it's horrible for Freya.'

'Can't she just play with someone else?'

'It's not that simple, though, is it?'

'So what can we do about it?'

'I'm going to speak to the school and maybe the girls' parents.'

'Sounds like you have it all in hand, babe.'

'Poor Freya, though. First the house move and now this. Sometimes I wish that Bella was still at primary school, to keep an eye on her. She'd stick up for Freya, stop any bullying.'

Oliver turned round to face me. 'You think she's being bullied?'

'I don't know. Maybe I'm overreacting. Perhaps it's just temporary friendship issues.'

'I have to say, it sounds like it to me. But we'll keep an eye on it.'

Oliver had never been bullied at school. But I had, and I remembered it acutely. The cruel hostility radiating from the popular group of girls who had chosen me as their victim. The sting of their mocking laughter. The pain of fear, loneliness and isolation. It didn't matter that they hadn't laid a hand on me, it had still hurt as much as if they'd physically attacked me and I wouldn't wish it on my worst enemy, let alone my daughter.

I tried to remember what I had done at the time. I hadn't said anything to my parents about it for weeks. But my mum had realised that something was wrong because I was so sullen and quiet, and I kept feigning illness to get out of going to school. Eventually, she had got it out of me and the next morning, she had marched into the playground, gone up to the girls and given them a piece of her mind in front of everyone. I think a few people might have even clapped afterwards, as Mum strutted away. The girls had left me alone after that.

I smiled at the memory. You couldn't get away with that kind of thing any more, you'd get into all sorts of trouble. But my mum had been my hero that day and I wanted to be Freya's hero too. I just had to work out how. *I wish you were here, Mum.* It had been a long time since Mum passed away but sometimes I felt her loss as acutely as the day she died and all I wanted to do was to pick up the phone and call her. She'd know what to do.

As Oliver and I settled down to watch TV, I couldn't stop

thinking about the misery on Freya's face when she told me that everyone hated her. It was etched into my mind and I couldn't distract myself from it. If only Summer and Luna hadn't moved here, I thought, then none of this would have happened. I could feel the seed of resentment towards them that had embedded itself inside me growing. And I knew it wouldn't take much to make it flourish.

9

Freya's scream pierced through the silence and I sat bolt upright before I'd even fully woken up. Beside me, Oliver stirred and opened his eyes.

'What's going on?' he asked sleepily.

'It's Freya. I'll go.'

I clambered out of bed and ran across the landing to Freya's room. When I pushed the door open, she was thrashing about, and I knew immediately what was happening.

'Freya,' I said, sitting on the side of her bed. 'Freya, it's Mummy.'

Freya's night terrors had started again. She'd gone through a phase of having them a few years ago, when she first started school, but then she grew out of them. Now they were back with a vengeance and I feared that this trouble with Aanya and Luna, combined with the house move, had triggered them. But I remembered what to do and I sat quietly, waiting for her to calm down. I knew that trying to restrain or wake her could frighten her even more because we had been here before. I just wished we weren't back again.

After a few minutes Freya stopped shaking and opened her eyes, looking at me in fright.

'It's okay, sweetheart, you had a night terror.' Gradually Freya's eyes came back into focus and she blinked a few times. 'You're safe, darling, Mummy's here.'

I was exhausted. Freya's night terrors had started just as I was getting over the insomnia that had plagued me for weeks. I couldn't remember the last time I'd had a full night's sleep, but it was probably when we were still in the flat. Instinctively I imagined our cosy old bedroom and thought of Summer tucked up in bed underneath the beautiful gold pendant light we'd splashed out on. We'd decided to leave it there as a gift for the new owner because it suited the flat so perfectly. Now I wish we'd brought it with us.

I stroked Freya's forehead, brushing away stray wisps of her hair, which had stuck to her sweaty face. 'Shall I get into bed with you?'

'Yes please.'

Freya shuffled over and I climbed in, moving a few stuffed toys out of the way and covering us both with the duvet. Freya pressed her body up against mine and we lay there for a while in silence, my mind whirring. Should I make an appointment with the doctor? We'd been before, when Freya first started having night terrors, and the doctor had said that it was something she'd probably grow out of in time. She'd also said that they could happen when a child was anxious or afraid. And I hated the thought of that. I blamed myself, for making Freya leave the flat and upheaving her life. For selling the flat to Summer and Luna.

Everything was going wrong, and it had all started when we moved house. The home I had dreamed of now felt like it was a curse. I knew that if I told Oliver how I felt he'd say I was overreacting, again. Creating problems that weren't really there. And maybe he was right. In a few months, when we'd fixed all the leaks and Freya's night terrors had stopped, I was sure that the world would seem like a brighter place again. But in the darkness of the night, lying next to my distressed child, I could only see, and feel, negativity.

Freya's breathing slowed and I turned to look at her. She was asleep again, thank goodness. If only I could be so lucky. But I was old and wise enough to know that everything would seem better in the morning. And I would talk to Freya again and see if I could prise any more information out of her about what was going on. *Everyone hates me.* Her words were haunting me. At least I wouldn't need a Halloween costume for the party, I thought wryly. With my pale face and dark bags under my eyes, I already looked like a member of the Addams Family.

I must have fallen asleep eventually because when I woke up, light was streaming through the curtains in Freya's room and she was awake and watching me.

'Hello, sweetheart,' I said, rubbing my eyes sleepily.

'I don't want to go to the Halloween party.'

I tried to get my wits about me as I roused myself from sleep. 'But you were so looking forward to it.'

'I don't want to go.'

I sat up slowly, the effects of sleep quickly wearing off. 'What about your bat costume?'

'I don't care. I'm not going.'

'Why don't we see how you feel after school? And if you're still not up for it, we can just go trick or treating on our own road, you and me. How about that?'

'I'm not going to school. I don't feel well.'

I studied Freya's face. She looked tired, but not ill. Did I push it and insist she go to school or let her have the day off? I knew that hiding away wasn't the answer to anyone's problems and if anything, her absence would only make Aanya and Luna's friendship grow stronger, but I also hated the idea of sending her to a place where she wasn't happy.

'Why don't I come into school this morning and speak to your teacher.'

'No!'

'Freya, I just want to help.'

'If you want to help, let me stay at home today.'

One day wouldn't kill her. And maybe she'd feel better by Monday after a restful weekend. 'Fine,' I agreed. 'But just today, okay?'

The relief on Freya's face stayed with me as I got up and went downstairs to make a coffee and prepare breakfast for the girls. When Bella came down, dressed for school, she looked at Freya's pyjamas suspiciously.

'Why isn't Freya dressed?'

'She's staying home today, she's not feeling well.'

'She looks fine to me.'

'Well, she's not fine, Bella.'

Bella shrugged and helped herself to some cereal. Bella loved going to school, I practically had to force her to stay at home when she wasn't well. She was always busy, going to some club or event, or rehearsing for an upcoming show with her stage school.

'I thought I might come to the Halloween party after all,' Bella said, munching on her cereal. 'Apparently Jack and some of his mates are going.'

Jack was Noah's older brother and he was in the year above Bella at school. I knew she had a crush on him because she went beetroot every time she saw him.

'We might not be going,' I warned her.

'Why not?'

'Because Freya's not well.'

Bella rolled her eyes. 'She's fine.'

'Bella, that's not helpful.'

'She just doesn't want to go to school because of what that girl Luna told everyone.'

I spun around to face my daughters. Freya's eyes had widened in horror and Bella had clapped her hand to her mouth, realising that she had just shared a secret she wasn't supposed to.

'What did Luna say?' I addressed both girls.

'Nothing,' they said in unison.

'Girls.' I used my sternest voice.

'I hate you, Bella!' Freya stood up and stormed out of the room, leaving me utterly perplexed but with a sinking feeling in my stomach.

I turned to my eldest daughter. 'Tell me, Bella.'

Bella looked conflicted. 'She made me promise.'

'Well, it's too late for that now. Please, Bella.'

Bella put her spoon down slowly. 'So, apparently Luna told everyone that she found Freya's diary in her bedroom when she moved into the flat. And Freya had written loads of mean stuff about all the other kids in her class.'

I was appalled. 'Freya would never do that! And anyway, we checked all the rooms when we moved out. There's no way she left a diary behind. I don't even think she has a diary.'

'Chill, Mum, I know.'

I started pacing the kitchen. 'Why would Luna say such a thing?'

'Probably to get people to like her instead.'

'When did Freya tell you about this?'

Bella looked sheepish. 'She didn't. Jack told me. Noah told

him. But then I asked her about it and she said that Luna had spread lies about her. She made me pinkie promise not to tell you.'

I slumped down at the kitchen table next to Bella. 'Why didn't she want me to know?'

'Because she didn't want you to kick off. Pretty much like you're doing right now.'

'I'm not kicking off.' But inside, I was seething. Clearly Luna was a nasty bully and she needed to be stopped before Freya, or anyone else, got even more hurt.

'Anyway, that's why she doesn't want to go to the party. She's not ill.'

I already knew Freya wasn't ill, but the rest of this revelation was news to me, and I was almost shaking with fury. I imagined my mum, striding into the playground towards those girls who'd bullied me and finally understood the single-minded rage she'd felt.

'What are you going to do, Mum?' Bella was looking at me curiously.

'I'm going to put a stop to it.'

'How?'

I was going to have to speak to Summer, mum to mum. It was the only way to make this problem go away. And I was already dreading it.

10

I had all weekend to fester. Freya hadn't changed her mind about going to the Halloween party and although I was disappointed, I didn't put any pressure on her. Asha, Rachel and Victoria had all messaged me to ask if everything was okay and I'd told them that Freya wasn't well. Bella had gone anyway, promising to stick to our alibi, and when Oliver picked her up, she bounded into the living room, full of beans, because she'd spent all evening hanging out with Jack. As she gushed about how fun it was, I glanced over at Freya and the disappointment on her face at having missed out broke my heart.

Later, when Freya had gone to bed, I asked Bella more about the party.

'Was Luna there?'

'Yeah, she was joined at the hip with Aanya. Her mum's really cool, by the way. Did you know she used to perform in West End shows?'

I knew that Bella would be impressed by this, but the idea of my daughter chatting with Summer made me inexplicably uncomfortable. 'Yes, I know.'

'And she's so beautiful, isn't she! She could have been a model, I bet.'

'What did you think of her hair?'

'What do you mean?'

'Don't you think it looks like mine?'

Bella scrunched up her nose. 'No, not really.'

So, there we had it. A damning verdict from my twelve-year-old. I was the only one who could see what was really going on. And I couldn't stop thinking about it.

On Monday morning, Freya didn't want to go to school but this time I stuck to my guns.

'You can't hide at home forever, darling,' I told her. 'And I'm going to have a chat with Luna's mummy this morning and see if we can't sort this out.'

Freya looked at me like I'd just told her I was selling Sparkle on Gumtree. 'Mummy, no!'

'I'm sorry, Freya, but what happened is not okay. And it can't happen again.'

'You promised!'

'I know, but it's the right thing to do. And I'm going to speak to your teacher too.'

'No, Mummy!'

'Freya.' I took my daughter's hand in mine. 'You've done nothing wrong, and everyone needs to know that. I just want you to be happy.'

Freya burrowed herself into her duvet. 'I'm not going to school.'

I threw the duvet back. 'I'm sorry, darling, but you are.'

Even the chocolate croissant from the cafe on the school run didn't soften the blow this time. When we arrived at the playground, I practically had to drag Freya inside. Spotting

Sharon, the headteacher, standing at the gates and greeting parents, I walked over.

'Sharon, any chance I could have a word?'

Freya was tugging on my sleeve, but I gripped her hand tightly and held firm.

'Of course, is everything okay?'

I looked up and saw a few of the mums I knew walking past.

'Could I pop in for ten minutes after the bell's gone?'

'Yes, absolutely, ask for me at the school office.'

I smiled gratefully. 'Thank you, I will.'

Freya was furious and refused to talk to me after that. But she didn't want to join the others either, so she clung to my side, her eyes lowered. I went to speak to Victoria.

'Are you okay, Freya?' Victoria asked, looking at my daughter in concern.

'She's fine,' I answered for her. 'Just a little tired still, from the virus she had.'

'Of course. I hope you feel better, sweetheart. We really missed you at the party.'

I glanced towards the entrance and saw Summer drifting in, resplendent in a trench coat and ankle boots. The autumn sun bounced off her shiny hair, emphasising her new colour. She was a picture of health and in comparison, I knew I was haggard. So much for thinking she'd want to look anything like me. I peered down at Freya who was scuffing her shoes on the playground floor, and decided I'd speak to Summer once the kids had gone inside. When the bell rang, Freya reluctantly walked over to join the line, standing alone at the back. Her solitude only reinforced my determination to get to the bottom of this.

'Summer!' I called, once the children had started to go inside.

She turned and smiled at me, holding up a hand in greeting. 'Naomi! Lovely to see you.'

'Can I have a quick word?'

'Yes of course.'

She walked over and I immediately smelled her fragrance. If I wasn't about to embark on such an awkward conversation, I'd have asked her what brand it was.

'Such a shame you couldn't make the Halloween party.' Summer's voice dripped with sincerity. 'It wasn't the same without you.'

'Thanks.' I took a deep breath. 'Listen, there's been a bit of trouble with our girls.'

Summer's expression morphed into concern. 'Oh no, what's happened?'

I tried to keep my tone as conciliatory as I could. 'It seems Luna told everyone that she found a diary of Freya's in the flat with lots of nasty things written in it about the other children. And it's simply not true. Now I know that children tell tales all the time, I'm sure Freya has done so herself. But it's really upset Freya, because she says now no one will talk to her any more.'

I held my breath and waited for Summer's reaction. Prayed she would be understanding.

'No, that doesn't sound like Luna.'

I gritted my teeth and pushed down the anger threatening to rise inside me. 'I didn't just hear it from Freya, Summer. One of the other kids was talking about it too.'

'Which kid?'

'It doesn't matter. The fact is, I'm afraid it's true and I'm hoping we can fix it amicably. I don't want Luna to get into any trouble, I'd just like to sort it out.'

I was aware of Victoria, Richard and Asha lurking at the periphery of my vision. They'd probably come over to say hello and then held back when they overheard our conversation. I was acutely self-conscious of their listening ears, but I'd come too far to back out now.

'Luna wouldn't lie.' Summer was still smiling, but her eyes were boring into me.

'All kids lie sometimes, it's part of growing up.'

'Not Luna.'

I was getting exasperated and the grip on my self-control loosened. 'Perhaps Luna really wanted to be friends with Aanya and so she used this to turn her against Freya?'

'Or perhaps Freya is jealous of Luna and Aanya becoming friends, so she's made this story up to get my daughter into trouble.'

'No.' My voice was rising now. 'No, that's not what happened.'

'Listen.' Summer held up her hands in what felt like a passive-aggressive gesture. 'We're all a little tense. Why don't we calm down and then meet for coffee later?'

But I didn't want to get a coffee with Summer. I wanted her to admit that her daughter was a lying little madam who had spread false allegations about Freya.

'No thank you.' As soon as I said it, I realised how churlish I sounded and I regretted it. 'All I want to do is to sort out this nonsense and get on with my day.'

By now, a small crowd had gathered around us. This was the juiciest thing that had happened in the playground for months and I hated that I was at the centre of it. But I kept thinking of Freya, and my own, brave mum who had defended me, and I refused to back down.

'I just don't think we're going to get anywhere right now.'

Summer's voice was as smooth as silk and I had a sudden, impulsive urge, to reach forward and throttle her.

'Yes, clearly we're not getting anywhere. I'm going to speak to the headteacher now.'

At this point, Asha stepped in and I looked at her gratefully. If ever there was a time that I needed some backup, it was now.

'Naomi,' she said quietly. 'Luna is a sweet girl. I'm sure this is all a misunderstanding.'

I looked at Asha in shock. Was she really defending Luna when she had known Freya for years? When our families had spent so much time in each other's company?

'It's not a misunderstanding,' I told her, aware I sounded shrill. 'I heard it from Bella too. Apparently it's even doing the rounds at the secondary school.'

'Well, I wouldn't base your evidence on teenage gossip.'

'If you must know,' Summer said, and her voice was shaky, 'Luna's really been struggling to settle in at school. She says some of the children haven't been kind to her.'

Maybe because she's a little shit-stirrer, I thought cruelly. But I held my tongue.

'And she told me that Freya is jealous because we've moved into your old flat so she's saying nasty things about Luna to anyone who will listen.'

I couldn't believe what I was hearing. 'Freya would never do that.'

'And Freya told Luna that you don't like me either.'

Oh my God. Was it true? I couldn't imagine Freya saying something like that and I'd never said a bad word about Summer in front of her. But she could have overheard one of my conversations with Oliver. It was possible. I wanted the ground to open up beneath me.

Instead, I held my ground. 'This is ludicrous. Of course I like you, Summer.'

'I've tried so hard to be friendly, I just don't know what I've done wrong.'

I looked at my friends, who all had grave expressions on their faces, and felt a sting of embarrassment and shame. And the weeks of stress and worry and sleepless nights and regret finally tipped me over the precarious edge I'd been balancing on.

I lost it.

'Well, here are a few ideas, Summer,' I shouted, prodding her in the chest. She staggered backwards. 'Stop copying my hairstyle. Stop trying to dress like me. Stop inviting all my friends around to your house for cosy drinks parties without me. Oh, and tell your daughter to stop spreading malicious lies about Freya.'

You could have heard a pin drop. Summer clutched her chest as if I'd stabbed her. I was too ashamed to look at my friends because I knew I'd gone too far. I'd been impulsive and made an idiot of myself. But it was done now, and I couldn't take it back. How I wished that I could.

'Parents.' Sharon strode towards us in her yellow tabard, her brow creased with disapproval. 'We need to close the gates. Can you please make your way outside?'

We obediently started heading out of the playground. Asha and Richard flanked Summer like protective bodyguards. She had them all wrapped around her little finger, just as Luna had the kids in the class wrapped around hers.

On the street, I turned to Summer to resume our conversation, but Richard stepped in.

'Summer's very upset.' His voice lacked its usual warmth. 'Let's leave this for now.'

'I didn't mean to upset her,' I said, and I meant it. 'But Freya's very upset too.'

'Look...' Richard looked between us. 'Why don't we go for drinks later this week and we can all have a chat. Clear the air.'

How had it come to this? A publicly aired argument that I'd had no intention of starting. And now we had to clear the air. All I'd wanted to do was to talk to Summer and see if we couldn't resolve things. But she had driven me to lose my temper with her faux 'woe is me' act and now I had unwittingly become the baddie. I was upset and I was mortified.

'Fine,' I said.

'I'd like that.' Summer blew her nose.

Asha took her arm. 'Come on, Summer.'

They turned away without even saying goodbye and I was left standing alone outside the school. It occurred to me that, even though we were adults and seemingly beyond petty behaviour, we were no better than the children. I was no better. I'd lost my temper in front of everyone and said some nasty things to Summer. They were all things I'd been thinking but I'd never meant to let them spill out of me. And now I felt sheepish and very, very alone.

But I also felt betrayed by my friends. They had only known Summer for a couple of months and yet they had immediately come to her aid, leaving me isolated and vulnerable. Tears pricked at my eyes. Then I felt a presence by my side. A hand on my arm.

'What on earth is going on, Naomi?'

It was Sharon, using the same voice I suspected she used on errant children who had been sent to her office.

'I'm sorry, Sharon.'

'This isn't like you.'

'I know.'

'Come inside for a cup of tea.'

I followed her, embarrassingly grateful that someone still wanted to talk to me. But now, instead of going in to discuss Freya, I'd somehow made it all about myself.

Sharon guided me into her office and disappeared for a few minutes, returning with two cups of tea. In her absence, I'd cried a few tears, blown my nose, and tried to calm myself down.

'I'm so sorry, Sharon,' I said as soon as she sat down.

'What happened?'

I told Sharon everything. Well, I omitted the bits about Freya telling everyone I didn't like Summer, or me accusing Summer of imitating me. I tried to make it about the children because this was the whole point anyway. Wasn't it?

When I was finished, Sharon plucked another tissue from the box and handed it to me.

'You know, Year 3 can be tricky, especially for girls,' she said. 'We often have friendship issues at this age. They're growing up, forming groups, establishing hierarchies and so on. You wouldn't believe how many worried parents I've spoken to over the years.'

I smiled. 'Thank you for the reassurance. But this felt like more. It felt personal.'

'It's always personal,' Sharon said knowingly. 'Girls know how to go for the jugular. Boys? They have a scuffle and then it's all forgotten five minutes later. But girls fester.'

I thought about my own festering over the weekend. 'Will you keep an eye on them, Sharon? I really want to sort this out. Freya's so unhappy.'

'Of course I will. And I'll speak to the class teacher this morning and ask him to do the same. But Naomi, you can't go around yelling at other parents in the playground.'

I reddened. 'I know. I'm so sorry. It won't happen again.'

Sharon smiled kindly. 'I know it won't. And I thought you and Summer were such good friends too.'

'We're not good friends,' I said quickly, before adding, 'We don't really know each other.'

'I must have got my wires all mixed up.' Sharon stood up. 'I'm so sorry but I have to dash. I have another meeting in five minutes.'

'Of course, I won't keep you any longer.' I stood up too. 'Thank you again.'

'Any time. And don't worry, we'll get this resolved, okay?'

I smiled. 'Yes, thank you.'

When I left the school, I felt marginally better. But the image of my friends' disapproving faces continued to haunt me. I had to try and sort this out otherwise I'd be miserable all day. I fished my phone out of my pocket and called Asha.

'I'm about to jump on a conference call.' Asha's voice was uncharacteristically curt.

'I won't keep you long, I just wanted to apologise for earlier.'

'It's not me you should be apologising to.'

I closed my eyes. 'I know. But I thought I'd start with you.'

There was silence and when Asha spoke again, her voice was friendlier. 'Listen, mate, what's going on? I've never seen you go off like that before.'

I could feel myself welling up again. 'I'm a bit down,' I admitted. 'The move affected me more than I thought it would. And this business with Freya has upset me so much. And I just...'

How did I tell her that it was all linked to Summer? She already thought I was acting like a freak. Even my own husband thought I was being irrational. And I knew now that I had to be careful of what I said in the house in future, in case little ears were listening in.

'Did you really tell Freya that you don't like Summer?'

'Of course I didn't.' At least that bit was true. 'I'd never do that.'

'Listen, I've really got to get on this call, but let's have a chat later, okay?'

'I'd like that.'

We hung up and I called Victoria next but she didn't answer. Nor did Richard. Were they avoiding me or were they busy? I knew I should call Summer, but I was still too riled. Instead, I went for a walk, treated myself to a coffee in the hope that it would cheer me up, which it didn't, and then headed home, feeling about as desolate as I'd ever felt.

When I reached our front driveway, I knew immediately that something was wrong but I couldn't put my finger on what it was. As I looked around, I got a strong sensation that I was being watched and the hairs on my arms stood on end. I spun round in a circle but the road was empty. Then I turned my attention back to the house and that's when I realised that the front door was ajar. My heart lurched as I remembered the sensation I'd had that Friday evening when I thought someone was watching us. I was certain that I'd closed the door before we left that morning, but I also knew that in previous rushes to get to school I had forgotten to close it, something Oliver had been both furious and amused about, asking me if it was a ploy to get a new laptop and TV. And I had been distracted this morning. Had I left it open?

I crept up to the door, opening it a crack and peering inside. The hallway looked exactly as I had left it. Coats hanging up on the hook, a few pairs of shoes scattered on the floor. No sign of any disturbance.

I stepped tentatively inside and looked around. 'Hello?' I called, in case Bella had come home for some reason. But there was no response, no sound.

I went into the front room first and spotted Sparkle, asleep on the sofa, oblivious to my discomfort. Next, I went into the kitchen but again, it looked the same as it had done when we rushed out of it this morning. With a cursory glance in the downstairs loo, I tiptoed up the stairs, my heart thudding, and checked the girls' rooms first and then the office. Nothing untoward. The last room to check was mine and Oliver's bedroom and at first glance, everything was in order. The hastily made bed. A bra strap poking out of the top of one of the dresser drawers. Then I looked at the back of the door and frowned. My silk dressing gown, a twelfth wedding anniversary present from Oliver, was missing. I always hung it on the back of the door.

I checked the bathroom just to make sure it wasn't there, and then lifted the lid of the laundry basket on the off-chance I'd chucked it in, even though I was sure that I hadn't.

It was gone. Someone had taken it. But how had they got in and why would they want my dressing gown?

Summer. There it was again. That gut instinct.

This time I didn't hesitate. With a shaking hand, I got my phone out of my pocket and called Oliver.

'What's up, babe?'

'Can you come home?'

Oliver's voice switched to concern in an instant. 'What is it? Is it the girls?'

'The girls are fine, but I need you to come home. I'm scared.'

11

When Oliver got back, his hair was awry and his face was sweaty.

'What is it?' he demanded, gasping for breath, and I knew he'd run all the way back from the Tube station.

'Someone's been in the house,' I said.

In the hour it had taken Oliver to get home, I'd paced the house, working myself up into a state. But, along with my panic, my resolution had grown too. I was done with doubting myself. I was no longer going to blame stress or worry about Freya or sleep deprivation. Someone had been watching me and someone had broken into our house. And the only person I could think of who might do that was Summer.

'You mean we were burgled?' Oliver was looking around the house in horror.

'Kind of.'

'Kind of? What does that mean?'

'I got home and the front door was open.'

'And what did they take?'

'My silk dressing gown.'

Oliver looked at me incredulously. 'Excuse me?'

'I know it sounds absurd. But I'm telling you, someone took my dressing gown.'

'Why would they do that?'

'I don't know!' I was becoming hysterical. I knew I sounded unhinged but he had to believe me. After the morning I'd had, I needed someone on my side.

'Okay.' Oliver's breathing started to slow down as he recovered from his sprint. 'Talk me through the whole thing.'

I explained it all to him, the open door, the discovery of the missing dressing gown. When I was done, I looked at him and prayed that his reaction would be the one I craved.

'Have you looked for it?'

'For what?'

'The dressing gown.'

'Of course I have. It's missing.'

'Okay.' Oliver walked towards the front door and inspected it before returning to the kitchen and sitting down on one of the bar stools. 'There's no sign of any forced entry. Which means whoever was in the house must have had a key. Who have you given a spare to?'

I thought about it. We'd got the locks changed when we moved in, getting some extra keys cut for friends and family. 'I gave one to Asha and one to Dad, but that's it.'

'Could your dad have popped round?'

'Come off it, Oliver. Dad can barely leave the house.'

'What about Asha?'

'I spoke to her just before I got home and she was working.'

'Right, okay. And you're certain you haven't given a spare key to anyone else?'

'Positive.'

'And you're sure one of the kids didn't accidentally leave the door open when you left?'

He was being kind. What he really meant was, are you sure *you* didn't leave the door open when you left, like you've done before?

'It was closed,' I said firmly.

Oliver rubbed his head. 'I don't get why someone would steal a dressing gown.'

'I know it sounds crazy. I just really need you to trust me on this, Ol.'

'I do but I'm struggling to work out who would do that.'

'Summer.'

He lifted his head and looked at me. And I knew what he was thinking. Not this again.

'We had a massive row this morning in the playground,' I admitted. 'It was awful.'

'What about?'

I told him everything, this time with no omissions. This was my husband and he deserved to know the whole story, warts and all.

'Jesus, Naomi, handbags at dawn in the playground, eh?' There was a hint of the Oliver I loved in his response. The wry humour sneaking into what was a pretty dire situation.

'I know, and I'm not proud of it, but there's a reason why I'm reacting the way I am to Summer. There's something off about her, and I can't help feeling it's to do with me.'

'Why would it be to do with you?'

'I don't know. Maybe because she bought our flat? But come on, Oliver. First she's telling me I'm beautiful, getting her hair cut like me and buying my dress. The next she's inviting all my friends around for drinks without me. Not to mention the time when I saw someone watching us from the window and I found that camera.'

'Yes, but you said the next day that there may not have been anyone there after all.'

'And now I'm sure again that there was. And remember when she turned up on our doorstep the day after we moved house when I hadn't even told her where we lived?'

Oliver was watching me carefully and I knew he was trying to get his head around all this. He loved me, he wanted to be there for me. But he doubted me.

'Believe me, I know how wacky this all sounds,' I said.

'I mean, it sounds seriously wacky.'

'Yes.'

He rubbed his head again. 'Right. Here's what we'll do. We'll get the locks changed again. And no giving the key to anyone, okay? Not for a while. And I'll get a little camera set up in the porch at the weekend so we can keep an eye on any comings and goings.'

In that moment I loved my husband more than ever. I threw myself at him, gripping on to him as tightly as I could.

'Whoa, what's that for?' he asked, squeezing me back.

'For being you. For getting me. For not having me committed to a mental institution.'

'Babe, if I did that, I'd have to solo parent and I'm not sure I'm cut out for it.'

I laughed, burying my face into his chest and felt comforted for the first time that day.

'Do you have to go back to work?' I asked him. I didn't want to be alone in the house.

'I'll work from home for the rest of the day. And I'll call a locksmith now.'

Oliver stood up and started fussing around, searching for his phone and getting his laptop out of his bag. I watched him.

'Oliver?'

'Mmmm?'

'I love you.'

He paused. Looked at me and smiled. 'I love you too, babe.'

* * *

We never did organise the drinks that Richard suggested. Or at least, if they were organised, I wasn't invited to them. Over the course of the following week, which felt like the longest of my life, I got in contact with my friends to apologise again and they all said the same thing. I should be apologising to Summer. I had known these people for years and I was confident that things would go back to how they were. I just had to put things right with Summer.

But I couldn't bring myself do it. Every time I started to write a text message to her, or my finger hovered over the dial button on my phone, I changed my mind. All week I dropped Freya at school ten minutes early, before most of the other parents arrived, so that I wouldn't bump into her in the playground. At every pick-up time my stomach was in knots as I walked towards school, fretting about coming face-to-face with Summer and worried about the stares of the other parents because word had spread about our row. But the gods were in my favour that week because Luna was poorly and didn't attend school for a few days.

I hadn't called the police about the break-in. Oliver and I had discussed it but decided there wasn't enough evidence. I knew Oliver still doubted my theory that Summer was involved but he loved me enough not to question me. We'd got the locks changed but I no longer felt safe any more. The dark November evenings were upon us and as soon as the sun went down, I went around the house closing all the curtains. I hated the idea of someone watching us. This house was turning into my worst nightmare.

Freya was still miserable too. She went to school, because I made her, but every afternoon when she came home, she was morose and I was struggling to get her to open up to me again. I had called Sharon in the middle of the week for an update, and she told me that the teacher had spoken to all the children about the importance of being kind. The school's inclusion mentor was going to start hosting lunchtime friendship clubs for the girls, including Freya and Luna, when she was back at school. And they were keeping an eye on things in the playground. The school was trying and I was grateful, but it didn't seem to be having an impact.

In contrast, Bella was blooming. She'd been given a main part in an upcoming play at her stage school and she was thrilled. The house was full of Bella; she was either singing, dancing around the room, practising her lines or playing the piano. And when she wasn't rehearsing, she was on the phone to her mates, chatting and giggling. Probably about Jack. Bella was living her best life – she had her own bedroom now, plenty of mates, a crush and a big play to look forward to. But her exuberance made the contrast between the two sisters even more stark. It was like Bella was growing and Freya was shrinking. And no matter what I did, I couldn't fix it.

By the weekend, I had finally accepted what I needed to do. It was time to apologise to Summer. It didn't matter that I now suspected her of being in my house, of watching me, because my daughter's happiness was more important. I'd clear the air and maintain a veneer of politeness whenever I was around her. That was all I needed to do. But I'd be watching her very closely from now on. And if she put a foot wrong, I'd pounce.

On Saturday morning, Oliver took the girls to their usual activities, and I made my way to our old flat, feeling the familiar pang of loss and regret as I reached the street we used to live on. I couldn't believe how much I still missed the flat but I could only remember the happy times we'd had there. My memory was selective because there had been difficult times too. But I could no longer recall those periods. All I could think of was dancing around the kitchen with Oliver, sleeping soundly in our bedroom, the giggles of Bella and Freya as they learned to crawl and then to walk. The pen marks on the wall by the bathroom where we'd charted Bella and Freya's growth. The photos we'd taken outside the flat of the girls on their first day at school. And the calm happiness that had spread over me whenever we returned from a weekend away or a holiday and I felt gloriously thrilled to be home.

Home. According to the saying, it was where the heart was. And my heart was still here, in this flat. The flat now occupied by the woman I suspected of stalking me.

And yet, here I was, ignoring the lump in my throat as I headed down the street I'd walked along a thousand times. Preparing to apologise to this woman. I had told myself that a face-to-face conversation was better than calling or texting, but in truth I wanted to take the opportunity to visit Summer's home. I wasn't sure what I was looking for. My dressing gown? A key to our house? Evidence that Luna was lying?

It was going to be excruciating, pretending to be remorseful, but I had to do it for Freya. The last thing we needed was to become the pariahs of the school. Even so, as I walked up to the front door and pressed the buzzer, I yearned to turn around and run away.

When Summer answered the door, I was greeted by the sound of children's laughter in the background. More than one child, I guessed. Clearly she had company.

'Naomi,' she said, smiling brightly at me, as though nothing was amiss. 'What a surprise!'

'I'm sorry to turn up unannounced. I just wanted to apologise.'

Summer looked briefly over her shoulder and I wondered who was there, with her.

'If it's not a good time, I can come back later,' I said hurriedly.

'No, it's fine. Come in.' Summer let me in. 'Asha and Aanya are here.'

My heart sank. Not only would I have to have this conversation in front of one of my friends, but I also felt a pang of envy that the two of them had got together on a Saturday morning without me. I wondered how often they met up now that their girls were such good friends. Whether Summer and Asha had, by default, become close too.

As I walked down the hallway, I was completely thrown. This was my home except it wasn't. Everything was both familiar and unfamiliar, just as it had been the last time I was here. And when we went into the kitchen, I saw that Summer had repainted the walls a dusty pink. It looked beautiful, I thought grudgingly. The woman had good taste. For a moment I wondered how the shade might look in our own kitchen. It would show off the grey cabinets perfectly. And then I realised that I was considering copying Summer, something I had angrily accused her of doing to me, and the thought sickened me. Dusty pink was off the list.

Asha was sitting at the kitchen table, sipping on a coffee.

Her eyes widened in surprise when she saw me and she smiled, but she looked wary.

'Hey, Naomi, what's up?'

'Asha.' I went over to kiss her cheek, but it felt awkward.

'Coffee?' Summer called from the kitchen.

'Erm, yes please.'

I looked at Summer and then at Asha, not sure where to go from here. I'd hoped for a private conversation and now it seemed I had an audience. But I had to get this conversation over and done with and maybe having a witness wouldn't be such a bad thing. Once Summer and I had sorted things out, Asha could report back to the rest of the school crew that it was all fixed and things could go back to normal again. It was all I wanted, things back to normal. But as I watched Summer making my coffee, I realised that, with her around, it was never going to happen. I was too suspicious of her now to ever truly be friends with her and yet, while my doubts about her escalated, my friends were getting even more chummy with her.

'We're disgustingly hungover,' Summer said as she placed my coffee down in front of me. 'We went to that new Italian restaurant last night and it got a bit crazy. We ended up in the dodgy old pub on the high street until goodness knows what time.'

We. I looked at Asha and saw that her face had reddened slightly. Clearly 'we' included Asha. And it did not include me.

Summer carried on, oblivious to the tension, or perhaps in spite of it. 'But we'd promised Luna and Aanya that they could have a playdate this morning so here we are, nursing our sore heads while the girls run around making a noise. That's karma for us.'

'Sounds like a great night!' I tried to keep my voice upbeat.

'It was a very last-minute thing,' Asha said quietly. 'It wasn't planned.'

Summer looked at me, her mouth forming a perfect O. 'Oh gosh, I'm so sorry, Naomi, we should have called you. But as Asha said, it was very last minute.'

I hated her then. I saw right through this woman and I knew what she was doing. She was elbowing her way into my group of friends and pushing me out. But why? What had I ever done to her to make her behave in this way? Other than scream at her in the playground. It was time to channel my inner Bella and put on the greatest performance of my life.

'Summer, I wanted to apologise for the other day. I behaved terribly and I'm sorry.'

Summer took my hand. 'Thank you, Naomi, that means a lot to me.'

'It won't happen again.'

'It's forgotten already.' Summer smiled sweetly. 'You know, ladies, we mustn't let these little tiffs between our children get in the way of our friendships.'

I wanted to say that falsely accusing Freya of writing nasty things about her peers was a lot more than a little tiff, but I kept my mouth closed. Kept my focus on the purpose of this visit. *This is for Freya. This is for Freya. I loathe you, woman. But this is for Freya.*

I sipped my coffee, playing for time while I worked out a suitable response. But before I got the chance, Asha interjected. 'I couldn't agree more. I was thinking that we should get the three girls together. I'm sure they will all become great friends. How about next Saturday? What do you say?'

I really didn't want to spend any more time with Summer than I needed to, but Asha was trying and I appreciated it. 'That sounds lovely, thanks, Asha.'

'Super!' Summer beamed, but her smile now seemed insincere to me.

We were interrupted by the children running in, asking for snacks. I took advantage of the moment to appraise Luna. She was a pale child, almost sickly looking, which seemed odd in comparison to the radiant health of her mother. But she was smiling, clearly at ease around Aanya. When she saw me, a look of terror flashed across her face and her eyes darted around, presumably looking for Freya. As soon as she realised I was alone, she visibly relaxed.

'Hello, Luna, how are you?' I asked.

She looked down at the floor and didn't answer.

'She's a bit shy with strangers,' Summer said. 'But once she gets to know you, she's very chatty. Isn't that right, Asha?'

'Oh yes. She's extremely relaxed when she comes to ours for playdates now.'

How many playdates could they possibly have had? They hadn't been living in Barnet for that long. And was Summer making polite conversation or was she eager to show me just how much she hung out with Asha and Aanya? Was she as innocuous as everyone thought or was she a jellyfish, deliberately stinging me with each comment?

And why was I subjecting myself to this? I'd done what I came here to do, and I didn't want to stay any longer. I downed my coffee and stood up to leave. 'I have to pick Freya up from her club soon,' I lied. 'I'd best be off.'

'Naomi! Come and see the kitten first!' Aanya said, hopping from foot to foot.

'A kitten?' I grinned at Aanya.

'She's the cutest thing ever. Come and see!'

Aanya took my hand and guided me towards Luna's room.

And there, lying in a little basket, was a tabby and white kitten. A replica of Sparkle.

'This is Jupiter,' she told me.

Summer. Luna. Jupiter. Was Summer going for the full solar system?

'She's very cute,' I said, staring at the kitten. Trying to work out if it was a coincidence that they'd chosen one that looked exactly like our cat.

Summer appeared behind me. 'Luna is absolutely in love with her. She's always wanted a kitten. Isn't she gorgeous?' She walked over and picked the kitten up, kissing her nose.

'She's beautiful,' I said. And she was. She was exactly how I remembered Sparkle when she was a kitten.

As Summer chatted away about their new pet, I looked around. A quick glance didn't unearth anything suspicious. It was a typical little girl's bedroom. Pink duvet cover and pillow with rainbows on it. A line of cuddly toys. A wardrobe and a chest of drawers. Some framed prints on the wall. A doll's house. I looked back at the kitten. Frowned.

'Well, I'd best go,' I said.

Summer put the kitten back in its basket and followed me down the hall. Just before she opened the door she leaned forward and embraced me.

'I'm so glad we've had this talk,' she said.

I forced myself to hug her back. 'Me too.'

As I walked away, I couldn't reconcile with what I was feeling. Relief at having successfully had the difficult conversation I was dreading. Pleasure that things were sorted out and I would no longer be seen as the troublemaker at school. Hope that it would improve relations between Freya, Aanya and Luna. Weirdness about feeling like a stranger in what used to be my flat. Envy that Asha and Aanya had been there and that they had gone out the previous evening without me. And incredulity over the lookalike kitten.

I was eager to tell Oliver about it. He was the only person I could discuss this with now because I couldn't talk to my friends. Not long ago I would have relished the chance to share it with the school gang. But it was too icky now that they were all friends with Summer. I already knew that they wouldn't understand. They would think I was being bitchy, or they would tell Summer and make things worse. So I was keeping it from them and this only made me feel more distant from the people I had not long ago considered to be like family.

I could talk to Dad, I supposed, but I didn't want to worry him. He had enough on his plate. And although I had other friends, mates from university or work colleagues I'd met along the way, we were more like acquaintances now, meeting up once or twice a year for a long overdue catch-up. My daily life was in Barnet, among the school parents who I saw all the time. Whose children played with mine. Or used to play with at least. I'd been friendly enough with the mums from Bella's class, but not as close as I was with Asha, and once the children went to secondary school and formed different friendship groups we'd lost touch a bit. I certainly didn't feel comfortable calling them now to tell them I thought the woman who bought my flat might either be obsessed with me or freezing me out. *I miss you, Mum.* The feeling was growing stronger the longer she was gone. What I would do to pop round to see her now. To get it all off my chest and take comfort in her confident, reassuring advice.

By the time I got home, I was almost burning with the anticipation of telling Oliver what had happened. But he was still out so I made a cup of tea and sat down at my laptop to catch up on some of the work I'd missed while I'd been out of sorts during the week. As I worked, my mind kept drifting, to the kitten and to Luna's bedroom. I pictured it all in my mind. The rainbow duvet. The cuddly toys. The doll's house.

The image began to grow stronger. The door on the little doll's house had been painted yellow, just like the front door of the house we now lived in. There had been some cute little window boxes outside, almost a replica of what we had added when we moved in. A creepy sensation came over me as I compared the little wooden house to the one I was currently sitting in. Was the picture in my head real or had my imagination skewed it? I was certain that it wasn't my mind playing tricks on me, but I had to know for sure. Already I was coming up with ways that I could visit the flat again and take another peek inside Luna's room. Suddenly it was of critical importance. Because if I was right, and if Summer had decorated her daughter's doll's house to look exactly like mine, and bought an identical cat to ours, then I finally had proof that there was something seriously sinister about her.

All the evidence was piecing together to form a coherent picture. Summer had, for some reason, become fixated on me. I just didn't know why.

Or how far she was willing to go.

12

A noise woke me up and my eyes snapped open as I listened keenly, my pulse racing. Was it Freya again? We'd gone a week without any night terrors and I was cautiously optimistic, hoping that the phase had passed. But something had disturbed me and I was instantly on edge.

The house was quiet and there was no sound coming from Freya's room. But then I heard it again, a scratching noise. I looked at Oliver, squinting at his silhouette in the darkness. He was lying on his side, fast asleep. I considered waking him up but the noise was probably Sparkle, playing with one of her catnip toys. She often had mad moments in the early hours, so we usually shut her in the kitchen at night.

I looked at the clock. It was two in the morning. I could just lie down again, curl up next to Oliver and drift off. But my nerves were tingling and I wouldn't be able to go back to sleep until I'd worked out where the noise was coming from. Reluctantly, I climbed out of bed, glancing at the empty peg on the back of the door where my dressing gown used to be.

I threw on last night's tracksuit bottoms and a T-shirt and crept out of the room, so I didn't disturb the girls. Pausing outside both their bedrooms, I listened for any sound but there was nothing. I glanced at the stairs to the dark hallway below. At night, the house felt ominous, its creaks and sounds unfamiliar even after months of living here. I almost went back to wake Oliver up but I imagined his reaction when he charged downstairs in the nude, only to discover Sparkle skidding around the floor, batting a toy mouse with her paw. No, I'd check myself and if I had any suspicions, I'd call up to him.

I tiptoed down the stairs, wincing as I stepped on a creaky board. The tiles at the bottom were cold on my bare feet and I hugged my arms to my chest as I walked towards the closed kitchen door. I heard a noise behind me and spun around in fright. There it was again, the scratching. Except it wasn't coming from the kitchen, it was coming from the front door.

'Oliver!' I screamed.

He was down the stairs in seconds.

'What is it? What's happened?'

'Someone's trying to break in.' My body was surging with adrenaline.

'Stay here.' Oliver marched towards the front door, yanking it open and looking outside. I heard a movement from upstairs, a light going on, and then Bella's head appearing over the banister from the landing.

'What's going on?' she asked sleepily.

'Nothing, go back to sleep.'

'I heard a scream.'

'It was nothing, Bella. Go back to your room.'

Oliver had disappeared, leaving the door wide open and I stood stock-still in the hallway, torn between rushing out after him and going to the kitchen to get some sort of weapon in case an intruder appeared in the doorway. My heart was thudding so loudly I could almost hear it.

I heard a scuffle coming from outside and I didn't hesitate. I ran outside, my fists clenched, ready to defend my husband. I found him, stark bollock naked, by the bins.

'What is it? What's happened?' I demanded.

He looked my way, but I couldn't make out his expression in the gloom. 'It was foxes.'

'No,' I said confidently. 'It wasn't foxes. Someone was messing with the front door.'

'Look.' He pointed at the upturned food waste bin. 'They were trying to get into the bin.'

'No.' I was adamant. 'I heard scratching. Like someone was fiddling with the lock.'

Oliver shivered and I remembered that the poor man had no clothes on. 'Come on,' I said. 'Come inside before anyone sees you.'

We headed back in and closed the door. Instinctively, I pulled the chain on, something I never usually did. Oliver headed straight upstairs and I followed him to our bedroom, turning on my bedside lamp and picking up my glass of water. My hands were shaking.

'It wasn't foxes,' I said. 'Oliver, I know it wasn't.'

Oliver looked at me and this time, I could see his expression clearly. He was weary and not just because he'd been woken up. He was weary of me. Of my paranoia.

'I'm sorry,' I said quietly. 'I shouldn't have woken you up.'

'What's going on, Naomi?'

'What do you mean?'

'Ever since we moved here you've been on edge. It's like you're convinced that someone's out to get you.'

I was convinced that someone *was* out to get me. And up

until now, I thought Oliver understood. 'I'm freaked out, you know that,' I told him. 'There's some weird stuff going on.'

'Is there, though? You found a kid's camera in the front garden and thought someone was watching you. You were just convinced we were being burgled and it was foxes.'

My disappointment at his reaction made me defensive. 'What about when I found the front door open?'

'You know as well as I do that you might have left it open yourself.'

'And my stolen dressing gown?'

Oliver rubbed his face. 'I don't know, Naomi.'

'What about Summer's lookalike cat? And the doll's house I told you about?'

He had no answer to that. Or he did, but he knew I wouldn't like it.

'This can't go on,' he said.

'I agree.'

'So what are we going to do about it?'

I already had a plan. The following day we were going to the playdate at Asha's house. After that I was going to tell Summer that Freya desperately wanted to see the kitten and hope that she invited us over to meet it. And while everyone was distracted, I was going to take a photo of the doll's house. When Oliver saw it, he'd finally believe me. I would be vindicated. I imagined showing him the photograph. His eyes widening in shock as he looked at it.

But until then, I had to keep my cool. 'I'm sorry,' I said again. 'Let's go back to sleep.'

We lay there, side by side, in silence. We were both awake but neither spoke to the other. Eventually, Oliver's breathing became steady and rhythmical as he drifted off. And despite being in a warm, cosy bed, inches away from my lovely husband, I felt painfully lonely.

I climbed out of bed and walked across the landing to Freya's room, pushing the door open gently. She was fast asleep, the only one of us who hadn't been woken up, and the little nightlight gave the room a soothing glow. I tiptoed over to her bed and lifted the duvet, crawling in next to her. She stirred, but she didn't wake. I curled up, lying on my side in the narrow space and trying not to fall off the bed. But as I rested my head on the pillow I felt something hard and I carefully lifted it up, expecting to see a reading book tucked underneath it.

It was a diary. One I didn't know about. It must have been an old birthday present I'd long forgotten. I glanced at Freya to check she was still asleep and then sat up and opened it. Inside was Freya's familiar scrawl. I tried to make out the words in the dim light. She had written 'I luv Sparkle' next to a picture she had drawn of our cat. On the next page was a drawing of the four of us, with the words, 'My familee'. I smiled. This was what a seven-year-old's diary looked like. Not the vitriol that Luna claimed Freya had written in her fictitious one. I flicked through the pages, comforted by the innocence of Freya's memos. Her favourite food. 'Chicken nuggits'. Her favourite television show. *'Floor is Lava'*. Her best friend.

My heart sank when I saw that she had crossed out Aanya's name. And then I saw what she had written next to it, and I visibly deflated. 'No-won'. There was a picture of a little stick girl on her own, with a sad face, and above it was a broken heart.

I closed the diary and put it back under the pillow. I didn't want to read any more. My daughter was suffering. And so was I. And it was all because of Summer and Luna.

Ever since they had arrived here, things had been going wrong for my family. They were playing with us, like we were toys in Luna's creepy lookalike doll's house. They were trying to turn our friends against us. It was one thing to mess with me but it was quite another to mess with my daughter. Something had to be done.

They weren't going to get away with it.

* * *

Freya was anxious the next morning. She was worried about the playdate with Aanya and Luna. In contrast, I was almost excited. I was a woman on a mission, and I was determined to expose Summer for the fraud she was, once and for all.

As we walked to Asha's house, Freya clutched on tightly to my hand and I squeezed it reassuringly. By the time we rang the doorbell, both of us were a little flustered. We'd been to Asha's house dozens of times before, it was almost like a second home, but somehow the presence of Summer and Luna made it feel like hostile territory.

Asha answered with a big smile, and I relaxed slightly, reminding myself that Asha was a good friend and this was just a regular playdate, even though it didn't feel like one.

'Welcome!' she said. 'So lovely to see you.'

I handed over the biscuits I'd picked up at the supermarket, leaning forward to kiss her, and then stepped inside, taking my shoes off. Freya did the same but she didn't run off to find Aanya like she usually did. Instead, she stood by my side, kicking the floor with her socked feet.

'Aanya and Luna are playing upstairs,' Asha said. 'Why don't you go up, Freya?'

Freya looked at me, her eyes pleading.

'Go on,' I said gently. 'I'll be in the kitchen if you need me.'

'I want to stay with you,' she said.

I felt Asha's eyes on us. 'Okay, darling, why don't you come and hang out with the grown-ups for a bit. Have a snack. Then you can go and join the girls.'

We headed into the kitchen and the first thing I saw was Summer, sitting at the table and sipping on a cup of coffee. She was wearing an oversized jumper and her bobbed hair was shiny and sleek, as though she'd just had it trimmed. Mine, on the other hand, was straggly and frizzy from the drizzle we'd walked through on the way over.

'Hi, Summer,' I said, keeping my voice as friendly as I could.

'Naomi! So lovely to see you.' Summer stood up to greet me, before turning to Freya. 'Freya, darling, the girls are upstairs.'

'Freya's going to hang out with us,' I explained. 'She's peckish and fancies a snack.'

'Do you want a cookie?' Summer pushed a cake tin towards us and I peered inside. There were a dozen chocolate chip cookies inside and from the smell of them, I guessed that they were freshly baked.

'Did you make these?' I asked her.

'Yes, this morning.'

'They smell delicious.' I looked at Freya. 'Go on, darling, help yourself.'

Freya reached a tentative hand out and picked up a biscuit, nibbling on it shyly.

Asha was making coffees. 'We missed you last night,' she called over.

Last night? What had happened last night? I looked at her questioningly.

'The PTA meeting. We were planning for the Christmas Fair.'

It had completely slipped my mind. 'I'm so sorry,' I gushed. 'I've had a crazy week and I totally forgot. I won't miss the next one, I promise. What did I miss?'

'Just the usual.' Asha poured out the coffees. 'Summer gave us an update on the raffle, so don't worry about that. You've worked so hard, I can't believe the prizes we have this year.'

In truth, I hadn't even thought about the raffle for the past couple of weeks. And I certainly hadn't sorted out any prizes yet. I looked at Summer, my eyebrows raised.

'Don't worry,' she whispered to me with a wink. 'It's all sorted. My clients have donated some prizes and I charmed a few local restaurant and beauty salon owners into giving us vouchers. They were just so accommodating when I asked nicely.'

Perhaps she meant to be friendly. Maybe she thought she was being helpful. But the raffle had been my baby for the past four years and now it seemed like she was taking that from me too. Thankfully I was saved from thinking of a charitable response by the arrival of Aanya and Luna, who bounded in wearing princess dresses.

'Oh girls, you look beautiful,' Summer gushed. 'Like peas in a pod.'

I glanced over at Freya who was still nibbling on the cookie. The girls ignored her, tucking into the tin of cookies and taking greedy bites.

'I've brought some biscuits too,' I said a little feebly. Next to Summer's home-baked cookies, my shop-bought treats paled in comparison.

'Luna, say hello to Freya,' Summer instructed her daughter.

A look of what I could only describe as disgust passed across Luna's face.

'Luna,' Summer said, a little more sternly. 'Did you hear me?'

'Hello, Freya.'

'Hello.'

Freya's voice was small and uncertain. I saw Asha beckon Aanya over and whisper something into her ear. Aanya rolled her eyes, reminding me that our girls were seven going on seventeen. But she walked over and stood in front of Freya.

'We're playing princesses,' she said. 'I have a spare dress upstairs. Do you want it?'

'Yes please.'

'Come on then.'

The three girls trooped upstairs and Summer looked at me with a satisfied sigh.

'There we go. All sorted. They'll be the best of friends by the end of the day.'

I wasn't so sure, but I smiled back and took the coffee that Asha had brought over. Then I remembered my mission and decided to get stuck right in.

'I told Freya about your new kitten and she was so keen to meet it.'

'Oh, you must pop round again.'

'That would be great.'

I waited for Summer to ask if we wanted to go that day, or to suggest another date, but she took a sip of her drink and started talking with Asha about the PTA meeting.

'I couldn't believe it when Angela suggested we get real-life reindeer for the indoor Santa's grotto. I thought poor Sharon was going to have a heart attack. Think of all the poo!'

Asha snorted with laughter. 'You should have been here last year. She wanted Santa to come down an actual chimney to surprise the kids. Poor Mr Jones, the teacher who has been our Christmas fair Santa for years, looked absolutely terrified.'

As they chatted about the meeting, and the various different characters who made up the PTA, I listened and laughed along with them, but I felt left out. It was my own fault, I should have gone to the meeting, but something about the way Summer had fitted so seamlessly into my place seemed deliberate. I remembered my promise to myself. I was not going to let Summer win. And I wasn't going to let Luna push Freya out either.

'I was thinking of holding a house-warming party next Saturday,' I said impulsively. 'An afternoon thing so that we can involve the kids too. We should have done it weeks ago, I know, but we've just been so busy. Are you free?'

Summer and Asha exchanged looks and I got a sinking feeling in the pit of my stomach.

'It's just that it's Luna's birthday next weekend,' Summer said hesitatingly. But I knew what was coming already. Luna was having a party. And Freya wasn't invited.

'It's only a very small do,' Summer continued. 'On account of the flat being so small.'

We'd hosted many children's birthday parties in that flat and always managed to successfully cram everyone in. That wasn't why Freya was excluded.

I forced a smile. 'No problem. I can do the house-warming another time.'

Already I was dreading the week ahead. The other children would be chatting excitedly about the upcoming party at school and Freya would feel left out yet again. I would have to think of something fun to do that day to make up for it.

A scream from upstairs made us all jump. We looked at each other and then, in unison, made a dash up the stairs to see what was going on. We found the three girls in Aanya's bedroom. Luna was crying and it didn't take long to work out why. Her princess dress was ripped. I looked at Freya who was cowering, her eyes lowered, like a terrified puppy.

'What's going on?' Asha demanded. 'What happened?'

'She ripped my dress.' Luna was sobbing in great gulps, tears dripping down her face.

'Who did?'

Luna didn't speak. Instead, she lifted a finger and pointed it directly at Freya. I stared at my daughter, who was still refusing to look up.

'Freya, what happened, darling?' I asked her, trying to stay calm.

But Freya didn't respond and it was left to Aanya to fill in the gaps.

'Freya wanted to wear Luna's dress but Luna didn't want to swap. So Freya ran at her and started pulling at it. Luna told her to stop but she wouldn't. And then it ripped.'

Was it true? If it was, then Freya needed to be told off. That kind of behaviour was not acceptable and Freya knew that. But if Luna and Aanya were telling fibs to get her into trouble, then punishing Freya would be cruel and heartless.

I hesitated, torn between scolding my daughter and defending her. I knew that Asha and Summer were waiting for me to do something, but I was in a storm of indecision.

Eventually, I said, 'Freya, come outside for a moment.'

She followed me out and I guided her towards Asha's room, closing the door behind us.

'What happened, darling?'

She looked at me then and I saw the guilt in her eyes. She didn't need to say anything.

'Why did you do it?'

'They were being mean.'

'What were they doing?'

'Luna said that even if I wore a princess dress, I'd still be ugly.'

I was incandescent with rage, but I swallowed it down. 'And what did Aanya do?'

'Nothing.'

'She didn't stick up for you?'

'No.'

'Was she mean to you?'

'No.'

So, it was between Luna and Freya then. They had unwittingly become enemies and Aanya was stuck in the middle. But although I could never condone what Freya had done, she had been provoked and that needed to be made clear.

'Leave it with me,' I said. 'I'll sort this out. But you still need to say sorry for ripping the dress, okay?'

I headed back to Aanya's bedroom, with Freya trailing behind me. Summer was on the bed, clutching her daughter to her as though she'd been viciously assaulted.

'Freya has something to say,' I told them and I turned to my daughter, who was hovering behind me.

'Sorry,' she said meekly.

'Freya is sorry,' I added. 'But apparently Luna said something quite nasty to her first.'

Summer was stroking her daughter's hair. 'Is that true, Luna?'

'No.'

We all looked at poor Aanya whose version of events was, unfortunately, critical. 'Luna didn't say anything.'

And that's when Freya finally found her fight. 'She did!' she shouted. 'You know she did!'

'Freya, it's okay,' I said.

'It's not okay. Luna was horrible to me and Aanya is a liar!'

It was like someone had flicked a switch in Freya. Weeks of hurt and rejection bubbled to the surface and suddenly she was crying and screaming like a toddler, pummelling her fists in frustration. As everyone else looked on in horror, I tried to pull her towards me.

'Freya, calm down, darling.'

'I hate them! I hate them!'

Freya was beyond reason. She had spiralled out of control and the only thing I could do was to remove her from the situation.

'We're going to go,' I said, picking up my daughter and wincing as my back groaned.

'Yes, I think that's for the best.' Summer was still clinging on to her daughter.

I glared at Summer, loathing her with every inch of my being and then turned and walked down the stairs. It was not a dignified exit. I was waddling under the weight of my daughter and I nearly fell down the stairs. Asha followed us down.

'I'm sorry,' I said, not sure why I was the one apologising.

'It happens, don't worry.' But I could tell from Asha's tone that she was unhappy.

I put my shoes on and somehow managed to get Freya into hers. 'Thanks for inviting us.'

'Of course.'

When Asha closed the front door, it felt like she'd slammed it in our faces. I took Freya's hand and walked away from the house as quickly as I could. It was only once we were out of sight that I stopped. I crouched down so that I was eye to eye with Freya.

'I believe you,' I said. 'I want you to know that. I believe that Luna was mean to you.'

'But no one else does.'

'It doesn't matter what anyone else thinks, okay? Look, I know you were best friends with Aanya but I think you need to stay away from her for now. Play with other children.'

Freya's lip wobbled. 'No one else wants to play with me.'

'I'm sure that's not the case.'

'It is, Mummy.'

'Well, here's what we're going to do. We're going to call Rachel and invite Noah over to play. You two have always gotten along so well. And maybe you can play with the boys at school? You love the playground games. Forget about the girls for a while. It'll all calm down.'

'It won't.'

To Freya, it was the end of the world. She'd lost her best friend and she'd been accused of things that she hadn't done. She had no friends and she dreaded going to school. I pictured Luna's face, the revulsion I'd seen when she was asked to say hello to Freya. But she was a seven-year-old girl, it was hardly her fault. No, the problem lay with her mother.

Enough was enough. I was going to arrange a meeting with the school and demand that they dealt with the situation. And I was going to get together with Asha, Rachel and Victoria and tell them my suspicions about Summer. I knew they liked her but surely their loyalty was to me? We'd been friends for years and the evidence against Summer was mounting up.

It would be better if I had proof, though. I remembered Oliver saying he would set up a camera in the porch. He hadn't got round to it yet, but I was going to make sure he did it this weekend. I was convinced it had been Summer at my front door, trying to get in. It occurred to me that she might have somehow got a copy of our spare key, perhaps stolen it from Asha, and let herself in the first time, when she took my dressing gown. And then she came back for another snoop, but we'd changed the locks and she couldn't get in. It would explain the scratching sound I'd heard. No one had a spare now, we were safe.

But Summer would be back, I was certain of it. And I was going to catch her in the act.

13

On Monday, Freya didn't want to go to school and I could hardly blame her. But I gave her a cuddle and told her that everything would be fine. I hated that I was lying to her. She cried on the way in and I felt so sorry for her that I almost took her straight home again. But she couldn't hide from her problems any more than I could.

In the playground I saw the usual huddle of Year 3 parents. They were talking animatedly, their heads together and when they looked up and saw me, I knew immediately that they had been talking about us. About what had happened at Asha's house on Saturday. A surge of anger flared inside me as I took in Asha's guilty expression. She was supposed to be my friend. They all were. But now Freya and I had become the subject of gossip and judgement. And then, as they parted slightly, I saw Summer in the centre of them. She was clutching a black and gold bag and I recognised it immediately as mine. I'd bought it last summer and had worn it pretty much every day until I had retired it a few weeks ago when a new one in the sale caught my eye. Had she stolen it from my house, along with the dressing gown, without me even realising? I was burning to go over there and say something about it but the group of parents, who had once been my comrades, now intimidated me.

I hovered, uncertain whether to say hello or walk away to another area of the playground. I felt sick and my palms were clammy. This is how Freya feels every day, I thought, and I hated it. But I had to set a good example for my daughter and I refused to be daunted.

I walked over. Smiled. 'Hi, everyone, good weekend?'

I was greeted by silence. It was probably only a second or two, but it felt like hours.

'Lovely, thanks.' Rachel smiled back at me. 'We went to see my parents.'

'Oh great, they live by the sea, don't they?'

'That's right. Although the weather was atrocious, so we didn't brave the beach.'

It was polite conversation at best, but I was grateful to Rachel for not freezing me out.

'How's the house going?' she asked me.

'The bloody boiler packed up at the weekend,' I said. 'Just what we need.'

'I know a great plumber if you want his number?'

'Thanks, but Oliver's already called someone.'

The house had been freezing all weekend and we'd had no hot water either. By Sunday evening we'd been as miserable as we'd been stinky. It was another thing that had started to make me suspicious. How could so many things go wrong with this house? It was like we were cursed. Or the house was. Either that or someone was tampering with things and causing them to break down. I hadn't told Oliver what I was thinking though. Things had shifted slightly between us ever since I'd thought we were being burgled. He was still Oliver, of course. He still came home from work, gave me a kiss and made the girls laugh. But I had sensed a change in him, in the way that he behaved towards me. It was like he was guarded, almost wary of me. And when I tried to talk to him about Freya, it was like he just didn't get it. He still thought it was run of the mill stuff, girls falling out, testing boundaries. He told me I was overreacting and making things worse for Freya.

'Remember when Bella fell out with her mates at the end of primary school?' he'd said. 'You told her not to worry, that it would all sort itself out, and it did. So why are you getting into such a state now about Freya?'

'Because this is different,' I'd said, amazed that he didn't see that. 'This is bullying.'

'Is it, though? I'm still not sure.'

'Well, I am. It's nasty stuff, Oliver.'

He'd held his hands up in surrender. 'Fine. Do what you have to do.'

I'd been angry with him then. Resentful that he wasn't supporting me or trying to see things my way. It didn't help that we were freezing cold of course, wrapped up in jumpers and hats to keep warm in the old, draughty house. But with all my friends slowly turning away from me, I needed Oliver more than ever. I just wished he realised that.

As Rachel and I chatted, my gaze kept drifting to Summer's bag. She must have sensed me looking because she met my eye and gave me a smile. Was it me or did she look smug?

I couldn't hold it in any longer. 'Summer, I see you have a new bag.'

She looked at me quizzically. 'What, this old thing? I've had it forever.'

'That's odd, I've never seen it before.'

I was aware that everyone was watching, listening.

'I bought it in the sale months ago, Naomi.' Summer was looking around at the others, her face a picture of confusion.

As I concentrated on the bag, I realised with a sinking heart that, although it looked like mine, it wasn't exactly the same. The stitching was different and so was the texture. It was time to retreat from battle. 'Oh, right,' I said, turning away.

I was relieved when the bell finally rang. I wanted to get the hell out of that playground as quickly as possible. I gave Freya a kiss and watched as she practically dragged herself to the end of the line, keeping her distance from the other children again. I noticed that no one said hello. They all kept their backs to her, blocking her out.

As soon as the children had gone in, I walked around to the office and asked to speak to Sharon. But the receptionist told me that she was in a meeting and would call me later. Deflated, I thanked her and left, heading out of the main gate and waving at some of the other parents I vaguely knew. I was glad that the Year 3 crew had already left because I had no desire to face them again. I fancied a coffee but I was too worried that I might bump into someone in the cafe or, even worse, see them all sitting together without me, so I headed straight home.

As I turned into my road, I heard footsteps behind me and I spun around to see who it was. But the road was empty. I stood there, frowning, my eyes scanning the street, before turning back round to continue my journey home. Suddenly I was afraid, convinced that someone was watching me. I heard the footsteps again but this time I didn't stop. I picked up the pace, until I was jogging and then running, breathless, up the driveway. I let myself in and slammed the front door shut, then dashed into the front room and peered through the gap in the curtains. I was furious with Oliver, who still hadn't installed the camera. To his credit, he'd been about to go to the shop to buy one but then the boiler had stopped working and he'd been waylaid, trying to fix it himself. I scanned the street, my heart pounding and my hands shaking.

After a few minutes my legs became stiff from crouching, and I admitted defeat. If someone had been following me, they'd clearly given up. I stood up slowly, wincing as my legs creaked and went into the kitchen to make a coffee. As I put the radio on, craving the comfort of background noise, I tried to calm myself down. I had a ton of work to do, and I couldn't waste another day being distracted. I was safe inside the house, no one could get in.

I typed out a message on the WhatsApp group I had with Asha, Victoria and Rachel, suggesting drinks later that week. It was part one of my plan to get my friends back on side again. There hadn't been much chatter among the group recently and I was keen to revive it and to eliminate any more awkwardness, like there had been in the playground that morning. Then I put my phone down and reached into a cupboard to get a mug.

Someone grabbed me from behind and I screamed, dropping the mug with fright. It hurtled to the ground, smashing to pieces and I spun around and pushed the intruder with all my might. It was only when they tumbled to the ground that I realised who it was.

'Jesus Christ, Naomi!'

'Oliver! What are you doing here?'

'The plumber called when I was on my way into work to say he'd be here around ten, so I thought I'd come back and work from home, in case you were busy.'

'I'm so sorry. You frightened the life out of me.'

He stood up and brushed his bruised bottom. 'Well, you frightened the life out of me.'

'It's just that I thought someone was following me on the way home and I...'

I looked at Oliver's expression and knew in an instant that he didn't believe me.

'Come and sit down,' he said quietly, taking my hand and leading me to a bar stool.

I sat down, half obedient, half defiant. 'I know what you're going to say.'

'What am I going to say?'

'You think I'm crazy.'

'No, babe. I don't think that. But I do think you're low and you're anxious. This move, and all this stuff with Freya, has really taken its toll on you. So I've been thinking. Why don't you go away for the weekend? A spa trip or something? Relax, recharge the batteries.'

Depressingly, my first thought wasn't, *What a lovely idea, this is why I adore my husband.* Or even, *I don't want to leave Freya right now.* It was, *I can't think of anyone to invite to come with me.* A couple of months ago I'd have messaged the ladies WhatsApp group within seconds, asking who was game. Now I wasn't sure I wanted to.

'It's a lovely thought, Oliver. But with Freya so upset, I'm not sure the timing's right.'

'Actually, that's why I think the timing is right. You and Freya, you're feeding off each other's anxiety. Winding each other up. Not on purpose of course, but you're both very sensitive and you can sense when the other is unsettled. And me and the girls will be grand. We'll go to the park, have a movie night. It'll be fun.'

It'll be fun because I'm not there being a total paranoid freak, you mean. But there was some truth in what Oliver was saying. Freya was empathetic and I knew she could sense when

I was stressed. My own anxiety was probably making hers worse and I felt guilty about it. And maybe a break from the house would be just what I needed. It had been so full on ever since we moved and as I worked from home, I didn't get any time away from it. My day was full of constant reminders of the things that were going wrong. A couple of days away could reset me and make me a better mum to Freya. The mum she deserved.

'Can we afford it? Things are really tight.'

'Consider it an early Christmas present from me and the girls.'

I capitulated. 'I think it's a lovely idea, thanks, Ol.'

His relief was palpable. 'Great, well, no time like the present. Why don't you look at places to go this weekend?'

Wow, he really wanted me gone, and fast. Paranoia seeped in. Was he that sick of me or did he want me out of the way for some reason? But I checked myself. Oliver was my husband, my partner in crime. He was the last person I should be mistrustful of. He was just worried about me and wanted to make sure I was okay.

'I'll do some googling,' I told him, already thinking about booking somewhere with a spa. Would Asha come with me? But then I remembered it was Luna's birthday party and she'd probably want to go to that, given how friendly she was with Summer. Rachel was always rushing about after her brood and needed several weeks' notice for any weekend plans. What about Victoria? I hastily typed out a message, asking if she was free.

I could go on my own. And if push came to shove, I would. But I was already feeling lonely and alienated by my friends and I wasn't sure that a weekend in my own company would be as healing as a couple of days with a pal to have a good chinwag with. I considered taking Bella along, but Oliver was right, I needed some time away from being a mum. I couldn't remember the last time I'd spent more than a few hours apart from them.

Victoria's reply was quick and brief. She couldn't make it. My heart sank as I thought about going alone, lost in my increasingly dark thoughts. And in my desperation I had a mad idea. What about someone who didn't fit in either? Who constantly lingered on the edge of our friendship group looking for a way in? Maybe she would understand how I was feeling more than anyone. The only problem was, she was intolerable.

But beggars couldn't be choosers. Before I could change my mind, I sent a message to Angela, asking if she fancied a spa weekend at short notice.

14

Angela picked me up in her SUV. On the back seat I spotted a Burberry holdall. I placed my tatty old backpack next to it and climbed into the passenger seat.

'Thanks for picking me up,' I said.

'Oh, it's my pleasure.' Angela was brimming with excitement. 'I haven't had a girls' weekend away in so long. It's going to be fabulous!'

I was already regretting my decision to invite Angela. I knew I was in for a long weekend of in-depth discussion about the best secondary schools, how important it was to find a pushy tutor, and why Sebastian was so gifted and talented. But it was too late to change my mind now and I was grateful that Angela could come at short notice. So if that meant listening to her wax lyrical about her son, while I slowly glazed over, then so be it. It would make a change from discussing how wonderful Summer was, in any case. And I was looking forward to two days without having to look behind my shoulder, fearful that I was being watched. I knew that the minute we drove out of Barnet, I would finally be able to relax.

We'd found a spa hotel about an hour's drive away and got a good rate for a last-minute deal. I felt guilty about spending money that should be going on the house, but Oliver had insisted that my well-being was more important. Angela and I had booked a massage and facial and I was planning to make good use of the hotel swimming pool and sauna. As we drove towards the motorway Angela was already discussing how Sebastian was sitting a piano exam that day and was on course to get a distinction. I murmured my admiration as I gazed out of the window, letting her words wash over me. Already I could feel the stress of the last couple of months start to leave my body. I was free and unencumbered for the next forty-eight hours. I'd taken Friday afternoon off work so that we could have two nights away and Oliver was picking Freya up from school. By the time I got home on Sunday afternoon, I hoped to be a new woman.

'How's Sebastian getting on at school now?' I asked Angela, remembering our conversation in McDonald's, when she'd said he was struggling to fit in.

'So-so,' Angela admitted. 'He's become friendly with a boy in another class, and they play together at breaktimes, so that's something. But our class seems troubled, don't you think?'

I turned to her, my curiosity piqued. 'What do you mean?'

'Well, it just seems a bit cliquey.'

'I'm so glad you said that, Angela, because I've been thinking the same thing.'

In truth, I had never thought it before Summer and Luna moved to the area. I'd always been grateful that we had such a fantastic class, full of lovely children and lovely parents. I'd made what I considered to be friends for life, and so had Freya. But now I was starting to come around to Angela's way of thinking. How quickly Freya's best friend had abandoned her when a shiny, new girl came along. How speedily the rest of the class had turned against her. And how fast my own friends had left me out in the cold. Suddenly I felt an intense pang of guilt for the way that we'd treated Angela. We'd never been cruel, but we'd often gone out without inviting her and we'd tittered more than once at her pushy messages in the class WhatsApp group. But here she was, accompanying me on a weekend away, and I felt a rush of affection for her.

'Sebastian says the boys only want to play football and he's not interested so they never play with him,' she told me. 'And the girls constantly seem to be rowing over something.'

I leaned towards her eagerly. 'What have you heard?'

'Well, reading between the lines of what Sebastian's told me, they've become a bit of a pack. You know, singling out one girl and excluding her on a whim. It sounds very nasty.'

Yes! This was exactly what I had been telling Oliver for ages now. It was nasty.

'At the moment the girl in question is Freya,' I admitted. 'I've spoken to the school and they said they're keeping an eye on it but it doesn't seem to be getting any better.'

'Well, that's the problem with state schools, isn't it? With thirty children to a class and not enough staff, they barely have time to teach them basic maths and reading, let alone monitor them constantly for any sign of bullying.'

I was tempted to ask Angela why, if she was so against state schools, she didn't just send Sebastian to a private school, given that she could clearly afford it. I loved North Hill and didn't have a bad word to say about it. And Freya would be going to the local state secondary just like her sister. Bella adored it there and was thriving. But I remembered that I was supposed to be seeing Angela in a more positive light and I bit my tongue. Anyway, I was keen to learn if she'd heard anything else from Sebastian about the issues between the girls in the class.

Before I got a chance to ask, Angela pulled over to get some petrol and by the time she'd returned to the car, she'd changed the subject. But in the evening, after I'd had the best facial of my life and we were sharing a bottle of wine over dinner at the hotel, I brought it up again.

'So, has Sebastian told you anything more about what's happening at school?'

Angela took a sip of her wine. 'Only that the girls are causing trouble. And apparently this Luna girl is at the heart of it all.'

This was music to my ears. 'How so?'

'Well, she acts all meek and feeble, but it seems that she's a fox among the chickens. Sly and cunning and sending everyone into a frenzy.'

'She's turned everyone against Freya,' I said, welling up. 'I don't know what to do.'

Angela looked at me intently. 'You need to tell Freya to stick up for herself.'

How did I tell a terrified seven-year-old girl to stick up for herself? And I wasn't sure that getting into a fight with Luna or the others was the best solution.

'Freya really doesn't like confrontation. And I don't want to cause any more trouble.'

'But someone has to stand up to this Luna. She's running amok.'

'She's a child, Angela.' I hesitated before saying, 'Maybe it's Summer that's the problem.'

Saying those words out loud was like a tonic. I could feel

some weight lifting from me as I finally aired the thought I'd kept locked away inside from everyone but Oliver. Now I just had to wait and see how Angela responded. I took a bracing glug of wine.

Angela's eyes narrowed. 'You don't like Summer?'

I shouldn't have said anything. I should have left it at that. I wasn't even sure I could trust Angela. But something about being away from home and having Angela's full attention, along with a large glass of wine, made me want to speak freely. 'I just don't really trust her.'

'Why not?'

So I told her. About how Summer had copied my hairstyle and clothes. The regular feeling that I was being watched. My dressing gown being stolen. The scratching noise at the front door. Angela clung on to my every word, her eyes wide. This was, after all, probably the best gossip she'd ever heard. But it wasn't gossip to me, it was real and it was frightening.

When I was done, I took another sip of wine and wondered if I'd just made the biggest mistake of my life by confiding in Angela. 'Do you think I've lost the plot too?'

'No,' she said slowly. 'But why would Summer do all of that?'

'I don't know. I really can't work it out.'

'Have you met her before? Perhaps years ago, and you don't remember?'

'I'm positive that I haven't.'

'Did any alarm bells ring when she bought your flat?'

'To be honest I was so relieved that someone wanted the flat after our last buyers pulled out that I thought the sun shone out of her backside.'

Angela was thoughtful. 'But isn't it strange that she still wanted it after all that time? Surely she would have found somewhere else while you were in negotiations with your previous buyers?'

I hadn't thought about it at the time. But now I began to wonder if Angela was right. There were plenty of flats for sale in and around Barnet. Why had Summer been so fixated on getting ours? And why, for that matter, had she chosen to live in Barnet? If she wanted to move back to London there were so many other places she could have picked. As far as I knew, there was no link to Barnet for Summer. I'd come away for the weekend to escape my intrusive thoughts but now Angela was feeding my hungry paranoia. And I knew it wasn't helping but I was still glad that she was entertaining my theory.

'Have you googled her?' Angela asked.

'A few times,' I admitted. 'But I can't find anything about her online, which I think it strange in itself, especially given that she was allegedly some big West End star.'

'That *is* strange. Unless she used a stage name.'

'I wondered that too. But I haven't found a way to ask her without sounding like I've been stalking her online.'

'Leave it with me.' Angela gave me a wink. 'I'll find out.'

Right then, in that moment, I loved Angela. She had given me what I craved. Support. Alliance. And even when she started talking about how Sebastian was three academic years higher in intellect than the other children, I didn't begrudge her. So she was proud of her son. And a little annoying with it. But we all adored our children.

By the end of the evening, we were sozzled. And when I went up to my room to go to bed, I thought I'd pass out immediately. But instead, I lay awake, thinking about what Angela and I had discussed. And I wondered why, if she had been so quick to believe me about Summer, Oliver still had his doubts. I had found an unlikely comrade and the fact that it was a woman I'd spent the past few years avoiding almost made me laugh out loud. But it wasn't Oliver's fault, not really. I'd been wound up like a coil recently and it wasn't the first time I'd had anxiety. And Oliver had supported me through these difficult periods. So it was no surprise that he just thought I was going through a similar thing now.

Only there was one big difference between then and now. And her name was Summer.

* * *

I woke up the next morning with a dry mouth and a sore head. When I looked at the clock on the bedside table I gasped. It was nine o'clock. I hadn't slept that late in years and clearly I'd needed it. I hurriedly got dressed and went downstairs to meet Angela for breakfast.

She was already sitting at a table with a cup of coffee when I arrived, and she was texting furiously on her phone. As soon as she saw me, she put her phone away.

'Naomi, hi. How are you feeling?'

'Like I drank a bottle of red wine last night.'

'Oh, me too, I'm... what do you say? Hanging.'

She didn't look hanging though. She looked like a woman who'd been up for hours, with plenty of time to style her hair and perfect her make-up. And text people.

Was she talking about me? Drunken remorse was kicking in. I'd been too candid with Angela last night. I'd laid all my cards on the table, and I had no idea what she was going to do with the information. What if she told everyone what I'd said? It didn't bear thinking about. I thought about how hurriedly she'd put her phone away when she saw me.

'Angela, about last night. I think I said too much.'

'Don't give it another thought.' Angela waved her hand dismissively.

'What I said about Summer...'

'Was very alarming. And I shall certainly be keeping my distance from her.'

I scrutinised her face. Was she telling me the truth? Did she really have my back? I wanted to believe it more than anything.

'Thanks for listening,' I told her. 'I appreciate it. And now it's time for a full English.'

Angela was horrified. 'Do you really eat that stuff? I've ordered fruit and yoghurt.'

Fruit and yoghurt with a hangover was not going to cut it for me. I needed hash browns and I needed eggs. I beckoned to a passing waiter so that we could place our orders and when I turned to Angela, she was on her phone again.

'It's Michael,' she told me. 'I left him Sebastian's full itinerary, but he's still clueless.'

It was the first time that Angela had mentioned her husband all weekend. I knew she was married but I hadn't seen the man at school once and presumed he worked long hours.

'I take it he's not used to looking after Sebastian?'

'He has no idea. Do you know, he never even changed Sebastian's nappy when he was a baby?'

I looked at her in shock. 'Are you serious?'

'Oh yes, quite serious. Michael said it was women's work.'

I couldn't believe what I was hearing. That men like that still existed. I remembered Oliver on the floor, changing the girls' nappies. Blowing raspberries on their tummies and making them giggle. God, I was so lucky to have him.

'So you raised Sebastian pretty much on your own?'

'Yes. Michael works hard, but he does his best to provide for his family. He's a proud man and he wants to make sure Sebastian doesn't want for anything. I always thought I'd have three children but to be honest, after Sebastian, I didn't think I could do it again.'

My heart went out to her as I realised how much I'd leaned on Oliver in those early years. And poor Angela, despite being married, had done it all herself with little support. I wondered if her pushy parenting was partly a result of pressure from her high-achieving husband. Perhaps he had high expectations of both his wife and his son. This weekend was making me see her in a whole new light and, once again, I felt bad for excluding her in the past. I'd been no better than those girls in Freya's class. And I wasn't going to behave like that again. I also felt guilty for assuming she'd been texting the other mums when I walked in. I'd got it wrong, again.

'Well, a weekend of solo parenting will show him just how much you do,' I told her. 'Maybe after that he'll be a little more grateful to you.'

'I doubt it. But it's nice to get away.'

We tucked into our breakfasts and then went for a walk around the grounds to digest our food. It was a cold, wet November day but the fresh air invigorated me and by the time we went to the spa, I was feeling calm and peaceful. It was a refreshing change and, I realised with a sinking heart, that I could stay here forever. I missed Oliver and the girls, of course, but it suddenly occurred to me that I didn't miss the house, or the now fraught school drop-offs and pick-ups. The lovely bubble that we had built for ourselves in Barnet over the years had burst. As I thought about returning home the next day – of lying awake at night listening for strange noises, worrying about Freya and fretting that my friends had turned against me – I felt the familiar knot of anxiety twist in my stomach. But I had another twenty-four hours to go and I was going to make the most of it, starting with a swim in the pool.

By the end of the day, I was feeling better again. We'd had the most glorious few hours in the spa and then I'd gone upstairs for a little nap before dinner. Just before I headed back downstairs, I'd video-called Oliver and the girls and they had all appeared on the screen, their faces squashed together, as they talked about the film they'd been to see at the cinema. I could tell from the way Freya was jigging about that she was on a sugar high and suspected that Oliver had let them go overboard with the pick 'n' mix. But she seemed happy and it was lovely to see.

'What are you doing this evening?' I'd asked them.

'Pizza takeaway,' they'd shouted in unison.

My stomach had rumbled then and I'd said goodbye and headed downstairs to meet Angela. After another delicious meal, and more wine, I was ready to hit the sack. Angela had spent most of the evening talking about the best universities – which her son would not be attending for another eleven years – and while I was determined to stick to my pact to be kinder and more tolerant, I'd hit my limit. It was time for bed.

It wasn't until I stood up that I realised I was tipsy again. I said goodnight to Angela and swayed along the corridor, letting myself into the room and collapsing on the bed. As I lay there, I wondered what Oliver was up to. The girls would be asleep by now, but he often stayed up late, especially if I was out for the evening. He liked to take advantage of my absence to watch films that I hated. He was probably halfway through a gory horror movie, a growing line of empty beer bottles on the coffee table in front of him.

I reached for my phone and sent him a WhatsApp message.

> Hey, babe. Just got back to my room. What
> you up to? xx

As I waited for the two blue ticks to appear, I scrolled through my Instagram feed, pausing when I saw a photo of some of the Year 3 girls. Asha had shared it and I realised that it was from Luna's birthday party. In the post, she'd written, 'Aanya had a great day celebrating her bestie's birthday'. I studied the photo. Luna was in the centre of it, smiling with the wariness that seemed to be a permanent feature on her face. Next to her, Aanya had an arm flung around Luna and was showing her gappy smile. There were several other girls I recognised in the picture. Girls who had come to playdates at ours and Freya's birthday parties over the years. Girls who had once been her friends.

I swiped to the next image, and it was of Summer and Asha. They were head-to-head, holding up a glass of champagne each. I looked to see if Asha had tagged Summer in the photo, which might lead me to her Instagram profile, but she hadn't. My eyes moved back to the photo. Summer looked beautiful, as she always did. She was wearing the same dress she'd been wearing when we went for coffee, the one that I also owned, along with gold hoop earrings. They really suited the dress, I thought grudgingly. I swiped again, and this time it was a group photo, kids at the front, parents behind them. I saw Victoria, Rachel and Richard, along with some other parents. So the small party was not so small after all. It didn't surprise me, but it still hurt.

I closed Instagram and returned to WhatsApp. Oliver still hadn't read the message. Perhaps he was already asleep? But in my inebriated state I was feeling needy and I wanted to speak to my husband. To tell him I loved him, and that I'd see him tomorrow.

I called his number, hoping that he would pick up, but it rang out. Disappointed, I tossed my phone on the bed and tried to muster up the energy to get up again so that I could brush my teeth and take my make-up off. I must have dozed off because the sound of my phone ringing woke me up with a jolt. Sleepily, I rummaged around for it and picked it up. It was Oliver.

'Hey, Ol.'

'Hey, babe. Did I wake you?'

'It's okay. I'd only just nodded off.'

'I saw your missed call.'

I sat up drowsily and rubbed my eyes. 'I just wanted to say hi.'

'Did you have a good evening?'

'Lovely, thanks. The food here is amazing. We should come together for a night, maybe Dad could mind the girls?'

'Sounds great.'

'How about you? Did you have a good evening?'

He paused before he answered. 'Yeah.'

'What did you get up to?' Another pause. Even in my sleepy state, I sensed something was amiss. 'What is it, Oliver? Are the girls okay?'

'The girls are fine. Fast asleep.'

'So what is it?'

'Let's chat tomorrow.'

Oliver's reticence was unnerving me, and I felt the effects of sleep rapidly wearing off. 'You're worrying me now. Was there another attempted break-in?'

'No, nothing like that.'

'So what is it, Oliver?'

'I just had a bit of an unexpected evening, that's all.'

'Unexpected in what way?'

He paused again. 'Did Summer know you were going away?'

My heart started pounding at the mention of that woman's name. 'Probably. Angela was telling anyone who would listen.'

'It's just that she turned up here.'

My blood ran cold. 'She did what?'

'She said her plans had been cancelled at the last minute and, as she'd booked a babysitter, she thought she'd pop by with a bottle of wine to discuss the Freya and Luna situation. She asked for you and I told her you were away for the weekend.'

But Oliver had asked if Summer knew I was away, which meant that he'd seen through her excuse. Finally. I thought back, trying to remember if Summer had been there when Angela was telling everyone in the playground that we were going to the spa. I was sure she had.

'What happened then?'

'Well, I invited her in. It seemed rude not to.'

It was crystal clear to me what had happened. The bitch had taken advantage of my absence to spend a night alone with my husband. My hands were shaking as I held the phone to my ear. I was furious. 'Oliver, how could you do that?'

'I didn't know what to do. She was just standing there expectantly with a bottle of wine.'

'Which I presume you drank?'

Another hesitation. 'Yes.'

'And?'

'And what?'

'What happened?'

'Nothing happened. Of course nothing happened.'

I was struggling to gather my thoughts. If I hadn't had a skinful I would have got in the car and driven straight home. But then I remembered that Angela had driven us anyway. I was stuck here until the morning at the earliest.

'How long did she stay?'

'A couple of hours.'

A thought occurred to me. 'Was she there when I called? Is that why you didn't answer?'

He hesitated again. I wanted to throttle him. 'She's just left.'

It was eleven o'clock at night! Which meant that she'd clearly stayed more than a couple of hours. I couldn't believe that this was happening. I couldn't believe the sheer gall of her.

'Did she try anything on with you?'

'Of course she didn't. Come on, Naomi, don't get all worked up. I genuinely think she has our best interests at heart. She's very keen to sort out this issue with Freya and Luna. She wants everyone to get along.'

Oh Oliver. Good-natured, naive Oliver. 'And she waited until I was away to do that?'

'Well, she asked for you. So perhaps she genuinely thought you were at home. Or maybe she thought it might be easier to talk to me, given the issues between you both.'

'Issues?' I could feel my voice rising. 'They're not issues, Oliver. The woman is crazy. She's going after everyone I love. She's following me. We need to call the police.'

'And tell them what? That a school mum friend popped round while you were out?'

'For fuck's sake, Oliver!' I was beyond reason now. All I could think of was getting home and having it out with Summer, once and for all. Enough was enough.

'Look, let's sleep on it and we'll chat tomorrow when you get home, okay?'

But I already knew I wouldn't sleep. I would be haunted by thoughts of my husband and Summer, sitting together on the sofa with a glass of wine. Her melodic laughter in response to one of Oliver's wry jokes. Her smooth, slender hand moving to his inner thigh as her bracelets jangled gently. And then the moment when she leaned in, engulfing him in her sweet scent, and kissed him. And then I dropped the phone and ran into the bathroom to be sick.

15

'She did what?'

Angela and I were driving home and I'd just filled her in on what had happened the previous evening. Her outrage and cynicism were the reaction I'd been hoping for and what had been lacking in Oliver's response when he told me.

'I'm certain she knew we were going away. Which meant that she timed her unannounced visit for when my husband was home alone. I told Oliver we should call the police, but he pretty much said I was being ridiculous.'

'I'm sorry but he's right. Not about you being ridiculous,' Angela added quickly. 'But the police aren't going to get involved in this.'

'What about the break-ins though?'

'There's not enough evidence.'

'So what the hell do I do?'

'Watch your back. And try to gather more proof against her.'

It didn't feel like enough. I wanted to do something. To make something happen. But Angela was right. As it stood, I had nothing but a strong instinct and some unexplained events in my armoury. I needed more.

'Do you think I should say something to the others? Asha and so on?'

'Not yet. They've all become pally with Summer. Until you can prove definitively that she's up to something, it may not go down well.'

'You mean, they may not believe me.'

'Well to be blunt, Naomi, it is rather far-fetched.'

I swivelled to face her. 'But you believe me, right?'

'Of course I do.'

Was she lying? Was she simply telling me what I wanted to hear? I didn't know her well enough yet to be able to tell. I turned my head away again, watching the rain spatter against the car window. Then, agitated, I opened Instagram to distract myself and noticed that I had a new follower. Their handle was Summer_Luna, so it didn't take a genius to work out who it was. I clicked on her profile, but it was set to private. She had nine followers which suggested that it was a new account. Perhaps she set it up to look at the photos Asha had posted of Luna's party. Did I send a follower request? The last thing I wanted was to have anything to do with Summer, other than see her arrested for harassment. But what was that saying? Keep your friends close and your enemies closer. This could be a window into her world, a chance for me to gather evidence against her. Against my instincts, I forced myself to press the button requesting to follow her. And then I waited to see if she would accept.

By the time we reached Barnet she still hadn't, and I was seriously considering blocking her from my own profile. But as we pulled up outside the house, Freya and Bella came dashing out to reach me and I pocketed my phone and climbed out of the car.

'Hi, girls, I missed you so much.'

'Did you bring us anything?' Bella was already rummaging around in my handbag.

'In my backpack. Hang on a minute.' I turned to say goodbye to Angela. 'Thanks for a lovely weekend. And for your listening ear. I really appreciate it.'

'It was my pleasure. We must do it again.' Angela leaned out of the window and said quietly, 'Keep me posted on all things Summer.'

We waved as she drove off and then I flung my arms around the girls and walked back inside with them. Oliver was in the hallway waiting and he sprang forward and took my bag.

'How was it, babe?'

'Rejuvenating,' I said, keeping my voice light and upbeat in front of the girls. Oliver and I had a lot to talk about but now wasn't the right time. 'Have you guys had fun?'

'So much fun,' Bella enthused, taking the backpack off Oliver and unzipping it, clearly looking for her present.

'It's the bodywash on the top,' I told her. 'The purple one. The pink one's for Freya.'

'Thanks, Mum!' Bella handed the pink bottle to Freya and then opened hers, taking a sniff. 'Smells delicious.'

'So, what did you all get up to?'

The girls launched into a colourful description of the weekend while Oliver wandered off to put the kettle on. I somehow managed to maintain an air of normality for the rest of the afternoon. It wasn't until we'd said goodnight to the girls that I finally got the chance to speak to Oliver. And he was clearly expecting it because he was looking decidedly uncomfortable.

'We need to talk,' I told him.

'Okay.' He sat down opposite me, his expression guarded.

'I know you think this whole Summer business is all in my head. But surely after last night you see her differently now?'

'I'm not sure.'

Something had changed. I could sense it in the air between us. 'What is it?'

'She's been texting me today.'

I managed to hold my temper. Just about. 'What's she been saying?'

'Nothing dodgy. Nothing at all, really.'

'So what's made you wary?'

He ran a hand through his hair. 'I dunno. It's just innocent chatter but it feels a bit inappropriate. I mean, we hardly know each other.'

'Have you been texting her back?'

He winced. 'Yeah. I didn't know what else to do.'

'Well, you have to stop, okay? Starting now.'

'But she'll think I'm being rude.'

Jesus, were we really having this conversation? Oliver was worried about upsetting my stalker? It would have been amusing if it wasn't so horrific.

'Stop replying, Oliver. You'll only encourage her.'

'Fine.' He nodded resolutely. 'You're right.'

'So do you believe me now?'

'I always believed you.'

'No, you didn't.'

'Well, I'm sorry if you thought that. But listen, I'm still a bit unsure about all this. Is it possible that she's just a really nice lady who wants to be friends with us?'

'No.'

'But what if we're wrong? We can't go accusing her of all

sorts of mad stuff if she's just trying to be nice. I mean, you loved her when you first met her.'

'That was before all the weird stuff started happening.'

'And what about Freya?'

I closed my eyes. Oliver had voiced the thing that worried me the most. 'I don't want to cause any trouble for Freya. I just want her to be happy.'

'Exactly. And maybe being friendly to Summer will help to make that happen.'

'But how can you ask me to do that? After everything that's happened.'

'I'm not asking you to do it. I'm saying I could do it.'

I couldn't believe how naive he was being. He was playing right into her hand. This was what she wanted. Oliver on her side. Me left out in the cold. Again.

'I don't think that's a good idea. Especially given that she probably fancies you.'

He grinned. 'Well, I am a catch.'

'Oliver, it's not funny.'

His smile dissolved immediately. 'I know it's not. I'm sorry. Look, just try and be nice to her, okay? For Freya's sake. I didn't realise how bad things had got until she told me last night.'

'I've been telling you for weeks.'

'I know, and I apologise. But if we can get Summer on side, we might be able to sort things out between Freya and Luna. Get things back on track at school again.'

He was right, and I hated it. 'Okay. I'll bite my tongue. I'll play nice. But stop texting the damn woman. And get that bloody camera installed in the porch, okay?'

He mimicked a scout's salute. 'On it.'

'Do you find her attractive?'

Oliver looked at me, frowning. 'Not particularly.'

'Come on, she's gorgeous.'

'Maybe she is to some people, but she's not my type.'

'So then, what is your type?'

He grinned, relieved that our serious conversation was becoming playful. But I needed this as much as he did. I needed to know that my husband still loved me. That he still wanted me. And I needed to prove to him that I could still be fun and sexy.

'My type is beautiful, and clever, and funny. And she just so happens to be my wife.'

'It's your lucky night then because I know a woman matching that exact description.'

He laughed and came over to me, cupping his hands around my face and leaning in to kiss me. 'Strap in, ma'am. It's going to be a bumpy ride.'

We made love that night for the first time in weeks. But every time he moaned with pleasure, I wondered who it was he was thinking of. Me or Summer.

* * *

At school on Monday, I forced myself to walk up to the Year 3 parents. To smile at Summer. To pretend that I wasn't furious with her about her behaviour at the weekend.

'Hi there, how was the birthday party?'

'Oh, it was fabulous, thanks so much for asking, Naomi. I'm just so sorry we didn't have enough space to invite everyone. But we'd love to have Freya around for a playdate.'

I remembered the doll's house. 'We'd love that. She's still so keen to meet the kitten.'

'Wonderful. We'll get something arranged.' But she didn't suggest a date.

Asha was watching me. 'How was your fun weekend away with Angela?'

'It was great. We had a lovely time. We should do drinks before the Christmas rush sets in and we're all fully booked. How about next Friday?'

Asha looked at Summer, almost waiting for her approval. It was astonishing to watch. 'What a great idea,' Summer enthused. 'I'll put a message out on the WhatsApp group.'

'Oh, I can do that now,' I said, pulling out my phone. I saw Asha and Summer exchange another look. 'What is it?'

'We didn't mean the class WhatsApp group,' Asha said quietly. 'There's another group, just a small one, with a few parents. I think Summer meant that one.'

So they'd started a new WhatsApp group without me. It was like being the last person picked for the team in a school sports class. Or not being picked at all, come to think of it. But I was determined not to show them how hurt I was.

'Oh, great. Yes, do send a message out there. I'll let Angela know.'

Asha laughed. 'Since when did you and Angela become so tight?'

Since you turned your back on me. 'Oh, she's really nice when you get to know her.' I hesitated, still thinking about that WhatsApp group. About my friendship with Asha. I had taken Angela's advice and told Freya to stand up for herself more at school. And now I needed to take my own advice. 'Asha, have you got time for a coffee after drop-off?'

'Sure, why not. Summer, do you fancy it?'

My disappointment was palpable. But then Summer surprised me. 'I'm sorry, I can't make it this time. Have a good one, ladies.'

I suppressed my relief. Smiled at them both. 'Never mind, next time.'

As usual, Freya went to the back of the line where she stood, alone. Aanya and Luna were at the front, talking to some of the other girls who had been at the birthday party. And then, as I watched on in surprise, Freya walked to the front of the line and manoeuvred her way into the group. I saw Luna look at her and then glance behind her shoulder at us. Almost as if she was checking to see if we were watching. Which we were. And then the next thing I knew, Luna had stepped aside to let Freya in and was talking to her. Was this a genuine peace offering or was it all a show because she knew she had an audience? Was she an actress, like her mother?

'Luna's really making an effort with Freya,' Summer said.

'I appreciate it,' I replied through gritted teeth.

I was still scrutinising the girls, waiting for Luna to put a foot wrong. But the conversation seemed, if not animated, harmonious at least. Then the bell rang and they all marched in, leaving me hopeful that our troubles, or Freya's at least, were behind us.

'Well, enjoy your coffee.' Summer waved and drifted away, resplendent even in a raincoat. Asha and I began to make our way to the cafe and I realised it was the first time we'd hung out, just the two of us, in ages. We used to do it all the time and I missed it.

'This is nice,' I said as we ordered our coffees and sat down.

'It is. Listen, Naomi, I'm sorry. I know I've been a bit distant. It's just all this business with the girls has been quite stressful. Aanya's really felt stuck in the middle.'

My heart went out to poor Aanya. 'I know and I'm sorry too. That's the last thing I would ever want.'

'And if I'm being honest, I've felt a bit stuck in the middle too.'

Asha looked downcast and I felt a pang of both guilt and annoyance.

'I wouldn't want that either,' I said truthfully.

'I've been spending a lot of time with Summer recently, on account of the girls becoming such good friends, and I'm really struggling to work out why you dislike her so much.'

'I don't dislike her.' My first lie.

'Come on, Naomi, it's pretty clear that you don't like her. You practically assaulted her in the playground.'

'That's not fair. We had a row about a very emotive subject.'

'Fair enough.' Asha held her hands up. 'I don't want to cause any more trouble. It's just that she's a nice person. A good person. And she adores you.'

I couldn't hold my tongue any longer. 'Does she though? I mean, she excludes me from everything. You've even got a new WhatsApp group that I'm not in.'

'Well, it's awkward, isn't it, because you clearly have a problem with her.'

'Are Victoria and Rachel in the group?'

Asha had the good grace to look guilty. 'Yes.'

'And what do they make of it all?'

'They're confused too. We just want everyone to get along.'

Which meant that they'd been talking about it. About me. I hadn't seen much of Victoria and Rachel recently as they were always rushing about. That's why we always made an effort to get together for drinks. But that hadn't happened for weeks.

I wanted to tell Asha. To confide in her like I had done with Angela. But I knew that I couldn't. She wouldn't believe me because Summer had already manipulated her into thinking that I was the one causing trouble. And knowing that I couldn't talk to her was crushing. In that moment, all I wanted to do was go home and have a good old cry. But then I thought of Freya and how unexpectedly brave she'd been that morning, going over to talk to the girls. I owed it to my daughter to smooth this out once and for all, even if only on the surface.

'I'll make more of an effort,' I promised.

Asha visibly exhaled. 'That's great. That's really great.'

We moved on to other topics, catching up on what we'd been up to. But the conversation lacked the easiness that we had enjoyed before. It felt stilted, almost forced. And I hated it.

We only stayed for the one coffee. We hugged on the pavement outside, as we always did, and then went our separate ways. I should have been overjoyed to have had some much-needed one-on-one time with Asha but instead I felt deflated. What had happened to my friendships? And how had they deteriorated in such a short space of time?

I'd almost reached the house when my phone rang and I looked down to see it was the school calling. Usually, they only called when Freya was ill and needed to come home but she hadn't seemed poorly when I dropped her off an hour ago.

'Hello?' I answered.

'Naomi? It's Sharon.'

'Hi, Sharon.' I smiled at the sound of the headteacher's voice.

'Could you come into school? There's something I need to discuss with you quite urgently.'

My heart sank. What had Luna done to Freya now? 'Is everything okay?'

There was a slight pause. And then Sharon said, 'No, I'm afraid it's not.'

16

I arrived at the school ten minutes later, out of breath and fearful. The school, which had once seemed so friendly and welcoming, now loomed threateningly in front of me. I didn't know what I was going to hear when I walked through those doors, but I sensed it wouldn't be good.

I pressed the buzzer and waited to be let in, listening to the sounds of children playing happily in the playground behind the school. They sounded so excited and carefree, and I hoped that Freya was among them, but I had a nagging, uncomfortable feeling that she wasn't. I signed in at the office and waited nervously for Sharon to appear. When she did, her usually warm, open face was uncharacteristically serious.

'What is it? What's happened?' I demanded.

'Come into my office, Naomi.'

I followed her and sat down but this time she didn't offer me a cup of tea. She took a seat opposite me and cut straight to the chase.

'I'm afraid there's been a rather serious allegation made against Freya.'

My eyes widened as my pulse began to race, and my maternal instincts immediately kicked in. 'No, you've got it the wrong way around, Sharon. Freya's the one being bullied.'

Sharon looked at me solemnly. 'I know that Freya has been having some friendship issues at school. I'm also aware that there is some history behind this incident and that it is completely out of character for Freya. However, the allegation is too serious to ignore.'

I frowned. 'What is Freya alleged to have done?'

'She kicked another pupil in the stomach.'

It was like I was the one who had been kicked in the stomach. I felt physically winded by Sharon's words. But I quickly rallied. This was untrue. Freya would never do anything like that.

'I only dropped her an hour ago, Sharon, and she went straight into class. It can't possibly have happened. There must be a misunderstanding.'

'The incident happened last Friday.'

It all became clear. It was so obvious. I thought back to my conversation with Asha and Summer in the playground earlier that morning. Summer had said she couldn't join us for coffee because she had plans. And now I knew exactly what those plans were. She had been right here, sitting in this seat only minutes before me, playing the part of the innocent victim's mother, and telling Sharon lies about my daughter.

'Luna, or Summer, is making it up,' I said firmly. 'It's not true.'

Sharon frowned. 'I haven't told you which pupil it was.'

'I know it was her, and I know it's not true. Luna has made Freya's life a misery since the day she started at North Hill. She's told everyone lies about her, she's turned all her friends against her. And now this. Surely you don't believe it?'

'Again,' Sharon said firmly, 'I haven't told you which child it was. However, there were witnesses, Naomi, other children who saw what happened.'

'Well, I saw Freya and Luna together just this morning,' I argued. 'And they were chatting perfectly happily. It stayed in my mind because it's the first time I've ever seen it. Surely Luna wouldn't behave like that if she had been kicked by Freya?'

'According to the child's mother, there were marks on her stomach.'

Marks which had probably conveniently faded over the weekend and were no longer visible. 'Perhaps she fell over,' I suggested feebly. 'Did any teachers see what happened?'

Sharon shook her head. 'No.'

'Well surely the teacher on duty would have seen it, if it really happened.'

'Naomi, with hundreds of pupils running about, we can't always see everything, no matter how hard we try. Listen, I know this is difficult and that Freya is usually a very kind and thoughtful girl. But you also know that we do not tolerate any form of violence at this school. Now, in theory this type of behaviour would mean a fixed term exclusion...'

'Exclusion!' I stared at Sharon in disbelief. 'She's seven years old!'

Sharon held up a hand. 'Please let me continue. As I said, in theory, this would mean a fixed term exclusion. However, Freya's record is impeccable, and as I said earlier, I know that she's been having a difficult time at school. I am also aware that Freya herself may have been the victim of some unpleasant behaviour. So we will not be excluding Freya.'

I exhaled. I knew I should thank Sharon. That I should be grateful to the headteacher. But it was hard to be grateful for what I believed to be a grave injustice in the first place.

'I have spoken to both pupils separately this morning,' Sharon said. 'And I will be doing so again. We'll be keeping a close eye on them. We also have a counsellor who visits the school once a week and I would like Freya to spend some time with her.'

'What about the other child? Will they have counselling too?'

'Yes.'

Sharon's handling of the alleged incident was fair and reasonable, and she had acted with compassion. But I was still outraged. This was all so unfair to poor Freya.

'Would you at least consider the possibility that it's not true, Sharon? That it's made up?'

She looked at me carefully. 'Other children saw it, Naomi. And I have to act on the evidence I have. But I hope that we can draw a line under this, once and for all. And remember, you are a role model for your daughter. Freya learns from your behaviour.'

I stared at the headteacher in horror. Was she thinking about my spat with Summer in the playground? Was she suggesting that this was my fault? Freya hadn't even been there at the time. Could she have seen it happen, though, from the window of her classroom? My throat constricted but Sharon's last comment had stolen my fight. There was nothing I could say to convince her that she'd got this wrong. The evidence was against Freya, just as it was against me.

But I knew it was lies, and I knew exactly what Summer was trying to do. She was no longer just coming after me, she was coming after my family. I wondered now if she had tried to persuade Sharon to suspend Freya. I bet she had. Thank goodness the headteacher was so reasonable. But Summer was clever, I'd give her that. Both Freya and I now looked like the guilty parties, again, while she and Luna came up smelling of roses.

For a brief moment I considered telling Sharon all of this, but I knew how it would make me sound. The silence stretched out and eventually Sharon stood up, ending our meeting.

'Thank you for coming in so quickly, Naomi, I do appreciate it. We'll talk again soon and if you have any concerns, you know that my door is always open.'

Trying to suppress my tears, I thanked Sharon and followed her back to the main entrance. I avoided the receptionist's eye as I signed out and left, keeping my head down. As soon as I was on the street outside, I turned to face the school, imagining Freya inside. What would school be like for her that day? Would the other children talk to her? Or would they believe Luna's false allegations and freeze her out, like they had done before?

I wanted to go round to Summer's and have it out with her. Rage was bubbling up inside me and threatening to pour out. But Sharon's words were ringing in my ears. *You are a role model for your daughter.* I knew that anything I did would get back to the other mums, and probably Sharon too. So, as much as it pained me, I had to keep my distance. Anyway, I'd tried to have a reasonable conversation with Summer before and look where that had got me. She knew how to play the game, how to push my buttons. And I couldn't let her do that again.

I started walking home but at the last minute I detoured via the high street. I didn't want to be alone, I wanted to be surrounded by other people going about their day. I paused as I reached the popular local coffee shop, looking in through the window out of habit to see if I knew anyone in there, and my heart stopped when I saw Summer at the counter. Instinctively I moved back, peering in to watch her. She was laughing with the barista, like she didn't have a care in the world and fury surged through me. How dare she? She was acting as though everything was perfectly normal, wonderful in fact, when she'd just turned my daughter's life upside down. It took every ounce of strength I had not to yank the door open, stomp up to her and confront her in front of everyone, and screw the consequences.

I watched carefully as Summer tapped her phone on the card payment reader, thanked the barista, and walked towards the back of the coffee shop, waving at someone who stood up to greet her. And then my breath caught in my throat as I realised who it was.

It was Angela. And by the way they warmly embraced one another, it was obvious that they were close friends. A lot closer than I had realised.

I moved away from the window, nauseous. How had I missed this? I'd never seen them together and there had been no mention of Angela attending the drinks and dinners that Summer had arranged with the others. Yet the evidence was right there, in front of me.

This was bad. This was very, very bad. The one person I'd confided in, the one person who I'd talked to about Summer, was now sitting opposite her having a cosy coffee and probably telling her everything I'd said, if she hadn't done so already. Was that why Summer had used our children as ammunition against me? Was it my punishment for confiding in Angela?

I'd been played, that much was clear. And it meant two things. One, that Summer knew I was on to her and that I despised her. And two, that I was even more alone than I had thought.

17

___

Christmas lights adorned the high street and every shop or cafe I entered had festive music blaring from the speakers. The girls were caught up in the excitement, writing long, elaborate letters to Santa, even though Bella had long stopped being a believer. We'd bought a tree and decorated it, and the fairy lights gave our living room a cosy glow. With the boiler back to full health, the house was toasty and nothing else had gone wrong for weeks. There had been no strange noises or open doors, and even Freya had turned a corner.

Everything was right but it had never felt more wrong.

When I had tried to talk to Freya about the incident with Luna, she had denied everything, explaining that another child had accidentally kicked Luna in the stomach with a ball during a game. She had been upset that evening because she had unfairly got into trouble and I had reassured her, telling her that it would soon be forgotten, and the school wasn't punishing her. I had assured her that I believed her and I had, yet again, suggested that she give Luna a wide berth and play with other children. I had worried that the incident would send

Freya spiralling but conversely, it seemed to have the opposite effect. She was happy again, chatting to me on the way into school and heading straight to her class line in the playground. I had watched her like a hawk and seen both Luna and Aanya move aside to let her into the group. Freya had not heeded my advice to avoid Luna and instead, they now seemed to talk to each other like they were the best of friends. I couldn't get my head around it. Why Luna would make up a lie about Freya and then decide to be nice to her. Why Freya would forgive her so easily.

Oliver had given me an 'I told you so look' when I relayed it all to him. He had told me from the start that it was playground politics and that the girls would sort it out between them.

'See, you had nothing to worry about after all,' he'd said. But his response only made me angrier. How could he not see what was going on right in front of him? That it was so much more than a schoolgirl spat? Our darling Freya had been bullied and victimised and it was only a matter of time before it happened again. Luna, like her mother, was not to be trusted.

'She's a child, Naomi,' was Oliver's response to that. 'She's not a criminal mastermind.'

Everyone else had moved on and I knew I should be happy. Freya was back to her old self, and it was the greatest Christmas present I could have asked for. But something still felt off.

While the children may have sorted out their differences, forgiveness had not stretched to the parents. There was a divide now and I hated it. I avoided Summer, which meant avoiding all my old friends too, who huddled around her like doting fawns. I kept my distance from Angela too, ignoring her texts and calls and refusing to engage with her in the playground, because I couldn't trust her either. I was an outcast in a place where I had once belonged.

Oliver still thought it was all in my head. He couldn't understand why I didn't just message Asha, Victoria or Rachel to arrange a meet-up. Or why I didn't just go up to them in the playground and have a chat, like I used to. But he wasn't there, he didn't feel the tension in the air or see the sidelong glances they gave me as I played on my phone, pretending that I was busy so that it wouldn't seem obvious that I was on my own, with no one to talk to.

I couldn't be anywhere near Summer and unfortunately that now meant that I couldn't be anywhere near my friends either. I had completely relinquished my responsibility of the raffle to Summer and so I didn't even attend the PTA meetings any more. The school's Christmas fair was that afternoon after school, and I was dreading it. Freya wanted to go, and even Bella was attending with some of her secondary school mates, who also had younger siblings. I had to go, even though the very idea set me on the verge of a panic attack.

With so much time to myself, my thoughts were going off on all different tangents. Why, when I had isolated myself from the group, had everything else stopped going wrong? There had been no more attempted break-ins or strange goings-on. Had Summer backed off? And if so, why? Was it because she had got what she wanted? She had succeeded in scaring me off. She had turfed me out of the gang and seamlessly taken my place. Or was she plotting something else? Something worse? And what did that mean for Freya, who now seemed to be pally with Luna?

I didn't know what to do about any of it. So I did nothing. But I was still watching. Summer had approved my follower request on Instagram and I pored over her feed, scrolling through her photos. Summer and Luna. Luna and Aanya. Summer and Asha. Summer and Richard. They were always smiling, laughing or pulling funny faces. It felt like a personal attack, as though she was trying to show me just what a great time they were all having without me.

And yet it didn't offer me any clues as to Summer's past. Her Instagram account had only started when she moved to Barnet, like she and Luna hadn't existed before then. And no matter how hard I had delved, I couldn't find any information about her that pre-dated this time. Eventually I had given up, throwing myself into work and into making the house look festive. I wanted the girls, and Oliver, to have a wonderful first Christmas in the house, one to remember. It would sort itself out in the New Year, I told myself. We'd all have the break we needed over the holidays, and I would start the year with renewed vigour and determination. If Summer and Luna could conveniently move back to Devon in that time, it would certainly help.

I cursed as I looked at the time. I had to leave for the school pick-up and then it would be straight into the Christmas fair. The children would be out of their minds with excitement. And I would plaster a smile on my face and pretend that I was having a great time too.

My phone pinged and I looked down to see a message from Oliver.

> Good luck at the Christmassacre fair. You got this, babe.

Oliver had been to one Christmas fair and had declared never again. They were always chaos: school halls packed to the rafters with screaming children and long lines for sweets and cakes that would send them even more loopy, not to mention the tat that ended up coming home in armfuls. But Oliver knew I was nervous about it and I appreciated him getting in touch. He was worried about me. He said I wasn't myself. But I didn't need him to tell me that because I already knew it. The problem was that I didn't know how to fix it.

I wrapped myself up in my winter coat and let myself out of the house, checking that the door was double locked before walking briskly towards the school. The closer I got, the more my stomach churned. I forced myself to keep going, smiling and nodding at a couple of faces I recognised, until I reached the playground. Thankfully Summer and Asha weren't there. They were probably inside, helping to set up for the fair. I spotted Angela looking at me from across the playground and I turned away, avoiding her eye. I reached for my phone, as I always did now, to pretend I was checking my messages, and then I felt a hand on my arm.

'Hello, stranger.' It was Rachel, smiling as if nothing at all was amiss.

'Hey, Rachel.'

'I haven't seen you for ages. Have you been hiding?'

I looked at her for a moment, confused. Surely she knew what was going on? She was friends with the others and I had no doubt that they had been talking about me. In my head I have visions of them gossiping about mine and Freya's behaviour over drinks in our old flat. Like mother, like daughter, I imagined them sniggering. But Rachel's face showed none of that.

'I've been busy with the house, and work,' I stuttered.

'Tell me about it. Christmas is our busiest time at work and the kids have been taking it in turns to get ill. I swear if I hear one more "Mummy, I've got a tummy ache" I'll lose my mind.'

I smiled, relieved that I was having what felt like the first normal conversation with a school mum I'd had in weeks.

'And now we've got the bloody Christmas fair,' Rachel said, rolling her eyes.

I leaned in. 'Oliver calls it the Christmassacre fair.'

Rachel laughed with delight, 'Oh, I like that. I like it a lot. We should do drinks before the festivities completely take over our lives.'

'Yes please. How's Noah doing?'

'He's grand. Annoying his older siblings as usual. How's Freya?'

'Good. Really good, actually.'

Rachel smiled. 'I'm so pleased to hear that. I know you were worried about her.'

I shouldn't have said anything. But the urge was too strong. 'Have you seen much of the others recently?'

'Not much, other than the usual after-school club pick-ups. A few of us went for drinks the other night. I was sorry to hear you couldn't make it.'

'I didn't know about it,' I said, unable to keep the hurt from my voice.

I saw red creeping up Rachel's neck and felt guilty for making things awkward for her. 'It doesn't matter,' I added hurriedly. 'Don't worry about it at all.'

Rachel still looked uncomfortable. 'I'm not sure what's going on, Naomi.'

'You and me both.'

'This thing with you and Summer, what's caused it? Why don't you like her?'

There it was again, the question that everyone seemed to be asking me. And I burned to tell Rachel why. But after the Angela debacle, I no longer knew who I could trust. Until I had figured it out for myself, and connected the dots, I was keeping quiet.

'It's just been a difficult term, I think,' I told her, my voice beginning to waver.

Rachel smiled sympathetically. 'You've had a lot on your plate.'

'I have.'

'And I know it must have been hard, seeing Summer move into your old flat.'

'That's not what this is about,' I spat, before I could stop myself.

Rachel didn't say anything at first. She just looked at me curiously. Finally, she nodded. 'Okay, no problem. Sorry for bringing it up. Anyway, I'd better go, I'm on the first shift on the tombola stall. Wish me luck.'

I forced a smile. 'Good luck.'

The children started emerging from their classrooms and I craned my neck, looking for Freya. There she was, walking with a couple of other girls in her class. She smiled when she saw me and, as soon as she was dismissed by her teacher, she raced over to me.

'I'm so excited about the Christmas fair!' she said.

'Me too, darling. Where do you want to go first?'

'The cake stall. Luna and Aanya are helping their mums out.'

I suppressed a grimace. 'Sure, let's do that.'

As soon as the doors opened, Freya grabbed my hand and dragged me inside. Lines were already beginning to form. Freya pulled me towards the cake stand and then released my hand and ran behind the tables to join Aanya and Luna, leaving me on my own. I came face to face with Summer, who was looking resplendent in a red jumper dress, with a chunky gold necklace.

'Naomi!' she said brightly, but her expression was cautious.

'Hi, Summer.'

'What can I get you?'

I looked down at the mixture of homemade and store-bought cakes and then across at Freya, who was chatting with the girls. 'Freya, which ones do you want, darling?'

Freya pointed at some cupcakes with green icing.

'I'll take four of those,' I said, digging into my purse for some money. As I waited for Summer to put the cupcakes in a bag, I glanced over at Asha, but she was busy serving someone else. Thankfully Summer had other customers waiting so she handed me my bag, took my money with a nod of thanks and moved on. It had been a completely innocuous exchange but as I stepped back and watched Summer and Asha working together as a team, I felt lost. I should have been there with them and yet I was on the other side, excluded. Then, as Summer tucked her hair behind her ear, my eyes wandered up to her earrings and my heart started racing. They were gold star studs, with rubies embedded in them. Oliver had given me an identical pair when Freya was born but I hadn't worn them for ages and the last time I saw them, they were at the bottom of my jewellery box. Was it possible Summer had the same pair? I was certain that Oliver said he'd bought them from an antique store rather than a high street shop, so the chances were slim. I thought back to the day when I came home to find my front door open and my dressing gown missing. Had she taken them then? And if so, would she really have the audacity to wear them in front of me? My hands were trembling as I instinctively put my hands to my own ears.

She must have felt me staring because she turned and looked at me, her gaze drifting up my arms and towards my ears. Then I swear to God, she smiled at me. And not a polite smile, a knowing one. In that moment she knew that I knew. And she took pleasure in it.

'Mummy, can we go to the toy stall?'

Freya tugging at my sleeve broke the spell and I stared down at her, confused and disorientated. When I looked back at Summer she had turned away.

'Mummy, come on!' Freya was impatient.

I was tempted to confront Summer, but I'd made that mistake before. No, I would go home first and check to see if the earrings were in my jewellery box. If they weren't, then I'd know that I was right. That it was definitely Summer who had snuck into the house and stolen from me. And then I would call the police and have her arrested.

I don't know how I made it through the rest of the fair. I was on autopilot, letting myself be dragged around by Freya, handing out cash as though it was Monopoly money to keep her happy because I couldn't cope with any level of confrontation, not even from a seven-year-old. At some point Bella turned up and I parted with even more coins which she snatched before running off with her mates. By six o'clock I was burning to get home and check for the earrings.

'Come on, Freya, let's find Bella and go.'

'But, Mummy, they haven't done the raffle yet.'

'They'll let us know if we win, don't worry. Come on.'

I took a reluctant Freya's hand and wandered around until we found Bella, getting a glitter tattoo. With both my girls beside me, I guided them out of the school gates.

'Can we get a takeaway on the way home?' Bella asked.

But I was the impatient one now. 'Let's go home and order from there,' I suggested. I didn't want to lose another minute.

As soon as I opened the front door, I raced up the stairs, hurtling into the bedroom and picking up my jewellery box. I turned it upside down on the bed, searching through the contents in a frenzy. After a few minutes, I was satisfied. The earrings weren't there.

'Mum!' Bella called from the bottom of the stairs. 'What are you doing? We're hungry.'

'One minute,' I called, staring at the mess of jewellery on the bed. I was excited and terrified. Excited because I had finally caught Summer out. And terrified because if I took this further, I was opening a can of worms that I would never be able to close again. I picked up my phone and prepared myself to make the call.

'Mum, we are dying of hunger down here!'

Bella's flair for the theatrical usually amused me but this time it annoyed me. 'I said in a minute,' I shouted angrily, and that silenced her.

My hand hovered mid-air as I gripped on to my phone. I imagined the police turning up, me making a statement, them going over to speak to Summer. And I felt sick.

I put the phone back down. I'd speak to Oliver first. He was my voice of reason and he would help me decide what to do. I scooped the jewellery up and put it back in the box before making my way downstairs, where the girls were waiting with matching frowns. Despite stuffing their faces with cakes at the fair, they were on the cusp of being dangerously hangry.

'Come on then, ladies, what will it be? Pizza? Fish and chips?'

'Pizza,' they shouted in unison.

I nodded and opened my app to place the order. Oliver couldn't come home soon enough. I had to tell someone about this, and I had to do it soon or I would burst. But a strange sense of calm had also settled over me. I'd got Summer this time. She was a wrong 'un and soon everyone would know about it. Soon I would have my life back.

18

Oliver bought me a new pair of earrings for Christmas. Perhaps he hoped that they would help me forget about the ones that had gone missing. The ones she had stolen.

When I opened them on Christmas Day, I smiled and thanked him for the thoughtful gesture. And then I put them on, letting the girls admire them before they lost interest and started tearing shreds of wrapping paper off their own presents. Toys, stationery, clothes. My dad watched on fondly from the armchair where he was sitting in the corner. It was picture perfect. If anyone had been watching, they would have thought it was the dream family Christmas.

Only Oliver and I knew that it wasn't. I hadn't called the police in the end, a decision made after both Oliver's advice and my own nagging fear that if I took that step, my life would implode, and so would my family's. Freya was happy at school and I didn't want to cause an earthquake which would get her caught up in the shock waves. I was hanging on to my friends by a thread as it was and if I went ahead and Summer wasn't caught, it would be social suicide.

Oliver had been diplomatic, telling me that because the break-in was so long ago and there were no signs of forced entry, the police might not take it seriously. But the undercurrent, while subtle, was clear. *What if you're wrong?* That was what he was thinking.

I hadn't had a single Happy Christmas message from the school gang. But I knew they'd met up for pre-Christmas drinks because Summer had posted about it on her Instagram feed. They'd all been there, at her flat, holding their glasses up to the camera. There had been another photo of the children all curled up in a makeshift den, watching a film. In the caption, Summer had written, 'Celebration with our besties to mark the end of term.'

Screw them, I'd thought. I wasn't going to let them ruin our Christmas. I'd spent hours buying and wrapping presents, preparing lunch and decorating the house. We'd been too busy for playdates anyway, what with the Christmas preparations and Bella's end-of-year performance with her stage school. She had shone on stage, word and pitch perfect, and Oliver and I had held hands and looked on proudly as our eyes glistened. The most important things in life were family and love, I'd decided then. The rest of it didn't matter.

But once Christmas was over, the children started growing restless. Oliver went back to work and the weather was too miserable to get out and about much. Bella got in touch with her friends and arranged her own meet-ups, but Freya was hanging around, bored.

'Can I have a playdate?' she asked me.

'Who with?'

'Aanya and Luna.'

My stomach lurched at the prospect.

'How about just Aanya?' I suggested. 'I think you'd really enjoy a bit of quality time, just the two of you.'

I held my breath while Freya mulled this over and finally exhaled when she nodded her agreement. Although things between Asha and I weren't great, contacting her was the lesser of two evils. And perhaps, with Summer out of the way, we might even be able to have a chat and start to mend the bridge between us while the girls played. I wasn't sure that things would ever go back to the way they'd been before but as long as we were on good terms, and it didn't affect our children's friendship, then I could live with that. I sent her a breezy WhatsApp, saying I hoped she'd had a fabulous Christmas and did Aanya want to come over to play? Then I waited for a response, checking my phone constantly to see if she'd read the message yet.

She responded a few hours later, saying that they had gone to stay with her parents and wouldn't be back until the new year. There was a time when I would have known that already but we'd barely spoken over the past few weeks. *No worries*, I wrote. *Give me a shout when you're back and we'll arrange something.* She replied with a thumbs up.

I tried Rachel next, but they were busy too. Freya wasn't that friendly with Victoria's son and had scrunched up her nose when I suggested inviting him over to play.

'What about Luna?' she asked. 'I still haven't met her kitten.'

The idea of contacting Summer sickened me. And I still didn't like the fact that Freya had become friendly with Luna after everything the girl had done to her.

'I'm not sure,' I said tentatively. 'Luna wasn't very kind to you.'

'But we're friends now.'

'Yes, but what if she's mean again?'

'She won't be.' Freya was determined. 'Because we're friends. Please, Mum. Please.'

And so that was how I found myself messaging the woman I loathed and inviting myself and Freya round to her flat. Or our flat, as I still thought of it. Summer replied immediately, suggesting the following day, and when I told Oliver about it, he raised his eyebrows at me. 'So, one minute you hate her and the next you're going round for a cosy coffee?'

'It's for Freya.'

'Just don't do anything stupid.'

'Like what?'

He looked at me carefully. 'Like going through her stuff, looking for the earrings.'

Of course I'd thought about it. Just like I'd thought of sneaking into Luna's room to get another peek at the doll's house. But I smiled sweetly at Oliver. 'Of course I won't.'

I didn't sleep well that night. I tossed and turned, thinking about the playdate and having abstract dreams about being a doll trapped in Luna's doll's house. In contrast, Freya slept like a log. Her night terrors had disappeared along with her reluctance to go to school, and in the morning she bounded into our bedroom and jumped on the bed.

'We're going on a playdate! We're going on a playdate!'

I wished that I matched her excitement. I felt nauseous as I made breakfast, sipping on my coffee and fretting about the day ahead. I considered dropping Freya and leaving, saying I had some chores to do, but I didn't like the idea of my daughter being alone with Summer and Luna. I had to stay and I had to be on my best behaviour.

Despite the cold drizzle, Freya practically bounced the whole way over to the flat, chatting incessantly about meeting the kitten and asking if we were staying for lunch. When we arrived, Luna was hovering behind her mother, and she immediately took Freya's hand and pulled her away towards her bedroom. I stood there, marvelling at children's ability to forgive and forget so quickly, and for a moment I forgot how nervous I was.

'It's so good to see you.' Summer leaned in and kissed me.

'You too,' I lied, following her into the kitchen. 'How was your Christmas?'

'Lovely,' she enthused, putting the kettle on. 'Asha knew that we would be on our own and so she invited us round to theirs for the day. It was marvellous, we had such a good time.'

'How nice,' I said, ignoring my flare of envy. 'Asha's family are wonderful.'

'Aren't they just. Tea? Coffee?'

'Coffee, please.'

I studied Summer as she made the drinks, looking at her earlobes, but she was wearing gold hoops. Her hair was growing out again, just as mine was, yet hers looked fabulous whereas mine looked horribly in between styles. She turned and beamed at me and for a moment, I forgot why I didn't like her.

Summer brought the drinks over, placing one in front of me, and sat down.

'How are you, Naomi?'

She said it in the way that a therapist might ask a client, as though her eyes were burning into my soul. But I wasn't falling for it.

'Good, thanks. We had a lovely Christmas too. My dad came over for the day.'

'Oh, that must have been nice. Does he live nearby?'

'Not far. I'm glad he's close to us because his health isn't great.'

'I'm so sorry to hear that. What are his health problems?'

I told her about his stroke, and how it had left him with limited mobility. She was attentive company, asking me where exactly he lived and how often I saw him. As I drank my coffee I relaxed, despite all my reservations about Summer.

After half an hour, we hadn't seen hide nor hair of the children and I began to feel uneasy again. Freya normally checked in on me during playdates and this wasn't a big flat, so it was unusual that the girls hadn't appeared yet.

'I might just check on Freya, make sure she's not hungry,' I said, preparing to stand up.

'Oh, leave them to it, they're getting on so well.'

I paused, my bottom mid-air, undecided. Glancing uneasily at the door, I sat back down again. Summer smiled at me, flashing her perfect dimples.

'I'm so happy that our girls are friends now,' she said. 'It was all I ever wanted. I hope we can put everything behind us and move on.'

'Yes.' I forced a smile. The more I thought of Freya, the more I wanted to check on her. But Summer was chatting away now, and it would be rude to interrupt her.

'Luna had such a difficult first term at North Hill. She really struggled to settle in, you know? I guess that's what happens when a child joins later and friendships are already established. If it wasn't for Asha and Aanya, I'm not sure what we would have done.' She looked at me. 'And you too, of course,' she added hurriedly.

It was a lie and we both knew it. I was distracted now, my thoughts constantly veering towards Freya and wondering what was going on in Luna's bedroom.

'But now she seems so happy. And I am too. I think we've really found our people here.'

I was no longer listening as I stood up abruptly. 'I'll just stick my head around the door and see if the girls want a snack.'

Summer looked at me, her eyes narrowing. She knew what I was thinking, what I was doing. For a moment I had a mad thought that she might try and stop me. But then her expression cleared. 'Good idea, I'll cut up some fruit.'

In the seconds it took me to get from the kitchen to Luna's bedroom, my mind had already concocted some terrible fates that might await me. Luna had hurt Freya. Freya was trapped, unable to call for help. Freya was dead. I flung the door open so hard that it banged against the wall and both girls looked up at me in fright. They were sitting on the floor, side by side, in front of the doll's house. The kitten, who had been lying beside them, ran away in fright and scrambled underneath the bed.

'Mummy, what did you do that for?' Freya was not impressed.

My eyes moved from Freya to Luna. Everything was fine. No one was hurt. And slowly I began to return to my senses. 'So sorry, darling, I opened it a little too hard.'

'You scared the kitten.'

'I really am sorry.'

'Don't worry,' Luna said in her quiet little voice. 'She'll come out again soon.'

I looked over the girls' heads, my eyes resting on the doll's house they had been playing with. It was not how I remembered it. The front door was pink and there were no flower boxes on the sills. A Sylvanian Family rabbit was sticking its head out of one of the open windows. It looked just like any other, generic, shop-bought doll's house. I blinked a couple of times, scarcely believing my own eyes.

I felt a presence behind me, and I smelled Summer before I saw her.

'Hi, girls, would you like some strawberries and grapes?'

The girls rushed past us into the kitchen and, with one last look at the doll's house, I turned and followed them. I was more confused than ever.

'Mummy, can Luna come to our house tomorrow?' Freya asked, stuffing her mouth with strawberries. 'I want to show her my bedroom.'

Put on the spot by my daughter, I scrambled for the socially appropriate words. 'Of course, if that's okay with her mum?'

'Oh, I'm sorry, Freya, but we're going to Devon tomorrow,' Summer replied.

Luna looked at her mother. 'I didn't know that.'

Summer's laughter tinkled. 'I told you, darling.'

'No, you didn't.'

'Sweetheart, I did. We talked about it.'

'No, we didn't.'

I saw it then. A flash of anger across Summer's face. 'I told you, Luna.'

Her voice was hard, cold. And the effect on Luna was immediate. She lowered her eyes, nodding slightly. Freya was oblivious as she helped herself to a handful of grapes. But I saw it. And I wondered what it meant. Was this simply a mother frustrated with her daughter for not remembering something they'd discussed? Or was there more to it?

Summer quickly reverted to her usual, smiling self. 'We're catching up with some old friends. We won't be back until the beginning of term. Perhaps we can do something then?'

I smiled. 'Great.'

Luna was quiet after that. Morose even. And no matter how hard Freya tried to engage her, she seemed to have retreated into herself. After another half an hour I called it, telling Summer that we had lunch plans. Freya started to protest but I shot her a warning glance and she got the message. Thanking Summer for her hospitality, we put on our coats and left.

On the way home, I took Freya's hand. 'Did you have a good time, darling?'

'Yes. Why did we leave so early?'

'Luna seemed a bit unhappy. I thought maybe she needed to chat with her mum.'

'It's because she doesn't like Devon.'

I looked at my daughter. 'She told you that?'

'Yes.'

'Did she tell you why?'

Freya looked away. 'No.'

I sensed she was fibbing, and I was curious to find out what Luna had said. But we'd had about as successful a playdate as we could under the circumstances, and I didn't want to taint it. Besides, I had enough on my mind already.

'Did you enjoy playing with the doll's house?' I asked her.

'Yes, Luna got it for Christmas.'

I stopped short. 'The Christmas just gone? Are you sure?'

Freya looked at me curiously. 'That's what she said.'

The doll's house was new, which meant that the old one hadn't been a figment of my imagination after all. Summer had replaced it and I didn't know why, or what it meant.

'I'm just a bit confused, darling, because when I went round previously, well before Christmas, Luna definitely had a doll's house in her bedroom.'

'Luna said it broke.'

I stared at Freya incredulously. 'It broke? How does an entire doll's house break?'

Freya shrugged. 'Dunno.'

My nerves were tingling and although I couldn't come up with a rational explanation, something wasn't sitting right with me at all. In fact, the missing doll's house was now troubling me more than anything.

Back home, I made myself a cup of tea and sat down on the sofa, stroking Sparkle absent-mindedly. But I was restless and so I decided to do a couple of chores before making lunch. Heading up the stairs, I located the laundry basket and started throwing the dirty clothes in, remembering that I had chucked a muddy pair of jeans on our bed that morning. As I went over to retrieve them, something caught my eye. There was a tiny piece of material poking out from under the bed and I recognised it immediately. I pulled it out, staring at my dressing gown in wonder. Had it been under the bed the whole time? How had I not seen it before? I sat down on the bed and held it in my hands, running my fingers over the smooth silk. As I did, I felt something sharp in one of the pockets and I reached in, pulling out one of the ruby red earrings. Putting my hand back in, I quickly located the other one.

'Mum, I'm hungry.' Freya was hovering at the door, peering in.

I looked at her and then back down at the dressing gown in my hands.

'What's that?' she asked.

'My dressing gown and earrings.'

'The ones you lost?'

'Yes, I found them under the bed.'

Freya shrugged, disinterested. The only thing she cared about right now was her stomach. But I was still flummoxed.

'I just don't understand how they ended up under the bed, or how I didn't find them before now,' I said, more to myself than to Freya. 'I must have looked there at some point.'

'Maybe Sparkle was playing with it. She likes going under your bed.'

It was true. But what Freya didn't realise was the implication of my discovery. It wasn't just about locating a couple of missing items. It was about accepting that Summer hadn't stolen them. That no one had broken into our house. And I wasn't sure I was ready to do that yet because it also meant admitting that I was wrong.

About everything.

19

Freya was in high spirits as we walked to school on the first day of term. She was looking forward to seeing her teacher and her friends. I, on the other hand, was nervous. I wasn't sure what kind of a reception I would receive when I got there, and I didn't know how to act around Summer. If I was wrong about her then that was on me. But I couldn't believe that I would be so mistaken about a person. And even if she hadn't stolen my things, she'd still isolated me from my friends and got my daughter into trouble unfairly. And then there was the business of the strange missing doll's house.

As we entered the playground, I remembered my New Year's resolution to get my friendships back on track. Instead of hiding in the shadows, I spotted the gang and walked up to them. I belonged here, I reminded myself. These people were my friends.

'Hi, everyone,' I said. 'Happy New Year!'

I knew immediately that something wasn't right. Their smiles didn't meet their eyes and they were shuffling about.

'What is it?' I asked, looking at Freya who had run off to see her buddies. I noticed immediately that Aanya turned away from her and the all too familiar trickle of dread appeared.

No one spoke for a moment and the seconds stretched out like hours. Finally, Richard was the one to tell me. 'Summer has pulled Luna out of North Hill.'

Hallelujah! This was the end of all my problems. Life could finally return to normal. But I very quickly realised that it wasn't that simple.

'What happened?' I asked, feigning concern.

'She's going to home-school her.'

'Why?'

Richard looked at Asha, who looked at Rachel. And Rachel, ever the diplomat, said, 'Summer found out some stuff over Christmas. Stuff that happened to Luna at school.'

I frowned, confused, but already the dread was expanding like a balloon as I feared what I was going to hear next. 'What kind of stuff?'

'Nasty stuff. Bullying. Luna finally told her everything that's been going on and Summer feels that the best thing for her daughter is to keep her away from school for now.'

All eyes turned to Freya and my cheeks flamed. Not this again. Not more lies. This was a nightmare and I was fast realising that I was never going to wake up from it. Summer's decision to leave the school wasn't the answer to all my prayers, it was the opposite.

'I don't understand,' I said. 'I saw Summer over Christmas and everything was fine.'

The awkward silence resumed but I felt the implication. I saw it too, in the way that they looked at Freya, who was trying to talk to Aanya and was getting upset at being ignored. I cast my mind back to the playdate at Summer's house. Freya and Luna had been left unsupervised for a while. Could something bad have happened? Could Freya have hurt Luna? But I couldn't believe it. I trusted Freya and anyway, the girls had been on good form – right up until Summer mentioned Devon. Suddenly I wondered if their trip to the coast had anything to do with this.

'I've asked Aanya not to play with Freya,' Asha told me, and her voice was as cold as ice.

'But Freya hasn't done anything wrong,' I insisted. 'She and Luna are friends now.'

'That's not what I've heard.'

I looked around helplessly, thrown into the deep end and fast sinking. 'Seriously. Freya has done nothing wrong and if Summer is suggesting that she has, then she's lying. Or Luna is.'

'Not this again,' Asha spat. 'Luna is sweet and kind. And so is her mother. Why you and your daughter have it in for them is beyond me, but enough is enough, Naomi. You've driven them out of the school, what more do you want?'

And with that she walked away, leaving me with no right of reply. The others followed suit. Rachel looked at me apologetically but she, too, turned and left. Tears pricked at my eyes as I watched them go and then I looked at Freya again who was staring at me, eyes wide, tears streaming down her face. I felt anger, guilt and horror all wrapped into one. And I had no idea what to do. Did I take Freya home or make her go into school and hope that it sorted itself out?

I felt a hand on my arm and saw Sharon beside me.

'I don't know what's going on,' I said, unable to stop my own tears from falling.

'Come inside after the bell goes. We'll have a chat.'

'They're saying Freya's done something nasty to Luna. It's not true.'

Sharon squeezed my arm gently. 'Come inside, Naomi.'

I nodded and watched as a teacher went over to a sobbing Freya and guided her into the building. The other children in her class stared as she went. And then I walked away, no longer wanting to be anywhere near all those people who had turned their backs on me. On us. I hovered by the main entrance and waited for the bell and then I went in and asked for Sharon.

She appeared a few minutes later and I followed her into her now familiar office. Before I even got a chance to speak, she started talking. 'I don't know what's going on Naomi, I really don't. I'll speak frankly because it's clear that you already know most of it. Summer has made the decision to take Luna out of school and home-school her. She claims that Luna was being victimised at school. Apart from the one occasion we have already discussed that involves Freya, I am not aware of any more incidents.'

'Freya hasn't done anything wrong,' I said. 'This is all a mix-up.'

'I'm going to get to the bottom of it.'

'All her classmates ignored her this morning. I think their parents have told them not to play with her. It's horrible, Sharon.'

'I'm going to speak to the form teacher and indeed the whole class. I'll put a stop to that right now.'

I looked at her gratefully. 'I don't know what the hell is happening here.'

Sharon smiled. 'That makes two of us. But we'll work it out.'

'Is Freya in trouble?'

'No, she's not.'

'She wouldn't do anything nasty to Luna. I'm certain of it.'

But I knew Sharon was thinking of the stomach-kicking

incident. She was just too kind, or professional, to say it. My own mind drifted back to when Freya had ripped Luna's dress. But she'd been provoked and her reaction, while unacceptable, was understandable.

'I saw Summer over Christmas,' I added. 'Everything was fine. Luna and Freya got on well. None of this makes any sense.'

'Try not to worry, Naomi. If Freya knows that you're upset, she'll only feel more anxious. Reassure her, let her know she's safe and loved. Leave the rest to me.'

As I left, though, I knew I couldn't do it. I couldn't stay out of it. Too much was at stake. It was time to confront Summer and have it out. It had been a long time coming.

I marched out and almost collided with Angela, who was hovering outside. I had ignored her for weeks and thought she had finally got the message, as her texts and calls had stopped and she no longer approached me. She had picked the worst possible time to try again.

'Whatever it is, I'm not in the mood,' I said sharply, brushing past her.

She reached out and grabbed me. 'Naomi, why are you avoiding me?'

I stared at her accusingly. 'I thought I could trust you.'

'You can.'

'No, I can't.' I brushed her hand away, too agitated to maintain any veneer of politeness. 'Please leave me alone.'

'Naomi, wait.' She ran after me, trying to keep up with my long strides. 'I need to talk to you about Summer.'

'I know all about you and Summer.'

'What do you mean?'

I stopped and glared at her. 'I saw you two together in a coffee shop before Christmas looking all cosy. You pretended you didn't like her to gain my trust and you lied to me.'

Angela's face was as white as a sheet. 'No, you've got it all wrong. Just listen to me.'

'Did you have something to do with all of this? Are you part of the plan?'

'What plan? What are you talking about?'

'You know she's pulled Luna out of school? She's blaming Freya, saying she bullied her.'

Angela stared at me. 'I don't know anything about that. I'm not friends with Summer.'

'Stop saying that.' I was almost shouting now. 'I saw you two together.'

'Yes,' Angela shouted back. 'I was doing it for you.'

Now she had my full attention. 'Excuse me?'

'I arranged to meet her for a coffee. I thought if I acted friendly towards her then I might get some more information out of her. Information that could help you.'

'But you were hugging and kissing.'

'Yes,' Angela said. 'You know what Summer is like, she acts as though everyone she meets is a long-lost friend. It was the first time, and the last time, I've ever met up with her.'

I frowned. Was it possible that Angela was telling the truth? I had trusted her before and lived to regret it. Now history was rewriting itself in my mind. Summer rushing towards Angela in the coffee shop and embracing her, like she'd done to me a dozen times. And we certainly weren't friends. I stared hard into Angela's eyes and all I saw was a slightly frightened, slightly defiant woman, silently begging me to believe her. A woman who struggled to make friends because everyone thought she was a snob. Who did not feature in a single one of Summer's Instagram posts. Who was an outsider, just as I had now become.

'You only met up with her for me?' I asked, still wary.

'Yes. Information gathering. I thought it might help you.'

'And did you find out anything?'

'At first, I didn't think so. Summer kept things light and didn't give much away. It quickly became clear to me that she didn't want to delve too much into her past, which made no sense given that she was such a big West End star. You'd think she wouldn't shut up about it.'

My heart sank. And then I processed her words. 'At first?'

'Yes. I realised later that she had made one slip-up.'

'Which was?'

'She told me about a long stint she had done as the main character in a particular West End show. So I did some research and I found her. But she wasn't the star, she was the understudy.'

'You found her?'

'Yes, I recognised her photo. But her stage name was Christina Caldwell. And the more I looked into her, the more it became clear that she didn't make it into the big time. She had a few short runs here and there but never a major part. I've googled "Christina Caldwell" extensively and nothing has come up other than a couple of very brief mentions. But then, I guess, if she wasn't particularly well known in the industry then that would explain it.'

So she had used a different first name back then. Before she created a new life here in Barnet. A new Instagram account. How many names had she used in the years in between?

'I found the dressing gown,' I blurted out. 'And some earrings I thought she'd taken. They were under my bed.'

'Could she have put them back?'

'I don't see how. I haven't invited her over and we changed the locks.'

'I still think you were right. There's something off about her. She's lying.'

'I was on my way to have it out with her right now.'

'Don't do that. Not yet. Trust me, it's not the right time.'

I had to make a choice. Did I trust Angela or not? It only took me a second to decide. 'Okay. I'll hold off for now but I'm not sure how much longer I can wait.'

'It won't be for much longer. We're going to find out what's going on.'

'Angela, the fact that you're doing this for me means so much. I'm so sorry that I got the wrong end of the stick. You didn't deserve the way I treated you and I can only apologise.'

She shrugged good-naturedly. 'I should have tried harder to explain it to you. But when you ignored all my calls and texts, I was a bit annoyed with you.'

'I don't blame you. I would have been too. You were trying to help me and I was downright rude to you. It won't happen again. I just didn't know who I could trust. No one believes me and I...'

Angela put her arm around me. 'It's okay, Naomi. I believe you.'

She would never know how much that meant to me. How it gave me the strength for everything that followed. Everyone else who I thought had my back had abandoned me. But I had found an unlikely friend and she had spoken the three words I needed to hear.

I believe you.

20

It had been three weeks and Luna still hadn't returned to school. I didn't pretend to be looking at my phone any more when I dropped Freya. I kept my distance from the old gang and they ignored me. If it wasn't for Angela, I'm not sure I would have coped. But she was there for me. She stood beside me, my own personal protection against the cold shoulders.

Behind closed doors, we were plotting. But we were struggling to come up with a way to prove that Summer wasn't who she said she was. The items I was sure she had stolen had been found. The house was as it should be. The old doll's house had been replaced by a shiny new one. Yet I was more convinced than ever that she was up to something. We knew Angela's research alone wasn't enough to prove that she was a fraud and that's when Angela came up with the plan. And the more she explained it to me, the more convinced I became that this might finally be the answer we had been waiting for.

I raised it with Oliver that evening.

'Why don't you meet up with her?' I said, out of the blue.

Oliver frowned, confused. 'Who?'

'Summer.'

'Why?'

'Meet her for a drink and then, when she comes on to you, it will prove to everyone that I was right about her all along.'

Oliver was incredulous. 'You want to use me as bait?'

'Kind of,' I admitted. 'It's all I can think of.'

'I'm not sure that's a good idea, babe.'

'It's the only one I've got.'

'And what if she doesn't come on to me?'

'She will, I'm sure of it.'

Oliver shook his head. 'I'm sorry, I don't like it.'

'Please, Oliver.'

'Was it you or your new best mate Angela who came up with this ludicrous plan?'

'It was nothing to do with Angela,' I lied. 'It was all my idea.'

'But why? What's the desired outcome?'

'To prove she's not as sweet as everyone says she is.'

'But she's out of our lives now. Luna doesn't even go to the same school as Freya.'

It was that simple to Oliver. But Summer was not out of our lives. How could she be when the shadow of the false allegations against Freya loomed? The headteacher had evidently spoken to the class, as she had promised to do, because Freya seemed okay. Her friends were talking to her again, and no one seemed to be accusing her of anything, although there had been no invitations to playdates. And she was still confused about it, asking me constantly why Luna wasn't at school and if she'd done something wrong. I always assured that she hadn't, telling her that it was nothing to do with her. I don't know if she believed me.

'She'll be back, Oliver. She's not gone.'

He shook his head. 'I love you, Naomi, you know I do, but this is madness.'

Madness. That's what I had been driven to. Using my own husband as a honeytrap. I took a deep glug of wine, ignoring the look that Oliver gave me as I did. Then I took another.

'Easy there, tiger,' he said, laughing nervously.

I looked at him defiantly, raising my glass to my lips another time.

'What's happened to you, Nims?' he asked.

'Summer,' I said, my voice unfaltering. 'Summer happened to me.'

He looked at me for a long time. And then he said, 'If I do this, will you draw a line under it all? Because this can't go on for much longer.'

I nodded as a wave of anticipation flooded over me. 'This will be the end. I promise.'

He ran his hand through his thinning hair and reached for his phone. 'I'll text her.'

I peered over his screen. 'What will you say?'

'Whatever you want me to.'

I hated how resigned he sounded. How tired. 'Maybe say you'd like to have a chat about the girls and suggest a drink at the pub?'

'Fine.'

He sent the message, pocketed his phone, and left the room. I knew he was frustrated with me. But I was triumphant. The wheels had been set in motion. I didn't allow myself to think about Summer being alone with my husband. I trusted Oliver 100 per cent and I knew he wouldn't let me down.

When I told Angela, she was giddy. 'Should we go and take some photos?'

'We can't do that,' I replied in hushed tones, ever paranoid. 'They'll see us.'

'But how can we prove it happened?'

'We'll have Oliver's word.'

'Will it be enough, though?'

'It'll have to be.'

Sometimes I wondered why Angela was helping me. What was in it for her. But I concluded that she enjoyed being part of something and, after years of being on the fringes of the gang, she finally had a friend. She had proven herself to be loyal, far more so than my so-called close friends had been.

It took Summer two days to respond. The waiting was brutal and I fretted that she was on to us, that she had somehow worked out our plan. But her reply, when it came, was breezy. She told Oliver that she'd love to have a drink and suggested that evening. I wondered again how she always seemed to be able to secure a babysitter at such short notice. But I didn't have time to dwell on it because I had to prep Oliver for the night ahead.

'Be your usual charming self,' I told him. 'A little flirty but not too much.'

Oliver, who was getting changed out of his work clothes looked miserable. 'I still can't believe I'm doing this. It's ridiculous.'

'It's only one time, Ol. After this, we can forget about Summer for good.'

I'm not sure who was more nervous, me or Oliver. When he left, he didn't kiss me goodbye like he usually did. He barely even said goodbye to the girls, who were doing their homework at the kitchen table. After he had gone, I paced around the house nervously, wondering what was happening, whether Summer had made her move yet. Freya sensed my anxiety and messed around at bedtime, refusing to put her pyjamas on and getting out of bed on several occasions to say she couldn't sleep. Eventually, I climbed into bed with her, keeping my phone in my pocket in case Oliver called, and read her a long bedtime story which did the trick.

While Freya slept, I considered going downstairs to make some dinner, but I had no appetite. I took my phone out of my pocket to see if Oliver had messaged me, but the screen was blank. I had no idea what was going on and I wondered if I'd made a huge mistake. I had sent my husband out for drinks with a beautiful woman. What if this massively backfired? Had I driven Oliver straight into Summer's arms? No, I couldn't think like that.

Waiting was torture, so I slipped out of Freya's bed and went downstairs to pour a glass of wine. Oliver thought I was drinking too much but I told him I had it under control. I was just under a lot of stress and needed to unwind in the evenings. Once this whole Summer business was over I'd get back to my old self. I'd cut down on the drinking and return to the gym. Maybe I'd change my hair colour too, go a bit lighter, so it no longer matched Summer's. And I'd grow it out. Just the thought of it made me feel better.

By ten thirty, I was in bits. I had expected Oliver back ages ago and I was doubting my decision more than ever. The wine bottle was empty but instead of feeling calmer, I was harried.

Finally, just after eleven, I heard a key in the lock and I rushed to the front door, pulling it open before Oliver had a chance.

'How was it?' I demanded, pulling him inside.

'Fine.'

'Tell me everything.'

Oliver scowled. 'Can I take my shoes and coat off first, please?'

'Of course, sorry. Sorry, Ol.'

Was it me, or did Oliver take his time? His movements felt as though they were in slow motion as he put his keys down on the sideboard and then sat on the bottom step to unlace his trainers. But then I realised he wasn't being deliberately slow. He was drunk.

'Well, someone had a good night,' I said accusingly.

'You're the one who sent me out in the first place.'

It was true, but the plan hadn't been to go on a jolly, it had been to catch Summer out. I watched impatiently while Oliver unlaced the other trainer and pulled it off his foot. Then he stood up, swaying slightly, as he removed his coat. And he said I was drinking too much.

Finally, he wandered into the kitchen and got himself a glass of water before sitting down at the table. I sat opposite him, waiting for him to debrief me.

'Go on,' I urged.

'It was fine, we had a good chat.'

'What about?'

'Everything, really. Life, work, the kids.'

'And did she, you know?'

He looked at me. 'Did she try to stick her tongue down my throat?'

I winced at his words. 'Come on, Oliver, don't be a prick.'

Oliver shrugged. 'No.'

My heart plummeted. This had all been a waste of time. 'Not even a tiny flirt?'

'No.'

'Tell me exactly what you talked about.'

'She admitted that she might have overreacted about everything. Apparently Luna got upset while they were down in Devon and said she didn't want to go back to school. Summer flew off the handle, thinking that it was because she was being bullied.'

That was it? That was Summer's evidence?

'She just wants to protect her daughter,' Oliver said. 'Like you do.'

'By taking her out of school and accusing Freya of bullying her?'

'She says she never said that to the headteacher. She just told her that Luna was anxious and she had decided to home-school her for a while, for her mental health.'

But she was lying, she had to be. Sharon had told me that Summer had blamed Freya. Hadn't she? My mind was scrambled as I thought back to the conversation I'd had with the headteacher. Had she explicitly said that Summer had made those allegations? The wine had made my head fuzzy and I was struggling to recall her exact words.

'But everyone hates me,' I said. 'The children wouldn't speak to Freya.'

Oliver rubbed his eyes. 'I'm tired, babe. I'm going to bed.'

I wanted to keep talking, to thrash this out with Oliver, but he had other plans.

'I'm sorry,' I said. I wasn't even sure what for any more.

He nodded. ''Night.'

I stayed in the kitchen after Oliver had left, thinking about how my plan had gone horribly wrong. There was nothing left for me to do. Summer had won but only I knew it, because no one else realised it was a game. I didn't understand Summer's motive but at least the sensation that I was being followed had stopped. She'd clearly got what she wanted and backed off. Maybe she'd grown bored of playing with us. Or perhaps she had hoped to seduce Oliver too but given up when she realised that she didn't stand a chance. At least I could claim victory to my husband, if not my friends.

Then I thought about Freya and Bella. They were my number one priority and always would be. Perhaps if I left Summer alone, she'd do the same. Oliver was right, it was time to stop this amateur sleuthing and move on. I needed to forget about Summer.

I turned off the light, ready to go to bed. But the second the kitchen was plunged into darkness I saw something outside. I dropped my glass and it plummeted to the floor, smashing at my feet. I was paralysed with fear, too petrified to move or even to scream.

Someone was out there. They weren't even trying to hide it. They were standing right on the other side of the patio doors, their face inches from the glass, dressed from head to toe in black. And they were staring directly at me.

21

As the figure disappeared into the darkness, I finally regained control of my body. I scrambled for my phone, dialled 999 and then ran up the stairs to wake Oliver. My entire body was trembling with shock and terror.

There was no doubt in my mind. I had seen them this time and it had been vivid, not a figment of my imagination. They had been watching me and if their goal was to terrify me, they had succeeded. When I shook Oliver awake, it took him a few moments to come round but when I told him the police were on the way, it soon had the desired effect.

By the time officers arrived, Oliver was dressed and he had patrolled the garden but found no evidence of anyone hiding. The police searched the garden too and found a trampled piece of grass at the back, by the fence.

'It was probably an opportunistic burglar,' one of them told me. 'There was another break-in on this road a few weeks ago and they accessed the property from the footpath that runs along the back of the gardens. You should consider putting a floodlight in your back garden and perhaps installing a security camera. And make sure your windows and doors are locked.'

At least they were taking me seriously. And so was Oliver, who seemed as shaken as I was. Thankfully the girls had slept through it, which was the only good thing to come out of all this. But I didn't tell the police I suspected Summer. What was the point? They wouldn't believe me. Other than their eyes, the intruder had covered their face and it had all happened so quickly that I hadn't had a chance to look at them properly or determine whether it was a man or woman from their stature. I did tell them about the other incidents though, when I thought I'd seen someone outside the living room window and when I'd heard someone fiddling with the front door one night. I could feel Oliver's eyes on me but he didn't interrupt or try to rationalise those incidents, like he had done before.

The officer looked solemn. 'There have been several burglaries in the area. It's possible they have been scoping out properties for a while.' He handed me a leaflet, with tips for keeping your home safe from burglars. 'There's some useful advice in here.'

'What are you doing about it?' Oliver demanded, taking my hand.

'Rest assured, sir, we're doing all we can. We believe that the incidents are linked and we're advising everyone to be extra vigilant and to report any suspicious behaviour.'

I would never feel safe in this house again and I bitterly craved the comfort of the flat. We hadn't had a single break-in while we had lived there and now my mind connected our old home with safety and security and our new one with peril.

After the police left, Oliver and I were too wired to sleep.

'I'm really sorry,' he said. 'I should have taken your concerns more seriously before.'

'You thought I was losing the plot.'

'It's this business with Summer. I couldn't understand why she would be trying to get into our house. But now we know the real culprits. Bloody burglars.'

'What if it wasn't burglars?'

Oliver looked at me incredulously. 'You still think it might have been Summer?'

Did I think that? The obvious explanation was that it was opportunistic thieves operating in the area. But my gut was telling me otherwise.

'I'm scared, Oliver,' I told him.

He took my hand. 'I know. I'm going to take tomorrow off work and get some security lights and a camera set up in the back garden.'

'But don't you have meetings?'

'It doesn't matter. This is more important. You are more important.'

We went to bed eventually, but I couldn't sleep and in the morning, I was shattered. When Oliver offered to take Freya to school, I was grateful. The idea of a morning off the awkward school run was bliss. But I was nervous about being in the house on my own too.

'It's daytime,' Oliver assured me. 'The burglars won't try anything. I'll be back as soon as I've dropped Freya and been to the shops to get all the security supplies I need.'

I said goodbye to the girls and then went upstairs to get dressed. But I kept hearing noises. A floorboard creaking. An unexplained rattle. Every sound sent me spiralling into terror and I couldn't shake off the feeling that someone was in the house. I went downstairs to make a coffee, glad that Sparkle was hanging around. She wasn't exactly a guard animal, but her company soothed me. I took my drink up to the office, calling to Sparkle to follow me, but I couldn't concentrate. Where was Oliver? He should have been back by now.

When my phone rang, I almost jumped out of my skin. A quick glance at the screen showed that it was Bella's school calling and I answered immediately.

'Mrs Burton? It's Joanne here, Bella's singing teacher.'

'Oh, hello, Joanne.'

'I was just calling to ask if Bella might be returning to choir?'

I was flummoxed. Bella had been going to after-school choir rehearsals on Fridays ever since she started at secondary school. 'What do you mean?'

'We haven't seen her since before the Christmas holidays and if she doesn't come back soon, I'm afraid I'll have to give her place to another student. But it would be a shame to lose her, she's such a talent.'

'I don't understand, I thought she was going.'

'I'm afraid not, Mrs Burton. I've asked her about it a few times, but she said you needed her for something at home.'

My mind was now whirring frantically, despite my exhaustion. Why was Bella lying? And if she wasn't at choir, where the hell was she?

'Thank you for calling me. I'll speak to Bella. She'll be back at choir next week.'

I hung up, trying to make sense of it. This was the last thing we needed right now. Was Bella secretly meeting up with friends? Or a boyfriend? She was thirteen now and the transition into teenage years often brought with it an overwhelming urge to rebel. But Bella had always been an open book. She was happy to tell me who she was hanging out with, and who she had a crush on, so why the secrecy? And how had she managed to get away with it for weeks? I kept tabs on Bella, checking her location on my phone to make sure she got where she was going safely. But I never checked on Friday afternoons because I assumed she was at choir. I reached for my phone now, but her location was at school, just as it should be. It would have to wait until she got home but I was desperate to find out what was going on.

When Oliver got back, with armfuls of supplies, I no longer cared that he had been gone longer than I expected. I was too anxious about Bella.

He frowned when I filled him in. 'So where has she been?'

'That's what I'm going to find out. I'm going to pick her up from school. Are you okay to get Freya?'

'Of course.'

The day dragged as I tried to get some work done but at least having Oliver in the house soothed my nerves. I left early for the school pick-up and hovered outside the gates, peering in at the buildings and willing Bella to appear. When the students started piling out in droves I looked keenly for my daughter, worried in case I missed her, and then I spotted her. She was chatting to some friends and would have walked past me if I hadn't called out her name.

'Mum, what are you doing here?'

I beckoned her over. 'We need to talk.'

Bella was confused. 'What about?'

'Joanne from choir called.'

Guilt was written all over her face. She said goodbye to her friends, and then turned back to me, her face pale. She knew she was in trouble.

'Come on,' I told her. 'Let's walk.'

I waited until we had turned onto a quieter street, away from Bella's mates, because I didn't want to embarrass her. I had been a teenager myself, I knew the drill. But Bella's safety came first and that meant knowing where she was.

'Where have you been, when you were supposed to be at choir?'

She didn't answer and I tried again. 'Bella, I need to know where you've been.'

'Nowhere.'

My patience ran out. 'Come on, Bella, you know that's not going to wash. So either you tell me, or I ask your friends instead.'

She looked horrified. 'Mum!'

'I'm serious. You've lied to me and I need to know why. Is it a boy?'

'No, it's not a boy.'

'A girl?'

'No.'

'Vaping?'

Bella had the audacity to roll her eyes. 'No, Mum. Not vaping.'

I stopped. 'So what is it, Bella?'

'I've been having acting lessons.'

This threw me. 'Acting lessons?'

'Yes.'

'But you go to stage school every Saturday. Are these private lessons?'

'Yes.'

How could Bella afford private lessons? Her pocket money barely stretched to a new lip gloss, let alone one-on-one sessions. I knew they wouldn't be cheap because her termly stage school fees nearly bankrupted us three times a year.

'Who are the lessons with?'

She visibly blanched. 'It doesn't matter.'

'Yes, it does. You're thirteen years old, Bella. If you're meeting up with someone, especially in private, I need to know who you're with.'

She had been backed into a corner and we both knew it. I wasn't giving up until I got the truth out of her. 'Don't be mad, Mum.'

But I could make her no promise. 'Who are you having lessons with?'

'Summer.'

My stomach lurched as I looked at my daughter in shock. How on earth had this happened without my knowledge? What was Summer playing at, and Bella for that matter?

'Are you paying her?'

'No. They're free.'

But nothing in life was for free. Especially when it came from a woman like Summer. 'Right, Bella, you're going to have to start from the beginning, because I'm really confused.'

We went to a cafe and I ordered a hot chocolate for Bella and a strong coffee for myself. I had a feeling that I was going to need it. As soon as we'd taken our first sip, I got straight to it. 'Tell me everything.'

Bella didn't resist. 'We got chatting at the Halloween party and she told me all about how she used to be a big West End star. And then I saw her again at the North Hill Christmas Fair and asked her a bit more about it. I told her that's my dream, to be on stage, and she offered to give me a few lessons.'

I didn't tell Bella that Summer had never been the big star she claimed to be. Not only would it shatter my daughter's dreams, but I had more important things to worry about.

'What happened then?'

'We swapped numbers and she texted me at the beginning

of January asking if I wanted to pop round that Friday. We've been meeting every week since.'

'Why didn't you tell me?'

Bella looked down at her drink. 'Summer suggested that we keep it between us. She said that you might not approve and she didn't want you to ban me from coming.'

I was incandescent. How dare Summer convince my own child to lie to me? The idea of that woman spending time with Bella, forming a friendship with my daughter, disgusted me.

'What about choir? You love choir.'

'I do, but Summer suggested Fridays and I didn't want to let her down. The lessons are really good, Mum, she's such a great teacher. I've already learned so much.'

'And you didn't think it was odd that she told you to keep this from me?'

'Not really. I know you don't like her.' Bella looked away guiltily.

'And have you stopped to think why I don't like her?'

'Because she bought our flat.'

'Bella, that's not the reason.'

Bella shrugged. 'You've been acting funny ever since we moved.'

What could I say to that? Bella was right, I had been out of sorts since we moved. I had spiralled but was it any surprise? The upheaval of moving, all the trouble with Freya, this business with Summer, my friends turning against me. People watching us. No wonder I was frazzled. But it was nothing to do with selling the flat.

'I'm sorry if I haven't been myself, Bella. I've had a lot on my plate. I'll be more present from now on, I promise. But that's no excuse for lying to me.'

Bella hung her head. 'I know, I'm sorry, Mum.'

'I want you to stop these lessons and go back to choir.'

Her head shot up again. 'No! Why?'

'Because I don't want you seeing Summer any more.'

'That's exactly what she said you would say. See, she was right all along.'

I couldn't believe what I was hearing. All these months I'd been focusing so hard on Freya that I'd somehow managed to miss this. I could kick myself. Summer had taken advantage of my distraction over Freya to muscle in on Bella. To turn her against me. And although I still didn't know why, I knew that this was a deliberate act on her part.

'Summer is not your mother, I am. And you're not seeing her any more.'

'I wish she was!' Bella shouted, causing other people in the cafe to stare at us.

Her words hurt, more than she would ever know. And as much as I tried to hide my distress from her, my expression betrayed me.

'I'm sorry, Mum, I didn't mean that. I just don't want to stop the lessons.'

'I'll arrange some private lessons with someone else,' I promised her, even though I knew we couldn't afford it.

'But I don't want to have lessons with someone else. I want to have them with Summer.'

'I'm sorry, Bella. It's not going to happen.'

Her temper flared again. 'I hate you, Mum.'

'I'm sorry to hear you feel that way because I love you very much. But this is non-negotiable. And if I catch you lying to me again, you'll be in big trouble. I'll be checking in with Joanne to make sure you're at choir each week.'

Bella's dark mood continued all the way home. It was so unlike her and I hated the tension between us. But I would take it because there was no way she was going over to Summer's again. When we got home, she marched up the stairs and slammed the door, causing Oliver and Freya, who were watching TV together, to look up in alarm.

'What's going on?' Freya asked.

'Bella's cross with me but it's nothing to worry about,' I assured her.

'Why is she cross with you?'

'She lied to me and she got caught.'

Freya's eyes widened. 'What did she lie about?'

'It doesn't matter.' I looked at Oliver. 'Ol, a word?'

He followed me into the kitchen and closed the door so we could speak privately. I filled him in on our conversation and his eyes widened when I mentioned Summer.

'She didn't say anything to me about it when we met for drinks last night.'

'Of course she didn't. She didn't want us to know.'

Oliver frowned. 'This isn't on. She told Bella to lie to us. Summer is a mother too, she should know better than to convince a young girl to deceive her parents.'

'Oh, I think she knew exactly what she was doing.'

This time when Oliver looked at me, his expression wasn't wary, or resigned. His suspicion matched mine. 'You think she did this deliberately?'

'I'm certain of it.'

'But why?'

'To get at me.'

He nodded. 'Okay.'

'Okay?'

'Yes. She's getting way too involved in our life. It's creepy.'

I thanked the heavens. Finally, he got it. 'So, what do we do?'

'Shall I talk to Summer?'

The last thing I wanted was my husband having another cosy drink with that woman. 'I don't think that's a good idea.'

'Well, you can't talk to her. It'll end up in a huge row.'

'Maybe it needs to. This has been brewing for months and it's come to a head.'

Oliver nodded again. 'I get what you're saying. But I still think it's better coming from me. She's been texting me a bit again today and I think—'

'She what? She's been texting you?'

'Yeah. Nothing serious. Just benign chit-chat.'

'Oliver, why didn't you tell me?'

'There was nothing to tell you. Or at least I didn't think so. Now I'm not so sure.'

'Welcome to my world.'

'Okay.' Oliver stood up. 'Here's what we'll do. I know you don't like it, but I'm going to speak to her. The dialogue is there between us and so it will seem more natural coming from me. I'll tell her to back off. A friendly warning.'

Was this what Summer wanted? Another reason to talk to Oliver? Another excuse to meet him for a drink? And how much confidence did I have in my husband not to fall for it?

'Fine,' I said. I had to trust him. 'But be careful.'

He grinned, a hint of the Oliver I hadn't seen for a while returning. 'Do you think she'll lure me in like the White Witch and I'll end up trapped in Narnia forever?'

'Yeah. She'll feed you Turkish delight and then turn you into a statue.'

'That doesn't sound so bad, actually. I don't mind Turkish delight.'

I punched him gently on the arm. 'Don't even go there.'

His expression turned serious again. 'I'm sorry, Nims. Sorry I doubted you.'

I took his hand. 'It doesn't matter. What matters is that you finally understand where I'm coming from. She's trouble with a capital T.'

And as I said it, I just had to hope that it would stay true. That Oliver would remain on my side, no matter what else Summer had up her sleeve.

22

Bella didn't emerge from her room until dinnertime and that was only because Oliver went up and coaxed her downstairs. She sat at the table scowling, her eyes shooting daggers at me. I had never seen her so furious. Oliver and I tried to draw her into conversation but she was having none of it so eventually we gave up. Freya, used to being frequently interrupted by her exuberant big sister, took advantage of the silence to talk incessantly.

'And then Noah did better in the spelling test than Sebastian, and Sebastian was crying, and then Noah told him it didn't matter because it was only a silly test, and then Sebastian...'

On and on she went, and I smiled, enjoying seeing my youngest daughter so animated. But the mention of Sebastian reminded me that Angela had rung me twice that day and I hadn't called her back. I'd been too caught up in this whole Bella business. I made a mental note to contact her after dinner and then turned my attention back to Freya.

'And then Aanya said that she wondered if Luna was ever

coming back, and then Ella said she'd heard a new child was starting, and then Maria said that wasn't true and then...'

'Speaking of Luna...'

We all stopped and stared at Bella, who had finally stopped giving us the silent treatment.

'Yes?' I said.

'I've been round to Summer's house several times.' She threw another venomous look my way. 'And I've never once seen Luna. Which I think is a bit random, given that she's supposed to be home-schooled.'

'Maybe she was just in her bedroom?' I suggested.

'Maybe. But I've been there for over an hour every time. And I've used the loo. You'd think I'd at least hear her moving about, even if I didn't see her. The door is always closed and I've never heard a peep. I wondered if she'd gone to live with her dad.'

I leaned across the table. 'Have you asked Summer about it?'

'No.'

Oliver and I looked at each other but we were both distracted by snuffling noises.

It was Freya, with tears in her eyes. 'I don't want Luna to move back to Devon.'

It was literally my dream that they'd move back to Devon. But somehow both my daughters wanted the opposite. 'I know you're friends with Luna now, darling, but you must remember that she wasn't very nice to you when she first came. Not very nice at all.'

'She didn't mean it. She said she was sorry.'

'And it's really important that she apologised. But it doesn't excuse what she did. She said some horrible things about you, Freya. She really upset you.'

'She didn't mean it!'

'Okay,' Oliver interrupted, shooting me a warning glance. 'We understand, Freya. I'm sure this is all just a misunderstanding and she'll be back soon. Perhaps she's gone to stay with her dad for a short while because her mum is busy working?'

'It's been weeks,' Bella interjected, chewing as she spoke. The dark cloud that had been hanging over her all afternoon seemed to be lifting and, in typical Bella style, it was like she'd almost forgotten about it. 'I've literally not seen her once.'

'Well, there'll be an explanation,' Oliver replied reasonably.

'She wouldn't go back to Devon,' Freya said quietly. 'She hates it there.'

Bella's eyes lit up at the prospect of gossip. 'Why does she hate it?'

'Because of the bad thing that happened.'

We were all staring at Freya, rapt. 'What bad thing?' I asked.

Freya looked away. 'I don't know.'

'Freya, this is important.'

She slammed her fork down. 'I don't know.'

The table was quiet as we all tried to process what scant information Freya had given us. Only Bella continued eating happily and eventually broke the silence.

'So, Kimberley messaged me and apparently she's joining the choir too so I'm well up for going next week. And remember you promised you'd get me more private lessons.'

I loved my eldest daughter for being able to get over things so quickly. I wished I shared the same trait. But as I looked at Freya intently, I knew that I would never be like that. And nor would Freya. So why was she protecting Luna? What did she know?

'Freya,' I said quietly. 'I need to know what Luna has told you.'

'Nothing.'

'Freya.'

'Nothing.'

Oliver put his hand over mine. 'Who wants dessert? We've got some ice cream.'

Once the girls were ensconced in front of the television, I asked Oliver why he'd stopped my questioning.

'She's just a little girl. I don't want to push her too hard.'

'But what if Luna's in trouble? What if she's not safe?'

'We don't know that. All we know is that Bella hasn't seen her. The most likely scenario is that she's at her dad's. And the bad thing Freya is talking about is probably Luna's parents splitting up. It must have been really hard on her, especially if her dad is as useless as you say.'

'But if he's that useless, she wouldn't be staying with him, would she?'

'We don't know the full story, and until we do, we shouldn't jump to conclusions.'

But I was worried now. For my family but also for Luna. She'd been nasty to Freya but she was just a kid and if her mother was as manipulative as I believed, then I didn't know what that meant for Luna. I thought about all the times that Summer had gone out and posted on her Instagram feed, as though she had a babysitter on speed-dial. Was it possible she had left Luna at home alone? Surely not? But I wouldn't put anything past her. Then, remembering that I owed Angela a call, I decided to strike while the iron was hot and get her take on it too.

'I need to make a phone call,' I told Oliver. 'Has Summer replied to your message?'

'Not yet, I'll let you know as soon as she does.'

Oliver took his bowl of ice cream to the living room and I called Angela.

'I've been trying to reach you,' she said when she answered.

'I'm sorry, I've had quite the day.' I filled her in on the Bella shenanigans and Freya's odd comments over dinner.

'Wow, Naomi, that's a lot of information to process. But right now, I have something important I need to tell you about last night.'

My hand tensed around the phone. So much had happened that it was hard to believe Oliver's drink with Summer was only the previous evening. 'Go on.'

'I know you told me we shouldn't go and spy on Summer and Oliver, but I couldn't resist. Don't worry, I was very subtle. I arranged to meet an old school pal in the pub and we had dinner right on the other side. She didn't see me, but I had a fairly good view of her.'

Despite everything, I had to stifle a smile at the image of Angela acting like an intelligence agent, going full surveillance on the enemy. 'Oliver's already told me everything.'

'So he told you about the kiss?'

My heart stopped. 'What kiss?'

'She kissed him, right there in the pub. I couldn't believe it.'

'You must be mistaken, they didn't kiss.'

'I saw it with my own eyes, Naomi. They kissed.'

My world was falling apart around me and I slumped down on a chair, unable to believe what I was hearing. 'Are you absolutely sure?'

'I'm certain. So he didn't tell you?'

'No, he bloody didn't.'

'I'm sorry, Naomi. But I thought you should know.'

'I'm glad you told me, thank you, but I've got to go. I need to speak to Oliver.'

I waited until he returned a few minutes later with the empty bowl. I watched him as he walked casually over to the sink and dropped it in, ignoring the dishwasher as he always did. Then he turned and smiled at me, raising his eyebrows quizzically when he saw my expression.

'What's up?'

'Why didn't you tell me that Summer kissed you?'

His face fell. 'How do you know about that?'

'It doesn't matter how I know. What matters is that you lied to me.'

He closed the kitchen door and came to sit down next to me, trying to take my hand. I snatched it away.

'She tried to kiss me and I pulled away,' he said. 'That was all that happened.'

'But you didn't tell me.'

'I knew you'd lose it, and I was worried. I didn't want to make things worse than they were.'

'But you've made things worse, Oliver, because you lied to me when I asked you outright about it. What else have you lied to me about? Did you kiss her back?'

He was outraged. 'Of course I didn't. You know I would never do that.'

'I don't know anything any more. I don't know what to believe.'

'You can believe me on this. I am not interested in Summer. I didn't tell you for your own good. You were already in a state and I knew this would send you flying off the handle.'

'But she did exactly what I thought she would do, and you protected her.'

'No, Nims. I protected you.'

So, he didn't get it after all. Perhaps he did genuinely think he was doing the right thing. I wanted to believe the best. But instead, I felt betrayed.

'You let me down,' I told him. 'You made me doubt myself.'

'I'm sorry. But you have to remember that this incident happened before all this business with Bella. I was confused but I get it now, I really do. I'm on your side.'

'But you still didn't tell me about it, even after you knew about Bella.'

'I was going to, but I haven't had the chance. The kids have been around all afternoon.'

I had a thought. 'Hang on. She tried to kiss you, but you still want to meet her again?'

'Yes, to warn her off. To tell her to leave us alone.'

'And you think she'll listen?'

'It's worth a try, isn't it? I'll make it crystal clear that I'm not interested, and I don't appreciate her going behind our back with Bella either.'

'You didn't make that clear to her before?'

'Of course I did. I pulled away as soon as she kissed me and I told her that it wasn't happening. I said I was happily married.'

I looked at him and I believed him. But I was still fuming.

'I can't look at you right now...'

'It won't happen again. I promise.'

I couldn't just forgive him, though. He had deceived me, even if he had believed it was for my own good. And it didn't escape me that two members of my family had been caught lying to me that day, and both times it involved Summer. I stormed out of the room and went upstairs to the bedroom, closing the door. And then, craving an ally, I messaged Angela.

> Will you spread the word about what you saw in the pub? Maybe everyone will finally believe me about Summer. It'll seem more believable coming from you.

She replied immediately.

> I was waiting for you to give me the green light. I'm on it.

So, it was done. And now all I could do was wait and see if it worked. If my friends finally saw Summer for who she was and came back to me.

The problem was, I still didn't know who Summer really was.

* * *

The next morning, I asked Oliver to take Freya to school on his way to work. I didn't want to face the playground because I didn't know if Angela had set the wheels in motion yet. I was fed up with the fear and the hostility. Instead, I walked with Bella, who was mortified about being accompanied by her mummy after having her independence for so long.

'How long is this going to go on for?' she demanded.

'Can't a mother walk her darling daughter to school?'

'Not when her darling daughter is thirteen and perfectly capable of going on her own.'

We compromised on me saying goodbye at the end of the road and she dashed off, eager to get away from me. As I began to walk home, I decided to detour. Among the many other worries competing for attention in my mind, I had been thinking about Luna and I decided on the spur of the moment to walk past the flat and see if there was any sign of her. I knew it was risky in case Summer spotted me because I didn't want to talk to her. I was too angry, too volatile, and I didn't trust myself. I would wait until Angela told everyone the truth and then when I had them on side, I would have the strength to have it out with Summer, knowing that she couldn't blame me this time. That my friends would finally support me.

I was half expecting my phone to start pinging with messages from Asha, Rachel, Victoria and Richard. I eagerly awaited the moment that they sent gushing apologies for their behaviour, telling me how embarrassed they were for getting it wrong about Summer. I would forgive them because I missed them, but it would take a long time for me to forget and I wasn't sure we'd ever be close again. In any event, my phone remained resolutely silent.

When I reached the flat, I walked past slowly, peering in through the window which I knew to be Luna's room, but the curtains were closed and there was no sign of any movement. I kept going, walking around in a large circle and then turned back, retracing my steps. Again, the curtains were closed. I hovered for a bit but, feeling self-conscious, I eventually headed home.

My phone didn't ping all day. What was taking them so long? Surely Angela would have spread the word by now? Why wasn't anyone reaching out to me? I messaged Angela.

> Have you done it yet? xx

But she didn't reply. Fortunately, Freya was at art club after school which meant that I missed the usual school pick-up time. As I was leaving the house to collect her, I realised I had a few minutes to spare and I detoured to the flat again, slowing down as I reached it. This time the curtains were open and I peered in, trying not to look suspicious. But there was no one there and I sped up again and hurried to the school so I wouldn't be late for Freya.

The first message came as we were walking home together and when I saw it was Asha, my heart soared. Then I read it.

> Summer says you've been lurking around
> outside her flat. What the hell, Naomi?

My hands trembled as I digested the message. How had Summer made me look like the one in the wrong again? And what did I say in response?

'Are you okay, Mummy?' Freya was looking up at me.

'I'm fine darling. What did you have for lunch?'

By the time we reached the house, I was still reeling from Asha's message. With dinner underway, I tried to call Angela, but she didn't answer. Why hadn't she told everyone yet? Should I tell Asha? Would she believe me? A surge of defiance ran through me. I had done nothing wrong and it was time that everyone knew about it. I got my phone out.

> Summer tried it on with Oliver. Ask Angela, she
> was the one who saw it and told me. And I'm
> worried about Luna because no one has seen
> her for ages. That's why I walked past the flat a
> couple of times.

My stomach churned as I pressed send and waited for the two blue ticks to appear, which they quickly did. I held my breath as I saw that Asha was typing back.

> From what Summer told me, it was Oliver who tried it on with her. She's been really upset about it. She didn't know whether to say anything to you, or if you'd even believe her. I'm sorry to be the one to tell you the truth but you deserve to know. And Luna's fine, I saw her yesterday.

Bile rose up in my throat as I read her reply. How the hell had Summer managed to come out smelling of roses again? She was lying, I knew it in my bones. Oliver may have fibbed to me but he was telling the truth about this. I wasn't giving up that easily.

> Summer is the one who's lying, Asha. Oliver has told me everything and I believe him. She's been texting him for ages. She has also been having secret lessons with Bella and she persuaded Bella not to tell me. Bella said that she's never seen Luna once, in all the times she's been there. I was worried about her, that's all.

The blue ticks appeared but this time Asha didn't respond. I tried to call her, desperate to speak to her, but she didn't answer. I tried Angela again but no response. Then I smelled burning and cursed as I realised I'd neglected dinner. I was fishing some very sorry-looking sausages out of the oven, and contemplating a glass of wine when my phone rang and I reached for it eagerly, hoping to see Asha's name on the screen. But it was my dad and, although I was agitated and in no mood for a chat, I didn't want to ignore him.

'Hi, Dad. How are you?'

His voice shook as he whispered. 'Naomi. I think someone's in the house.'

I dropped the tray of sausages with a clatter. 'What? Have you called the police?'

'No, I called you.'

'Call the police now. I'm on my way.'

I shouted for the children and bundled us all in to the car, driving as quickly as the rush-hour traffic would allow. Bella and Freya kept asking what was going on and I didn't want to scare them, so I told them that Granddad had fallen over and needed our help.

I skidded to a halt outside my dad's house and saw the police car outside. Clearly they'd beaten us to it and I was relieved because if there was an intruder in the house, I didn't want to be the one to confront him, especially with the children in tow.

I opened the front door with the spare key I kept and strode into the living room to see Dad in his chair, while two uniformed police officers sat on the sofa opposite him.

'Girls, go and see if Granddad has any biscuits in the kitchen,' I ordered. The two girls, who were staring openly at the police officers, obeyed without argument. As soon as they were out of earshot I turned to Dad. 'Are you okay? What happened?'

'I was upstairs in the bathroom,' he said shakily. 'And I heard a noise downstairs and what sounded like someone moving about. I called out but there was no answer. And then I called you. You know how long it takes me to get down the stairs, it's a military operation. Anyway, by the time I got down here, whoever it was had gone.'

I looked around the room. 'Did they take anything?'

'Not that I can see.'

I turned to the police officers. 'Do you know how they got in?'

One of them nodded. 'The back door was open.'

'Oh, Dad.'

'I'm sorry.' He hung his head, like a small child. 'I went out for some fresh air and must have forgotten to lock it behind me. I was certain that I did, but apparently not.'

I could hardly berate him for it. I'd done the same thing with the front door. Or had I? This was surely too much of a coincidence. First the attempted break-in at our house and now Dad's.

'We've spoken to your father about making sure the doors and windows are locked,' one of the officers said with a friendly smile. 'He was lucky that nothing was taken. I think he must have scared the intruder off when he called out.'

The girls had reappeared, clutching on to a packet of biscuits and staring at the police. They ripped the packet open and started munching, their eyes never leaving the two officers.

'Are you okay, Dad? Do you want to come and stay with us for a bit?'

'No, love. I'm fine. Honestly, I'm fine. It was all a fuss about nothing.'

But it wasn't nothing. Someone had preyed on a vulnerable, elderly man and it made me furious. My brain whirred as I tried to make sense of what was going on. It couldn't be Summer this time because even if she was out for me, she had no business with my dad. And how would she even know where he lived? Then I remembered our conversation at the playdate, when she had asked about Dad. She had been extremely interested in him, although at the time I hadn't thought much of it. Had I given too much away?

Confident that my dad was okay, I decided to take the girls home. They asked me a million questions in the car, but I assured them that all was well, and that Granddad had panicked when he fell and called the police. They seemed to believe me. The last thing I needed was Freya getting worried and her night terrors starting again. With all the excitement, I had forgotten about Asha, but our awkward conversation came back to me on the drive home and as soon as I parked up, I checked my phone for any missed calls or messages. There were none.

When Oliver got home, I told him what had happened and he, too, suggested that Dad come and stay with us. But when I called Dad to ask again, he wouldn't hear of it. Promising to go and see him the next day, I hung up and looked at Oliver.

'He won't come.'

'We'll just keep an eye on him then. By the way, Summer still hasn't messaged me back.'

'Maybe she knows we're on to her. Speaking of which, you'll never believe what Asha said to me.'

I showed him the messages and his eyes widened when he read the bit about him coming on to Summer rather than the other way around.

'It's not true,' he said, his eyes pleading.

'I know it's not. But it seems like she's convinced everyone that it is.'

I still hadn't got over the fact that Oliver had lied to me about the kiss. It came back to me constantly, accompanied by a sharp stab of anger towards my husband. Sometimes I found myself looking at him and wondering what else he hadn't told me. But I needed us to remain a united front, now more than ever. I needed Oliver. And if that meant doing my best to let it go, then that was what I had to do. It was easier said than done.

'But listen, Nims, you need to stop walking past Summer's flat, okay?'

'I only did it twice,' I said defensively.

'Yeah, and that's two times too many. You're making it worse for yourself.'

'I was worried about Luna.'

'I know, but it makes you look like a stalker.'

I laughed coldly. '*I'm* the stalker?'

'I know you're not. But until everyone else does, just back off, okay?'

He was right. But that night, I couldn't stop thinking about Luna, isolated from her friends, and in the morning, I knew that I couldn't stay away. Luna had behaved terribly towards Freya but I was beginning to think she had been driven to it by her mother. And I was feeling increasingly sorry for the girl and worried about her welfare.

As soon as I had dropped Freya at school, ten minutes early to avoid bumping into Asha and the rest of the gang, I headed towards the flat. I would just be more careful this time, so that Summer didn't see me. I stopped before I reached the building, hiding behind a van parked on the opposite side of the road. I peered around and saw that the curtains to Luna's room were open. From my vantage point I had a clear view of the windows and I stood there for while watching, not sure what I was waiting for but compelled to stay.

My patience was rewarded because ten minutes later, Luna appeared at the window. I watched as she pressed her palms up against the glass. And then her eyes met mine.

My heart was in my throat as I quickly ducked behind the van. How had she known I was there? Had she felt my gaze? After a few seconds, I peeked out again. She was still there and she was still looking at me. I glanced in the other windows to see if Summer was watching too but there was no sign of her. My eyes drifted back to Luna.

She was mouthing something, I realised, and I tried to

make out what she was saying. I craned my neck, studying the movements of her lips, desperate to work out what it was. She seemed to be saying the same thing over again. What the hell was it?

And then it hit me, with the full force of a train. Because I had worked out what the little girl was mouthing and it chilled me to the bone.

Help me.

23

It was the third time I had spoken to the police in as many weeks. But this time, they didn't look at me sympathetically and hand me generic leaflets about keeping my property safe. Instead, they interrogated me. What exactly had I seen? When did I last see Luna? What was my relationship to Summer? Had I contacted Social Services?

By the time they left, I was exhausted. The children, who had been banished upstairs, crept back down and came to sit next to me on the sofa.

'Mum, what's going on?' Bella asked.

'Nothing you need to worry about,' I told her.

'You told me not to lie to you. But you're lying to us.'

She was right. I was doing it to protect my children, but I owed them the truth, or part of it at least. 'I was worried about Luna so I've asked the police to make sure she's okay.'

Bella was aghast. 'Because of what I told you?'

'Not just that, darling. Other things too.'

'But what if Summer finds out that I told you? She'll be angry with me.'

It rankled that Bella cared so much what Summer thought. 'The important thing is making sure that Luna is okay. Summer never needs to know that you told me.'

Freya was quiet. I took her hand and squeezed it. 'Are you okay, darling?'

'I'm worried about Luna too.'

'I'm sure she's absolutely fine.'

'What if she's not?'

'She will be,' I said, more confidently than I felt. This had gone beyond the rift between Summer and me. This now involved a child.

I had no idea what to expect. If Summer had hurt, or imprisoned, Luna, would she be arrested? Would the police keep me updated? I thought about what Asha had said. She claimed to have seen Luna and that she was fine. But Asha hadn't seen what I had seen. She hadn't witnessed a terrified-looking girl, begging for help.

The evening dragged on, painfully slowly. Oliver tried to distract me, suggesting that we put on a comedy, opening a bottle of wine. But my desire to drink had vanished. It only made my anxiety worse, and I was more determined than ever to think rationally. I had to be seen to be the reasonable one, and finally prove that I had been right all along.

Then it was the weekend and my phone remained silent. I tried to keep busy, taking the children to their various activities and then shopping to buy some new clothes that they were constantly outgrowing. We went to visit Dad. I tried Angela but she still wasn't answering and I hadn't heard from Asha, or any of the school gang. By Monday, there was no word from anyone and I had to take Freya to school because Oliver couldn't be late for work. I tried to leave early again to avoid the crowds, but Freya dragged her heels, spending ages looking for her spelling book, and then ensconcing herself in the toilet with a book. By the time we left, I was completely stressed out.

'Come on, stop dawdling,' I snapped.

But Freya seemed intent on stopping to look at every snowdrop she saw, then declaring that she was so hungry she couldn't think straight, despite having had breakfast, so we had to detour to the cafe. By the time we reached the gates, the playground was packed full of parents.

I saw Summer first. She was in the centre, surrounded by the Year 3 mums and dads. My spirits soared as I spotted Luna, looking perfectly well, in her school uniform. Thank goodness she was okay. But then they plummeted again as I realised the implication of this.

I had been wrong.

Summer must have felt my gaze because she turned to look at me, her expression unreadable. Then Asha turned and hers was as clear as day. It was disgust. They both turned their backs on me, whispering quietly. Freya, oblivious, saw Luna and raced over, embracing her tightly. I saw with relief that at least Luna hugged her back, although she kept stealing glances at her mother. Had she been told not to play with Freya?

And where the hell was Angela? My only comrade had been missing in action for days and I was starting to worry. Was she okay? Had something happened to her? Or Sebastian? I couldn't see him in the playground. I looked back at the school gang and a couple of them were scowling at me. It was horrible. Absolutely horrible. And I couldn't take it any more. I turned and fled, making it to the exit just in time before my tears fell. I hadn't even said goodbye to Freya.

At home I scoured the local news and social media, looking for any mention of a woman matching Summer's description being arrested, even though I knew it was pointless. Unable to resist, I called the police for an update. But no one could help me.

It was over. I had committed the ultimate betrayal. I had reported another mother to the police and although I had done it for the right reasons, no one would ever forgive me. Would I forgive me if the shoe was on the other foot? Probably not. Because the evidence was clear for all to see. Luna was safe, and now, for some reason, she was back at school too. Why had she returned now? Was it so Summer could prove to everyone that she was fine?

I was too defeated to analyse it. Abandoning all pretence of work, I climbed into bed and pulled the duvet over me. I would never be able to get Summer out of our lives. She had infiltrated us, wrapping herself around us all. I would have to face her every day, just as I would have to face the hostile stares of the other mums and dads who knew what I had done. And nothing I said now would make any difference. I was officially an outcast, and it was a life sentence. My only hope now was that we could keep the children out of it, but I knew it was unlikely.

The sound of my phone ringing roused me from my misery, and I reached for it, seeing my dad's name. I didn't want to talk to anyone, but I needed to make sure Dad was okay.

'Hi, Dad, how are you?'

'Fine, love. Are you busy?'

'No. Do you want me to come round?'

'Only if you've got time. It's not urgent.'

'And you're sure you're okay?'

'Yes, love, I'm sure.'

I climbed out of bed. 'I'll be over in half an hour.'

When I arrived, Dad had already boiled the kettle and put

tea bags in two mugs. I finished making the drinks and took them over to him.

'Are you all right, Naomi? You look tired.'

I didn't want to worry him. 'It's been a busy couple of days but I'm fine.'

'Everything okay with Oliver and the girls?'

'Yes, Dad, they're fine. Very well. How are you?'

'I'm okay, love, it's just that something odd has happened.'

Fear pricked at me. Had the intruders returned? I looked around the house, but everything seemed as it should be. 'What is it?'

'I was having a nostalgic moment, so I went to get the family photo album. You know, the one with all the photos of you as a child.'

'Okay.'

'Only it wasn't there.'

I frowned. 'Are you sure?'

'I'm quite sure. It's been in the same place on the bookshelf for twenty years.'

I glanced at the shelf and sure enough, there was an empty space where Dad kept his old photo albums. 'Could you have moved it and forgotten about it?'

'No.' Dad sounded certain. 'I always put it back in the same place.'

'Then what's happened to it?'

'Well, that's the thing. I'm wondering if the intruder took it.'

'Why on earth would the intruder take a photo album?'

'I don't know, that's why I'm confused.'

The cogs were turning in my mind. Intruders at both my house and Dad's. And now a missing photo album. Dad's health wasn't great, but he was meticulous with his organisation. If he said the album was missing, then I believed him.

Which meant that whoever got into his house wasn't an opportunistic burglar. They had been looking for something.

That was the link. On the face of it, the attempted burglaries were isolated incidents. But now they both had one thing in common. They both involved me.

Summer. She had gone to my dad's house to steal childhood photos of me.

'Dad,' I said suddenly. 'Do you know anyone called Summer?'

He frowned. 'No, I don't think so.'

'What about years ago when I was a child?'

'I'm sorry love but my memory's not great. And I worked a lot, so your mum always handled the school events and parties and so on. Why do you ask?'

'Don't worry about it.'

Once I was certain that Dad was okay, I made him another cup of tea and said my goodbyes. As I drove home, I wondered what to do. I couldn't call the police because after what had happened last week, they probably wouldn't believe me. They would think I was some sort of mad fantasist. I tried Oliver but his phone was off.

Then I thought of Angela. Where was she and why wasn't Sebastian in school? A nagging fear developed in my gut as I wondered if I had been wrong to trust her again. Had she pretended to be my friend when really she was on Summer's side? But that didn't explain her absence, unless something bad had happened to her. With everything else that had been going on, it wouldn't surprise me. I felt like I was living in a parallel world, one which seemed normal on the outside but was far from it. And I didn't know how to escape from this nightmare.

I parked up and tried Angela again, praying for her to answer.

Someone must have been listening because just before it rang out, I heard her voice.

'Angela, are you okay? I've been worried about you.'

'Sorry, Naomi, my mother fell ill suddenly and Michael was away on business so Sebastian and I drove down to Sussex. We're still here.'

'Oh my goodness, I'm sorry. Is she okay?'

'Heart attack. She's still in hospital. I'm sorry I've not had a chance to tell everyone about Summer, I've been all over the place.'

'Don't worry about that. You concentrate on your mum. When are you coming back?'

'I don't know. Sebastian needs to get back to school and he has his tutor tomorrow. I might drive back this evening, if my mother doesn't deteriorate. How are you?'

'Well, you'll never guess who turned up at school today.'

I told Angela about Summer and Luna being back and how everyone had ghosted me when she told them I'd reported her to the police.

Angela was shocked. 'You called the police?'

'I didn't know what else to do. I was worried about Luna.'

'But you've played right into Summer's hands. Now everyone thinks you're in the wrong again.'

'I know, but we're talking about a little girl.'

'I wonder why she's back at school. Perhaps, after the police visited her, she wanted to prove to everyone that Luna is fine.'

'I thought the same thing.'

'I'm sorry I'm not there for you, Naomi.'

'You *are* here for me. And you're the only one. I'm so grateful.'

'Have you talked to Oliver about the kiss?'

'Yes, and he says Summer initiated it.'

'But why didn't he tell you?'

'He was worried about how I would react. Tell me, from what you saw, did it seem that the kiss was all from Summer's side?'

Angela was quiet for a few moments. 'I didn't see the whole thing. All I know is that I looked over and their lips were locked.'

'How long for?'

'Not long. And to be fair to Oliver, he did pull away.'

I closed my eyes. 'Okay. Thank you. Listen, you look after yourself, okay? Forget about everything that's going on here. And if you need any help with Sebastian, just let me know. He could stay with us for a few days if that would help? I could take him to school?'

'Actually, that would be great, if you don't mind?'

'Of course not. I'm home all day so why don't you drive him over when you're ready.'

'Thank you, Naomi, I really appreciate it.'

I hung up and let myself into the house, determined to try and do some work. But instead I found myself scrolling on Instagram and, inevitably, Summer's profile. She'd posted a photo of Luna in her school uniform, the logo covered by an emoji heart. And she'd written:

Back to school for my darling Luna. Thanks so much to my bestie, Asha, for all your support. I know that with the gorgeous Aanya by my girl's side, she can tackle anything. You go girl, you've got this.

Rage built up inside me. The insinuation was clear. But Luna didn't have to tackle anything. Freya had been delighted to see her and any suggestion otherwise was false. The post already had seventeen likes and when I looked through the list of who had liked it, it was all my old friends. Richard had left a comment. *So proud of you both.*

I thought of Freya and hoped everything was going okay at school. Then I forced myself to do some work, stopping only to make a quick sandwich, and by the time it came to pick Freya up from after-school club, I desperately needed some fresh air. I hovered by the school entrance, keeping my head down, but thankfully none of the gang were there.

Freya came out full of beans, talking about the fun she'd had with Luna at school.

'I'm so happy she's back,' she said before leaning in conspiratorially. 'She asked me to be her best friend and I said yes.'

This was the last thing I needed. But how could I tell a seven-year-old that she couldn't be friends with the person she now, for some reason, adored?

Instead, I said, 'What about Aanya?'

'We're friends with her too, Mummy.'

'Speaking of friends, Sebastian is coming to stay with us for a few days.'

Freya looked appalled. 'What? Why?'

'His nana is poorly and his mummy needs to stay with her in the hospital.'

'What about his daddy?'

'His daddy is away. And I want you to be nice to him, Freya. Make him feel welcome.'

'But he's such a show-off.'

'He's a nice boy, really.'

Freya didn't look convinced. 'Where will he sleep?'

'In the office. I'll make up the sofa bed. Angela is dropping him this evening.'

She scrunched up her nose. 'How long is he staying for?'

'Just a few days. And remember what I said. Be nice.'

When Angela dropped Sebastian that evening, Freya hovered in the hallway looking uncertain, and Sebastian didn't look any more enthusiastic. He glanced at his mum pleadingly.

I took his hand. 'Come on, Sebastian, I've made pasta for dinner. Your mum said it's your favourite.' I looked at Angela, who mouthed, 'Thank you.'

'I'm hoping to come back tomorrow, or the next day at the very latest,' she told me.

'Take your time. Sebastian will be fine.'

'I really appreciate this, Naomi. I've packed all his school things.'

I took the bags she was proffering. 'It's my pleasure.'

Dinner began as a stilted affair. I sat down with them, even though I wasn't eating until later. Bella was reading a script while she ate, and Freya and Sebastian sat next to each other in stony silence. I hoped it wasn't going to be like this for the next two days.

'Are you looking forward to going back to school tomorrow, Sebastian?' I asked. I got a shrug in response, but I kept trying, 'I bet you've missed your friends.'

Then I remembered that he didn't have many friends and I changed tack. 'Hey, it's your school camping trip in a few weeks. Are you excited?'

The Year 3 camping trip was a rite of passage at North Hill and Freya had been talking about it for ages. She had been anxious about it too and so I had nominated myself to go along as a parent volunteer, which had assuaged her concerns. Now, though, I was worried about the other parents who might be going. I didn't want the tension to spoil it for the kids and I was terrified about being ignored by everyone, but I couldn't let Freya down.

'I'm not going,' Sebastian said glumly.

'Why not?'

'Mummy doesn't want me to.'

A few parents opted out of the trip every year, saying the children were too young, but the school had been doing it forever and I was confident that it was well organised. Thinking about it now, I wasn't surprised that Angela had said he couldn't go, because she wrapped him up in cotton wool and I felt bad for bringing it up. This conversation was going from bad to worse.

'I wonder if Luna will go,' Freya said.

I hoped not. I was about to say something neutral about the possibility but then Sebastian piped up. 'Why would she go if she doesn't even go to our school any more?'

'She's back,' Freya told him, elated. 'She came back today.'

Sebastian's expression was stormy and I picked up on it immediately. 'Are you okay, Sebastian?'

'I don't like Luna,' he said quietly.

'Why not?'

'She lies.'

I had to hide my eagerness. 'What does she lie about?'

'Everything.'

'That's not true!' Freya jumped in to defend her friend, even though she had been central to Luna's pack of lies.

'Yes, it is,' Sebastian retorted. 'Remember all that stuff she said about Devon?'

My ears pricked at this. 'What did she say?'

'Stop it, Sebastian!' Freya was furious.

But Sebastian ignored her. 'She said they had to run away because her mum was in trouble.'

I listened, wide-eyed, as Freya pushed Sebastian in a fit of fury. 'Shut up, Sebastian!' she screamed. 'We weren't meant to tell the grown-ups.'

'It wasn't true anyway,' he retorted.

I was fizzing with anticipation. Sebastian had given me the most vital piece of evidence yet against Summer. She had a past that she didn't want anyone to know about. My relief was palpable, but the battle wasn't over yet. Because while I now had a critical clue, I didn't know what to do with it, or who would believe me if I told them.

Whatever it was, though, I would find out. I had nothing left to lose.

24

The children were running around in a frenzy of excitement, as already-frazzled teachers tried to line them up. Bags were being loaded on to the coaches and parents huddled together, waiting to wave their offspring off. I hovered by the coach, pretending I was busy.

I'd been relieved when I went to the camping trip briefing and discovered that my fellow parent volunteers were from the other Year 3 class. I recognised them but I didn't know them and, from the way they smiled politely at me, I guessed that they had no idea that I was public enemy number one. I was hoping it would stay that way.

The school run recently had been a daily nightmare. Every morning, I woke up with a sense of foreboding and I had to steel myself for the simple act of taking my daughter to school. Oliver did it whenever he could, but he was busy with work and I had no one else to ask. Everyone, except Angela, hated me. And now Angela's mother had passed away and she had enough on her plate without me begging her to take Freya to school, so I had no choice.

I was on my own. I tried to leave as early as possible to avoid the rush and I never stayed for the bell to ring. I left Freya in the playground under the watchful eye of the teachers on duty. But it was impossible to avoid everyone all the time. Freya often dawdled in the morning, and I had to pick her up in the afternoons too, so I inevitably saw the Year 3 parent gang. Every time I did, I looked away from their hostile stares, red creeping up my neck and my stomach churning.

As a couple of the dads who were also volunteering came over to say hello, I thanked the heavens that the whispers about my behaviour hadn't infiltrated the entire school community. Yet. But Freya was so excited about this trip and I had to keep my spirits high.

'Marcie can't volunteer any more,' one of the dads told me. 'Her car was broken into overnight and she's waiting for the police to come.'

'Oh no, poor Marcie. Does that mean we're a parent volunteer short?'

'They were trying to get another parent but I don't know if they managed it at short notice.'

I felt a sinking feeling as I considered the possibility that one of the gang would step up. But I doubted it. They all had jobs and other children to juggle, and I couldn't imagine them being able to organise the logistics in time. Anyway, they knew I was going as the names of the parent volunteers had been included on the briefing letter, so I was sure they'd stay away. They didn't even want to talk to me, let alone share a tent with me.

I relaxed a fraction as the teachers started ordering the children on to the coaches. No one else was coming, it was going to be fine. Suddenly I heard a commotion and spun around to see

Summer, running down the road, a huge backpack on her back, as she pulled Luna along.

'So sorry we're late,' she called. I saw Freya's face light up at the sight of Luna. I still hadn't told anyone, apart from Oliver, about what Sebastian had told me. I had suggested to Oliver that we go to Devon to do some investigating, but he'd said it would be like looking for a needle in a haystack. I hadn't given up, exactly, but I was lying dormant, waiting for Summer to make a mistake. Surely, she'd have to eventually? It sounded like she had done in Devon. Our house was like Fort Knox now, with cameras and floodlights everywhere and it had helped me to feel more secure. But I hated that we'd had to resort to these measures to keep that crazy woman away from us and I loathed the fact that there was nothing I could do about it.

I had attempted to prise more information out of Freya, but she refused to tell me anything and so instead, I had come up with my own theories, both plausible and implausible. Summer had stalked another woman in Devon and had been caught? Or she'd been sacked from her job for gross misconduct. Perhaps she'd actually hurt someone?

I watched her from the corner of my eye, waiting for her to hug Luna goodbye and go and stand with all the other parents. But then, to my horror, she went over to greet Sharon and then started to climb onto the bus. I stood, frozen to the spot, as I realised that Summer was coming on the trip too. She had stepped in to replace Marcie.

Sharon walked over to me. 'All set?'

'Is Summer coming too?'

'Yes, that's right. Will everything be okay between you?'

I forced a smile. 'Of course. Everything will be fine.'

But everything would not be fine. I now had to spend two days with the woman I despised and feared. The woman trying to steal my life. For a brief moment I considered feigning illness and telling Sharon that I couldn't go after all. But then I saw Freya waving to me from the window and I knew that I couldn't do it. I owed it to my daughter to get on that coach.

I glanced at Asha, Rachel, Victoria and Richard but they were waving at their kids and if they felt my gaze, they didn't respond to it. It was like I no longer existed in their world. I was dead to them. With a sinking heart and an even deeper sense of dread, I climbed onto the coach.

On board it was chaos. The children were chatting loudly, their voices competing to be heard over each other. Some kids at the back were already looking mischievous. I waved at Freya and then took an empty seat at the front, studiously ignoring Summer who was sitting on the other side of the aisle. This was going to be the longest two days of my life.

I sent a message to Oliver.

> Summer is coming on this trip! Send help!

I pocketed my phone and looked straight ahead at the seat in front of me, wondering what the hell I was doing on a coach with the woman I wished I'd never laid eyes on.

The journey wasn't without drama, but fortunately none of it involved me. Two of the children were sick and another one started crying because she missed her mum. The teachers had it covered but I tried to help where I could, changing sick bags and cleaning up. It churned my stomach, but it was no worse than the feeling I already had in my gut about being in close proximity to Summer. We avoided each other, a mutual under-standing perhaps, but I wasn't sure how long it could go on for. At some point we would have to communicate.

By the time the coach pulled up at the campsite, I wasn't

sure who was more eager to alight, me or the children. They all jostled to get off and once we were on firm ground, I looked around at the tents which were mercifully set up already, and prayed that I wouldn't be asked to share with Summer.

Mr Bentley, Freya's class teacher, came over to me. 'Everything okay, Naomi?'

'Fine, thanks, Mr Bentley.'

He smiled. 'You can call me Tom.'

'I'll try but it feels alien to me after only knowing you as Mr Bentley.'

He laughed. 'You'll be pleased to hear that you have your own tent.'

He had no idea just how pleased I was. 'That's great, thank you.'

I was feeling better already. The fresh air, along with a good weather forecast, lifted my spirits. I stood by and watched as the teachers organised the children, allocating them into tents while they waited eagerly to see if they would be with their buddies. When Freya and Luna were put together I wasn't surprised as I suspected they had requested it. Aanya was in another tent and I wondered if Asha had asked the school for her to be separated from Freya. I risked a glance at Summer, but she was beaming at everyone, the sun reflecting off her glossy hair. She already seemed to have the dads wrapped around her little finger. They kept stealing glances at her, no doubt admiring her beautiful floral midi-dress, which was ridiculously impractical for camping. I was wearing combats and a T-shirt and felt like a troll compared to her.

Insecurities were already flooding in. Was Oliver attracted to her? Everyone else seemed to be. Had he been telling the truth when he had insisted that she kissed him and he pulled away? Why had he lied to me? Why was Summer lying to everyone?

I tried to focus on the children. But my dark thoughts were consuming me and I was filled with rage that she had somehow managed to ruin this trip, as well as everything else. Her mere presence was an insult, as well as a reminder that I couldn't escape her. She was there, constantly, haunting me.

Then another thought crept in. If she really was as unpredictable as I thought, was I safe? This was a woman I suspected of breaking into my home, and my dad's. Of watching me through the window and maybe even following me. Of locking her child in her bedroom. I had to be on my guard and I knew that I wouldn't be getting much sleep that night.

Summer was talking to the dads and they both turned to glance at me before quickly looking away. What was she saying to them? What lies was she telling them? But I couldn't march over there and confront her, not in front of nearly sixty children. Then I watched as she took out her phone and took a selfie of herself and the dads. She was sandwiched between them. It would probably be on her Instagram in the next five minutes. I imagined her caption.

Having the best time on the Year 3 camping trip! These guys are awesome!

I turned away in disgust and noticed Mr Bentley watching me curiously. I fixed a smile on my face and went over to ask if he needed any help.

By the time the kids had gone to bed, I was shattered. We'd had a crazy afternoon, kayaking on the river, making a fire, cooking sausages, telling stories, toasting marshmallows. The children had been buzzing and even though they were exhausted, I suspected that their little faces would be poking out of the tents in no time, asking for missing teddy bears or the toilet.

The grown-ups lingered around the fire. Summer was on one side, between the dads again, and I was on the other with Mr Bentley. The other teachers had gone to do a round of the tents, to make sure that everyone was okay. I had stuck close to Mr Bentley – who I kept forgetting to call Tom – because I was now too afraid to talk to the other parents in case they ignored me too. I was worried about what Summer had told them about me.

Exhausted by the constant paranoia, I decided to call it a night. 'I'm going to hit the sack,' I said. 'We've got a busy day ahead.'

Mr Bentley smiled. 'Good call. I won't be far behind you. Sleep well.'

I went to the shower block to brush my teeth and wash my face and then crawled into my tent, thankful that I'd already laid everything out. I snuggled up in my sleeping bag and pulled out my phone. Oliver had messaged to ask if I was okay and I sent him a quick response, saying that I was holding up. And then I closed my eyes and willed sleep to come.

There was no chance. I was in a strange, unfamiliar place, sleeping on the floor, surrounded by dozens of children and acutely aware that Summer was nearby.

For a while, I tuned into quiet murmurs in the distance but soon the campsite fell silent until all I could hear was an owl hooting and the odd rustle. It should have been peaceful, but it was the opposite. I was on edge, my senses heightened. If it wouldn't have mortified Freya, I'd have found her tent and snuck into the sleeping bag with her. But she'd been on top form all day, barely acknowledging me as she had fun with her friends. I wasn't here to cramp her style, I was here to support her if she needed me. Now I wondered if it was the other way around.

The minutes turned into hours and still I couldn't sleep. I was desperate to put my headphones in and listen to an audiobook, but I wanted to hear everything, just in case. What I was waiting for, I wasn't sure. Summer was hardly going to do anything to me here, with all these people around, was she? And what exactly did I think she was going to do to me anyway?

I was spiralling. And the dark, still night wasn't helping. It felt ominous and frightening and I craved the warmth of my bed at home. I scrunched my eyes shut and tried to imagine it. Curled up under the duvet with Oliver, looking up at our beautiful pendant light.

My eyes snapped open. I had been imagining the flat, not the house that we had lived in for months. Why, after all this time, was the flat still my happy place? I closed my eyes again, trying to picture myself in the house, but every time I did all I could see was the dark hooded figure in the garden, staring at me. I could hear the scratching at the front door.

The crunch of a twig had me sitting bolt upright. It had come from right outside the tent. Did I go out and see who it was, or did I stay in my sleeping bag and pretend to be asleep? I felt like a child who had just been told a terrifying ghost story. I listened keenly, my heart thudding.

There it was again! Someone was right outside my tent. I was immobile with fear, adrenaline coursing through my body. I heard them moving and it sounded like they were walking right around my tent, circling me like a predator.

Then I smelled it. The sweet floral scent that I had come to loathe. It was her.

25

I flung myself out of the sleeping bag, landing in an ungainly heap, and yanked the zip of my tent up, forcing my way outside and standing up to confront Summer. My mind and body were spoiling for a fight. But as I looked around in the darkness there was no one there.

I hadn't imagined it. She had been there. Was she trying to scare me, or had she been attempting to get in? I listened keenly for the sound of someone running away, or movement nearby, but there was nothing but silence.

With a final glance I went back inside the tent, zipping it up tightly and climbing back into my sleeping bag. I was shaking with fear. I thought about going to wake Mr Bentley but he would think I was pathetic. All round us seven- and eight-year-olds were sleeping like babies and I was the one getting freaked out. No, I was on my own. I lay there, wide awake, listening for more noises but there were none. Summer had clearly given up and gone back to her own tent.

By dawn I had, as expected, been unable to sleep a wink. It had been the longest, and most terrifying, night of my life and the prospect of having to do it all again was unbearable. I felt like I'd been hit by a ton of bricks. My eyes were dry, my head and limbs heavy, and now I had to go out there and be a good sport. I had to kayak and climb ropes and cheer the children on. Yet all I wanted to do was go back to Barnet, lock my door, and never leave the house again.

I forced myself to get up and climb out of the tent, stretching my arms up into the air and looking around. A few people were starting to emerge and I decided to head to the shower block before the rush. A quick blast of water might wake me up and help me to feel more human. I located my washbag and towel and headed over, slipping into a cubicle and sighing with pleasure when I realised that the water was hot. This was what I needed to shake off the night I'd just had. Well, this and seventeen cups of coffee.

As I turned the shower off and reached for my towel, I heard someone come in and then the sound of a washbag being opened, its contents moved around. I dressed hastily and slipped out, my eyes meeting Summer's in the mirror above the sink. She was putting make-up on and she paused, lipstick hovering in her hand mid-air, as she appraised me.

'Good morning, Naomi,' she said at last. 'How did you sleep?'

'Terribly,' I said, watching her carefully for any sign of guilt.

'Oh no, I'm sorry to hear that. I slept so well. I love being at one with nature.'

How could she do it? How could she chat away to me as though we were friends after all she had put me through? After she had prowled around my tent only hours ago?

I went and stood alongside her, looking at my own reflection in the mirror.

'I heard you,' I said quietly, not meeting her eye.

'Excuse me?'

'I heard you last night.'

Her tinkling laughter echoed around the shower block. 'What are you talking about?'

'Outside my tent.'

'Naomi, I wasn't outside your tent.'

'I smelled you.'

She swivelled her head to look at me. 'You smelled me?'

'Yes, your perfume.'

She put a hand on my arm, and I pulled it away angrily. 'Naomi, are you okay? Do you need some help?'

'Not from you,' I snapped. 'You may have fooled everyone else, but you haven't fooled me. I know all about you, Summer.'

She was still looking at me curiously. 'What do you mean?'

'I mean, I know. Everything.'

She was silent for a moment and I wondered if I'd hit a nerve. But then she said, in a steady voice, 'Why don't you like me, Naomi?'

I stared at her incredulously. How did she have the gall to ask me that? When everyone else had asked me that question I'd tried to sugar-coat my answer. But I was well past that now.

'Because you're a lying, manipulative fraud who is trying to ruin my life.'

'I've never been anything but nice to you.'

'How can you say that? You tried to imitate me. You accused my daughter of bullying. You stole all my friends. You tried it on with my husband.'

She was infuriatingly calm. 'Naomi, I'm really worried about you. I think you need help.'

'How dare you? I don't need help. It's you who needs help.'

'I think you've created this fantasy world, Naomi, where

you're convinced these things are true. But they're not true, honey, it's all in your head. I promise you.'

I wanted to strangle her. 'Are you saying you didn't kiss my husband?'

Her face dropped and her eyes lowered. It was the perfect act. 'He kissed me, Naomi. And I was so upset about it, I didn't know what to do. I wanted to tell you, but I wasn't sure if you would believe me. I know how much you dislike me.'

'I dislike you because you tried to kiss my husband. Did you break into my house too? And my dad's?'

'Naomi, what on earth are you talking about?'

'Did you steal my dressing gown and earrings?'

'What earrings?'

'The red rubies. I saw you wearing them at the Christmas Fair.'

Her eyes moved to my earlobes, and she frowned. 'Those red rubies?'

Damn. I'd forgotten I was wearing them. 'I saw you wearing them,' I insisted.

She tried to take my arm again and this time I pushed her away forcefully and she fell back against the sink. 'Get off me!' I screamed.

'What's going on?' I turned to see one of the female teachers looking at us in shock.

Summer immediately crumpled. 'I'm so sorry, I don't want to cause a fuss.'

'What's happening here?'

I looked from the teacher to Summer. How did I even begin to explain it?

'It's nothing,' I said meekly.

'It doesn't look like nothing. Do we have a problem here, ladies?'

'I don't have a problem,' Summer said, her voice perfectly contrite. 'I just wanted to come here to support the children. To make sure they had fun.'

The teacher turned to me, and I reddened. 'That's what I want too.'

She gave us both a shrewd look. 'Do I need to call Sharon?'

'No,' Summer and I answered in unison. At least we agreed on one thing.

'Well listen, sort it out, okay? We're meant to be setting an example to the children.'

She gave us one last glare and then retreated. I had the strong suspicion that Sharon would be hearing about this when we got back and she'd already given me one warning. And, as always, I would look like the one in the wrong.

I furiously packed my washbag and turned to leave. But I wasn't done yet.

I spun around. 'I'll catch you out eventually, Summer. Just like they did in Devon.'

It had the desired impact. Her face immediately clouded over and she looked angrier than I'd ever seen her. For a few seconds, Summer finally dropped her mask.

'What did you say?' she demanded.

I decided to call her bluff. 'I know what happened in Devon. I know everything.'

The mask reappeared as quickly as it had vanished. 'I have no idea what you are talking about. I tried to be nice to you. I tried to help you. But it's clear you're not interested.'

'Damn right I'm not.'

'Fine.' Summer sighed and turned away. 'Have it your way. But don't say I didn't try.'

* * *

Somehow, I made it through the day. Summer and I were put into separate groups and I suspected that the female teacher had done it deliberately. I was with Freya and the only silver lining to this trip was watching her have a whale of a time. She was so brave, my little girl, tackling the activities with gusto, more animated than I had seen her in ages. Clearly the fresh air was good for her and I made a mental note to enrol her into Beavers when we got home.

But I was tired, so very tired. The adrenaline from my argument with Summer had left my body and I was struggling to keep it together. By the time we all gathered for the evening activities, I thought I might pass out in front of the fire.

Luckily the children were exhausted too and when the teachers told them it was bedtime, there were only a handful of protests. Most of the kids went off to their tents without any arguments. I cuddled Freya goodnight and then stood up to make my way to my own tent.

As I was leaving, I felt a hand on my arm. It was Mr Bentley.

'Is everything okay, Naomi?'

'Yes, fine, thanks. I'm just tired.'

'It's just I heard there was a row this morning. And you've been quiet all day.'

I glanced over at Summer who was laughing at something one of the dads had said. I'd kept my distance all evening, refusing to engage in conversation with her. And with all the children acting as a buffer between us, I didn't think it had looked obvious. But it was clear that the teacher who had walked in on our argument had shared it with the others.

'I'm sorry about that. It won't happen again.'

'I know there have been some issues with Luna and Freya,' he told me quietly. 'And I imagine that tensions might be high as a result. But it's all resolved now. They've sorted it out.'

I leaned in towards him. 'Did you ever see Freya bullying Luna?'

'Not personally, no.'

'What about the other way around?'

Poor Mr Bentley looked decidedly uncomfortable. 'This isn't really appropriate, Naomi. If you want to make an appointment through the school office when we're back home—'

'Of course,' I interrupted. 'I'm sorry. I didn't mean to put you on the spot.'

I felt a pair of eyes on me and I turned again to see Summer watching me and her mask had slipped again. The expression on her face was one of pure hatred and it sent shivers up my spine. I was not safe here any more, I realised with a sudden clarity.

'Did you see that?' I said to Mr Bentley.

'See what?'

'The way she looked at me?'

'The way who looked at you?'

'Summer.'

Perplexed, he turned to Summer and then back at me. 'She's not looking at you.'

'She was, she...' My voice petered out. What was the point? Everything I did made things worse. Every word I uttered reinforced the negative perception Summer had created of me. To everyone else I was losing my mind and accusing her of things that weren't real.

I would have to be on my guard all night. My body ached from the lack of sleep and the day's exertions but my mind was alert, and I was afraid.

'Never mind,' I said. 'I'll see you tomorrow.'

'Will you be okay?'

I couldn't even muster a smile. 'I'll be fine.'

I crawled into my tent, checked it was closed tightly and got into my sleeping bag. As I lay there, staring into the darkness and listening to voices in the distance, I was counting down the hours until this was all over and I could go home. I thought I had another long night ahead of me but after a while I felt my eyes drooping, sleep unexpectedly pulling me down. I tried to resist, but the urge was too strong and eventually I capitulated to the blissful oblivion.

When I awoke again, it was the middle of the night. I had probably been asleep for a few hours but there was no hint of the dawn light yet. I was groggy at first, unaware of what had woken me, but then I heard a noise outside and I was instantly on alert. I scrambled up into a sitting position and looked around for my torch, which I'd placed by my sleeping bag. I turned it on and waved it around and that's when I saw a shadow pass by the tent.

I didn't hesitate. I unzipped the tent and hurried out, standing up as quickly as I could and coming face to face with Summer. As my pulse began to race, I instinctively glanced down at her hands, looking for any sign of a weapon, but she wasn't holding anything.

'Hello, Naomi.' Her voice was devoid of its usual warmth. 'I think we need to talk.'

26

I looked at the tents surrounding us, full of sleeping children. 'Not here.'

'Follow me.'

Summer started walking away from the campsite towards the river, using her torch to light up the uneven path ahead. As I followed with my own torch, I questioned whether this was a wise idea but curiosity, and indignation, had got the better of me. Finally, Summer wanted to talk and I suspected it was because of what I'd said about Devon. I had provoked her and although I'd been lying when I said I knew what had happened, my insinuation had been enough. Summer was afraid of being exposed. So what did she want? To cut a deal? To persuade me that no one would believe me anyway? Or to silence me?

I was afraid but I kept walking. This felt like a final show-down, and although I didn't know what was going to happen, I wanted it to be over. I could no longer live like this, and it seemed nor could Summer. Logic told me that Summer was not going to attempt to harm me in the middle of a primary school camping trip and I clung tightly to this knowledge. But it was cold and it was dark, and neither of these facts alleviated the tingling in my body.

When we reached the river, Summer sat down on a bench overlooking the water and I hesitated before taking a seat next to her. For a moment we didn't speak but the tension was electric in the gloomy night air. Neither of us knew where to start.

Finally, she said, 'How do you know about Devon?'

I stared into the beam of my torch. 'Luna told some of the children in her class.'

I regretted it as soon as the words were out. Now I'd got poor Luna into trouble, and I had no idea what the ramifications would be for her.

'That damned child.'

I looked at her in horror. 'She's your daughter, Summer.'

'She's nothing but trouble. Always has been.'

I couldn't believe what I was hearing. I cursed myself for not bringing my phone along so that I could secretly record Summer. We were embarking on the most critical conversation, the one that finally exposed her, but without any evidence would anyone believe me?

I decided to change tack. 'Why did you do it, Summer?'

I was talking about her behaviour towards me, but she clearly misunderstood, assuming that I was referring to whatever had happened in Devon.

'I did nothing wrong. And Luna had no right to tell people I did.'

I considered my next words carefully. 'But you still left.'

Summer ignored me. 'Luna doesn't know what she's talking about. It's her stupid father, poisoning her against me. Trying to win her over.'

But Summer had said Luna's father wasn't interested in

being involved in his daughter's life. So why would he do that? Something wasn't adding up, but I had to tread carefully because I didn't want Summer to know that I was bluffing.

'You used to call yourself Christina. Why did you change your name?'

If she was surprised that I knew this, she didn't show it. She shrugged. 'Christina was my stage name. I used it for a while but in the end I reverted back to my real name, Summer.'

'Why are you trying to ruin my life?'

She fixed her gaze on me and, even in the darkness, her expression sent shivers up my spine. 'I really tried to be friends with you, Naomi.'

I almost laughed. 'By turning everyone against me?'

'You did that to yourself, not me.'

'You told lies about me. And Freya.'

'Because you forced me to.'

I was aghast. 'How did I force you to?'

'You made it painfully clear that you didn't like me. And you were threatening my new start. I knew you were close to the others and if you told them to avoid me, they would. So really, I had no choice but to exclude you instead. It could have been perfect, Naomi, if only you'd let it. I admired you so much. We could have been so close.'

This woman was out of her mind. I called her bluff again. 'Is that why you stole my dressing gown and earrings? Because you wanted to be friends with me?'

If she denied it, there was nothing I could do. After all, both items had turned up again in my house. I waited for her response, wondering whether she would admit to what I suspected.

'You have no idea how lucky you are, Naomi. You have a

beautiful home, beautiful children, a beautiful husband, beautiful things. And you take it all for granted.'

It wasn't an admission of guilt, but it wasn't a denial either, so I pushed on. 'How did you get into my house?'

'Oh, it was easy. I took the spare keys from Asha's house when we were at a playdate. They were labelled with your name and everything. A bit careless of her, really.'

I closed my eyes and exhaled. I finally had the truth. But why was she telling me? Why was she giving her confession so easily? Was it because she knew there would be no record of this conversation? Or was she simply tired of living the lie?

'Why, if you stole my things, did you then give them back?'

'I didn't.'

'I found them in my house.'

'Yes.' Summer shook her head, almost sadly. 'Freya put them there.'

'Freya?'

'That's right.'

I was struggling to comprehend it. Freya knew about this? What else did she know? And why on earth was my little girl protecting Summer?

'I don't understand,' I said, perplexed.

'When you came over for that playdate after Christmas, the little madams were playing in my bedroom. Freya recognised them and when Luna realised what had happened, she made Freya promise to put them back and not tell you.'

'Why would she do that?'

Summer's demeanour changed in a flash. 'Because she's self-righteous little meddler. And she had to be punished. She had to know that her behaviour was unacceptable.'

Understanding dawned. 'That's why you pulled her out of school.'

'The other kids were turning her against me. I should never have let her go to school, I should have kept her at home like I did in Devon. So other people couldn't poison her mind.'

Kept her trapped at home more like. I remembered what Sebastian had told his mother about Luna. It's like she's never been to school. He had been right. The poor girl had been denied it, not because of her mother's well-researched decision to home-school her child but because of her madness. No wonder Luna had struggled so much when she started at North Hill. Or why she had begged me to help her when I saw her looking out of her bedroom window that day.

'Did you lock her in her bedroom, Summer?'

'Oh, don't be so PC, Naomi. Parents have to discipline their children. It's the only way they learn. She was hardly starved, was she? I feed her, I clothe her. But that time she had to learn. You see, Luna isn't like your children. She's a miserable, defiant little thing. Freya is such a good child. And Bella, well she's special, isn't she? I've always dreamed of a daughter like Bella.'

She had a beautiful daughter of her own and yet she was jealous of mine. Poor, poor Luna. I wondered if the little girl knew how her mother felt. She probably did. Any shred of hostility I harboured towards Luna for the way she had first treated Freya was long gone. She'd had no experience of social-ising and I had no doubt she'd been spurred on by her mother too.

'Luna is a wonderful, clever, delightful little girl.'

Summer snorted. 'She's a pain in my backside. Like her dad.'

I couldn't reason with this delusional woman. 'So why did you let her go back to school?'

'I had no choice, did I?' Summer snapped. 'When the police came round, thanks to you sticking your nose in, my hand was forced. I had to show everyone that Luna was just fine, thank you very much. And actually, I found that I missed the camaraderie of school myself. Asha, Richard and so on. Such a great gang, don't you think?'

I used to think it. But they had turned against me so easily and they had allowed themselves to be manipulated by Summer. And the relief I felt about finally uncovering the truth about her was short-lived because I also knew that she would deny everything.

'What about the damage you've caused, Summer? You used our children as pawns. Did you convince Luna to make up those lies about Freya?'

'Luna didn't like Freya. Not at first. She wanted to be friends with Aanya, and Freya kept getting in the way. I made a suggestion, that was all. It was her choice to act on it.'

'Are you listening to yourself? You persuaded a seven-year-old girl to turn everyone against her classmate. To accuse her of bullying.'

'Well, it all worked out in the end, didn't it. They're besties now.' Summer's voice dripped with disapproval. 'Luna felt sorry for Freya and decided to stop heeding my advice. More fool her, but she made her choice. And now, Naomi, it's time for you to do the same.'

Her words chilled me. 'What do you mean?'

'You can stop all this nonsense. We'll return to the campsite as a united front and we can get on with our lives. We can be the best of friends and we'll have so much fun together. All will be forgotten, and I'll make sure you're brought back into the fold.'

'And if I don't?'

'Then you'll continue to make life very difficult for yourself. And your daughter.'

It was tempting. I could never be friends with Summer but I could go double agent; pretend that I wanted to bury the hatchet until I had the proof I needed to expose her. Did I want to, though? I was exhausted and I just wanted my life back. Suddenly, I yearned to go home. Not to the flat but to our house, to Oliver and Bella. To walk through our yellow front door and be back in the arms of my family.

That made me think about the mini replica of our home that I had seen in Luna's bedroom. It wasn't a coincidence, it couldn't be. There was still something that I was missing.

'Luna had a doll's house,' I said. 'What happened to it?'

'Excuse me?'

'The doll's house with the yellow door and the window boxes.'

Summer was quiet for a moment before speaking. 'It was a gift from someone. Someone very special. I've had it for years, although it's had a few refurbs over its time.'

'Who gave it to you?'

'It doesn't matter.'

But suddenly finding out what happened to the doll's house was of critical importance. 'What happened to it?' I repeated.

I was shocked to see Summer wiping her eyes. 'It broke. I don't want to talk about it any more.'

Summer had been candid about everything else, so it made no sense to me that she'd be reticent about this.

'Why did you decorate it to match my house?'

'I don't want to talk about it!' It was the first time she had raised her voice.

My mind was on overdrive as I tried to figure it out. Why had Summer held on to a children's toy for so long? Why was she so emotional about it? And that made me think about the break-in at my dad's and the missing photos of me as a child.

'Why did you steal the photo album from my dad's house?'

She didn't respond at first, and then she said, 'How well do you know your father?'

'Very well. We're extremely close.'

'He'd never lie to you?'

I shook my head vehemently. She wasn't driving a wedge between Dad and I too. 'No.'

'Well, I'm sorry to tell you that he has. He's lied to you your whole life.'

I snapped. 'What the hell are you talking about?'

She looked at me contritely. 'I'm so sorry to be the one to tell you this, and I don't do it lightly, but that man is not your biological father.'

The world began to close in on me and I involuntarily put a hand on my chest. Was she lying? It was highly probable, but why? And how would she even know that? I didn't know whether to scream, shout, deny it, hit her or cry, but my composure was long gone. I was falling apart, my life shattering around me and I was playing right into her hand.

But suddenly it all clicked into place and I knew, with a brutal stab of foreboding, that she wasn't lying to me. Summer had not chosen me at random. She had not moved to Barnet by coincidence. We had history, only I hadn't known about it. And I was about to discover what it was. I needed to know but I dreaded what I was about to hear.

'If he's not my father, then who is?'

'I don't know, I'm afraid. But I do know who your mother is.'

'I know who my mother is too.' I thought of Mum, the woman I had worshipped all my life and still missed with every inch of my body.

'You think you do, but you don't. Because the woman you thought was your mother lied to you too.'

'For God's sake, Summer, stop messing about. What are you trying to tell me?'

Summer hesitated before reaching into her coat pocket and pulling out a couple of photos, directing the beam of her torch so that I could see them. I recognised one of them because it had been in the family album that went missing. It was a picture of me as a toddler, sitting on a ride-on car. My hair looked as if had been cut with the help of a mixing bowl placed on top of my head and my cheeks were chubby and flushed.

My eyes moved to the second photo. It was a dated photo of a woman I didn't recognise. She was slender and her long brown hair blew in the wind as she gazed into the distance. I think she intended to look wistful, but my immediate thought was that she seemed sad.

I pointed at the photo. 'Who is that woman?'

'Your mother.'

I stared at the photo, trying to keep myself from losing it completely. Clinging to a life raft to stop myself from drowning in the tidal wave Summer had sent my way.

Then Summer's next words punctured it beyond repair. 'She's also my mother.'

27

I slumped, a shattered woman. Summer patted my arm gently, as though I'd fallen over and hurt my knee. My life was collapsing and yet she was serene again, like she had just told me the weather forecast rather than the fact that my whole life was a lie.

'Are you trying to tell me that we're sisters?'

She beamed. 'That's right. You've got it. We're half-sisters.'

'You're wrong. This is all lies. How could you do this?'

She ignored me as she looked down at the photo. 'Her name is Sandra, by the way. And, in case you're wondering, Sandra is not a good person.'

'That is not my mother. My mother is dead.'

'Your adopted mother is dead, yes. Your biological mother is very much alive and kicking, unfortunately.'

'Why are you telling me all of this?'

She looked at me quizzically. 'Because you asked.'

'I don't believe you.'

'Yes, you do.'

'If it is true, and I still think you're lying, how do you know?'

'Because she told me. Sandra's a drunk and when she's had a few, the truth comes out. I mean, it literally pours out of her. You can't shut the damned woman up.'

'So were you adopted too?'

'No. Sadly for me, I had to stay with her.'

'I don't understand.'

'You're a bit slow off the mark, aren't you, Naomi? And I thought you were the intelligent one. Okay, here's how it went. Our mother, the useless waster, got pregnant with you. God knows who the father was, she probably didn't. Anyway, social services took you away and off you went to live with the perfect parents, where you had the perfect upbringing.'

'And you?'

'Well, here's the fun of it. A few years later she fell pregnant with me. And this time she convinced social services that she had turned her life around. She persuaded them that she had stopped drinking and that she was ready to be a mother. And the idiots believed her.'

'So they let her keep you.'

'That's right. So you see, Naomi, you got to escape but I was stuck there.'

The doll's house. The beautiful family home Summer never got to live in, but I did.

'And that's why you hate me?'

'Oh, Naomi, you've got this all wrong. I don't hate you. I love you. We're sisters.'

I stood up, distraught, bordering on hysterical. 'Why are you doing this, Summer? Why are you telling me this pack of lies? Why are you ruining my life like this?'

'I only ever wanted to get to know you, Naomi. For us to become close. I never meant to tell you the truth, I wanted to protect you. But yet again, you made this happen, you forced my hand. And now I hope we can draw a line under all this.'

She had just ripped my world apart and she wanted to draw a line under it? I had to get out of here. I had to speak to Dad. I imagined his gentle voice on the phone, telling me that of course Summer was wrong.

I turned to leave, no longer wanting to be anywhere near this vile woman. But she reached out and grabbed me, her fingers wrapping themselves tightly around my arm.

'Get off me,' I shouted, trying to pull away.

'We're not done yet, Naomi. You haven't made your choice.'

'I need to speak to Dad.' Summer was surprisingly strong and I couldn't free myself.

'You can leave when you've made your choice.'

'Get off me. I'm warning you.'

'Stop being so unreasonable. I've asked you a simple question and I want an answer.'

'Here's your answer,' I screamed, my shrill voice carrying over the silent air as I shoved my torch full beam into her face to distract her so I could get away. 'You are a crazy, dangerous and manipulative fantasist and I never want to see you again.'

The torchlight exposed her anger. But her voice was steady. 'Naomi, I'm disappointed in you. I thought you were better than this. But you've made your choice.'

She reached into her pocket and I saw the glint of something silver. Recoiling in horror I realised that it was a knife. Did she mean to stab me, out here, just metres away from where our children slept? I used the full force of my fear and rage to push her away but she dug the knife into my side and I felt it pierce my skin. I froze in terror.

'Don't try anything silly, or you'll regret it.'

As I felt a warm, trickling sensation in my side, I didn't

doubt her. It was terrifyingly clear that there were no limits to what Summer was prepared to do.

She started pulling me in the direction of the river and I had no choice but to let her lead me, my eyes glued to the knife pushing into my side.

'You're going to go for a nice swim now, Naomi,' she explained, as though I was a child on the way to the local pool. 'And in the morning, when they find you, everyone will remember just how strangely you've been acting recently. How out of character.'

I started to struggle but she pushed the knife into me again, not enough to seriously wound me but as a warning. I was trying to think straight, to come up with a plan, but I was petrified and my mind was a mess. I would not go down without a fight but I had to work out how to get myself out of this without ending up with a knife in my stomach.

'I've changed my mind,' I said, thinking on my feet. 'I want us to be friends.'

'It's too late for that.'

'But we're sisters!'

'Yes, we are. But I'm not sure you're a very good sister, Naomi.'

We were getting dangerously close to the water's edge and the river looked ominous. I was running out of options, my mind rapidly formulating an escape. I was a fairly strong swimmer and already I was envisaging going underwater and then swimming across to the other side, climbing out and going for help. How long could I hold my breath for? Would she see me come up for air and what would she do if she did? How strong was the current? And would I survive the cold? But I was a fighter and I would keep swimming, even when I couldn't feel my limbs. This would not end tonight, no matter what Summer thought. She was not going to win.

'I'm so sorry it has come to this, Naomi,' she said, sounding genuinely remorseful. 'I promise you that I wanted things to be different. If I'm honest, I expected more of you.'

'You're crazy,' was all I could manage.

'Don't worry. I'll look after Freya and Bella. And Oliver too. They'll be safe with me.'

As I tried one last time to move away from the knife, I lost my balance and fell backwards. The icy cold water immediately sent my body into shock, and I flailed, trying to find my footing so that I could push myself back up again. The water was deep but the current wasn't strong and I eventually felt the ground beneath my feet and launched myself up, gasping for air.

She was waiting for me. And before I could turn and start swimming she reached down and pushed my shoulders, forcing me under the water. I scrambled, feeling for the bottom of the riverbed again but I was disorientated and freezing. My clothes felt like lead weights, pulling me down. Finally, I touched the floor and I pushed with all my might. The surface was centimetres away and I was feeling dizzy, my body desperate for oxygen.

My head pushed through the surface and was immediately plunged back down again, and again. I kept on fighting, using everything I had to get her hands off my shoulders and to push myself back up again. My survival instinct was in full force and, realising it wasn't going to work, I reached up and grabbed her arms, pulling her down with me until I heard the splash as she entered the water. I took advantage of her momentary shock and confusion to release myself from her grip and I used my legs to kick her away from me, aware that she might still be holding the knife. It was too dark to see anything and I had no idea where the torches were any more, so I had to trust my other senses. I turned and began to swim and then I felt her hand around my ankle, pulling me back. I kicked out but then her hand wrapped itself around my other ankle and I couldn't get her off, no matter how hard I tried. My lungs were screaming for air and I knew that if I didn't go up soon, my body would shut down. In a flash, I swivelled myself around, scrambling in the blackness until I touched something solid. I didn't know what part of her body it was but I pushed down with all my might, and felt the grip loosen on my ankles.

I swam upwards, gasping as I hit the surface but then she came up next to me, the moonlight reflecting off her hair. I immediately reached for her shoulders and pushed her down, using every ounce of strength I had. I didn't know what I was doing, all I knew was that I had to survive. I had to get out of this river. She was struggling, but my grip was firm and I kept on pushing, on and on, using the last remaining strength I had in my legs to keep myself from going under too. Then suddenly I felt her resistance begin to slacken.

I let go and scrambled for the water's edge, gripping on to a rock and trying to pull myself out. As I looked up, I saw lights in the wood, darting left and right and a few seconds later some dark figures appeared. Thank God. Help was finally here.

'Help me,' I screamed. 'I'm here!'

A figure loomed above me and then a hand stretched out. I grasped it and let myself be pulled out of the water, collapsing on to the grass and stones and gasping for breath.

'What the hell is going on? Are you okay?'

I immediately recognised Mr Bentley's voice.

'She tried to kill me,' I managed to say between breaths. 'She tried to drown me.'

'Who tried to drown you?'

'Summer.'

'Summer? Where is she?'

'She's in the river.'

He didn't hesitate. As I curled up on the floor, shivering in my sodden clothes, the stones grazing my frozen skin and my teeth chattering, Mr Bentley jumped into the river. Two people appeared beside me, calling out to him to be careful, and I realised it was the other teachers, including the woman who'd caught Summer and I arguing that morning.

'Help me,' I whispered, desperate for a towel or some warm clothes to stave off the painful chill that had taken over my body. But either they didn't hear me or they ignored me. They kept their gazes fixed firmly on the river, using their torches to light up the water.

'I can't find her,' I heard Mr Bentley shout. 'I'm going under again.'

I didn't want them to find her. My darkest hope, while fleeting, was intense. She had tried to kill me and she deserved to die.

Then I heard a commotion and the two other teachers rushed forward. I watched from the floor, immobile, as they pulled Summer out. Her eyes were closed, her wet hair stuck to her face and her skin pale in the moonlight.

'Is she breathing?' someone said.

'I don't know. Call an ambulance.'

Mr Bentley heaved himself out of the water, landing beside me. I turned to face him, my lips too frozen to speak. He clambered up and rushed over to Summer, taking her wrist and feeling for a pulse before starting chest compressions. It was as though I was invisible. I watched on, exhausted. My body was beginning to shut down, my eyelids drooping and oblivion offering blissful relief. I had no strength left to resist and I wasn't sure I even wanted to. I craved the nothingness. Then I saw a light in the distance. I was oddly calm now, almost peaceful, as I walked towards the light, feeling the warm glow dry my clothes and my skin. When I reached it, I turned around and saw Oliver and the girls watching me, and behind them was Summer.

'No!' I called, realising my mistake. I tried desperately to go back but I was being pulled in. The last thing I saw before I fell unconscious was Summer standing with my family, smiling.

28

The next thing I became aware of was an intermittent beeping noise. I was confused, disorientated, and my mouth was dry. Was I hungover? My head felt heavy, like I'd had too much red wine. For a few moments I wondered if I'd been out the night before, and then it hit me with full force. The argument with Summer, falling into the river. Being pulled out by someone. Seeing a strange light and being compelled towards it. Fighting to resist.

Was I dead? I tried to move my hands and toes. I couldn't tell what belonged to my body and what didn't. I wasn't cold any more, though. And I didn't feel wet. Something was covering my face, and I felt a strong urge to rip it off. Stay calm, I warned myself.

I slowly opened my eyes and saw someone staring at me. I squinted, trying to make out the blurry face. I didn't recognise it. Gradually it came into focus and then I realised where I was. The face I was looking at belonged to a nurse and the thing on my face was an oxygen mask.

'Naomi, can you hear me? Blink if you can.'

I blinked and the nurse nodded, satisfied. 'Well done, Naomi. You're in hospital. You had an accident, but you're going to be fine. Your husband's on the way.'

I was slowly regaining control of my limbs and I lifted my arm. It felt like a dead weight but I managed to manoeuvre it to my face, pulling at the mask.

The nurse leaned over to help me, lifting it from my face.

'Summer,' I croaked.

'Your friend is okay. She's down the hall.'

'She... she tried... she tried to...'

It was too much effort to get the words out. My hand dropped to my side again and I felt myself being pulled back down into sleep.

When I awoke again, light was streaming through the windows and I felt more alert. It was less effort to open my eyes, no longer a battle to move my fingers. I turned my head to the side and saw Oliver sitting in a chair, staring at his phone. He must have sensed my gaze because he looked up, dropping his phone onto the chair and taking my hand.

'Naomi, thank God. Are you okay?'

I opened my mouth and realised that I was no longer wearing the mask. 'The kids.'

'Bella is with a friend and Freya is with a teacher. How are you feeling?'

'Better, I think.' I tried to sit up and felt a sharp, unexpected stabbing pain in my stomach. Then I remembered it was where Summer had cut me with the knife. Oliver took my sides, gently helping me up and then he passed me a glass of water. I took a few sips.

'Naomi, what the hell happened?'

I swallowed the water, which stuck to my dry throat, and tried to get the words out. 'Summer. She tried to drown me.'

'What?'

'She says she's my sister. She says I'm adopted.'

Oliver pulled a face. 'That's ridiculous. No way.'

'I need to speak to Dad.'

His expression rang alarm bells. 'You need to speak to someone else first.'

Surely, he didn't mean Summer? 'Who?'

'The police. They're outside.'

'Good.' I nodded. 'Send them in.'

'There's no rush, you've only just woken up.' Oliver looked up at the door nervously and then back at me. 'Naomi, be careful what you say. I think we should get a solicitor.'

'Why do I need a solicitor? Summer's the one who needs a solicitor.'

Oliver was so clearly uncomfortable that he was making me nervous. 'I overheard some of the teachers talking. They think that you tried to drown Summer.'

'That's ridiculous. She had a knife, Oliver, I've got a wound in my stomach.'

He gripped my hand. 'I believe you. You know I believe you. But you have to be careful. You don't know what she's said. We already know we can't trust her.'

'You think she'll say it was me?'

'She might do. And it will be your word against hers.'

'What about my knife injury?'

'She could say it was caused by the rocks near the river.'

I considered this, dread pouring over my exhausted body. Summer had a successful track record of manipulating people, so why would it be any different now? The teacher would say she saw me pushing Summer in the shower block. Even Sharon had witnessed me shouting at her before. My friends had accused me of stalking her.

The walls began to close in on me.

But no. This was not fair. I was the innocent party and I had a mark on my stomach to prove it. She would not get away with this. I would tell the police about Devon, warn them to investigate. I would make sure the doctors confirmed that I had a knife injury. Summer had gone too far to talk herself out of it this time. Damn it, why hadn't I recorded our conversation?

I slumped back against the pillow and tears began to spill out as I considered the battle that lay ahead of me. I was determined to win it, but I knew that my opponent would not play fair and that was what terrified me.

Oliver leaned in and hugged me. 'I'm here for you, Nims. We'll get through this.'

'I need to speak to Dad,' I managed. 'I need to know if what she said is true.'

'We'll speak to him soon, but you need to rest now. Anyway, I'm almost certain that she was lying. Your dad wouldn't have kept something like that from you.'

'I don't know, at the time I sensed she was telling the truth.'

'She's a compulsive liar, Nims. You can't trust anything she says.'

But I couldn't let it go. 'I need to speak to him now, Ol.'

Oliver looked reluctant but he reached for his phone. 'Okay. I'll call him.'

Before he'd even unlocked his phone, the door opened and I saw a nurse lead two uniformed officers in. My moment of reckoning had arrived, and I wasn't sure I was ready for it.

'Five minutes,' the nurse told them. 'She's still recovering.'

They nodded before introducing themselves to me. 'Mrs Burton,' the female officer said. 'Can you remember what happened?'

'Yes, I remember everything.'

Oliver interjected. 'I think we should wait until we have a solicitor present.'

The officer fixed her steady gaze on him. 'We only want to ask your wife a few questions about what happened last night,' she said.

Oliver looked at me uncertainly and I nodded. I had nothing to hide and I wanted to make that crystal clear from the start. With a hoarse voice, that grew gradually stronger, I told them everything. About the break-ins, which Summer had admitted to, the allegations about us being sisters, the knife in my stomach and finally the moment when she tried to kill me.

I have no idea if they believed me. Their expressions remained stoic, with only the smallest, occasional raise of an eyebrow as my story unravelled. But it was true. No matter how far-fetched and extreme it sounded, every word I uttered was the truth.

By the time I had finished I was dog-tired, and the nurse was hovering by the door. The officers stood up and thanked me for my time. And then they were gone.

'You did great, babe,' Oliver said.

'Do you think they believed me?'

He couldn't hide his trepidation. 'I don't know.'

'You believe me, right?'

'Of course I do. I've already told you that.'

'What about everyone else?'

'We'll make them. We'll do whatever it takes. Do you still want to talk to your dad?'

But my conversation with the police had depleted my energy. I shook my head and closed my eyes, ready to let sleep take me again.

The next time I woke up, the room was dark. I turned, expecting to see Oliver, but the chair was empty. He must have gone to collect Freya. She was probably beside herself, the poor girl. And what about Luna? Who was looking after her?

I sat up with a wince, hoping a nurse would come in. I didn't want to be on my own, surrounded by sick and dying people. I felt alone and afraid as I recounted my conversation with the police. They had probably already spoken to Summer too and I feared what she had told them. For a moment, on the edge of the river, I had wished her dead and now I felt culpable for even thinking it. Was wishing someone dead a crime? If so, I was as guilty as charged.

And what about now? Did I still wish that she had drowned?

No. I wouldn't wish anyone dead, not in my right mind. And anyway, Summer had to face the consequences for what she had done to me. I needed to believe that justice would prevail. But the fear was still nagging at me, haunting me. What if she gets away with this?

In the middle of the night, my insecurities were like evil monsters. She had lied her way out of so many things already and she had turned an entire community against me. There were no witnesses to our argument by the river and the odds were in her favour. Was there seriously a chance that I could be arrested for this? Attempted murder carried a long prison sentence. I could be locked away for years and I wouldn't survive it. It would destroy me and rip our family apart. The children would be damaged beyond repair. Oliver and I would probably divorce. He might even get together with Summer.

Stop it. I was spiralling. I wanted to go home, to the house that I had moaned about for months. Now my gripes seemed trivial and pathetic. I hadn't realised how lucky I was. How privileged to have a beautiful family and home. I would never take it for granted again.

Where was Oliver? I prayed for him to appear, to lie on the bed next to me and put his arm around me. But he was probably with the girls, and that was where he needed to be.

I wondered if Oliver had called Dad to tell him what had happened to me. Could I still call him Dad if he wasn't my father? I had to speak to him and I considered discharging myself and going over there right away. But I wasn't strong enough to leave yet and, anyway, the police might think I was absconding. Oh Jesus, how had I ended up in this situation?

Summer. She was responsible for all of this, and she was somewhere in this hospital. Should I go and find her? Demand to know what she had told the police or beg her to tell the truth? The corridor was quiet and I reckoned I could sneak out without alerting a nurse. But I could end up making things even worse, because she would probably then tell the police I tried to coerce her.

This was hell. And most horrendous thing about it was that I knew it was far from over.

* * *

By the following morning, Oliver still hadn't appeared and I was in bits. I tried to eat some breakfast but the toast felt like cardboard as I forced it down my throat.

'When can I go home?' I asked the nurse.

'When the doctor has been to see you. He should be doing his rounds shortly.'

'Do you know where my husband is?'

'I'm sure he'll be here soon.'

I was so afraid of what lay ahead. Every time I heard a movement in the corridor, I expected the police to appear with handcuffs. I located my phone and started googling solicitors. I had no idea where to start. I felt another yearning for Mum, wishing that she was here with me. But she wasn't my mum. Or was she? With each hour that passed, I began to doubt Summer's outlandish story even more. There was only one way to find out and I needed to do it now.

With trembling fingers, I called Dad.

'Hello, love, how are you?'

I could tell from Dad's relaxed tone that Oliver hadn't filled him in. This was no time for pleasantries, and I cut straight to it. 'Dad, I need to ask you something.'

'Of course, is everything okay?'

'Am I adopted?'

I waited for his bemusement, amusement or even annoyance but none came. Nothing came at all and the longer the silence stretched out, the more fearful I became.

Finally, he spoke. 'Where has this come from, love?'

'Please, just tell me, Dad.'

He sighed and I imagined him sitting in his favourite armchair. 'I'll tell you everything but first you need to tell me why you're asking me this.'

'I've met a woman who claims to be my sister. I think she's the same person who broke into your house and stole the photo album.'

'This woman, what's her name?'

'Summer.'

'And what has she told you?'

'That my birth mother was forced to give me up but then she had Summer a few years later and kept her. Dad, what the hell is going on?'

His voice was thick with emotion. 'I'm so sorry that you had to find out this way.'

I froze in horror. Summer had told me the truth. My whole

life was a lie. 'How could you keep this from me?' I asked, my voice barely above a whisper.

'It was different back then. There was none of this openness and transparency that you have around adoption these days. And you were just a baby when we got you, we'd only missed the first few months of your life. You were ours. You always have been.'

'Except I'm not.'

'Yes, you are. Never forget that. You are ours.'

'I'm not.' My voice was rising now and I noticed a passing nurse pause outside my door.

I was too shocked to cry but our conversation had the opposite effect on Dad. He was sobbing now and part of me wanted to comfort him, to tell him it was okay. But I couldn't do it. He had deceived me and so had my mother. The woman I had idolised.

'Your birth mum wasn't in a good way when she had you,' he continued. 'She was an alcoholic and a drug user. You were taken away from her and put into care soon after you were born. Your mum and I were desperate for a child. We'd tried and tried but we hadn't been blessed with a baby, and so we had applied to adopt. When they called to tell us about you, we knew that you were ours. Right from the start, we knew.'

'Did you ever meet my mum?'

'No. We sent letters and photos for a few years, via the agency. But she never responded and, in the end, we stopped writing. I had no idea that she had another child.'

'And you never thought about telling me?'

'Oh we did, a hundred times. We discussed talking to you when you were older, when the time was right, but the right time never came. We were the only parents you had ever known, we were Mummy and Daddy, and we didn't want to take that away from you.'

'So you did it for me? Not for you?'

'We did it for us too, I admit. You were our daughter and we wanted it to stay that way. I'm so sorry, Naomi. I hate that you've found out this way. But you have to know, we both loved you so very much, from the second we set eyes on you. Nothing can change that.'

'Except that everything has changed. I have a sister I never knew about. Who, by the way, tried to drown me.'

'What did you just say?'

I was losing my grip on reality, the revelations making my head spin. 'If I'd known about this, then things might have been different.'

'Naomi, where are you? What's going on? What are you talking about?'

'I thought she was lying. But she was telling the truth.'

'Naomi, you're scaring me. Tell me where you are.'

I looked up at the door and saw two police officers hovering. Their expressions were grave. I knew why they were here, it was the moment I had been dreading, and yet I felt numb. I had no energy left to resist. It had been sapped out of me by my conversation with Dad, anger and denial now replaced by defeat. Up until now, I had led a sheltered life, with the innocent belief that the world was fundamentally a good and just place to live in. Now I knew how wrong I had been. The world was not the safe haven I had thought it was and bad things happened all the time, every second, and to anyone. Including me.

'Dad, I have to go.'

'Naomi, wait!'

I put the phone down and waited for the officers to

approach me. I could accuse Summer of lying until I was blue in the face. I could protest my innocence and try to make everyone believe me. And I would do both of those things in due course. I was a fighter who wouldn't give up until the bitter end. But, right then, I was not battle-ready.

As the officers began their spiel, telling me that I was being arrested on suspicion of attempted murder, I thought about Summer. She must be feeling so smug right now. She would be thinking that she had won. And maybe she had. Because even if I found my way out of this desperate situation, she had stolen something from me that I could never get back. Something that made turning my friends against me and trying to seduce Oliver seem insignificant. She had destroyed my past, my history, my memory of my mother.

And with it, she had destroyed me.

29

I sat in my holding cell, clutching the wound on my side and shivering. I was still reeling from what Dad had told me, but I knew I had to get my wits about me and fast. I could drown myself in self-pity over the fact that my parents had lied to me when this was all over.

If it ever ended.

I had gone straight to the police station from the hospital. As I'd handed over my possessions and had my fingerprints taken, I had felt as though I was having an out-of-body experience. This couldn't really be happening. It was a nightmare, it had to be.

But with each hour that passed as I waited in custody, reality returned to me, along with a nausea in the pit of my stomach that wouldn't go away. This was no bad dream, this was my life and I had to be very, very careful. I was walking a tightrope, and I could topple any second.

Where the hell was Oliver? Why had he abandoned me when I needed him the most? Insecurities were making me doubt my husband. And now I had no mobile phone, no way of connecting with the outside world. My solicitor, one I had chosen at random and in a rush, was apparently on the way. Until then all I could do was wait and try to drown out the thoughts that were screaming at me from every direction.

I pictured the girls, cosy at home, perhaps watching TV or eating a snack, but I could feel the image fading away from me. They would be worried about me, poor Freya would be in pieces. She would be asking for me. The picture-perfect image I had of them was not real. Stop wallowing, I told myself firmly. Concentrate on getting out of this. Find a way to prove that Summer is lying.

I had the wound she had inflicted. I had my unwavering story of what had happened. Oliver and Angela would hopefully come to my defence and corroborate parts of my story. Was that enough? Could I persuade the police to look into whatever had happened in Devon?

At least I knew why she hated me now. She resented me for getting away from our mother while she had been left behind, to be raised by someone unfit to care for her. She thought I had taken the life she deserved, and, as revenge, she wanted to take mine.

But it still didn't add up. She had tried to be my friend at first. She had even claimed to admire me, copying my hairstyle and clothes. She had modelled a doll's house on our home. Had she honestly wanted to form a relationship between us? Had her seeds of resentment only grown when I had rejected her?

Was this all my own doing?

No, this wasn't my fault. Summer's behaviour had been erratic. She had broken into my home, and Dad's. Her behaviour had been obsessive, not friendly. There was no way that we could have become friends after she acted in the way she had. There was no point in blaming myself for the irrational thoughts of another human being. One who happened to be my sister.

The thought that we were related sickened me. I had dreamed of a sibling growing up, imagining playing with a brother or sister, sharing a bedroom, making up games together. But this was not how I wanted it. My innocent childhood fantasies were far removed from the situation I was in. Because my new sister was a psychopath.

I counted down the hours in my head, starting at twenty-four because I knew that was how long the police had to hold me before they either charged or released me. Twenty-three, twenty-two. Time moved at the pace of a snail. I wanted to get going now, I hated being stuck in this cell, out of control, unable to defend myself. I needed to do something. To speak to a solicitor and tell my side of the story. What was keeping them? Where was Oliver? Did he still love me? How could my mum and dad have lied to me? Would I ever prove my innocence? How were the children going to cope with this? My incessant thoughts twisted, turned and tormented me while I tried to keep my mind focused on my story.

But it kept drifting. I wondered if the children were at school. If Freya was being treated as a pariah again, as word got out about what had happened. If the gang were huddled in a corner, talking about me, their faces grim with shock. 'Poor Summer,' I imagined them saying. 'Naomi is a real psycho. I can't believe we never realised it before.'

I wanted to scream and shout. 'No! No, you've got this all wrong!'

But no one could hear me.

Hope ebbed and flowed as I oscillated between conviction and doubt. The discovery that I was adopted had battered my defences and left me exposed to the storm. I thought about all the ways Summer might manipulate what had happened. If I told the police that she'd come on to Oliver, she could use it against me as evidence that I was angry with her. If I accused her of manipulating my friends, her well-curated Instagram feed would paint a different picture, one of a group of mums and dads having a great time.

And then another thought came to me. Had this been Summer's plan all along? Not to kill me in the river but to force me to defend myself and then claim that she was the victim? I wouldn't put it past her.

How could she do this to me? To Freya and Bella? But given how she had spoken about her own daughter, it was obvious that she had no empathy. She would probably love it if my name and photograph were splashed all over the newspapers. She would revel in the gossip about me, the discussions had over cocktails in her flat. She would be a shoulder for Oliver to cry on, maybe even offering to help with the girls. And my husband's absence made me wonder how much he would resist the attention of a beautiful woman.

The knife! Energy surged through me again. The wound on my side was proof of her intent to harm me. But where was the weapon? Had it been found or was it lying on the riverbed, having been pushed along by the current, never to be seen again?

Twenty-one hours, twenty. Something must be wrong. They should have questioned me by now. Where was my solicitor? Where was Oliver? How could my parents lie to me? How could I prove Summer was lying? I was off again, an endless cycle, an internal torture.

When the door finally opened, I had almost resigned myself to an eternal lifetime of being stuck in a cell.

'Mrs Burton, come with me.'

I stood up and immediately felt light-headed. I hadn't eaten in hours, refusing the food and drink offered to me. I took a few deep breaths to steady myself. My wound throbbed. I nodded at the officers and followed them outside, grateful that I wasn't being put into handcuffs.

We passed some rooms with closed doors and I imagined Summer inside one of them, weeping crocodile tears as she told the police that she'd tried so hard to be nice to me. That she didn't know what she'd done wrong. It sickened me that she might be close by. I could almost smell her perfume and it made me want to gag. We paused at some double doors and I looked through the glass panels, my neck craning to see my solicitor.

But the door opened on to the reception area and Oliver rushed over to me.

'Thank Christ. Naomi, are you okay?'

'What's going on?' I was confused.

'Mrs Burton, you're being released without charge,' an officer told me. 'You're free to go.'

'But you haven't even questioned me!' Someone handed me my things. I took them, baffled. 'Where is my solicitor?'

'I've spoken to him,' Oliver told me. 'It's all sorted.'

'I don't understand. What's sorted?'

Oliver took my hand. 'I'll explain everything. Let's get you home.'

Even as he helped me into the car, I still didn't know what was happening to me. Perhaps I was due back at the police station tomorrow. But no one had said anything about returning the next day. There was no talk of bail. *You're free to go.* Why? What had I missed?

Oliver leaned over and gently put the seat belt on me, as

though I were a small, incapable child, and then walked around to the driver's side.

'Where are the girls?' I demanded.

'They're with Asha.'

'Asha? But she hates me. She won't let Aanya play with Freya.'

'Let's get you home and we'll talk.'

'No.' I couldn't wait a second longer. 'Tell me now. Where have you been, Oliver?'

'I've been sorting this mess out once and for all. I should have done it long ago.'

I was in a fever of impatience. 'How? I don't know what you're trying to tell me.'

He turned to me, took a deep breath. And then he started talking. And the more he told me, the more emotional I became, as I finally understood with the biggest rush of relief I'd ever experienced in my life, that I wasn't alone at all.

Because help had come from the most unexpected quarters.

30

It was the people who I'd thought had abandoned me who finally freed me from the hell I was living in. Together, Asha and Richard did what I had been unable to do for all these months. They had proven Summer's guilt and, subsequently, my innocence.

But they would never have been able to achieve it alone. It was the children, the ones we were supposed to protect and keep safe, who had ultimately saved me.

When Asha had taken Luna home with her after the camping trip, the little girl had been shaken. Asha assumed it was the shock of hearing that her mother was in hospital. She had been stunned, she later told me, when she learned through the rumour mill that I had tried to drown Summer on a school trip. But she had also been cynical, scarcely able to believe what she was hearing. She was convinced there must be another explanation. Despite what she perceived as my recent track record of irrational behaviour, her gut feeling told her there was more to it.

And as that feeling grew stronger, so did her suspicion.

She called Oliver to find out what was going on. But he was already on the way to her house, with Freya in tow, to tell Asha what he had just learned. Because when Freya, my brave little girl, realised the gravity of the situation, she hadn't hesitated to break her promise to Luna. She'd confessed to Oliver that Summer stole my dressing gown and earrings and she had snuck them back into my room on Luna's urging. She'd told him that Summer was previously in trouble for harassing a woman in Devon. That she often trapped Luna in her room. And she admitted that together they had woken the teachers, when they discovered Summer and I missing, on the night that she tried to kill me, fearing that something terrible was about to happen.

Oliver and Asha had sat down together with Luna, taking her hand and telling her that she was safe. It was time to tell the truth, they'd said, and Luna hadn't needed much encouragement. Without her mother breathing down her neck, she was ready to let go of the fear she'd been carrying around with her for so long. She confirmed that everything Freya had said was true. She and Summer had fled Devon. Her mother had often locked her in her bedroom, as well as gone out in the evenings and left her on her own. She said that Summer made her falsely accuse Freya of bullying her and she had felt so guilty about it that she had decided to stop, despite her mother's wrath. She also admitted that it wasn't the first time her mother had told her to lie.

And then she had cried and said that she was sorry.

Asha, her heart breaking and her temper rising, had called Richard, who then – with Luna's help – managed to track down Luna's father. He had driven straight up from Devon as soon as he got the phone call, embracing Luna tightly and telling her that she was safe now. He had whispered into her ear that she was coming to live with Daddy and that her room was being prepared for her as they spoke. Her little half-sister and brother were excited to see her again.

Once the children were settled down in front of a film, munching away on pizza, the adults had closed the door softly and decamped to the kitchen, where Luna's father had told them everything. He said that when he first met Summer, he had fallen head over heels for her. She was beautiful, enchanting and, he thought, a free spirit. But as the months went by, her behaviour became increasingly obsessive, and he began to suspect that she was lying about her past too. Something didn't add up but he couldn't put his finger on what it was. When he tried to end things with her, a year into their relationship, she told him that she was pregnant. Despite his misgivings about her, he wanted to be a good father and so he stayed.

It got worse, he said, after Luna was born. Summer no longer tried to hide her true colours. She tracked his every move, attacking him verbally, and sometimes physically, if he did something that she disapproved of. Sometimes she would be tearful and apologetic afterwards, telling him that she had been let down in the past by people she trusted and her behaviour was a legacy of this. But other times she was unrepentant. Before Luna had even celebrated her first birthday, he'd left. He had never gotten over the guilt of leaving Luna, he admitted, his voice shaking. But he insisted that he had always been in the little girl's life. They made a custody agreement and he had Luna for two nights a week. Often she would stay for longer, if Summer wanted to go out or travel to London, which she did with increasing frequency.

For a while, he said, things were going as well as they could under the circumstances. Luna seemed happy. His voice broke as he said that he would never have left her with Summer if he thought their daughter was in any danger. He knew Summer was unpredictable but she had always been loving and kind towards Luna. If anything, she was overprotective of their daughter.

But then he met someone else and when Summer found out, everything started to go wrong. She refused to let Luna stay with him and told Luna that he didn't want her. Then she became obsessed with his new partner, stalking her until she was so terrified that she threatened to call the police. Fearing for Luna's well-being, he started proceedings to get full custody of her and soon after, Summer disappeared, taking Luna with her. He had been trying to track her down and had already started legal action against her. When Richard filled him in on what had been happening in Barnet, he had agreed to contact the police immediately and report Summer for child abduction and harassment. Luna would never live with her again, he had vowed.

Asha had called the police too and relayed everything she had learned to them. And she had contacted Angela and urged her to do the same thing. While I was sitting in a cell, awaiting my fate and wondering what the delay was, my friends and family were working tirelessly to clear my name.

It had been enough. The police had arrested Summer, and I was free to go.

And so the school gang had come together for me when I needed them the most. A formidable force at the best of times and a critical one now. They had exposed Summer. So their treatment of me over the past few months somewhat paled into insignificance, as I processed the fact that they hadn't hesitated to act when they finally saw what I had already done. Summer was a fraud.

I cried when Oliver finished telling me this story, and he took me into his arms, stroked my hair and told me that it was all over. I was safe.

'I'm so sorry you went through all of this,' he whispered in my ear.

'Me too.'

'I'll never forgive myself for letting this happen.'

We had a lot to talk about. I was still angry, rightly or wrongly, about being made to feel alone. But right then, I didn't care about that. 'I want to see the girls,' I told him.

'They're waiting for you. We'll go to Asha's right now.'

As we drove my fingers twitched with anticipation. I needed to hug Bella and Freya, to hold them in my arms and tell them that I loved them. Despite my ordeal, my tiredness had vanished, the pain from my knife injury fading to a dull throb as I focused on the girls.

There was something nagging at me, tearing me away from my elation. Oliver had said it was over, but it wasn't. There would be a court case and Summer would probably deny everything. I would have to give evidence and spend countless nights worrying that the jury wouldn't believe me. There might be media attention, my family's lives splashed all over the tabloids and the internet for the world to see. And I also had to find a way to come to terms with the fact that not only was I adopted, but that I was related to the person who had tried to ruin my life. For a moment it was all so overwhelming that I wasn't sure I was going to be able to get past it all.

But the minute we pulled up outside Asha's house, the door opened and Freya and Bella came running out. And for a few, blissful minutes, nothing else mattered. I leaped out of the car and rushed towards my girls, taking one in each arm and clinging to them tightly. I told them I loved them and I sobbed on their shoulders until I had no tears left.

And when I was done, I looked up at Asha and mouthed two words. 'Thank you.'

31

Everyone said I was mad to go ahead with it. Considering the recent events, it was an interesting choice of word. But I had to do it. I needed to see her one last time.

At least the shoe was on the other foot this time and I took comfort in that. Summer was the one accused, the person who had lost everything. I had my freedom, my family, my friends, my life. I had everything she had tried to take from me. Well, almost everything.

It had been five weeks since Summer was arrested. She was being held in custody, awaiting trial. She had, unsurprisingly, pleaded not guilty. I had given my full statement to the police and so had everyone else. Luna was living with her dad and Richard had kept in touch and reported that she was doing well. He said her dad was a decent man and his partner was treating Luna like one of her own. The siblings were all getting used to the change. Luna had started going to her local primary school and was settling in well. It would take time, her dad had told Richard, after everything that she had been through, but she would get there. They were taking each day as it came.

Freya had already written to her three times and Luna had written back, enclosing a photograph of her cuddling the kitten, who she had taken with her, and inviting Freya to come and visit in the summer holidays. Freya had been ecstatic when I told her that we could go, and I had already started looking for an Airbnb in Devon.

Asha, Richard and the rest of the school gang had been visiting me constantly. A day didn't go by when I didn't get a message or call from at least one of them. They told me over and over again how sorry they were. How much they regretted what had happened. That they knew they didn't deserve forgiveness, but they'd never let me down again. Although I still felt angry when I thought about how they had treated me, they already had my forgiveness. Summer had fooled them and for a while, she had almost fooled me. But they had come through for me in the end and that was what mattered. Without them, I might be the one in prison, awaiting trial.

Instead, I was wearing a visitors' badge as I made my way to the hall. When I'd applied to visit Summer, I'd wondered if she would refuse the request, but she didn't. Perhaps she was curious. Or maybe she was just bored. I had no idea what to expect, whether she'd be defensive, contrite, angry, or remorseful. I didn't know if she'd give me what I needed. But I had to try.

I had spoken to Dad a few times. He had cried and told me that he loved me. I knew that already, and I knew that Mum had loved me too. But I needed some time to process it all and to come to terms with it. I was determined that we would find a way through it because I wasn't going to let Summer rip us apart. My dad was getting on and it was more important than ever that he got to spend quality time with me and the girls. But the revelations had opened up a door and I was itching to walk through it. I had to know where I came from and I wanted to meet my birth mother. Dad had agreed to help me track her down, but Summer was the only one who knew exactly who she was and where she lived. I refused to acknowledge her as my sister, but the cruel truth was that she had vital information that could help me.

I fidgeted nervously as I waited for Summer. My gaze drifted across the hall, taking in the other visitors – men, women, children. It could have been Freya and Bella here, visiting me in prison. It had come so dangerously close to that. And the idea of this was a stark reminder that Summer wasn't to be trusted. She was dangerous and I had to be careful.

When she appeared, I wasn't prepared for the sight of her. She looked awful, her face contorted into a grimace and her usually glowing skin pale and wan. Her hair was straggly and unkempt. It looked like she hadn't brushed it in days. I had once thought she was glorious. Now I saw a weak, despicable woman. But the moment she locked eyes on me her demeanour shifted and I sensed that she hadn't given up the fight yet. It sent shivers up my spine.

She sat down opposite me and cocked her head to the side.

'Naomi, how nice to see you. Thanks for coming by.'

It was as though I had popped over to the flat for a cup of tea. What game was she playing? Her calmness unnerved me and I wondered again why she had agreed to see me. I had to stick to my script, I couldn't let her derail me.

'How are you, Summer?'

She shrugged, then laughed lightly. 'Not great, thanks to you.'

I swallowed my fury. 'You're here because of your own actions.'

'Don't tell me you still believe that?'

'You know the truth, Summer.'

'Yes, I do, Naomi. And soon everyone else will know it too.'

She was delusional. Absolutely crazy. But that made her even more of a threat.

Stick to the script. 'I came here to talk to you about our mother.'

She leaned forward with a look that frightened me. 'What do you want to know?'

'Everything.'

She smiled, leaned back again and folded her arms across her chest. 'I'm sure you do.'

Summer knew this was the one thing she controlled, and she wasn't going to make it easy for me, but I had been prepared for that. 'You don't have to tell me anything, of course. My dad's already helping me to track her down anyway.'

'No!' she screamed, causing several prison officers to turn their steely gaze on her. 'No,' she repeated in a quieter voice. 'You mustn't do that.'

'Why not?'

'She's bad news, Naomi.'

I almost laughed. It wasn't my birth mother who was bad news. 'Why do you care so much? You hate me anyway.'

Summer shook her head. 'No, I don't hate you. You've got it all wrong.'

'You tried to kill me.'

'No, I didn't. You still don't get it, do you?'

Was she joking? How had she not tried to kill me?

'I was hurt,' she said, her mouth forming a childish pout. 'I had dreams of us becoming close, the family I always wanted. You were so beautiful, so happy, I just adored you. And then when you rejected me, I felt betrayed. I only ever wanted to be part of your life.'

I was rapidly going off script. 'By murdering me?'

Her mouth formed a thin line. 'You did a bad thing and you needed to be punished. To see the error of your ways. But I didn't want to kill you. You're my sister.'

I was so dismayed at the way this conversation was going that it took me a few seconds to gather my thoughts. 'You pushed me under the water.'

She waved a hand as though trying to drown me was a minor inconvenience. 'As I said, you needed to learn. I was always going to let you go. Sometimes we just need a bit of a shock to see things how they really are.'

'That's your defence, is it? That you were teaching me a lesson?'

'My defence is that you actually tried to kill me. You pushed me under and you meant it.'

Her words terrified me because they were true. Attempted murder. Was this how she was going to get me? Did she have a chance of winning? I couldn't even think about that right now.

I tried to get back on track, aware that I was in danger of accidentally incriminating myself. 'I'm going to find my birth mother, with or without your help.'

Summer's nostrils flared. 'Then why are you here?'

'I wanted to give you the opportunity to tell your side of the story.'

Summer leaned forward suddenly and hissed, 'You have to get me out of here.'

I moved away from her. 'Excuse me?'

'Get me out of here and I'll tell you everything.'

'I can't do that.'

'Of course you can. Tell the police you made a mistake. You're the key witness, they'll drop the charges if you tell them you were wrong. Come on, sis, do this for me. We're family.'

I stared at her incredulously. She had completely lost the

plot and I realised now just how desperate she was. This was why she had agreed to see me because, in her delusional state, she had genuinely thought there was a chance that I would get her out of this.

'Summer, you tried to kill me and I'm not changing my story.'

She leaned back and glared at me, her entire body radiating hostility. 'Well, then I'm not telling you anything. And good luck in court when I tell the world what really happened that night in the river. Or about how you lurked outside my flat and falsely reported me to the police for child neglect. You won't look so shiny and innocent then, will you?'

This visit had been a terrible idea. I didn't know what I had been thinking. She was never going to help me, she only cared about herself and the illusion she had created, where she was the innocent party. I stood up and signalled to the nearest prison officer that I wanted to leave.

'We're done here,' I said.

'Naomi, please! Please!'

I gave her one last look. 'Goodbye, Summer.'

As I walked away, I heard her call out, but it took my brain a few seconds to process what she'd said. The hairs on my arm stood on edge as it hit me. She'd said, 'This isn't over.'

I spun around to face her, but she was already being led away.

* * *

Oliver was waiting for me in the prison car park.

'How did it go?' he asked as I climbed into the car.

'Not well. She didn't tell me anything about my mother. And then she had the gall to beg me to help her. And she accused me of trying to kill her and said the world would soon know it.'

'Christ, you didn't say anything stupid, did you?'

'Of course I didn't.' But already I was mentally rehashing our conversation just in case.

Oliver put a hand over mine. 'I'm sorry.'

'Me too. Do you think she's right? Is there any way she can turn this on its head and prove that I tried to kill her?'

'Of course not, because you didn't try to kill her.'

'It was self-defence,' I said feebly.

'Yes, it was. You have nothing to worry about, Nims, seriously.'

I absorbed his words like a sponge, feeding off his reassurance, and gradually my pulse began to return to normal. 'I can still find my birth mother without her anyway. Dad has found an old address and we're checking to see if she still lives there.'

'And you're sure you want to find her?'

'No. But I have to.'

'I understand. We'll do whatever you need. But no visiting Summer again, okay? It could land you in a whole lot of trouble and it's just not worth the risk.'

'Don't worry,' I scoffed. 'I have no intention of speaking to that woman ever again.'

'Do you feel ready to go and see your dad yet?'

'I think so. I'm going to take the girls this weekend.'

'How are you feeling about it?'

I smiled sadly. 'Strange. And worried it will always feel this way.'

'It won't, I promise. Whatever has happened in the past, he's still your dad. It's not about who gave birth to you, it's about who has loved and cared for you. That's what makes parents.'

I closed my eyes as I fought back tears. 'I know.'

Oliver looked at his watch. 'We have to pick Freya up soon. Do you want to come?'

Oliver, Angela and Asha had been doing the school runs for me, but I knew the time was fast approaching when I would have to take over. I couldn't hide forever. I wasn't sure what I was so afraid of. Everyone was on my side again, yet I still dreaded the playground and the stares. But I had to get on with my life and today was as good a day as any.

'I'll go,' I said.

'On your own?'

'Yes. I'm ready.'

He squeezed my hand. 'You are.'

Oliver dropped me at the school gates and as I climbed out, my legs threatened to give way beneath me. I took a few, bracing breaths and then started to walk slowly into the play-ground, my head down as other parents streamed past.

Sharon was by my side immediately. 'Naomi, it's so good to see you back. How are you?'

'Fine, thanks, Sharon.'

'I'm so sorry about everything. I can't begin to imagine what you've been through.'

'Thank you.'

'If you need anything, anything at all, you let me know.'

I nodded. 'I will.'

Sharon leaned in. 'Freya's doing great at school. She's very happy and she and Aanya have grown close again. You have nothing to worry about.'

I already knew it, but hearing Sharon say the same was music to my ears. I thanked her and made my way gingerly into the playground. Asha and Angela were already there and they rushed towards me.

'Welcome back!' Asha said, her expression slightly cautious as it always was around me these days because she still felt awful about what had happened.

'How did it go?' Angela asked. She knew I'd been to see Summer.

'Not great, but it's done now and I can move on.'

Richard came over and gave me a hug. 'Lovely to see you, Naomi.'

I bathed in the warmth of being back among my friends. Of not being afraid of the school community any more. These people had let me down spectacularly but none of us were perfect. I certainly wasn't. More than anything, I wanted to put it behind us and move on.

'There's a new boy in the class.' I understood immediately what Richard was saying. The new child had taken Luna's place. My breath caught in my throat as I panicked. What would the new mum be like? Would she divide our community as easily as Summer had done?

'He's come from another local primary school where he wasn't happy. I know the dad from the football league. They're a really nice family.'

I closed my eyes and exhaled. It would take a while to stop being on edge but with each day that passed, it would get easier. Summer was locked up and she wasn't coming back. I'd have to face her in court and then I would never have to see her again.

When I opened my eyes again, the children were coming out of the school building and I saw Freya's eyes light up when she spotted me.

'Mummy!' she called as the teacher dismissed her and she ran over.

I gave her a cuddle. 'Hey, darling, how was your day?'

'Good. I got full marks in my spelling test and Aanya and I played at lunchtime and Mr Bentley said that we might get a school pet and...'

And she was away, chatting at a thousand miles per hour, just as she should be doing. I glanced around, but everyone was busy greeting their own children. No one was looking at me, I realised. The stares and whispers I had feared had not come to fruition.

I took Freya's hand. 'Shall we go home?'

'Can we have chicken nuggets for tea?'

'I don't see why not.'

We said goodbye to the others and walked home together. I couldn't wait to get back. The house was no longer the nightmare I had made it out to be, it was my safe haven. A place I no longer feared or fretted about. The garden was blooming and we often had the patio doors open. Sparkle liked to wander in and out, chasing bees and rustling about in the bushes. At night-time I slept peacefully, wrapped up in Oliver's arms. I was working again, holing myself up in the office with cups of coffee and ploughing through my backlog. Soon we would have enough money to get the leaky window fixed and buy a new dishwasher. The house was home, because home was where the people I loved were, and that meant Oliver, Bella and Freya.

I had clung on to the old flat for too long, wrapped up in nostalgia, but it belonged in my past. The present, and the future, was what mattered to me. It was time to make new memories. To say goodbye to our old life, once and for all.

And with it, it was time to say goodbye to Summer too.

32

I parked up outside the small terraced house, on the edge of an estate. There was a playing field on the other side and some children were kicking a football about. A middle-aged man with a Labrador was walking around the perimeter. I watched him, trying to calm my nerves. Then, with shaking hands, I opened the car door and stepped out onto the pavement.

I had written to my birth mother a few weeks ago. Dad had helped me to write the letter and he had come with me to post it, even though walking to the postbox was a mammoth task for him. I knew it was important to him that he was there for me.

We were getting there, Dad and me. We were finding a way to repair the damage that had been done to our relationship. I had reconciled with it in my head, understanding the difficult situation Mum and Dad had been in and their desire to protect me. They had loved me, raised me, and they would always be my parents. No one could take that away from me.

But the itch hadn't gone away and that was how I had ended up here, ready to come face-to-face with my birth mother. Summer's mother too. I pushed that thought away.

Dad had offered to come with me, and so had Oliver, but this was something I had to do alone. I didn't know if it would bring me peace or if it would make things worse, but I had to find out either way. I walked up to the door, feeling sick to my stomach. Summer's words were echoing around my head, warning me to stay away from this woman. How bad could she be? But it was just a short visit, a cup of tea and a biscuit at most. No time to do any lasting damage, surely? And if she was rude or offensive, I would simply leave and never see her again.

I had created a mental picture of my birth mother. I imagined a haggard-looking woman, worn down by years of alcohol and drug abuse, a guarded, hostile expression on her face. But the woman who greeted me looked nothing like that. She was neatly dressed, her shiny brown hair cropped, her expression anxious but not unwelcoming.

'Naomi?'

'Sandra?'

'Yes, that's me. Come in.'

I could tell she was as nervous as I was, and this reassured me. I stepped into the hallway and took in the small console table which had flowers and a candle on it. The house was neat and tidy, clearly well looked after which, again, surprised me. I had assumed that this woman lived a chaotic life. I had prepared myself for mess and decay.

I had been completely wrong.

Sandra led me into a living room with a shaggy carpet and gas fire, and I sat down on a worn armchair and watched her carefully as she took the sofa opposite me. Did she look like me? The hair colour was similar and I thought perhaps the angular shape of her face bore a resemblance to mine. Or was I just looking for something that wasn't there?

'I'm really glad you wrote,' she began, saving me the job of initiating the conversation.

'You are?'

'Yes. I've always wondered if I would see you again. I hoped I would.'

I was struggling to reconcile my mental image of Sandra against the reality. 'Really?'

'Yes.' She nodded vehemently, as if desperate to show she meant it. 'I was devastated when they took you away. I never wanted to give you up, you must believe that. But I also realised later that it was the right thing for you and that's why I never tried to contact you.'

'What happened?'

I could tell she was prepared for me to ask. 'I was young and I was stupid. I got together with this no-good boy and started drinking and taking drugs. I was a mess, Naomi, but I didn't care. I had no interest in seeking help. And then I got pregnant.'

'It was unplanned?'

'Yes.' She spoke frankly and I was grateful to her for being honest. 'Someone at the hospital must have contacted social services as they became involved. I admit that during my pregnancy I didn't want you. I didn't look after you in the way I should have done and I will regret that for the rest of my life. But when you were born everything changed.'

She wiped a finger under her eyes before she continued. 'I loved you and decided that I would sort myself out and be a good mum. I persuaded social services to let me keep you and promised to get clean. They came to see me often and at first, everything was going well. They said I was doing a good job. But I was on my own, Naomi. Your dad was long gone and my parents had no interest in helping me. It was hard, really hard.'

I knew how hard being a mother was, and I'd had a strong support network. I imagined this woman, a young girl, trying to raise a baby while battling her own demons. And although a part of me resented her, perhaps even hated her, deep down I empathised too.

'The wheels came off. I wasn't a good mother, I know that. And when they took you away, I made a right fuss. Screaming, shouting, threatening, all sorts. Once you'd gone, I went even more off the rails. I didn't care any more. I was angry at the world.'

There was so much more I wanted to ask her. What had she done to get me taken away? Or was it simply that she had done nothing? Left me on my own while she got drunk or high? But she needed to keep talking and I didn't want to interrupt her so I stored my endless questions up until I could finally ask them all. I sensed from her candidness that she would tell me whatever I wanted to know.

'Something bad happened to me. I'll tell you more one day if you want to know but for now, let's just say it was a wake-up call. After that, I got clean, sorted myself out. Got a job. You had been adopted by then and I got letters and photos from your new parents. You looked so happy, and I knew then that I would never try to get you back.'

'You never wrote back to them,' I said.

'I didn't want to tarnish your new life. I was damaged goods and you were pure and innocent. I wanted you to have everything you deserved. A good life with decent people. Tell me, were you happy? Were they kind to you?'

I nodded. 'Yes, they were. They were amazing.'

'Thank God. It was all I ever wanted for you.'

'But then you had another child.'

She looked at me, stunned. 'Yes, that's right. I didn't realise you knew that. A few years later I fell pregnant again. Things were different, I was clean and I was looking after myself. My partner was a decent bloke and he stuck around. I promised that this time it would be different.'

But it wasn't different. Because clearly, at some point her partner must have disappeared, before she'd fallen off the wagon again. I wondered why social services hadn't taken Summer away too. Had she been better at hiding it? Or had she slipped off their radar by then?

'How did you know about Summer?' she asked, looking at me curiously.

'I met her,' I said. 'She's the one who told me about you.'

Sandra put her hand to her chest. 'I had no idea the two of you had met. I told Summer about you. You weren't a dirty secret, I wanted her to know she had a sister. But I didn't realise she'd gone looking for you. I wonder why she never told me.'

Because she hates you, I thought. And yet I was confused. This woman was nothing like the cruel, drunk person that Summer had insinuated she was.

'I miss her,' Sandra said, wiping away another tear. 'I hope you don't mind me saying that. I missed you too, of course, but Summer and I were incredibly close.'

Close? I looked at her, confused. Something didn't add up here. Had Summer lied again? Or was Sandra in denial? She had been honest with me up until now, so why wouldn't she tell the truth about this too? Perhaps they had been close once, before it all went wrong.

'Did you know she has a daughter?'

Sandra looked at me, almost angrily. 'Excuse me?'

'She has a daughter. Luna.'

'No, she doesn't. Summer never had a child.'

'She does. I've met her. She went to the same school as my daughter for a while. That's how I met her.'

Sandra was becoming increasingly distressed, and her reaction perplexed me. Something was seriously wrong, but I couldn't work out what it was.

'No,' she said again, shaking her head. 'You've made a mistake.'

'Look,' I said, getting out my phone and opening Instagram. Summer's account had been dormant since her incarceration, but it was still there. I scrolled to a photo of Summer and Luna and proffered it at Sandra.

'Here. That's Luna. She's eight.'

Sandra was staring at the screen in shock. I waited for her to crumple, to start sobbing about missing out on being a grandmother, to talk of guilt and regret.

'That's not Summer.'

I stared at her, my mouth hanging open. 'What did you say?'

'That's not Summer.' Sandra looked up at me. 'Why do you think that's Summer?'

'Because she told me. She told me all about you.'

'Naomi, Summer died ten years ago.'

The walls began to close in on me. Scenarios were flying around my head as I struggled to work out the implication of this. Summer wasn't who she said she was. She had lied, again. She was not my sister and the relief of this was immense. And yet she had known I was adopted and that I had a sister. How? And why had she told me yet another story?

Sandra was squinting at the phone. She pointed accusingly at the photo. 'That's Christina.'

Christina. Alarm bells rang with recognition of the name.

'Yes, Christina. That's what she used to be called. But she

calls herself Summer now. Why would she take your daughter's name? I don't understand.'

Sandra stood up and went to a cabinet, pulling out a photo album and flicking through the pages until she found the one she was looking for. She turned it round so I could see it and pointed at a photograph. It showed Summer, or Christina, or whatever the hell her name was, with another woman. They must have been in their twenties and they were beaming at the camera.

'That's Summer,' she said, pointing to the other woman. 'And that's Christina.'

I looked at the real Summer, my half-sister, and felt an intense pang of regret that I'd never met her. A strange sort of grief for someone I'd never even met. And then I looked at Christina who was, without a doubt, the woman we had all known as Summer.

'Summer and Christina were flatmates in their twenties,' Sandra explained. 'Summer wanted to be on stage and she moved to London to chase her big break. She did well too, she was cast in some lead roles. I was so proud when I saw her name on the programme. Summer-Mae Jones, right there on page one along with her photo.'

That was why Angela and I had failed to make the connection when we googled Summer. Summer Caldwell had never existed, Summer-Mae Jones had. And Christina Caldwell, a minor player in the theatre business who never hit the big time and so was barely mentioned. We just hadn't been looking in the right place, or for the right person.

I was still staring at the photograph. 'How did they meet?'

'They met at an audition. They hit it off and ended up renting a place together. A poky little flat but they were happy. They were always busy, working or partying. Whenever I went to stay in London, we'd go out for dinner and they seemed like two peas in a pod. Things soon turned sour, though. Summer was doing well, she was getting all these roles and Christina was struggling. She was always cast as the understudy, and I sensed that she was jealous of Summer.'

'Did you talk about it with Summer?'

'Yes, but Summer always shrugged it off. She said they were good friends, and she told me not to worry about it. But I did worry. And then some strange things started happening.'

I sensed what was coming. 'What things?'

'Summer told me that Christina was starting to dress like her. She got her hair cut and coloured blonde like her too. Some of Summer's things went missing and she found them in Christina's room. Summer was worried that she was becoming infatuated with her.'

'Like she almost wanted to be her?'

'Yes.' Sandra nodded emphatically. 'Exactly that. I told Summer to move out, to get away from her, and she agreed it was a good idea. But it was too late. She died a few weeks later.'

'Can I ask what happened?'

Sandra's face twisted in pain. 'Her body was found in the flat. Drug overdose.'

My heart lurched. 'I'm so sorry.'

'But it never added up, not to me. I'd always been honest with her about my past and she knew what drugs did to a person. She wasn't interested in that stuff. I told this to the police, I swore that she wouldn't have taken the drugs, but I could tell they didn't believe me. Her fingerprints were on the syringe, and they found all sorts of paraphernalia in the flat.'

It was so sad, but the truth was plain to see. Summer had gone to London and got mixed up with the wrong crowd. Partied too hard and perhaps recreational drugs had paved the way for heavier substances. It happened all the time and of all people, Sandra should know that. But she had idolised her second daughter and her refusal to accept it was understandable.

Then a thought crept in, one which deeply unsettled me. Summer. Christina.

'Did you suspect Christina of having something to do with it?'

'That bitch.' Venom spilled out of Sandra. 'I know she was involved. She was crazy, I'm telling you. One minute she was all sweet and adoring, the next she was a green-eyed monster.'

It was all starting to make sense because what Sandra had described was exactly how I felt about the woman I now knew to be called Christina. She had told me I was beautiful, she had tried to infiltrate my life but her admiration had quickly morphed into something else. A desire to almost become me, to step into my shoes. And, eventually, to get rid of me.

She hadn't succeeded in her attempt to kill me. But was it possible that she had done with Summer, and she had got away with it?

'Did the police ever investigate her?'

'They questioned her, of course, but she won them over. She was always manipulative, you know. She could charm people so easily, but she never fooled me. I knew she was involved but I couldn't prove it. I tried, I really did, but no one would listen. It almost killed me until, eventually, I wondered if I was going mad. Seeing things that weren't there.'

I knew exactly how she felt because I'd been the same.

'She tried to kill me,' I said.

Sandra's eyes widened. 'She what?'

'A few months ago. After she told me about you, she tried to drown me in a river. I'm certain she wanted me dead. Like with the real Summer, she'd started to style herself like me and she stole my belongings too. She turned my friends against me and she even tried to seduce Oliver, my husband. I had no idea why she was doing it but now I'm starting to see a pattern.'

'Where is she now?'

'In custody, awaiting trial for attempted murder.'

Sandra let out a loud sob as pain, anger and relief poured out of her, as I told her the full story. 'They got her. They got her in the end. Justice for my Summer.'

'You need to talk to the police,' I said urgently. 'It might not be too late to have her charged for Summer's murder too. But what I still don't understand is why she fixated on our family so much? Why she did what she did to Summer and then, years later, came after me?'

'I can't give you an answer for that. I do honestly think she met Summer by chance and then became obsessed with her. Why she came looking for you, I don't know.'

'She called herself Summer. Maybe she convinced herself that she was actually the real Summer? That I was her long-lost sister?'

'Maybe. But she'll never be my Summer. Summer was a sweet, kind person. She wouldn't hurt a fly. Christina is a monster. And I'm so glad that she's been caught.'

I thought about Christina's words when I visited her in prison. *This isn't over.* A shiver ran down my spine. But surely, we had more than enough on her now. If Sandra told the police what had happened to the real Summer, there was no way Christina could get away with it.

'She warned me not to come and see you,' I told Sandra.

'She didn't want you to find out the truth. She played a dangerous game and she lost.'

I sat back in the armchair, completely dumbfounded. This

was not the conversation I had expected to have with my birth mother. I had imagined a stilted affair, awkwardness, maybe recriminations. But now I saw that we were united, not by blood but by something else. By our hatred of the woman who had, for some reason, invaded our lives like an ugly weed.

I could have died. She quite probably killed one sister and then she came after the other. I already knew I was lucky to be alive, but I felt it even more acutely then. And she had robbed me of the chance to ever get to know my real half-sister.

'I'll help you,' I told Sandra. 'I'll make sure she doesn't get away with what happened to Summer. Everyone will know what Christina did. I know it won't bring her back but it's a start.'

'Thank you.' Sandra looked at me earnestly. 'I don't deserve your help, and I don't deserve your sympathy. You have every right to hate me.'

'I think a part of me was expecting to hate you,' I admitted. 'But you've already lost one daughter in the worst possible way, and I don't want you to lose another.'

As I said it, I realised that I meant it. Sandra would never take Mum's place, but I wanted to keep in touch. Possibly not ever as mother and daughter, but as something else. Maybe we would grow close or maybe we wouldn't. I had no idea when, or even if, I would introduce her to my family. But I knew one thing for sure. Together, we would bring Christina down.

Justice for Summer. For the innocent sister I never met.

I stayed for a couple of hours, talking more about Summer and Christina, planning our next steps, and then telling Sandra about my life and family. When I left, I promised to be in touch soon and to keep her updated about Christina. In turn, she said she would contact the police right away. I drove straight home, where Oliver and the girls were waiting. Freya and Bella didn't know about Sandra yet. But they must have sensed that something momentous had occurred because they curled up next to me on the sofa, snuggling into my sides.

I breathed in the scent of them, realising how close I had come to losing them. And then I gazed out of the window, watching the sun streaming in through the open curtains. I thought about how my half-sister had once been a performer and how Bella dreamed of doing the same. Was it in our blood? What else had I inherited from a family I didn't even know existed? There was a whole part of me that I had yet to discover. I thought about Sandra and the pain she had been through, some self-inflicted but much of it unfairly brought upon her. And I thought about the past year and how it had almost ripped our family apart.

But it hadn't. We had survived. I had survived. And Christina was locked away where she belonged. A surge of strength and optimism ran through me. We had to rebuild now, find a way past this mess and make the most of every moment. My sister had never got the chance and I wasn't going to waste mine. Life was too precious.

I smiled as I kissed the girls on the tops of their heads, and the weight I had been carrying around with me for so long finally began to lift.

Yes. We were finally free.

EPILOGUE

Once the words start flowing out of me, I can't stop. It's the best thing I've ever written. I tell her about how beautiful she is, how special. How I know it's difficult between us now but I miss her. I ask her to write back. I'm certain she will because we have a unique bond. I knew it from the first moment I met her, and she knew it too, I could tell. We're soulmates.

I used to feel that way about Summer. I still remember the first time I met her. We were auditioning for a role and she sat next to me, fiddling with her script. She smiled at me, and it was as though the whole world lit up. She was wearing this intense floral perfume and it was intoxicating. I still wear it now and it reminds me of her. She was heavenly.

We got chatting and I didn't want our conversation to end. Summer was vivacious and charming, she was everything I dreamed of being. I watched her mannerisms, studying them carefully, so that I could practise them in front of the mirror at home later. When she finished her audition and waved goodbye, I was bereft. I couldn't bear the thought her leaving. We had to be best friends, I felt it in every bone in my body. With her by my side, I would be invincible. People would look at me. They would love me. I could do anything, be anything.

Of course she got the lead role, and I was cast as her understudy. But I didn't mind because it meant that I could see her again. We rehearsed together every day and soon we were going out for drinks afterwards. It was the happiest time of my life. The play was called A Doll's House and one evening, after a few drinks, Summer told me that she'd never had one as a child, so I scoured charity shops until I found one and bought it for her. The amazement on her face when I turned up with it will stay with me forever.

When she got kicked out of her flat, I suggested that we share a place and then held my breath, terrified, to see her response. Had I gone too far? Been overkeen or pushy? But she said it was a great idea and my world flooded with joy at the prospect of living with my best friend. We moved in and the doll's house I had given her took pride of place in the living room, a beautiful reminder of how we'd met.

At first things were amazing. More than amazing. We worked hard, we partied hard. We ate breakfast together every morning and giggled over television shows in the evening when we were too tired to go out. Summer was getting some great roles, but I was never jealous of her, despite what her interfering busybody of a mother told her behind my back. I was Summer's biggest cheerleader, her right-hand woman. I supported her more than anyone. I held her hand when she cried because she didn't get the part she wanted. I looked after her when she was ill. All I wanted was to be there for her and to know that she was there for me too.

Then she went and ruined everything.

It started with a subtle shift in her behaviour, a wariness around me that became more obvious. She didn't like that I'd cut and coloured my hair like hers or that I was wearing the same clothes. I mean, talk about overreacting. She should have been flattered, touched even, by my devotion. I sensed that she had told our so-called friends about it because I could feel the whispers even though I couldn't hear them. Soon she started going out more without me, almost as though she was avoiding me, and I was deeply hurt. And then she got the boyfriend.

Summer's mother thought the sun shone out of her backside, but she was wrong. This boy was bad news and soon he was giving her drugs, which she took willingly. When I begged her to stop, she wouldn't listen. She shouted at me, said I was creeping her out, ordered me to stop being so obsessed with her. She talked about moving out. Her words broke my heart and I didn't know if I would ever recover. I lived for Summer, I yearned for her when she was absent.

But, as time went on, my grief turned to anger as I realised that I had made a terrible mistake. Summer wasn't the perfect angel I had thought she was. She had pretended to be my friend, but she had used me. Chewed me up and spat me back out. She had said nasty, cruel things and turned our friends against me. She and her lowlife boyfriend laughed at me to my face, calling me a sheep and making baa-ing noises. They said our precious doll's house was silly and put the dolls in rude positions for their own amusement. I watched on, seething. How dare she treat me like that! She did not deserve to stand on the pedestal I had put her on.

It was time to get her off. And I was ready to take her place.

I had earned it. I had spent months studying her, learning to move and speak like her. I knew everything about her, what she wore, what she ate, her mannerisms. And the thought of becoming Summer consumed me as I plotted my next move with mounting excitement. I would no longer be the understudy in my own life, I would be the lead role. And I was a far better Summer than the original because I was a good person, and she was a selfish, shallow liar.

It was really very easy. The thing with drugs is that it's not hard to overdose, especially if you're off your face and you don't know what's going on. And so I watched as she self-administered the last dose that she would ever have. The one I had carefully tampered with.

I didn't feel guilty because it was her fault. She had extinguished her own light when she became a druggie and cruelly cut me out of her life. I would have helped her if she'd let me. I would have kept the boyfriend away from her, forgiven her for all the things she had done to me, and supported her to get clean. But she didn't want me.

I moved away from London soon after she died, ready to forget the stage and start my new life. I knew that I couldn't take Summer's place in London because too many people knew her, but a change of location and career would soon fix that. After changing my first name by deed poll, I shed Christina and became Summer, in a place where no one knew the woman I modelled myself on, and at first it felt so good. I made new friends, got myself a handsome and successful boyfriend, and they all adored me. Everyone knew me as Summer and I enjoyed playing the part so much that sometimes it was hard to imagine that Christina ever even existed. I settled down and had a baby, carefully unpacking the doll's house I had taken with me to Devon and putting it in the nursery for my daughter to play with when she was older. I painted the doors and windows to match our home and considered my life as perfect as the dolls who lived in that little wooden house. But over time, I became restless and agitated. I had plenty of money, courtesy of my partner, but I didn't enjoy motherhood and I wasn't prepared for just how much I missed Summer, how lonely I was without her in my life. I felt lost at sea, drifting around, looking for an anchor. And something kept coming back to me.

Summer had told me that she had a sister she'd never met. The conversation stayed with me for years, pricking my curiosity, until eventually, I decided that I wanted to find her. It wasn't easy but at least I had a starting point. Summer had shown me some old letters from her sister's adopted parents, which she had brought with her to London in case she ever decided to track them down. I had taken a photo of one of the letters on my phone when she wasn't looking. I only wanted to help her, to do some research of my own and be the one to reunite Summer with her long-lost sister if she ever decided to go ahead. In the end, she hadn't wanted to, but I still had their names. Keith and Rita Cook. They had called the baby Naomi. And so, with a bit of online sleuthing and a lot of determination, I had eventually found her. I even had her home address because, as a self-employed accountant, her company was registered to where she lived. I couldn't wait to meet her. What if she was just like Summer but better? Kinder? The thought made my body tingle with anticipation.

I watched Naomi from a distance, getting the measure of her. I went to Barnet whenever Luna was staying with her father. Oh, she reminded me of Summer! She had the same glow about her, the easy confidence, and her two daughters were to die for. They were full of life, especially the older one, who was like a mini version of Summer, always dancing and singing. She was the exact opposite of pale, miserable little Luna who tiptoed around me like I was the wicked witch. How I ended up with a daughter who treated me like that I'll never know, but I blame her father and his stupid girlfriend, the one who had the gall to say I was stalking her. As if I'd ever be interested in someone as boring as her. I was merely watching her for my own amusement.

The more I watched Naomi, however, the more I realised, with excitement, that I'd backed the wrong horse. Summer had let me down, but Naomi? She was the real deal. She was the anchor I was looking for, the light I needed in my life. I was a moth but, in her flame, I would become a butterfly again.

When I saw the for sale sign outside her flat, I couldn't resist posing as a potential buyer so that I could have a snoop around. But then I fell in love with the place and I had the most tremendous idea. I would buy it, and we would become best friends. Soulmates. She wouldn't let me down like her sister had done, I was certain of it.

I told my ex that Luna and I were being evicted from our rental flat and I wanted to buy somewhere so we'd have more security, and he gave me some money to put a deposit down on the flat. He's a useless excuse for a man but he's got one thing going for him – he's rich. Of course, he thought the flat was in Devon and I didn't correct him, but the location was really none of his business. And with the money I was earning from my job, and the monthly maintenance payments from my ex, I could afford the mortgage. It was all perfect and I was so excited when I called the estate agent to put in my offer.

Then Naomi turned me down and I was furious with her for messing everything up. I went back to my ex to see if he'd give me more money but he refused. Said flats in Devon didn't cost that much. Determined to see my plan through, I started coming up to Barnet more regularly, looking for other flats nearby, and then the estate agent contacted me a few weeks later to accept my offer. It was fate. We belonged together, Naomi and me. And so I moved to London and did all I could to win her favour. To be the best friend she never knew she needed. She was my inspiration and I was ready to be her muse. I repainted the doll's house to match Naomi's house and imagined the dolls inside as the two of us, the best of friends. Sisters, even.

But she didn't want me either. It was like Summer all over again, only it was worse. I tried to impress her. I watched her every move, styled my hair like her, dressed like her, but it backfired. She started avoiding me too, just like her sister had. She tried to freeze me out of the school gang. With a sinking heart I understood that she wasn't the person I thought she was either. She had let me down, just like her sister. I wished I'd never met that damned family. I was so angry that I smashed the doll's house to pieces in a fit of rage, my dreams splintering as easily as the old wood.

And in my fury I decided that, just like Summer, Naomi had blown her chance.

I tried to do it the easy way. To exclude her so she knew what it felt like to be an outsider. I won over all her friends, slowly turning them against Naomi. I cosied up to her husband, using my best seduction tactics, the ones I learned from Summer. After I kissed him in the pub, I couldn't wait to race round to Naomi's house and watch from the back garden as he told her what had happened between us. And my anger mounted as I watched their conversation and realised that they weren't arguing. That he hadn't bothered to tell her.

I realised with a sinking heart that my plan hadn't worked. And so, Naomi had to go.

I was genuinely sad about it because I had wanted things to be different between us. But she brought it upon herself when she rejected me. In truth, I was bored of being Summer anyway and I was ready for a new lead role. And so it was time to shed my skin again. To take Naomi's place. I imagined being Oliver's wife, a mum to Freya and Bella, and my heart burst with anticipation. To call those girls my own would be everything. Who needed a doll's house when I could have the real thing?

When I found out that the school needed volunteers for the camping trip, I realised that this was my opportunity to finish what I started. Unfortunately, I was too late and I was put on the reserve list. But I soon resolved that by smashing the windows of Marcie's car and when Sharon called me to ask me if I could step in at the last minute, my bag was already packed.

To my credit, I gave Naomi one last chance, but she didn't take it. And so I instigated her downfall. I'd already set all the wheels in motion because everyone thought she was losing the plot. It was easy because she'd been so stressed about moving house and all the things going wrong that she'd worked herself up into a right tizz. She'd even accused me of stealing her cat, which was nothing to do with me. Although I will admit that a few things I did may have fuelled her paranoia. Painting the doll's house, getting the matching kitten. She'd sensed my presence a few times when I followed her but she couldn't prove it was me. So instead, she started doubting herself and when I successfully turned everyone against her, that was the final nail in the coffin. Everyone would be sad when she died but I would be there to help them get through it. I'd even imagined the dress I would wear to her funeral.

But somehow I've ended up in a prison cell while she gets

to go on with her life like I never even existed. She's screwed me over royally and that's not fair. I'm a good person, I know I am. It's everyone else who is bad. Who stomp on my kindness and throw it back in my face.

I'm not crazy. I've just been let down by everyone I've ever loved.

I glance at the photo on the wall and hope surges through me. It's a selfie I took with the person I know is my true soulmate. We are grinning at the camera, our heads together. We look magnetic. Unstoppable. She won't let me down, I'm sure of it. She's different, she gets me. Already I'm tucking my hair coyly behind my ears like I've seen her do so many times. We'll keep in touch and, when I get out of this place, hopefully sooner rather than later if the court case goes to plan, she'll be waiting for me.

I smile as I sign the letter with a flourish. I know she'll write back soon and she'll keep our secret. I would trust her with my life. This is it, my final move. Together, we'll change the world and to hell with everyone else. She is a part of me and I am a part of her.

I stuff the letter in an envelope and write the name and address on the front, before banging on my door so that I can give it to the prison officer to post. I can't wait for her reply. It will keep me going during the long, lonely days and the even lonelier nights. She is now my shining light, and I can't wait to be a butterfly once again.

The prison officer appears and takes the letter, looking beyond bored.

'It's for someone very special,' I tell her, even though she hasn't asked. I'm just so excited, I can't keep it to myself.

The officer shrugs and turns to leave.

'Make sure it gets posted as soon as possible,' I call to her retreating back.

It feels so good as I picture her smile when she gets the letter, imagining her rushing straight upstairs to write back to me. And I'll be waiting.

A warmness spreads over my entire body as I whisper her name.

Don't worry, Bella. We'll be together very soon.

ACKNOWLEDGEMENTS

I'd like to start with a huge thank you to my very own school gang. We've laughed, we've cried, we've drowned in class WhatsApp messages, we've managed endless face-painting stalls, we've drank copious amounts of wine, we've gone on tour, and we've supported each other through the good and the bad. A special mention to Laura Walmsley, the ultimate class rep, wonderful friend, avid reader of all my novels and all-round special person. And to Joana Oliveira, who introduced my books to the Brazilian contingent – love you all! – and is one of the strongest, loveliest ladies I know.

To the team at Boldwood Books for all your support, expertise, advice and for making the journey so enjoyable. Special thanks to my editor, Isobel Akenhead, my copyeditor, proofreader, and the wonderful and talented marketing and production teams.

To my family, Jon, Rose and Alice, who are my biggest cheerleaders and supporters. And finally, to you, my readers. Thank you.

ABOUT THE AUTHOR

Natasha Boydell is an internationally bestselling author of psychological fiction. She trained and worked as a journalist for many years, and decided to pursue her lifelong dream of writing a novel in 2019, when she was approaching her 40th birthday and realised it was time to stop procrastinating! Natasha lives in North London with her husband, two daughters and two rescue cats.

Sign up to Natasha Boydell's mailing list for news, competitions and updates on future books.

Follow Natasha on social media:

 facebook.com/NatashaBoydellAuthor
 x.com/tashboydell
 bookbub.com/authors/natasha-boydell
 instagram.com/tashy_boydell
 tiktok.com/@natasha_boydell

ALSO BY NATASHA BOYDELL

The Fortune Teller

The Perfect Home

The Doll's House

THE
Murder
LIST

**THE MURDER LIST IS A NEWSLETTER
DEDICATED TO SPINE-CHILLING FICTION
AND GRIPPING PAGE-TURNERS!**

**SIGN UP TO MAKE SURE YOU'RE ON OUR
HIT LIST FOR EXCLUSIVE DEALS, AUTHOR
CONTENT, AND COMPETITIONS.**

SIGN UP TO OUR
NEWSLETTER

BIT.LY/THEMURDERLISTNEWS

Boldwood

Boldwood Books is an award-winning fiction publishing company seeking out the best stories from around the world.

Find out more at www.boldwoodbooks.com

Join our reader community for brilliant books, competitions and offers!

Follow us

@BoldwoodBooks

@TheBoldBookClub

Sign up to our weekly deals newsletter

https://bit.ly/BoldwoodBNewsletter

Made in United States
North Haven, CT
14 January 2025

64403871R00192